For Better

OR MONEY

A NOVEL BY AMY MINTY

ISBN-10: 1477618783
ISBN-13: 9781477618783

For Caryn

For all those who ever worked in the service industry,

this book is for you.

Stealing comes with practice, lying comes with ease

But neither one is faster, than falling to your knees

—*Nickelback*

Part 1

Rob and Pam

Manhattan, NY

SEPTEMBER 2002.

Shortly before Rob proposed to me, a male customer approached me at Lime. He was a guest at a big holiday party. I don't remember this man's name or any striking details about him. He didn't possess any. Dressed in a charcoal gray suit and a light blue button-down shirt, he blended in with at least thirty other narcissistic shareholders who were guzzling gin and tonic and discussing the benefits of their 401K. All I recall is that he offered me two hundred dollars to kiss him.

My reaction should have been immediate. If I'd had any self-respect, I would have rolled my eyes and walked away. But I just stood there, staring at him blankly. My lack of reaction spoke volumes. It wasn't shock or surprise that caused me to hesitate. It was the money.

"Four hundred," he countered. The number sunk deep into my fickle soul. He was self-assured and confident—and close enough for me to smell mint on his breath and Creed on his neck. I glanced down at his wedding band and straight back up at him.

"What qualifies as a kiss?" I asked, my voice unrecognizable.

"I guarantee you'll enjoy it," he answered in a boisterous tone, which somehow seemed inappropriate. Possibly out of character, had I known the guy. "I turned forty yesterday. I need to know women still find me attractive."

I remained still, my lips moving with sudden destructive tendencies. "Four hundred dollars would be my only incentive." He was clean-shaven and a reasonable dresser, but that was all he had going for him.

"Yes, but if I were truly ugly, you would never do it," he challenged.

"Not necessarily," I said, squinting.

"You're lying."

"You just met me and solicited me in the same two minutes. How would you know if I was lying?" I was peering at him now from somewhere outside myself.

"It's a natural inclination to lie to strangers," he retorted. This intellectual assertion I agreed with, but the general conversation was getting us nowhere.

"FYI, I'd kiss my deranged boss for four hundred dollars." This was most certainly a lie—not because JT was unattractive or gay but because he was a psychotic, dangerous drug addict. Yet I still nodded in his direction. JT, the general manager of the hellhole in which I worked, was emitting a universal glare while downing an Amstel Light as if he were minutes away from entering the gas chamber. Feeling my eyes on him, he snarled at me, inhaling sharply on his cigarette. I refocused my attention on this stranger, having effectively proven my point.

"Meet me in the pay phone in two minutes," said Charcoal Suit, traipsing off in that direction. I stood there frozen, wondering why he had chosen *me*. Donna and Mimi, my pals and coworkers in the evil cocktail lounge world, were just as attractive as I was—well, maybe not Donna, but Mimi certainly was—and we were all waiting on the same slaphappy group. Did he detect a sluttish vibe in my walk? Did my eyes scream tramp? Or was I just so damn approachable that I was worth the gamble?

I retracted my steps slowly back to the computer, still balancing an unclaimed drink on a small tray. It was sweating into a wet, cold puddle. I took a small sip and concluded a customer was missing a gin and tonic; it tasted like a cold, unwelcome pinecone falling from a damp tree when winter refused to end. I continued to drink from the glass, hoping my common sense would return at some point. I also wondered how this man knew of the *perfect* setting to make out with the waitress. The pay phone was the only private space in the entire establishment! I hoped he wasn't planning to kill me in the phone booth and leave me for JT to discover when he smoked his next joint.

I drained the remainder of the icy pinecone and sneaked off to the pay phone. And of course, he was waiting for me with a big smile and four crisp bills.

Shutting the door behind me and trapping us both in, I plucked the bills from his claws and placed them in my pocket. "Hi," I said.

He cupped the right side of my face with confidence and tilted my head back. When his lips connected with mine, I counted to five and then turned away. "Wow, did I enjoy that! Thanks!" I said enthusiastically, full of shit as usual. *Whatever. It's four hundred dollars I didn't have yesterday.*

"If you kiss me like you mean it, I'll give you two more bills," he said, his hand still holding my squirming face.

I smiled widely, relaxing for the first time, and indulged him in the dirty phone booth, the same small space where I had once seen a mouse attempt to scale the smudged glass.

I emerged soon after, head buzzing with unrelenting self-awareness. I had just earned six hundred dollars for perhaps only a minute of my time? Ten dollars a second! You can't beat that. After all, you get what you pay for in life, and here was a guy who *finally* understood that. I hadn't met someone of his caliber since I'd quit dancing and was delighted this rare species had not reached extinction.

Looking back, he must have known I would agree to his sleazeball approach once he laid eyes on me. I was sickened by my behavior. *But* when I felt the crisp hundreds between my fingers, I was also exhilarated. I stuffed the money further into my pocket and casually walked back to the party as if nothing out of the ordinary had just taken place.

The ease with which I recovered from my nefarious activities amazed me. I had spent more than three years trying to turn my life around—going from one inhumane job to the next (hence the cocktail waitress position at Lime) to avoid the life I'd been drawn to—and it seemed to have caught up with me anyway. For me, this encounter in the pay phone was like enduring three years of AA, only to allow a stranger to pour champagne down my throat. I had broken my seal of good behavior, and I felt euphoric instead of guilt-ridden. After almost three honest years, clandestine situations resulting in cash payoffs still excited me! Despite my conflicting thoughts regarding this specific incident, I spent many nights wishing this mystery man would reappear. And reappear he did—in the form of Jake.

***

When I met Jake several months later, I was so obsessed with my upcoming wedding that I didn't realize my former self was slowly seducing me. It happened gradually, like watching a plant die.

People come into your life for a reason; this is what I've always believed. Not the minor characters—like the guy who sells you a pretzel on the corner—but the major players who enter our lives and stay put for a while. I think, sub-consciously *we* choose *them*. Somehow, in the deepest crevices of our mind, we pick our angels to guide us and our demons to tempt us. I can't prove this, but I know it to be true, for as hard as I tried to modify who I was and where I was heading in life, I remained impervious to change. No matter how much I tried to fly with the angels, my demons kept catching up with me.

I met Jake at Lime. Naturally. It was a boring Tuesday night, and Mimi and I were working together. I had a few tables, but as usual, I was ignoring them. Sitting at one of our VIP booths, I was drinking from a can of Pepsi and playing electronic Connect 4, enjoying the fact that JT was home with a near-death hangover. Mimi was working the other side of the room, and I glanced up in time to see an odd look cross her face. This, in itself, was not unusual, as her expressions didn't always match her thoughts. She reminded me of a Judy Jetson character with her blond hair cut diagonally longer in the front and her extremely light eyes. She was so fair that her white skin canvassed her calm detachment from the world. Her blue eyes were round and fairytale-like and I often thought she would maintain the same reaction whether she was watching a Broadway musical or witnessing a UFO landing.

"Pam," she said, tapping me on the shoulder. "Check out table eighteen. The blond dude. He looks like James Spader."

"Who?" I couldn't put a face to the name.

"*Pretty in Pink*. Duh. The rich kid. But this guy is older."

I glanced over at the table. "What about him?"

"See the pretty blond woman opposite him?"

"Uh-huh," I mumbled, my eyes already back on my electronic game. I was making a crucial move, and Mimi was famous for her nothing conversations.

"Well, when Spader went to the bathroom just now, the woman pulled me aside and told me if I called him a loser to his face, he'd give me a hundred bucks."

I shook my head and dropped an electronic black chip down the middle row.

"I'm serious."

I stared at the table with a tad more interest. "Well, what are you waiting for? Go call him a loser. Chance of a lifetime."

"You think I should?"

"A hundred bucks is a hundred bucks. Call him a bunch of names; maybe he'll give you *more*."

"What if it's a setup?" Mimi persisted, perpetually paranoid. "If one more customer complains about me, I'll be fired for sure."

"Get over there!"

"Are you sure?"

"Yeah, come on. I'll follow you." I dropped my portable game in favor of this new development. We marched over there together, and I watched Mimi step toward him, respecting her for perhaps the first time.

"Hi. Your girlfriend told me if I called you a loser, you'd give me a hundred bucks," Mimi accused. I smiled at her classy, ladylike approach and watched the gentle introduction between them unfold. Formalities were rather passé, after all, I considered.

The man looked up expectantly. I gazed at the muscles in his face and the angular set of his jaw. He did remind me of James Spader. Ten years ago, maybe. He was an older kind of sexy now, yet there was something combative lurking underneath his pleased expression. His short blond hair and light brown eyes gleamed under the flickering overhead light, and I had to admit I was intrigued.

I scooted over to Mimi. "Show us the money," I demanded, feeling a little like Cuba Gooding in that obnoxious football movie.

Spader looked startled by my sudden outburst but still managed to produce a hundred-dollar bill and set it on the table. I glanced at Mimi and nodded.

"You fucking pathetic loser!" she shouted, waving her hand and knocking his drink over so the contents spilled in his lap. She snatched the bill off the table. "You suck," she added before spinning on her heels, leaving me staring after her. The dude laughed and clapped, not seeming to feel the ice in his lap, and I turned and followed her back to the other side of the room.

"That was pretty good for someone worried she might get in trouble," I commented.

"Well, I rather enjoy yelling at people. Especially for cash."

"I was happy to coach you," I said, pleased with myself for being so encouraging in a critical time of need. Another good deed and I'd be up for a humanitarian award. "What else did

the woman say to you before?" My brain was already thinking
of other possibilities. I wanted to call him a loser too! Taking
money from people was the best. So much easier than stealing
or heaven forbid, *earning* it.

"Well, when she first called me over, she said she was with
this guy who often paid people to humiliate him. According to
her, he prefers blondes."

"How unfair. Oh look, they're leaving." Spader was helping
his date with her coat. She was probably an escort, I guessed,
noting the designer purse and expensive-looking boots yet ill-
put-together outfit.

"That was, like, so weird," mumbled Mimi.

"The world is a strange place. Full of unusual characters."
My eyes followed them closely as they left the lounge. I was
paying way too much attention...

8 MONTHS EARLIER

Lime Bar was where I plotted my engagement. I had met JT, the manager of this particular dive, working a private party in one of the penthouse suites of the Palace Hotel. A Japanese tycoon/acquaintance who knew me from the lounge hired me one evening to make drinks for him and his friends. JT was among his eclectic bunch of comrades. When JT offered me a line of cocaine and I politely declined, he cried, "Holy shit! How about that? You need to come work for me, you fucking bitch!" He said this rather good-naturedly. "I can't hire a single cocktail waitress who's not fucked up on nose candy twenty-four-seven. If you don't snort, smoke, or shoot up, you're my best employee—before I even hire you!" He laughed uproariously at his own testimony.

Perhaps most people wouldn't have jumped at the chance to work with a bunch of drug addicts, but hell, I did. I was unemployed and sick of hitting the pavement, and even though I didn't like drugs, drug-users were my kind of people. Having worked in a strip club for five years, I was accustomed to that type of atmosphere and preferred it to the uptight environment of a fancy restaurant.

Unfortunately, after eagerly accepting the position, I found that working for JT was probably comparable to spending quality time with Mussolini. His personality was largely dependent on the amount of crystal meth coursing through his veins, so you never knew where your next challenge might lie. But since I spent fifty hours a week at this Park Avenue hellhole and was able to avoid JT's wrath about half of the time, I put my nose to the wedding grindstone and enlisted the help of my two coworkers: Donna and Mimi.

Donna was a veteran. She'd been putting herself through college with a large portion of the restaurant's sales and was a pro at scamming. Naturally, this impressed me, and we became especially close after I caught her pocketing the cash for a bottle of Veuve Cliquot. I held it over her head until she relented and gave me half the profit. In the process, I earned her respect, and we became a team. Her quick math and knowledge of off-limit computer codes combined with my dynamite knack for obtaining drinks without a ticket was an exceptional combination.

Mimi, on the other hand, was simply too lazy to steal and couldn't be trusted with any information other than the type of hairspray that held my hair the best. Her employment at Lime had been brief, and more often than not, she called in sick. Sometimes she didn't even bother to call, and I often wondered how she got away with it. It may have had something to do with supplying JT new and improved pharmaceutical products, but it was difficult to be sure as she was hardly dependable. When she did work, however, she provided desperately needed comic relief. In addition to being cynical and jaded, she was also blessed with a charming amount of bitterness, which she applied heartily to the job. This I truly enjoyed, especially when a customer would receive the worst, most intense lashing of pointed sarcasm and take it as a direct compliment, blushing and waving her away with fake modesty.

While my two friends weren't exactly wedding planners, they each had a unique perspective on marriage. Donna wore a pinkie ring, which she referred to as a pre-engagement ring, and Mimi—for all her twenty-six years—had already been divorced twice. I figured they could offer some unconventional wisdom and aid me in my mission.

The three of us clustered in our usual section, next to the service bar and miles away from the customers. "If he doesn't want to discuss marriage, then fuck him, plan the wedding around him!" Donna yelled over the loud, obnoxious techno booming from the speakers. She ripped open a bag of freshly popped microwave popcorn as if we were in her living room watching pay-per-view. "I don't see why you're complaining when you haven't even tried the obvious."

"So mind games and manipulation are the obvious approach?" I shouted back. Steam billowed from the bag. *How had she used the microwave without JT noticing?*

"Just act like the two of you are getting married and he'll catch on. Men just have to get used to an idea, and then they're fine with it," claimed Donna.

"So I just start talking about it as if it's already decided?" I asked, frowning.

"Absolutely. Begin littering the apartment with bridal magazines and sample invitations. Flip through them when he's watching TV, and comment on dresses. That's what I did."

"But you're not engaged," I pointed out.

"Yes, *I am.* I just don't have the ring yet. This symbolizes our engagement," she raged, throwing her pinkie ring from Tiffany & Co. in my face.

"OK, calm down. Let me just get this straight. You did all this, and Rick went along with it?"

"Yeah. That was ages ago."

"And you never thought to mention this?" I wondered why Rick still hadn't produced a diamond, if this was all *ages* ago.

"You never asked." She quickly stuffed the popcorn behind the computer while simultaneously picking up a canister of Lysol. This maneuver signified the inevitable appearance of JT. I automatically followed suit, grabbing the closest rag. Donna sprayed the counter, and I began to wipe it clean. Mimi just stood there glassy-eyed.

"Tell him you want to go shopping for rings," suggested Mimi, not caring about JT's impending wrath. She was one of those people that you would never know was paying any attention until she offered her advice.

I glanced at Donna as JT hurled himself through the upstairs door. "Who the hell has popcorn, and why the fuck hasn't anyone offered me some?" He stormed toward us like the vampire he was. I pushed the computer back against the bag, a mere reflex, which confirmed its hiding place. JT pushed me aside and grabbed the popcorn. "Bitches," he hissed, swiveling around flamboyantly. The office door slammed shut.

"Good job, Pam," said Donna.

"Oh please. Residents of Staten Island could have smelled that."

"Pam, Mimi is right. Call Rob this second and tell him you want to shop for rings next week. See what his reaction is, and we'll go from there," instructed Donna.

"Seriously?" No wonder her boyfriend had produced a pinkie ring.

"Yes! You have to exert your power. Take control of the situation!" She raised her fist into the air like George W., pre-Iraq. Which fit her rather unique character, which was totally undefined and rather masculine.

"He'll be at work." I hadn't expected to be so enlightened from a single conversation.

"So? Will he answer his phone?"

"Yeah, probably," I said, stalling. It would no doubt sound absurd to him.

"OK, so call him."

I turned to Mimi. "Where do I say I want him to take me shopping? I can't say anything unrealistic like Harry Winston because he'll think I'm just fucking with him."

"Well, he works in Long Island, right?" asked Mimi.

"Yeah." I was amazed she remembered.

"Tell him you want him to take you to the mall. There's a big mall in Long Island named after an old president. That's where Ferdinand bought my second ring."

"Somehow, I think I need to be more specific."

"Tell him Fortunoff. Bargain hunters love that store," said Donna.

"Totally," agreed Mimi. "There's a Fortunoff near that mall."

"OK," I mumbled, my brain processing these random bits and pieces.

"Just don't go pear-shaped," warned Mimi. "My first ring was pear-shaped, and the marriage *didn't* work out."

"Interesting. To what do you attribute the failure of your second marriage?"

"Ferdinand didn't speak English, and the sex was so boring."

"I see."

"But ten thousand dollars is ten thousand dollars," she conceded.

I squinted at her. "I'll be right back." I didn't need to delve deeper into the business intricacies of Mimi's romantic arrangements. Wandering into the woman's bathroom, the only section in the restaurant that was off limits to JT—although it rarely deterred him from entering—I straightened my god-awful uniform and quickly dialed Rob's cell.

He answered on the first ring.

"Hi. What are you doing?" I said.

"I'm in the office doing the ordering."

I smiled. He sounded important. "Guess what?"

"What?"

"Mimi was telling me about this great place to shop for engagement rings. It's in Long Island." I awaited his reaction, staring at myself in the mirror.

"Rings?" he finally said.

"*Engagement* rings." I wanted no confusion.

"Um, you want to buy a ring?"

"No, you idiot, I want *you* to buy *me* a ring." I cleared my throat, reminding myself that being sweet was always more effective than being direct.

"OK," he answered tentatively. "Where in Long Island?"

"Fortunoff. Do you know it?"

"I'm not that out of the loop, Pam." Although I knew better.

"We can go to the Fortunoff near that mall," I said enthusiastically.

"Which mall?"

I wrinkled my forehead. "You know the one. It's named after a former president?"

"Roosevelt Field?"

"Yes!" I guessed. In the background, one of Rob's male coworkers yelled, "Robbie baby, make that fourteen pounds of ground beef! And ten pounds of bay scallops!" *Robbie baby?*

"I should go. JT could walk in here at any minute. So, we're on for shopping?"

"Sure," he said, surprising me. Could he actually like me taking control? I reminded myself that I had earned this. I had spent six days with my mother in New Jersey proving I could live without him. That had been no walk in the park.

"Next Monday?"

"Ah, OK, baby."

"Cool." I smiled.

***

The funniest thing about Rob proposing to me was he seemed unaware of just how much effort and manipulation I had applied to make it a reality. He also failed to realize a wedding would be the inevitable result.

Although I was ecstatic to be planning my wedding reception with Rob's actual consent, work was still a major inconvenience. However, the massive amounts of stolen cash I was leaving with at the end of my shift inspired me to return each day. Lime was operated under pretentious French rule, and I treasured their unwitting sponsorship.

Donna and I were still running the scene upstairs with the occasional help from Mimi—when she wasn't too coked up or crashing down too hard. Lime functioned on a similar system to communist Cuba, and us three rebels formed the branches of congress under JT's (Castro's) totalitarian regime. Consequently, this evoked a multiplying group of agitated customers. But we didn't care about them. All was right in a misguided world.

Lime's clientele was a bee's nest swarming with petite, rich college girls. This, in turn, attracted all the boys looking to hook up with petite, rich college girls. The young clientele, however, proved advantageous because serving drinks turned into a cash business. No young person trusted their friends enough to run an open tab on a credit card so they insisted on paying for each drink with cash. I didn't complain. With the right bartender, the majority of the money was going directly into our pockets. We made deals and agreements. It was a fifty-fifty-zero situation: half for the bartender, half for the waitress, and nothing for the French. However, it took skill and concentration, and quite naturally, it was one of the few things at which I excelled. My coworkers and I kept a running tally in our minds and sold as much cheap liquor as possible over the course of a night.

The technical name for it was grand larceny, but why get technical in the service industry? We would have been fools not to benefit from the situation, especially considering the French mob was stealing from its ridiculous clientele, filling up bottles of premium vodka with the cheap well equivalent and passing it off as the real stuff. In addition, the owners were rude assholes who treated us like slaves.

Lime ran on unspoken agreements. If the owners caught wind of us pocketing money, we had our blackmail prepared. I'd personally etched the phone number of the Better Business

Bureau into every female bathroom stall. It was as simple as that, a modern system of checks and balances in the shady underworld of New York nightclubs.

Around the end of August, JT's assistant manager quit (apparently he did not take well to JT's sexual advances), and the owners replaced him with a young man straight out of a distinguished Ivy League school. Originally from Alabama, Del-Raymond Jefferson didn't fit the drug-inhaling, profanity-spewing profile, and no one at Lime could understand why he'd accepted such a position. We called him Del-Ray, which he detested, but he was far too intimidated by Donna and me to express any displeasure. Naturally, he was completely useless, a key attribute to successfully overseeing the upstairs lounge.

It was fun to watch Del-Ray's obvious amazement when it came to our stellar, Upper East Side, underage clientele. He simply didn't understand the dynamic of wealthy, spoiled children running an establishment and couldn't comprehend why the same group of kids always sat at the best table and never paid for anything. "Why does Alexis always get the circular booth and free bottles of Veuve?" he asked one evening, clearly perplexed. Since he rarely spoke (it must be difficult to whistle and talk at the same time), Donna and I perked up. We preferred that he didn't become too observant when we were ordering a round of drinks without a ticket.

"She sleeps with both the owners," answered Donna without blinking. "Probably in the same bed at the same time." She tossed her mane of unruly brown hair behind her. Usually confined to a ponytail, her curls bounced with frenzied uncertainty.

"Both Jacque and Alec are happily married," stated Del-Ray with smug assurance. Donna rolled her deep-set brown eyes. I kept my eyes peeled on Jeffrey, the bartender. He was weird as shit but intensely handsome in a vampire way. His chiseled face was hardened and tan, and the whites of his eyes gleamed in the gloomy setting. More to the point, we had similar work ethics. Glancing sidelong at Donna, I shifted closer to the edge of the bar and winked at him. I was counting on Donna to distract Del-Ray. He didn't usually hang near the service bar, claiming it smelled, which it did.

"As if you would know," muttered Donna. I decided just then that her profile was much more complementary then her dead-on glare. Her nose was rather pretty, like a bunny slope.

"I've known Jacque for years, and Alec is my brother-in-law." I smirked at his delusional mind-set, finally understanding why he'd been hired in the first place.

"Del-Ray, I don't know where you're from, but this is New York City. You never know *anyone.* It wouldn't matter if those two fucking assholes were your twin brothers. Now get over here and tell me why the single-malt-scotch button won't work," shouted Donna, slamming the computer with her fist. That particular feature hadn't worked in months, but Del-Ray had no way of knowing that, especially since Donna's protests were complemented by a perfected look of wide-eyed irritation. In addition to her quick thinking, she was also a rather skilled actress.

Del-Ray appeared stunned that she would be so bold in referring to his next of kin in such derogatory terms, but he slowly emerged from his trancelike state and ambled over to her. "I hate this Del-Ray slang, you know," he mumbled. "My name is Raymond."

Donna sneered. "Whatever."

I gave Jeffrey the peace sign. We'd developed a pitcher/catcher type of communication for when management lurked nearby. The raised index and middle finger indicated I needed two Cosmopolitans, straight up. Jeffrey signaled he understood with a quick nod and reached for the shaker.

"Now, tell me what's wrong with the computer again?" Del-Ray asked.

"This button never works. Every time I need a Glenlivet, I have to ring in a top shelf whiskey and modify it. I don't have time for this shit."

I scratched the top of my head and tapped my thumb on the bar twice. This meant I also needed two vodka tonics. We never bothered with actual liquor name brands since it was all the same crap. Jeffrey locked eyes with me and tightened his jaw, another sign of his steadfast comprehension.

"Umm," Del-Ray hummed, peering into the screen.

Donna shifted her eyes in my direction, an all-systems-go signal to move when I received the handoff.

"So, no one knows anyone in your *big* city?" Del-Ray resorted back to the previous conversation, striving to act like he wasn't insulted. "It's a soulless town? Is that what you're saying?" He was stalling; he had no idea how to fix the restaurant computer. He might have mastered Lotus in the fifth grade, but the simple mechanics behind Lime's archaic operating system had him stumped.

"What I *meant* was, get with the program," said Donna. "Everyone has an agenda. Except maybe you."

"Well, I don't think Jacque is sleeping with anyone other than his wife, and I know Alec isn't cheating on my sister."

"Right. Sure. Can you fix this or not?"

"I don't know how," he finally admitted while I loaded my tray with drinks and walked calmly past both of them.

***

Later that night, the door to the office swung open and JT came flying out. An unforeseen surprise attack—similar to a bat— Donna and I settled on a mutual cringe.

"Hey! What are you lazy fucking bitches doing? Get to work! Clean something!" A bottle of Windex sailed through the air. I hopped quickly to my left as it whizzed past my right ear. Working for JT had sharpened my reflexes considerably; I could duck and weave better than Sonny Liston in his prime. JT pivoted and flounced away, briefly out of range.

"I'm *totally* sick of his psychotic outbursts," declared Donna.

"You've been here too long. I've only just gotten used to them." I grabbed the Windex off the floor and began spraying the computer in what could have appeared to be cleaning. I was determined to break the damn thing. Any type of liquid could upset its delicate balance. I smiled and sprayed. Smiled and sprayed.

"Are you fucking with the computer, again?"

"You're a logical person, Donna. What do you think?"

"I got blamed the last time. Remember?"

"No, you got blamed for breaking the printer. Which you did break. *I* got blamed for breaking the computer. Which I broke beautifully."

"Same difference. JT knows our tricks." As if on cue, our devout megalomaniac darted back through the door and appeared in front of us faster than Satan himself. I felt fortunate that I was still holding the bottle of Windex he'd thrown at my head.

"Pamela! Donna!" he screamed. "Where the fuck is Mimi? It's nine o'clock!"

Donna and I exchanged nervous glances. We knew she was going to be late due to her participation in an anti-war convention in Union Square Park—of all ironies.

"You both know where she is! Speak up, you butt-ugly, fat-as-a-house *bitches*!" he screamed at the pinnacle of his tarred lungs.

I stared at the giant, pulsating vein popping from his skinny pinhead. Working for him was always such an ego booster. Not waiting for a reply, he handed us a torn piece of notebook paper. "Eight people at ten o'clock. Seat them at table five. They're friends of mine. Fucking leech scumbags who think they can come here and drink on the house. Cocksuckers! Let me know if they don't give you a decent tip. I'll beat the shit out of them!" And that was the bottom line: for all the mean, dysfunctional bones in JT's skeletal body, if it came down to money, he always stood up for us. "And Pamela, you fucking whore! Stop trying to break the mother-fucking computer! I had it sealed the other day!"

***

Lunching with my mother at Christina's Restaurant on Second Avenue was a ritual based largely on its proximity to the multiplex theater next door. I picked my way through a Caesar salad while Sarah enlightened me on the disadvantages of Martha Stewart's decorative wedding cakes. Rumor had it that cutting into one of her art gallery exhibits was like knocking down the first domino in a chain. Apparently her cakes were symbolic of her empire. I hadn't let myself contemplate the wedding cake as of yet; I expected it would cost me a fortune and therefore was avoiding such speculation.

My mother, or Sarah, as I liked to call her, had surprised me by being genuinely excited about my upcoming wedding. She had come full circle. When I first announced our engagement over the phone, her enthusiasm lay dormant, and she refused to terminate her other call to discuss my exciting future. I was lucky to receive a "Congratulations on a job well done!" before she clicked back over to her accountant. Not that I expected balloons and a fruit basket, but her full attention would have been nice.

When my sister and I were growing up, my mother said to us, "You have a choice. You girls can either go to college or you can have a wedding. I can only afford one." And despite the fact that I was only ten, I recall thinking a wedding sounded like much more fun! Taking this into account, I found it particularly unnerving that she was leaning over the marble table, chatting away about what makes a wedding cake practical yet still fashionable. It being edible was not a chief concern.

"Sarah," I scolded. "You seem far more excited about this wedding than you were four weeks ago when I got the ring. Why the turnaround?"

"I know! Funny, isn't it? My coworkers totally cheered me up."

"Really?" I blinked. *She had to be cheered up?*

"My chief in command said it best. 'You're not losing a daughter. You're gaining a son.' I always wanted a son!" I was the older of two daughters, so this explained a lot.

"Well, I'm not sure if he fits the golden mold, but I'm glad you're feeling better about it." I sighed and pushed a canned anchovy to the edge of my salad plate.

"Don't get me wrong. I've always liked Robert. I just never thought *you* did."

"What?" I looked up sharply.

"I just never got that impression."

"What impression? Did you think I was living with him all this time just for the hell of it?"

"Well, Manhattan is pretty expensive."

"I pay half the rent. It's not like he's a free ride overlooking the park. Obviously, I love him."

"I know you say that, but it's more like you *chose* to."

"Elaborate. You've lost me." I set down my fork and reached for my Sprite, placing the straw to the right side of my mouth; the left side couldn't tolerate cold or sugar.

"*Choosing* someone to love is different than *being* in love. Being half of a partnership."

I humored her. "Continue."

"It's a subtlety. It can be revealed in something as simple as a nuance or a glance across the room."

"And you haven't spotted any of your so-called telltale signs? Is that it?"

My mother shrugged and studied her hearty meal of grilled vegetables.

"You don't think I ever *fell* in love with him?" I asked more specifically.

"It's more about having a connection," she said calmly, sipping Evian. Sarah thought tap water was utilized strictly for bathing.

"Well, we do. We must." I glanced behind me, feeling as if I was being filmed and broadcast in front of a large studio audience.

"Darling, I know that Robert is a wonderful, sweet man. I just hope he's enough for you." She punctured a spear of asparagus with her fork.

"Apparently our mutual infatuation isn't obvious to the common eye." I watched her slice the asparagus in quarters. Anyone else would have eaten it like a raw carrot. We were dining next to the sidewalk on Second Avenue, cars and cabs whizzing by like freight trains.

"I never detected it, Pamela."

"So, let me ask you. When Dad was still alive, was he enough for you?"

"Yes." It was a hard, convincing yes; a resounding, affirmative answer that warranted no further interrogation. If only he hadn't died at forty-one, leaving her alone with two angry kids.

"You mean to tell me that you were with him for twenty years and you never *desired* anyone else?" I persisted, unsure of why I was challenging her on this subject—especially since I didn't particularly want to hear the answer.

"Of course I did. Every woman thinks about it from time to time. But I never *needed* anyone else. He was consuming, your father."

"I know." My recollection of him was still strong after fifteen years of not hearing his voice. "But you never acted on it? Not ever? Even when Dad was being, um, a tyrant?" I chose my words carefully. It was difficult to speak ill of the dead, especially those who had exercised complete authority over you since birth.

"Never. I would tell you—and thank God, I didn't. It was a wonderful relief to me, knowing I'd always been faithful. There were no regrets." She dabbed her fingertips on her napkin.

"I don't even know how we got on this topic," I muttered.

"Pam, there is something you should know about relationships." *Another unsolicited opinion!* "There are two kinds of women in this world," she continued, pausing for effect. "Women who dream and fantasize but would never act on it and women who can't help themselves." I raised my eyebrows and took another sip of my soda, wishing I had ordered vodka. "I feel sorry for the married women who feel it necessary to chase their every desire. Not because of their guilt—most feel justified—but because deep down they are truly unhappy people. These women are like plants that suck up the rain but are still dehydrated. Unlike the cactus, which doesn't need moisture to grow and thrive."

I sighed. It was no secret that cacti were ugly plants. "What the hell are we talking about?" I finally said.

"Nothing, forget it. I've talked enough for one day. The cake. How many tiers?"

"Wait a minute. If you think this about Rob and me, why are you suddenly happy for us?"

"Because marriage can be a wonderful and fulfilling lifestyle. And it's a step in the right direction for you. It's not like you're career orientated."

"Hey, I'm writing another book, don't forget."

Sarah ignored me. "It wasn't until I started telling my friends that my older daughter was engaged that I realized the impact this will have on your life."

"Oh. I'm not sure I like when you put it that way."

"It illustrates that you've grown up."

"But I've wanted to get married for years."

"Yes, I know. And your determination has paid off. That says something. Especially given how stubborn Rob is. Is he still set on moving you both to Hawaii in the spring?"

"Yes. Don't remind me."

"You're going to have to think about it soon. And for the record I think it's a bad idea."

"Yes, we are in agreement on that." I cleared my throat. "What were you saying before? About me being so 'grown up'."

"Yes. You'll be entering into another stage of your life," she carried on, a running stream of distilled water. "It was only three years ago that you were working in that awful, seedy club doing God knows what."

"I liked that awful, seedy club," I said.

"By the way, how is Lexi? Still gorgeous?"

"Yes. And why is okay for her to still work there and not me?"

"Oh Pam. She's way tougher than you ever were." Sarah rolled her eyes like I was an idiot for asking such a question.

"Gee thanks. I am glad you like her better than me."

"Differently. I like her *differently*. She's always been a very good friend to you. Please give her my best."

"I will. Jeez. She's also engaged, by the way—and a bridesmaid so you'll be able to tell her soon how much you still worship her. At two separate weddings."

Sarah waved her hand as if swatting a fly.

"I miss that seedy club," I said, staring at the remains of my salad.

"No you don't. I see tremendous growth."

"But *I* haven't changed," I said. "I wish I was still working there and earning an honest living instead of stealing at my current job."

"Pamela! I don't want to hear about any underhanded thievery you may be involved in! I don't have the money to bail you out of jail! Do you hear me?"

"Would you lower your voice, please?"

Collapsing back in her chair, Sarah squinted, sizing me up Mafia style.

"Relax. I won't be at Lime much longer. Once we move to Hawaii—God help me—I'm going to rewrite my fairytales. They have potential," I added confidently. Writing had been my latest venture into the creative realm, and I'd been working on a collection of revised fairy tales. I took happy stories intended for kids and reformed them back to their original horror, twenty-first-century style.

"You haven't had much response yet, I take it?" She saw right through my bullshit.

"No, not yet. The retelling of popular allegory is a tough market. Which is totally ridiculous—it cries out marketable. I just have to target the right readers—mainly bitter, angry people with lots of time on their hands."

"I did think your retelling of Cinderella was quite good," she admitted. "Her scene in the bathroom when she overdoses was *hysterical*. And the taxi turning into an ambulance at the crack of midnight was sheer brilliance."

"Thank you," I sniffed.

"Anyway, the wedding cake. Let's get back to that. Does the reception hall choose it or do we?"

"We, as in you and me, or Rob and me?"

"You and me, of course."

October 2002

Late one evening, while I was looking over piles of church jargon, Mimi called me from work. I figured she was just bored. The excited tone of her voice, however, led me to believe otherwise.

"Pam! He's here again! But he came alone!" squealed Mimi.

"Who's there?"

"James Spader. The dude I called a loser last week!"

"No way." I was instantly envious.

"Yes way. And get this—he wants to buy my socks for two hundred!"

"The ones currently on your feet?"

"Yes. Isn't that fantastic? I told him that they were all sweaty and disgusting, and he said, 'All the better.'"

Rob stared at me from his position on the couch and made a face. I booked it to the bathroom. "What does he want them for?"

"Why should I care? He's willing to pay top dollar."

"Well, did you ask?"

"I'll call you in a little bit," she whispered.

"You better call me back—" The phone disconnected.

I walked back into the kitchen dejectedly. There had been something about James Spader that I couldn't stop thinking about. He'd been so good-looking in a responsible way, yet when Mimi had yelled at him, his eyes had lit up in what I could only describe as reckless abandonment.

"Who was that on the phone?" asked Rob.

"Mimi. She's at work. Just bored, I guess." I picked up the religious material again. "Rob, do you think the bishop approved of us? As a couple, that is? Taking our vows in his precious church."

"I have no idea, Pam. What's it matter?"

"I wasn't convinced Father Bob liked me, and the feeling was mutual."

"Oh no? He doesn't meet your high standards?" Rob said, snickering.

"He seemed a little judgmental."

"It's his job to be critical."

"I disagree. I think he enjoys being intrusive and nosy under the pretense of working under God."

"Whatever, Pam."

"Did he tell you how the church encourages *offspring*? Are we characters in a V. C. Andrews novel? That totally creeped me out."

"He mentioned it."

"And?"

"And what, baby?"

"What was your response to such a bizarre statement?"

"Nothing, really."

I stared at him "Rob, I know I said we'd move to Hawaii, but I really don't want to anymore. I'm a New Yorker. I just got scared after the bombings."

"Pam, I'm more of a New Yorker than you, and we're going. It's been decided."

"You decided."

"No, *we* decided."

"I want to retract my earlier statements."

Rob shook his head. "Retraction denied."

Two hours passed before Mimi called me back. I did a flying leap over Rob for the phone and picked it up on the second ring. "Guess how much money I just made?" she said, bragging.

I walked quickly to the bathroom. "Goddamn it. How much?"

"Eight hundred."

"I'm dying my hair blond tomorrow," I said.

"It doesn't usually have so many advantages," said Mimi, inhaling a post-work cigarette. I knew she was at the end of the long bar with her legs crossed nursing a vodka soda. In the background, I could hear JT screaming at his "friends."

"I'm assuming you sold him more than your socks. Are you still wearing underwear?" I teased.

"How did you know?" said Mimi.

"Wild guess. What other crazy things did you have to do?"

"I served him dog food on a plate."

"And he ate it?" It was, indeed, already a fact, as Mimi did not have the energy or enthusiasm to lie. "Canned or dry?"

"It was actually in this plastic packet, so more like canned."

"And he enjoyed this?"

"He seemed to."

"Right." I tried to picture this fiasco.

"And for dessert, he had me mix dirt in with his crème brulée. It looked like crushed Oreos."

"That is ridiculous. What is this guy's name?"

"Jake. He has a slight accent. He might be English. I'm not sure. Maybe Welsh?"

"You paint a vivid picture. More importantly, how did you serve him dog food without JT noticing?"

"I had to give him a cut—naturally."

I nodded at my reflection in the spotted mirror, alone in the bathroom with the door shut. My long dark hair was pulled back into a ponytail, and my cheekbones appeared severe with my pale coloring. "How much did you give him?"

"Fifty bucks. He wanted a hundred, but I promised him six Ambien as well."

"So let me get this straight: this guy, Jake, gave you two hundred for the socks. How much did he give you for the underwear?"

"Just a hundred."

"That doesn't make any sense."

"He said socks turn him on. He's got a serious foot fetish. He told me to save my disgusting tennis sneakers and he'd pay me for those as well."

"This guy is far too attractive to be up to such mischief! How *exactly* did you earn the other five hundred?"

"Well, between the dog food and the dirt and, oh, every time I spat in his drink, he'd hand me twenty bucks."

"You spat in his drink?"

"Yeah, I also flicked the ashes of my cigarette in his beer. Oh my God! I hope that anti-smoking law doesn't get passed in April. That would suck," Mimi said, sounding worried.

"Don't get sidetracked. So he drank this concoction of spit and ash? You watched him drink it?"

"Yep."

"Where did he get dirt in Manhattan?"

"He pulled it out of a small Hermès shopping bag."

"Hermès? This is just crazy. Will he be back?" I asked eagerly.

"He said he'd return next Monday. He likes when the lounge is quiet, and I told him Mondays were always dead."

"Eight hundred. Jesus. He *must* be loaded," I marveled, staring at my thin, threadbare, once forest-green towels, hanging like moss on the rack. I then stared back at my reflection thinking my once bright-green eyes appeared rather dull.

"Yeah, but you know what—apart from the odd eating habits and the foot fetish—he seemed rather nice."

"Sure, Mimi. I'd think he was nice too if he handed me all that money."

"I earned it!"

"Yes, you did." I agreed.

I walked back into the living room and sat down next to Rob. Suddenly my life seemed very dull. I tried to remember the last time I'd seen Rob without the clicker in his hand. I was staring at him so intently that he finally glanced up at me.

"Hey baby," he said, placing his hand on my knee.

"Hey." A repeat of *Seinfeld* was on. Again.

***

While I was preparing for my wedding, Jake, the sexy sock collector, visited Mimi every Monday for the next six weeks. I listened to the various exploits and was dying to be included in this fantastic economic opportunity, despite its outlandish circumstances. According to Mimi, Jake was encouraging her to meet outside of the workplace for further humiliating prospects! Perfect, I thought, encouraging her to expand the parameters. I viewed it as an opportunity to make money in a JT-free environment with fewer overall distractions. However, Mimi still felt uneasy, so I volunteered to be her sidekick/bodyguard on this chance encounter.

Mimi was the frigging genius who worked it out so we would both receive seven hundred in cash upon our arrival at our selected meeting place. Since I was the queen of dining out, I was in charge of choosing the restaurant. I decided on the downstairs lounge at AZ based on the fact that it was dark and swanky, and the service was notoriously bad. This guaranteed the waitress wouldn't notice anything irregular.

I suggested Mimi come to my apartment beforehand so we could arrive together. This also minimized the chance of her chickening out. At half past seven Mimi entered my apartment decked out in a particularly disturbing gothic ensemble complete with a matching oversized purse. Enclosed in this hulking mass of black vinyl were two cans of dog food, a sandwich bag full of dirt, and a can opener, which I pointed out was unnecessary given the pull tops.

"Where did you get this?" I asked, holding the dirt up to the light. It had little stems and weeds in it, possibly a worm or two. I shivered.

"I scooped it out of my plant."

"It's not a poisonous plant, right? No red leaves? Committing murder by accident would be bad," I added nervously.

"No, it has no leaves."

"OK, I won't ask. What else do you have in that purse? It's huge." She pulled out three packs of Parliament Lights, a black, plastic lighter, purple lipstick, a tiny blue straw, and a small bag of white powder.

"Looks like you're covered." All I needed was her getting too high and leaving me alone with this crazy dude.

We headed out of my building and hailed a cab heading up Sixth Avenue.

"This guy does know I'm tagging along, right?" I asked.

"Yes. I told him all about you," Mimi said, digging in her purse.

"What exactly did you tell him?"

"Just that you are my friend and you used to be a stripper."

"Oh, that's great. He's going to assume the worst. I prefer the term *dancer*, by the way."

"Whatever. He seemed intrigued."

"I'm sure he is. We have quite the reputation—the majority of it being true. I hope he doesn't think I'm going to sleep with him. I was a dancer, never a hooker," I added in a warning tone. It was hard to trust Mimi at times.

"He knows you're engaged. Seriously, all we have to do is treat him like shit. It should be great fun!"

"Truer words have never been spoken." We exchanged sly glances, and the lights changed as we stopped at a traffic light. "Does he remember me from that night at Lime when you first called him a loser?"

"I don't know. I think so. Whenever he asks to take me shopping, I keep mentioning your name because I know you and Donna are always discussing labels."

"He wants to take you shopping? You never told me that!"

"Yeah, he mentions it every time. He wants to buy me shoes at Saks. I've never even heard of the store."

"That's Saks Fifth Avenue, you idiot! Tell Jake you want him to take us *both* to Saks. Say you'd feel better if you brought a friend—just like tonight. I could use some new shoes."

"You would go with me?" asked Mimi, sounding surprised.

"Mimi, if Charles Manson wanted to take me shopping and buy me Christian Dior, I'd probably go." I worried about her sometimes.

The cab made a right onto Seventeenth Street, and we pulled up in front of AZ. As I gazed out the window, I could see James Spader lurking by the door waiting for us. I paid the taxi and hopped out of the cab before Mimi could finish sniffing a straw full of cocaine. Dying to make a good impression, I was wearing the Prada boots I'd bought at a sample sale two years ago and a short black skirt to show off my stocking legs. According to Mimi, Jake had enjoyed eating her cut-up nylons one night, adding them as garnish to a dish of linguini with clam sauce.

I walked up to him and officially introduced myself. "Hi. I'm Pamela, Mimi's chaperone for the evening. Nice to officially meet you."

"Nice to meet you too. Thanks for coming. She insisted you were the only friend she felt comfortable bringing."

"Isn't she sweet?"

"Where is she?" he asked, glancing around. He had a nice voice to complement his nice face. He sounded like he was half-laughing each time he spoke. I pointed at Mimi, who was only just emerging from the cab. Together, Jake and I watched her stumble toward us, her dress trailing behind her.

They exchanged requisite formalities, and I was surprised that Mimi greeted him so shyly. She wasn't bashful when it came to insulting him.

As we walked into the lounge area, Jake remarked, "This place is cool. I've never been here. It's nice and dark. I hate bright places."

"You've never been here before?" I asked.

"No, I live on the East Side," he stated.

"I used to come here a lot. The waitresses have a hard time remembering a drink, much less a face." The place was practically empty, and since there was no one there to greet us, I led Mimi and Jake to a table in the far corner of the room.

Jake smiled and sat down. Mimi positioned herself opposite him on a thin black couch, so I grabbed the space next to Jake. A small glass table wobbled dangerously in the center.

"Do you know how hard it was to get Mimi to meet me outside of your workplace?" Jake told me. "I'd almost given up, and then she mentioned she had a friend who would also like to humiliate me."

"Mimi has such a way with words."

"Those were your words!" claimed Mimi, indignant.

I picked up a cocktail menu. I was definitely going to need a stiff drink.

"Did Mimi tell you what we've been doing at Lime?" asked Jake.

"Every last detail," I said, thinking she left out the most important one: shopping!

"Mimi is awesome at coming up with new ways to embarrass me. Last week she had me drinking other people's leftover drinks, and the week before that I was only allowed to drink from the drink bucket," he said, smiling at her.

"And you know how disgusting that is," said Mimi, lighting up a cigarette. I pictured the filthy bucket where we tossed the customers' leftover drinks.

"What does it taste like?" I asked Jake.

"Mostly just like watered-down alcohol."

"We put everything in that—even dump the ashtrays. This includes everything from cappuccino to blue martinis," I informed him.

"I know," said Jake, winking at Mimi. "It tastes great. It's so pathetic that she makes me drink it."

I watched Mimi act coy. The girl was a fucking chameleon.

"Were you one of those kids in school that would eat and drink awful concoctions of food in the cafeteria?" I asked Jake.

"Only if a hot chick wanted me to do it."

I nodded. "Where did you grow up?"

"The Berkshires."

"Were many hot chicks forcing chemistry experiments down your throat?"

"Actually, yes. Quite a few."

I giggled and stood up. I knew it would take effort and patience to get the attention of a waitress. Catching sight of a tall woman dressed in black, I waved.

"Good," said Jake, watching me. "I could use a Beefeater and tonic."

"How about my piss in a glass?" offered Mimi. "That's more what you deserve."

I didn't comment, just stared at the both of them. Thankfully, the waitress appeared. A good six feet tall, she towered over the low table. "Yeah, I'll have a dirty Grey Goose martini. Straight up. And a Cosmopolitan," I told her. "This nut will have a Beefeater and tonic," I added, pointing at Jake.

"Two drinks. Impressive," said Jake, studying me more carefully.

"I'm going to drink her dirty martini, after she takes only one sip," said Mimi to the Seattle Needle. "Can I also have two ashtrays?" The waitress walked away, rolling her eyes, and I returned my attention to the two crazies with whom I was set to spend my evening.

"Do you do that?" I asked Jake.

"Do what?"

"Drink women's pee?"

"Not usually. But I've drank Mimi's."

"From a glass?"

"So far she hasn't allowed me to drink it directly."

"And whose idea was that?"

"Mine," bragged Mimi. "Loser here isn't inventive enough to think of something so demeaning."

Jake laughed, enchanted.

"I can see Mimi is a positive influence on you," I scoffed.

"Yes she is, and I am her willing slave."

"OK, let me get this straight," I said. "You drink women's piss—and you never get sick?"

Jake smiled and shook his head. "I've only sampled Mimi's. It's not as if I've compared and contrasted all over the world. I think people today are just paranoid. Germs aren't bad for you. They aren't on everything people touch, or if they are, they're not dangerous. I never get sick. I haven't been sick in years."

"That's wild. And to think some people won't share their toothbrushes," I marveled.

"Most people are assholes," said Jake with a shrug.

"Well, if I had known about *you* during my childhood, I wouldn't have been so upset about dropping my ice cream cone," I said, feeling rather cheated.

"I think Jake has formed antibodies against all germs at this point," snapped Mimi.

"Where are our drinks?" asked Jake. The way he shelled out money, he probably wasn't used to waiting, I thought, scanning the empty room for the Seattle Needle. A few seconds later, she set two martinis down in front of me, a gin and tonic in front of Jake, and two ashtrays in front of our fellow chain smoker. Jake handed her a credit card. "Keep it open," he said, looking her up and down—and then up again. She wasn't bad looking, just wicked tall and painfully thin. She belonged in Paris.

"Cheers," I said, holding up my dirty martini. "To new experiences." Jake raised his glass, and Mimi raised her cigarette half-heartedly.

"Give me that," Mimi said to Jake, grabbing his drink before he could take a sip. "Fucker," she hissed, spitting in the glass. Jake then handed me his drink and I gingerly accepted it. Apparently, it was my turn.

"It's so hot to have two beautiful girls spit in my drink and humiliate me in public," he stated.

I spat into the glass and handed it back to him, forcing a smile.

He took a sip and glanced over at Mimi. "Drink it fast," she ordered. "I have to pee and I need the glass. Open your mouth and stick out your tongue."

At this point, I honestly had no idea what she was going to do or say from one moment to the next. Jake obliged, and she took her lit cigarette and flicked ash into his open mouth. The silver embers sizzled on his tongue. It was a lovely sight, beautiful in its absurdity.

"Do you smoke?" Jake asked me.

"No. Yes. No. Sometimes."

"That's too bad," he said. "I love being a woman's ashtray."

"I'd be happy to take it up again." I polished off my Cosmopolitan in one shot. Mimi knew me too well. I handed her my full dirty martini.

"What shoes are you wearing?" Jake asked me.

I picked up my foot and bravely placed it on his lap. He felt the brown leather and the base of the rounded heel. "I normally don't like Prada, but this is well made," he said, studying the sole. "Most of their shoes are too masculine."

"I think so too!" I was tickled pink that he could tell the brand just by looking at the design. I thought briefly of Rob, who couldn't distinguish Prada from Payless.

"May I?" he asked.

"You may." I smiled, wondering what I was agreeing to.

Taking my leg, Jake carefully pulled it up in the air and started licking the soles of my boots. I watched his tongue go back and forth over the arch and the heel. I could honestly say that no one had ever done that to me before. It was so abstract; it was almost sexy. There I was in a public restaurant, one leg up in the air, allowing this stranger to lick the soles of my boots clean. What was the world coming to? And as the Cosmopolitan began to provide that rising feeling of floating, I started to relax. I began to think that perhaps this behavior wasn't all that unusual. In fact, it was admirable. In a game of truth or dare, he'd definitely have us beat. And as he reached in his pocket and pulled out two folded sets of Benjamin Franklins, I felt completely at ease. Almost as if I'd come home again.

Mimi opened Jake's can of gelatin-covered Purina and plopped it on a plate. It kept its original shape, similar to a traditional tartare. I held my breath.

Jake picked up his fork with seemingly genuine enthusiasm.

"Do you *like* the actual taste of that?" I asked.

"It tastes pretty awful," he answered, scooping it into his mouth. "But I love that you two are making me eat it." I exchanged glances with Mimi, who just shrugged.

"Did I say you could dig in yet?" bellowed Mimi, refreshing her power. "It's not even ready. It needs dirt!" She grabbed her mother-of-pearl caviar spoon and scooped a couple mounds of dirt onto the plate of dog food. Talk about an injustice to an item of silverware. "There, now you may eat. Loser," she added with disgust.

Jake smiled, delighted.

I held tight to my own caviar spoon and sipped my second Cosmopolitan. "So Jake, how did you get started in all this?" I asked carefully.

"Would you step on this piece of bread for me?" He handed me a small round roll from the breadbasket.

"Um, sure." I dropped it on the floor and flattened it with the ball of my foot, hoping I was doing it right. Was there more than one method?

"I was young. Like five or six," began Jake. "It's one of my first clear memories. There was this girl, a neighbor who used to play with me. Her older sisters would paint her toenails in glittery colors, and they sparkled and gleamed like jewels. And of course, being kids we were always barefoot. I used to just stare at her feet for hours, mesmerized."

"So, at the tender age of five you were already smitten with the female foot?" I said, unable to remember being five years old. Or six or seven or eight.

"Something like that. Kids have no idea what they're doing at that age."

"Yet you seemed to."

"Well, I used to love to kiss her toes. And I guess she liked it too, because whenever she had a new polish on she'd come rushing over to show me. She was the first girl whose feet I noticed."

"I'm assuming there were others?"

"Yeah. A few years later, my father's company started to take off, and we moved to a small town in upstate New York. I was about eight or nine when we moved in across the street from this other family. They had a daughter named Cassie who was my sister's age—three years older than me. I was utterly infatuated with this girl. Of course, she became friends with my sister because they were in the same class. Anyway, Cassie used to come over to our house after school. We'd all be watching TV, and she'd catch me staring at her feet instead of the television."

"I can just see you as a young kid," mocked Mimi, desperate for attention. "Open your mouth," she ordered, flicking more ash onto his tongue.

"Continue," I ordered.

"At the time, my only experience with girls was pink glittery toenails, so I found myself always watching Cassie's feet.

She caught on, and she liked it. She'd call me her foot slave and make me clean her shoes. She loved to order me around. 'Jake,' she'd say, 'go get me a glass of orange juice.' Or, 'Jake, give me the cookie you're eating.' And of course, I would. I did anything she asked."

"She sounds like a real brat," said Mimi.

"Look who's talking," I said sharply. "What did Cassie look like?"

"Very mature for her age. She had moved from New York City to upstate and had a lot of attitude. For twelve years old, her body was developed and she dressed differently: bell-bottom jeans, red Converse. Not preppy, like the rest of the kids. She was confident, which was unusual. At that age, girls try to hide their bodies. At least they used to."

"Was she blond?" I had to ask.

"Yes. Tall and blond. Blue eyes. Her skin was always tan, and she wore tight shirts that showed off her chest."

Mimi rolled her eyes.

"How did all this escalate into eating dirt?" I asked.

"Cassie kept raising the stakes. She was utterly unabashed. She knew she had power over me, and she used it. Soon, she was telling me to kiss her feet and lick the bottom of her shoes. By that time, we both realized I had a serious foot fetish. We didn't know the proper name for it, but she knew I liked her feet enough to do anything she asked."

"Did your sister know about this?"

"Oh, God no. All she knew was that I was obsessed with her friend. She didn't know about the role playing."

"So Cassie never did it in front of her?" I asked.

"No, she'd wait until the phone rang and my sister would run off to get it, or when she was in the bathroom."

"Wow. I didn't learn the benefit of discretion until I was at least twenty," I said.

"And once Cassie realized I was getting off on it, she'd remove her socks and let me kiss her bare feet. At first I was upset her toenails weren't painted, but I soon adapted to the natural look."

"Did you want to kiss her face? Her lips? Or just her feet?" I asked.

"Well, at the time, kissing her feet was like fireworks going off below my belt. I didn't think much beyond that. Probably because I was so young."

"Did the other girls catch on and start shoving their feet in your face?" Mimi asked, smirking.

"No. Cassie was the only one I experimented with before high school."

"How special. Now eat your fucking dog food," said Mimi.

"Yes, ma'am," Jake said, nodding.

"How long did this continue?" I asked, ignoring Mimi's glare. I was trying to understand *why* this made such a lasting impression on him. I was sure that other kids went through periods similar to this and it didn't have such a profound impact on their psyche.

"Years. It would have gone on longer, I think, but her family moved again by the time I was a freshman in high school."

"So it was just a lot of shoe and feet kissing?" I probed.

"And a few other things. After she realized that she had total control over me, she got creative. One winter she dragged me to this dirty pond in our neighborhood. It was low and muddy, and she stepped in it with her winter boots—you know—the big blue snow boots that kids used to wear. Well, she picked up her shoes one at a time and ordered me to lick all the mud off the bottom. She knew I would enjoy it."

"OK, but why? *Why* did you enjoy it? Did you know?" I pressed.

"She was hot. Even at twelve years old, it was already a sexual game. She knew what buttons to push."

"Right. I see. So you liked being her toy," I clarified. I was on my third Cosmopolitan by now, hoping all this random information would come in handy one day.

"Essentially," said Jake. "How's that bread doing down there?"

"Oh, it looks good," I said, having forgotten all about it. "It's like a dirty CD, but I'm assuming that's what you had in mind."

"Great. Let me see." He held out a small plate for me to place it on. I gingerly picked up what was left of the roll and passed it to him, thinking perhaps I should have worn gloves.

"I think there is something psychologically wrong with you," stated Mimi, watching this interaction. She drained her third martini ignoring my warning look.

Jake shrugged. "You could be right."

I was doing my best to give him the benefit of the doubt. "It shows your devotion. You were doing what Cassie asked because *she* wanted you to, right?" Mimi gave me a wry look, which I ignored.

"I think the Son of Sam had that problem as a child," said Mimi. "I read that somewhere." Both Jake and I turned to her. "I'm serious. Maybe you're a psychopath. Where the fuck is the waitress? She really sucks."

"You're not a psychopath. Trust me, I've met psychopaths," I reassured him, while Mimi stalked over to the bar. "Where is Cassie these days?" I asked.

"She lives in Nebraska. She's married with four kids and doesn't appear to have half the confidence she used to."

"You saw her after she moved?"

"Not until much later, but yeah, I looked her up. She told me she was engaged and moving to Texas. I was devastated; I always felt that she was the girl for me."

"Did you see her after that?"

"Not until her wedding."

"Oh my God, you went to her wedding! How did she look?"

"Beautiful. Like a goddess."

I stared down at the breadcrumbs on the floor, wondering if any man would ever describe me as a goddess. If Rob stumbled over the word *cute*, then goddess was probably out of the question.

"You said she doesn't have half the confidence now. What makes you say that?" I asked.

"Well, after college she married that guy and had kids right away. She never had a job. She's been a housewife for the last fifteen years, and I think she lost most of her individual expression. She's probably one of those people born in the wrong time. She liked to be in a position of power but was afraid that was a bad thing. I'm pretty sure that's why she never told anyone about the things we did. She would have made a great lawyer or politician, but I think she was afraid of her own abilities."

"That's sad. How old is she now, then?" This was my clever way of asking Jake's age.

"Um, I'm forty-one, so she must be forty-four now."

I smiled, liking that he was older. It made his choices more important.

"That bitch is finally going to bring us another round of drinks," announced Mimi, collapsing back on the couch. "You're not done with that gourmet meal yet!" she roared, staring at Jake's half-empty plate.

"Not yet, mistress. Please allow me to finish it. It's very good," said Jake, looking Mimi in the eye. It was obvious he really liked her.

"It needs more dirt," she declared, reaching into her massive bag again. "Stop eating just the topping, you bad boy! You know what happens to naughty boys who only eat the frosting. They get spanked!" I laughed in spite of myself. This role really suited her.

"Do you two want to go shopping for shoes on Sunday afternoon?" asked Jake, glancing from her to me. "Mimi needs serious help." He looked pointedly at her retro combat boots.

"Yes!" I exclaimed.

"Mimi?" asked Jake, turning back to her.

"If Pam goes, I will," she said, acting shy again. I raced to keep up with the two sides of her personality.

"Mimi said you might want to go to Saks?" I asked casually.

"Yeah, they just got some new lines in that are pretty good."

I clapped my hands together and sat up straighter in my chair. "What time is good for you?"

***

I had called in sick to go out with Jake and Mimi, so I wasn't at Lime when four waiters from the downstairs restaurant quit. According to Del-Ray, they all marched out in unity at 11 p.m. I found this out when I returned to work the following day and I laughed so hard, I practically wept.

When the shift started, I was standing by the computer in that uncommitted way, pretending I was still under the weather on the off-chance JT would let me leave early. I took extra care not to speak above a whisper, applied no makeup, and chose not to wash my hair. This ensured that I appeared as ill as humanly possible. With the combined effect of Lime's cry-for-help, psychiatric patient uniform, I resembled a listless escapee from the nearest mental institution.

Unfortunately, in my few self-appointed days off, Lime had surpassed my negative expectations. Every time a customer or member of the staff flushed any of the toilets, raw sewage came flooding up through the kitchen. It was a sanitary nightmare for those who wash their hands twenty times a day. The plumbers (notice the plural tense) arrived every two hours in full body suits, complete with extensive hosing equipment, to suck up the mess on the kitchen floor. This was so our culinary experts from Mexico could continue to work despite the gagging smell and slippery tiles. Funnily enough, these disgusting circumstances didn't faze the resilient kitchen staff, and they continued to fry calamari as if nothing was amiss. The cooks attached plastic bags to their shoes with rubber bands and forged on as

if they were troops in Vietnam, not underpaid servants to the
French.

At any rate, I held my own, arms folded across my chest,
watching the people wait in vain for the bathroom, which
had been out of commission for hours. How an establishment
that seats 250 people can stay open without working public
restrooms still remains a mystery to me. Where is the health
department when you really need them? Didn't they ever go
out to bars and stumble upon these situations? And at the time,
Lime already had a few disturbing violations that could have
used checking up on.

Rob had recently unearthed a website that informed the
average person of the health risks involved in eating out.
Naturally, the article listed Lime as one of the worst. "Vermin
and other live animals appear to be present in food storage units
at Manhattan's Lime Bar," he had quoted. *What other live animal
could they be referring to?* Squirrels? Raccoons? Where did the
truth lie? It seemed a shame that these critics had been so vague
in their evaluation. *Close us down already!*

I didn't *like* it, but I was accustomed to tripping over
mousetraps and smashing cockroaches with ketchup bottles. I was *not* used to wading through sewage whenever
I needed a wine bucket or a clean tray from the kitchen. It
actually reminded me I was due for my second hepatitis vac-
cination. In short, the state of Lime had officially begun to
compromise my morals, which was saying a lot. I was grateful that my penance would be ending shortly. There was no
way I was waiting tables after I got married, and I silently
thanked the Lord that I was, indeed, officially engaged and
this was not one of my famous empty threats with nothing to
back it.

Standing in the kitchen, where the floor was covered a half-
inch deep in piss, I couldn't help but think of Jake. When he
and Mimi had been discussing the pros and cons of drinking
urine, I had been more focused on the *why* of the situation. If

I understood *why* Jake was this way, I could handle it and in this particular case, capitalize on his peculiarities. I just had to remain calm and listen, understand, and accept, and I would be on top of my game. No one ever likes a new job at first. This was technically no different.

As I walked back up the stairs, I noticed the employee bathroom had yellow tape surrounding it like a crime scene. JT had pinned a note on the door that stated, "If you have to piss, go the *fuck* home. Cocaine sniffing only." I found this amusing, despite needing to pee. It could not have been any other way without raising a suspicious doubt that my life was not going according to God's peculiar plan for me.

As if things could get any worse, Alec, the more-annoying owner of this pathetic enterprise, was sitting at one of my tables, eating a cheap cut of strip steak as if nothing was amiss. The line for the bathroom continued twenty yards past his table, and still he remained unfazed. I was not the least bit surprised. He was a bastard, and I hoped that one day he would sample some bad cheese from his own restaurant and become terribly sick. I comforted myself with this fantasy since the chances of this happening were actually quite high and elevating with each passing moment.

My eyes shifted from my pompous prick of a boss to a couple holding hands at a corner table. Their drinks remained untouched and no longer cold, their table merely an excuse to have a place to sit and stare at each other. They didn't seem to mind that nearby customers were shouting insults at each other, and their "Grey Goose" on the rocks was really vodka made by misfits in a basement somewhere in Brooklyn. Their closeness piqued my curiosity. With my wedding only four short months away, I was constantly pondering how couples stayed together over *time*.

For example, earlier that evening I'd been waiting on one of my regulars, a Bruce Willis look-alike, and I realized with a sharp pain in my gut that he and I would never have a future together. His dead-sexy good looks hadn't concerned me before, but suddenly I was immobilized with remorse.

I reminded myself how wonderful it was to finally be getting married. *Will Rob still want to have sex with me after we tie the knot?* The thought had been entering my head during the strangest of times. I knew the statistics were not in my favor, although I didn't see how a marriage certificate could make such a tremendous difference. Would he glance at the piece of paper periodically and consequently begin to frequent topless bars? It was actually more probable that *I* would keep going to strip clubs since that was my favorite thing to do.

Still concerned with my devotion to someone who only resembled Bruce Willis, I approached Rob the second I got home. As luck would have it, I caught him in a rare moment when he wasn't watching TV. "Rob, do you think married couples have less sex than couples who live together?"

"Why? You don't think we have enough sex?" he answered, his nose stuck in *Food Arts*, feet up on the coffee table.

"No. Well, maybe. I'm just hoping nothing will change after we both sign on the dotted line."

"Trust you to be worried about something like that." He had a way of dismissing important subjects without ever answering my questions.

"I'm not worried; I just want you to reassure me." I wasn't just agitated—by this time I was in a mind-blanking panic! "Have any of your married friends complained to you about not getting it enough?"

"No. And given the babies they're producing, I don't think sex is an issue."

"That's not what I want to hear!" I yelled.

"Pam, calm down." Suddenly the philosopher, Rob plunged into a monologue about couples over the procession of time. According to his mysterious sources, after so many years the urge for sex lessens, but it doesn't have anything to do with marriage, just being together in general. Discomforted by his theory—and the fact that he was able to explain it in detail—I changed the subject, feeling thankful I was getting another ring out of the deal.

***

Working at Lime continued to be a rough gig. Looking back at the countless hours I spent wearing that prisoner uniform while putting up with customers' bullshit—in addition to JT's manic episodes—it is not surprising that I was excited by the prospect of a handsome, rich man taking me shopping. Granted, he wanted to be humiliated in exchange for gifts, but I was fine with that. When I really thought about it, it seemed very little to ask.

I suppose the reasons that brought me to Lime in the first place had something to do with the stepping-stones I'd hopped, stumbled, and tripped over my whole life. It is my belief that I was a product of the times. After all, the early seventies was a difficult period to be born. By the time one earned a college degree, it was about as useful as graduating eighth grade. And if one wasn't prepared to network and kiss ass, well, then, welcome to the world of Wendy's, the fastest-growing chain. But moreover, my generation was one confused bunch of kids. We didn't know what we wanted out of life and lurched through the years hoping we'd figure it out. In the meantime, the need for money overrode the need for moral correctness.

The only time I ever earned an honest living was when I was dancing. People *gave* me money—handed it to me nicely for the excellent service I provided.

The truth was, I grew up stealing. I'd been born with the necessary chromosomes to justify this behavior. My earliest recollection goes back to the third grade. I used to pocket all the *silver* coins from my mother's purse to buy candy for all my friends. (Even at eight years old, I felt that pennies were a useless commodity.) Sharing was also in my veins. I'd steal, and then I'd share. I would swipe a necklace just to give it to a homeless person on the street. And although my parents caught and scolded me numerous times for this behavior, I didn't understand why it was so wrong. *It felt right.* Take from the rich and give to the poor.

I am, however, unsure of why I was predisposed to think this way. Perhaps there is no solid explanation to rationalize who I was, and more importantly, who I was slowly becoming. I soon developed into a person who simply hated working.

My first real job, if you discount babysitting, a short-lived experience due to a lack of patience and the inability to tolerate cartoons, and shoveling driveways, in which I was served up by my parents for free child labor in the neighborhood, was at a clothing store in New Jersey. It was located in an outlet mall near the edge of town, and the tiny shop sold overpriced woman's clothing that catered to the over-forty age bracket. I was fourteen, and I earned $4.25 an hour, minimum wage at the time.

In addition to the pittance of a salary, I despised the uptight bitch who managed the store. She was seventy-five years old and wouldn't let me near the cash register. She didn't trust me, which contradicted her decision to hire me in the first place. Especially considering she'd employed me to keep my eyes open for any suspicious behavior (a.k.a., shoplifters with a penchant for Liz Claiborne). Back then, most privately owned stores hadn't yet installed cameras, so I was in charge of giving the very menacing, teenager evil eye while folding and refolding the same brown wool sweater for six consecutive hours.

I worked alongside two other girls roughly my age. The place was well staffed for a tiny storefront. Apparently the old woman had been going for quantity, not quality. We used to take shifts leaving; two girls would stay and man the ship while one would be free to gallivant through the strip mall. We alternated on the strictest of hourly schedules. My last day on the job, the nasty owner limped by me with her cane. I was eating a waffle cone and zapping bouncing fruit in a game of Ms. Pac-Man at the nearby arcade when I should have been refolding the same brown sweater. I wasn't cut out for retail. What I didn't yet realize was I wasn't cut out for working—period.

My second job was based upon the encouragement—or rather, the insistence—of my parents. I taught swim lessons to assorted tykes of various shapes and sizes at our local YMCA, which was where I first met Tina, who became my lifelong best friend and number one partner-in-crime. This job was short-lived as there was no expansion for growth. (As in no way to steal.)

I seized Tina on my way out the door. It so happened that she had an in with a crazy, perverted old man who owned a fast-food truck stop on Route 22 in New Jersey, and we both found ourselves pocketing as much money as we could for the next three years.

After high school—the day after graduation, to be exact—I rode the bus into Manhattan with no idea what I wanted to do with my life. The eternal artist, I was convinced New Jersey was limited. I needed a versatile city to allow my creative talents to reveal themselves. And so the pattern ensued, one waitress job after another, struggling to pay my rent in cockroach-infested studios. College was a mere afterthought based on the paranoid persistence of my mother.

By the time I was twenty, I didn't care what stigma was attached to a local strip joint in my neighborhood. I didn't want to scrape by anymore. And as I settled into a world of neon lights and pink money, I was only aware of my life becoming less laborious. For the first time, management treated me with respect. I had clients as opposed to customers, and I finally had the upper hand. More importantly, I still considered myself a good person, despite the misgivings my friends and family had about me. Tina was the only friend who thought it was cool. When I first told her the news, she exclaimed, "Maybe you'll meet Robert Downey Jr.!"

The bottom line was I was earning an honest living, and I could afford to eat something other than reduced-price bagels. In fact, I was delighted to be using the same capitalistic system that had used me for so long. Did it change who I was? Probably. Those five years made me into a stronger and more resilient person.

At twenty-six, when everyone found out I'd moved in with Rob and quit the business altogether, they perceived this as personal growth: the ability to walk away from the life without a drug problem and more than a few dollars tucked away in the bank. According to everyone with whom I associated, I was making a valid effort to improve the quality of my life. Only I knew the truth: I was actually careening backward, resorting to my former service industry crutch for less money than I had made in the early nineties.

In addition, I had to adjust to the shock of working for someone other than myself. I returned to dealing with bullshit from managers on a power trip and customers who assumed they were superior beings. Moreover, in the five years I'd been away, the bar and restaurant world had turned corporate, forcing me to find more independent enterprises, seeking cracks in the structure. In short, I was back to the dishonest lifestyle. I'd come full circle.

THREE YEARS EARLIER

"You're fifteen pounds overweight and you know it. I can't put you on stage." My dick of a boss frowned, his disgust apparent. His ruthlessness was slightly concealed behind odd-shaped spectacles and an unrealistic tan. "What the fuck did you do? Eat your way across the country? Or was it all the Vegas buffets?"

I ignored these insults. I knew he didn't want a true explanation. "Give me two weeks," I protested. "I'll work out every day, eat nothing, dance here, and I'll be skinny again."

Catching the mean glint in Jerry's eyes, I sucked in my stomach, reminding myself it was closer to ten pounds—not fifteen. Unfortunately, I wasn't that tall, so the pounds spread horizontally as opposed to vertically.

"You dancers are so frigging stupid. You disappear for months, let your body go to shit, and then expect to jump back into work. I must have told a *thousand* girls this over the years: come see me when you've lost the weight!" He tumbled away— a massive mountain of pizza and burgers rocking the concrete floor. I watched as he plunked down near the stage, my appearance already a scant memory in his mind. Soon he'd be yelling at another slightly overweight girl, and then he'd be back at the pizza place stuffing a calzone in his mouth.

I was left standing alone by the bar, the only woman dressed in street clothes. A few of my stripper acquaintances waved at me from the stage, their expressions revealing inner glee at the sight of my rounder face; one fewer girl to compete with.

"Fine," I muttered, glancing around the club.

The lighting seemed darker, the smell of cigars stronger, and the same men rested on their chairs like peeling wallpaper. I nodded at a few, and they peered at me, uncertain of my identity. Ridiculous. Take away the makeup, put on a shirt, and nobody knew who the hell you were. I'd only been away four months, but the energy in the room shuddered louder with negativity. Taking a deep breath, I stormed out of the rundown basement, back up the two flights of stairs, and out into the fresh air of Times Square, determined to get my job back. Not because I needed the money or particularly loved working there but because Jerry had insinuated I was fat, and I wanted to prove to him I was still hot. And certainly no more overweight than I had been when he first hired me in '95. Four years later, the standards were just higher, and when I say higher, I mean ruinous to the female mind-set; if you weren't super thin, you were nobody. And you certainly couldn't work at Dream Girls on Forty-seventh and Broadway.

At the time, I lived on the Upper East Side in a one-bedroom condo I had purchased in '97 with my considerable dancer's income. I even owned a thirty-five hundred–dollar gym-caliber Precor Elliptical exercise machine, and I went home that day and plugged it back into the wall. I was huffing and puffing on it when I realized working out alone was not going to do the trick. While I was living in Las Vegas, I had let myself go. My ex-boyfriend supported me, and the combination of not working, not sleeping, drinking excessively, and our regular table at the Palm had done me in. Two packs of cigarettes a day hadn't improved matters; I could barely breathe as I pumped my arms and legs, glancing disapprovingly at my profile.

I bit my lip, reminding myself that if I was strong enough to leave that asshole and move back to New York, I could easily

fix the minor mess I was in. I just had to stop drinking gal-
lons of wine and only snack on things. No meals. And rejoin
the gym. There was no feasible way I was going to rely on the
Precor. And knowing myself like I did, I knew I had to keep
busy. Frankly, I needed a job, if only to keep my mind off how
hungry I was going to be. But doing what?

Before I'd entered the world of pink money and fluorescent
lighting, I'd waited tables. Not particularly glamorous, but it
had kept me occupied. But oh God, dealing with strangers was
the utmost worst and something I could only do when I was
making a hundred bucks an hour. Dancing topless in a G-string
was simple; it was the conversation that was draining.

Furthermore, I'd been a terrible waitress, organization and
multitasking not being my greater strengths. I sighed and
opened the *New York Times*, flipping to the classified section. It
felt weird to be looking for a job at twenty-five, so I turned to
the hospitality section, the only area in which I had any experience, if not natural ability. An ad caught my attention. "FOOD
RUNNER WANTED, popular West Village restaurant. Must
be able to do stairs!" it warned. I circled it. Food running?
I wondered to myself what the waiters did if they no longer
served the food. At any rate, it sounded great. I wouldn't have
to talk to anyone, and the stairs would take care of my large ass.

***

I went to the address listed in the newspaper the next afternoon and was interviewed by a woman who, upon hearing my
request, stared at me as if I were insane. Laurie was her name.
She was tall, and her long, straight brown hair was pinned back
by two brown Goody barrettes. Her deep-set eyes pierced mine,
and her nose was a sharp triangle. Everything about her was
pointy.

"You want to run food?" she repeated back at me, barely
moving her lips.

Just for a couple of weeks! "Yes, I understand you're hiring."

"Why?" She stared at me blankly. "We're also hiring waiters. You have the experience." Surprisingly, my fabricated resume had impressed her, and I was now being offered a higher position.

I need to lose weight, and I don't want to talk to any customers. "I need a change."

"Well, we could also use a hostess."

"No!" A happy hostess was the very antithesis of my personality. "I'd rather run food," I reiterated, lowering my voice.

"The food runners make half what the waiters do," she prissily informed me, her triangular nose twitching. I squinted. Since I was used to making between six and eight hundred dollars a night, this detail wasn't relevant to me; I wasn't interviewing at Moon Restaurant for the money.

I nodded my understanding.

"There are three levels to this restaurant. We're sitting on the ground level, and the kitchen is in the basement," she stressed. Apparently Jerry wasn't the only one who thought I looked unfit.

"I can handle it." I hoped this would be true.

"We've never hired a girl runner before," said Laurie thoughtfully.

"So let me train," I countered, thinking she should be so lucky. I spoke English, and I was a legal citizen with no criminal record! What was the problem?

She tapped her triangle and finally relented. "OK, come tomorrow at three p.m. and trail with Franklin. He's been here the longest. Oh, and wear all black," she added. "That includes black socks."

I smiled. I hadn't worn socks to work in five years. A random pair of thigh highs, perhaps, but never socks. *Foot Locker, here I come!*

***

The next day at 3 p.m., I followed Laurie's stick-thin legs down a narrow staircase into Moon's kitchen, feeling like a donut stuffed in pants. In preparation for this experience, I had squeezed myself into a standard black button-down shirt and a new pair of black pants, sickened by the inside tag that announced the number eight to anyone who was talented enough to yank them down over my hips.

This is only temporary, I reminded myself, stepping into the cleanest and brightest utilitarian kitchen known to man. Glancing around, I did another double take; all the employees were white! There wasn't a single Mexican lurking next to the dishwasher or near the door. Was I on *Candid Camera* wearing size-eight pants? I panicked.

"This is Franklin," Laurie said by way of introduction. "Franklin, meet Pamela. This is the girl I told you about."

Franklin was stoned, and his expression was one of perplexed delight. He looked like he'd been plucked from a Californian beach with his short, spiky hair, tan face, and chiseled features. He seemed to lean rather than stand.

I continued to glance around nervously, still wary of hidden cameras given this was the best-looking group of people I'd ever seen operating a kitchen. Franklin stared hard at my chest while he introduced me to the rest of the kitchen staff. I met the executive chef first, and it was clear he was a conceited asshole. "Do you know what chervil is?" he grilled me.

I cleared my throat. "Is this a trick question?"

"No," said Big Chef flatly.

I felt my face flush. "I don't know. What is a chervil?"

"It's a fancy name for parsley," Franklin explained quickly while Big Chef glared at me. "We use it as a garnish," he added, guiding me in another direction.

"Ah," I said, nodding. So this was how the pretentious big boys rolled in a precelebrity chef culture, to which I was on the verge of being exposed.

"He's a real dick," whispered Franklin. "And he won't grow on you, trust me."

Numerous men, all clad in chef whites, gradually marched over with rigid formality to introduce themselves. Had they been dressed in suits, they could have passed as stockbrokers. None of their names registered, partly because there were so few distinguishing characteristics between them. During this meeting of the minds was when I first met Robert Trombetti, although he didn't stand out at the time. He slipped under a high steel table holding a frying pan and shook my hand quickly before slinking off again. It wasn't love at first sight.

As the restaurant became busy and the food orders came in, Franklin taught me the correct way to hold and balance plates. Of course, the stairs added a whole other dimension to this, as did the plates themselves, which were heavy and extremely hot. I was essentially the conduit to the customers receiving their thirty-dollar entrées.

When I had time to glance up, all I could see and hear was Big Chef barking orders to his constituents behind the line, and as the plates of food were prepared and spat back out at him, Big Chef subsequently shouted at Franklin and me. We ran up the stairs with thick, white napkins protecting our arms from third-degree burns, and I tried to remember table and seat numbers. I slammed the plates down in front of the customers and ran back down the stairs, ignoring pleas for extra dressing and additional silverware. *I'm just the food runner. Take it up with your waiter,* I thought, grinning. I didn't have time to wonder how I'd gone from successful exotic dancer to volunteer indentured servant.

The night wore on. It may have been December, but the kitchen was hot like Ecuador. When I dropped my first expensive plate of duck and the ceramic bowl shattered on the tile floor, I cried. This spurred Big Chef to curse at me before transferring his anger to Assistant Big Chef, who then shot a series of deadly looks in my direction. Had this been *my* idea to come here? And more importantly, had I lost the ten pounds yet? The ultimate irony was that food running made me hungry, and my home base was a kitchen! The smell of steak and lamb and pasta wafted in the air thick like passing clouds. And there is no harder mental exercise than eating a cardboard-flavored PowerBar with the aroma of bacon trapped in your nose.

***

I surprised everyone—including myself—by showing up the next day (partially because I didn't have anywhere better to be). Not that I didn't wish to be downing watermelon martinis at the Independent or watching three consecutive movies at the Angelika, but my only goal was to lose weight and I knew that would most certainly happen if I kept up the militant performance. I could tell my coworkers wondered what my deal was, but I just ignored their puzzled looks. I especially ignored Big Chef, whose official name was Big Dick as far as I was concerned. He was the type of person who knew one fact pertaining to every subject and never hesitated to make you feel stupider than you already felt. He treated me like I was a racehorse training for the Grand Prix.

"Chop, chop, this is a business here, not a coffee bar!" he'd chant. One flight up, I could still hear him saying, "Keep the plates level! Level!"

I continued to work at Moon, slowly adapting to my rather tenuous position. The weight wasn't peeling off as quickly as I had hoped, but surprisingly, I wasn't livid. And even though I was still confined to a basement—by some odd coincidence—I had to admit I felt better working with a few clothes on and a little overhead light. Or maybe it was the people, with the exception of Big Dick and Assistant Big Dick. The energy was different. I didn't dread going to Moon the way I feared walking into Dream Girls. I didn't think of it as a vacation by any means, but after a couple of weeks, I didn't feel so out of place and was able to joke around with some of the staff. I wasn't sure if this was because I trusted the job would be temporary or if it all just felt a little more *normal*. But I had to wonder, if it wasn't all about losing weight or making money, what was I really doing there?

***

I was the only woman who worked in the kitchen at Moon, and it slowly dawned on me that this group of culinary wizards had known each other quite a long time. After overhearing a conversation about a barbecue in '93, I turned to Franklin and asked, "How long have these idiots been working together?"

Franklin was staring at an empty plate. "Huh?"

I waved my arm around. "Please tell me this isn't Big Dick's entourage."

"A pathetic example, but yeah, I guess it is. They all came together from some snobby catering hall out on Long Island. That was over two years ago. They brought their own expeditor and dishwashers too. A major crew."

"Well, no wonder they all speak in private tongue. I thought it was just me."

"No. It's *them*. They're all crazy. With the exception of Rob and T-Bone. They're pretty cool guys."

"Which one is T-Bone?" I asked.

"He's normally a line cook, but he's been on the dessert station since our pastry chef quit. He's in the corner over there, fiddling with the sorbets. Pretending he's busy."

"I see. And Rob's the dude who always wears the bandana?"

"Yeah, ponytail, bandana, beard, mustache. Can be super, *super* loud at times."

"Right, the music boy," I said, nodding. His high-pitched laugh could always be heard above the Alice in Chains blaring from his 80's boombox. (I assumed it was *his* because he arrived and left with it every day, along with about thirty CDs.) "I've noticed he does most of the cooking while Big Dick and Assistant Big Dick do most of the yelling."

"That's for sure," agreed Franklin. "Have you ever thought about how this plate is comprised solely of molecular energy?"

"What?"

"This plate is *just* energy."

I stared at Franklin and pursed my lips. "Um, I have given it some thought actually, yes. Not that *particular* plate, but the scientific theory you're referring to."

"Trillions upon trillions of dense particles voluntarily stick together to create this matter," he said seriously.

"I'm not sure it's *voluntary*," I said with a smile. "I think it's more magnetic."

"So that means..." Franklin squinted. "If I were to smash this plate, the energy would spread and create new plates. Kind of like when the Gremlins touched water, they multiplied."

"I left something upstairs in my locker." Science frightened me, especially when it was spouted from a philosophical twenty-year-old with seemingly no goals and no sense of time. I wasn't afraid of him being crazy; I was afraid of him being too smart.

Walking to the locker room for no reason, I noticed the dining room had begun to fill up, which meant soon the kitchen would be flooded with food orders, and I'd be racing up and down the stairs like a lunatic. I counted to ten and was heading back to the kitchen—eyes peeled on the floor in case a customer needed anything—when I heard a variation of my name being bellowed through the restaurant. "Little Pammy!"

I turned full circle in panic. *Already, I'd been discovered!* Before me stood a gigantic African American waitress with a huge Afro and spectacles dangling from her nose. She looked vaguely familiar, and then it dawned on me. "Victoria?" The flashbacks came hard and fast. Six years earlier we had opened Fashion Café together, a short-lived theme restaurant in Rockefeller Center. Visions of us in our quilted bright blue vests drinking Long Island Iced Teas at ten thirty in the morning gripped me. So did the late nights at clubs getting in drunken brawls with other girls in bathrooms. At the time, I'd been walking a dangerous

plank into a dark world, and ironically, relocating to a strip club
had straightened me out. "Holy shit. You work here now, girl?"
I marveled, still in a frightened state of awe.

"Yes. What are you doing running food? Are you crazy?
Why aren't you waiting tables? And where have you been for
the last five years?" she demanded, shaking me. She was the
type of person who invaded your personal space and then proceeded to rock you like a rag doll out of drunken exuberance. I
smelled the Scotch on her breath and felt somewhat comforted
to know that after six years, Victoria still reeked of alcohol.

"I've been in New York, just different gigs, ya know?" I
wasn't about to spill my guts to someone who was probably the
gossip hound of the restaurant, if not the entire West Village.

"Hey, we have some secrets from a long time ago," she continued. "We have to keep those under wraps, if ya know what I'm
saying!" She chuckled heartily and glanced to her left. "Would
you fucking look at that table just scowling at me? Can't they
see I'm busy?" Victoria gave me another shake. "Little Pammy!"
I turned my head and noticed an angry couple glaring at us. I
smirked while Victoria continued to yak. "When I first walked
over to take their drink order, they asked for menus. *Menus*! Can
you believe that? This is an upscale joint. We don't just hand
out menus before they order a cocktail. This ain't no fucking
diner."

I nodded. Nervously. "Vic, I've been working here two
weeks. How come I'm just seeing you for the first time?"

"I was on probation," she whispered, clutching my arm and
moving in close again.

"I need to get back downstairs. We'll catch up later!" I
exclaimed, running away.

Unfortunately, Big Dick had entered through the side
door during my little chat and was already ordering around his
devoted followers. "I need two chicken, two lamb—one mid-
well, one medium rare. Chop! Chop! Rob, where's that fucking
rib eye!"

"Where were you?" Franklin asked nervously as I slipped into sight. "We need to take these six apps to table fifteen. Now." I grabbed three of the plates and followed Franklin up the first flight of stairs and toward the front of the restaurant. This was where all the underage socialites and teen stars liked to sit and order Moonapolitans. I set down a tuna tartare in front of a not-yet-ostracized Tara Reid and tugged on Franklin's sleeve as we headed back down to the kitchen.

"Hey," I said. "I know Victoria from another job."

"Oh Jesus. Don't tell anyone that. The kitchen can't stand her. She's always messing up," he warned.

"That comes as no surprise, believe me. It must be very difficult to wait tables when you're drunk, stoned, and confused to begin with. Throw in an attitude problem and the racial issues..." I muttered while Franklin layered my arms with plates.

"Yeah, totally. You're pretty funny, dude," he said, nodding and grinning.

"Get the food upstairs!" yelled Big Dick.

***

After a month of working at Moon, I'd only lost five pounds. This was partly because working in restaurants drove me to drink. Instead of going home after my shift to eat Lean Cuisine, I went to the neighborhood bar with Victoria, and we put back liquor like it was 1995 again. Reliving the not-so-golden days, I called it.

The job itself was also starting to suck. Big Dick seemed to have it out for me, and Assistant Big Dick was also riding my ass with additional kitchen duties. The restaurant had slowed down after the holidays, so when I wasn't running food, I was rolling cookie dough or separating egg yolks for custard. Sometimes husking corn, shelling peas, chopping celery, you name it. By February I was practically a prep cook.

Franklin's friend Rob, apparently third-in-command, didn't help matters either. He always seemed to be there to stop me from sitting on the kitchen counters during late nights or sneaking any food. For someone who came across so chill, he was a closet stickler for the rules. Moreover, at the end of his shift, he always made himself a giant sandwich and scoffed it down in front of me—usually picking one of my hungrier moments to do this. I'd often point out how inconsiderate his behavior was, and he'd just shrug and turn up the volume on his boom box.

***

Obviously, my demotion from food runner to food runner/prep cook was a time filled with turmoil. I didn't feel comfortable going back to the big stage, but Moon was also unbearable. One slow night after cleaning the walk-in cooler—per Assistant Big Dick's instructions—I actually relented and told pointy-nose Laurie I would wait tables a few nights a week. It was a dangerous decision, but at least I could walk away from my tables. In the kitchen, I was trapped.

One Sunday night, Franklin said I should have a drink with him and T-Bone after work. "Assistant Big Dick asked me to work the late night," I mumbled, turning my head in his direction. ABD was fussing with a bunch of meat on the grill, and the whole place was sizzling to the sound of his inner anger.

"Fuck that. They don't need a runner between midnight and three. It's Sunday night."

"True," I agreed.

An hour later, we slipped out the side door and rounded the corner onto Seventh Avenue. We were headed to Fiddlesticks, a bar I'd never heard of. "Do you think Assistant Big Dick will be mad when he realizes I'm not there?" I asked Franklin, jogging to keep up with his long strides. I'd already consumed two glasses of white wine during work—care of Victoria—and didn't care in the slightest, but I asked this anyway.

"Of course. He'll be furious. It's just him and Vic, and he *hates* her."

"Um, he hates me too," I pointed out.

"Not as much as he hates her. Trust me."

It was freezing outside, so we both began to jog to Fiddlesticks. T-Bone was waiting for us at the horseshoe bar, staring into his dark pint of beer. His nickname didn't suit him. He was tall and lean, with fair hair and eyes. Perhaps Wishbone would have been more appropriate.

"Dude, don't look so glum!" Franklin bellowed, pounding him on the back and scaring the crap out of him.

"Hey, dickwad, try spending your entire night making fairy desserts for rich little cunts, and we'll see how ecstatic you look by the end of the day," he retorted.

"Oh come on, you don't do *anything* back there," claimed Franklin. "I saw you clipping your nails over the wastebasket earlier."

T-Bone finally noticed me behind Franklin and urged us to sit down. A Corona was ordered for me, so I requested three shots of tequila.

"Are all those shots for you?" asked Franklin.

"No, moron. You, plus me, plus T-Bone, equals three," I explained, doling them out.

"You don't fuck around," said T-Bone, accepting the shot. We drained them, and I guzzled half my beer, ignoring the lime and salt. "Oh, hey," he added. "Rob said he'd meet us when he was done placing the orders."

I narrowed my eyes. I associated Rob with the two Big Dicks. "Will he be bringing his own music?" I quipped. Both Franklin and T-Bone laughed. "Seriously, what is it with him and that stereo? I can't believe he lugs that thing around with him every day like he's John Travolta."

"Well, he only lives a block away," said T-Bone.

"Yeah, he's on Ninth Street," added Franklin. "Cool pad, actually. Big for a one bedroom."

"What? How can he afford to live there?" I asked. He didn't dress or act like he could pay two thousand a month in rent. "Oh, shit. What if he squeals on me to Assistant Big Dick?"

"Nah, he wouldn't do that," assured Franklin. "He doesn't like working for them any more than you do."

"Gosh, you'd never know it," I said, worried. After a few drinks, I knew I'd be telling him how obnoxious I thought he was. I pulled another twenty from my purse and intentionally ordered three more shots.

"How much money did you two losers make tonight?" asked T-Bone. "It's been so slow lately."

"Probably just sixty bucks or something," Franklin said, sighing. "Sad, but at least I can chill. Pam has to do all this extra shit. Jeff, or Assistant Big Dick, rather—as Pam refers to him—is totally on her ass."

"Yeah, I've noticed," said T-Bone, turning to face me. "Where did you work before you came to Moon?"

I wrinkled my nose, unable to think of a suitable reply. "I wasn't. Working, that is. I was spending some time in Vegas with a friend." I bit my lip, hoping the scant truth sounded innocuous enough.

"Oh," they both said, the mystery deepening. However, they didn't get the chance to probe because in walked Bandana Rob, toting his stereo. He grabbed the empty seat next to me and plunked the boom box down by my feet. He looked at me as if I were vaguely familiar and said, "What's up?"

"I'm sorry, is it still 1985?"

"If I don't bring the tunes, no one will," he said smoothly, unruffled. And then he started whaling an unfamiliar lyric to an unfamiliar song, strumming an invisible guitar to his own beat. "I'll take a Killian's, man. Thanks," he said to the bartender while I continued to stare at him. He removed a thick, flannel, black-and-white-checkered coat and an underlying Levi's jean jacket to reveal a faded Pink Floyd T-shirt and extremely tight, stonewash jeans. A rusted silver cross attached to a silver chain escaped the confines of his shirt and dangled dangerously close to my arm as he reached for the pint of beer. I shifted my body closer to Franklin. "Cheers, dude," Rob said to the bartender. "Cheers, everybody." He glanced at all three of us before taking a rather long swig. I picked up my bottle and avoided his eyes, thinking about the sandwich he never offered me.

When Franklin and T-Bone stepped outside to smoke a joint, I turned to Rob. "I'm Pamela, by the way."

"I know your name. You've been there two months."

I just blinked. I had nothing else to say to this person.

"How do you like it so far?" he asked.

"It's fine," I said stiffly. "Actually, I hate Tom and Jeff. I refer to them as Big Dick and Assistant Big Dick, respectively."

"Oh," he said, smiling. "We all have *much* worse names for them." And he hooted, a high-pitched birdcall of sorts.

"You're no basket of fruit either, by the way."

"What?" he said, coughing.

"You're not very nice. You're always yelling at somebody. Or laughing at something that no one else can understand so they automatically feel stupid or just being a jerk in general." Rob blinked. A ridiculously large range of motion considering his eyelashes were incredibly long and his brown eyes were enormous. "And you kill me with that fucking sandwich. I'm always starving, and you wolf the whole thing down in front of me. It's so rude."

"I think you mentioned that before. I thought you were kidding."

"No, actually, I wasn't. It *really* bothers me."

He looked behind him, probably praying for the return of Franklin and T-Bone. "Um, do you want another beer?" he asked.

"No, but I'll take a vodka grapefruit. I hate beer. I just drank it to chase the shots."

"You guys did shots?"

"Yeah, tequila. You missed it."

"Thank God. I don't mess with tequila."

"Some people can't handle it. Oh, and please do not mention to Assistant Big Dick that I was here tonight. He wanted
me to work the late night."

"OK, but he's probably coming by after he closes the
restaurant."

"What?" I yelped.

"Just kidding. He won't. And I won't say anything," he said
quietly.

"Thanks." And I smiled at him for the first time.

Franklin and T-Bone returned to the bar cackling, cold
steam billowing from their lips. We all continued to drink into
the early morning, and I was rather drunk when Rob asked me
what I did for fun. "You're witnessing it now, dude. Certainly
nothing intelligent or athletic," I answered. "But I like to see
movies. If I have the whole day off, I sometimes see three or four
in a clip."

"No kidding? I like seeing movies in the daytime too. If
you ever go, you should call me up," he said loosely, scrawling
a phone number on a bar napkin. My eyes were crossing; the
numbers looked more like Arabic symbols.

"Right, sure, OK," I remember saying. But I was thinking,
Why on earth would I want to see a movie with you and your stereo?

***

Strangely enough, after our first encounter speaking in complete sentences, Rob acted nicer toward me at work. I was only
running food on Sundays and waiting tables the other nights,
but when I did have the misfortune of being in the kitchen,
Rob and I would often synchronize our irritation. Whenever
Big Dick would say something particularly cocky or intoler-
able, I'd shoot Rob a look. Deep down, he shared my hatred
for the combined team of head chef and management and even
began offering me some of his late-night sandwich, a true testament of his newfound respect for me.

On Valentine's Day, I volunteered to work to avoid any social expectations. Between passing out heart-shaped desserts and guzzling pink champagne at breakneck speed, I mentioned to Rob how much I despised Hallmark's most-celebrated occasion. "Fucking losers out tonight, big surprise," I muttered.

"Yeah, it's a bullshit holiday," he agreed, kicking a red carnation across the floor.

I went to bed that night and dreamt he and I had sex in the walk-in cooler, among the numerous wooden crates of organic fruit and vegetables. The sex was surprisingly good but came to an abrupt stop when Rob remembered a rack of lamb still smoking on the grill. I woke up in a sweat and thought of little else until I saw him again in the flesh.

As the days passed, I pushed aside all thoughts of him and impending hookup scenarios, but it proved difficult. The fact that I was even *considering* Rob as a potential one-night stand was positively unacceptable. I'd never fallen for that rock-star-in-training look, and he simply didn't possess that polished and refined glow. He was neither rich nor powerful nor distinguished. I detested his long hair and simply didn't understand how anyone could smoke pot twelve times a day and not be permanently stupid. In addition, his wardrobe of concert T-shirts and tight jeans was worrisome. And what was up with the Levi's jean jacket? It wasn't like he was sixteen. He was thirty.

He did have great eyes, however: huge, brown orbs with dark, long lashes that stared at me in the form of a question mark. Eerie or enchanting? All I knew is that after a few weeks of ignoring his dumbfounded gaze, I got annoyed when he stopped doing it. Suddenly I was the one watching him. Could I actually be attracted to a chef who was convinced he was Jimmy Page? I fretted. Truthfully, it had been so long since I'd met a man outside the strip club setting that I was unfamiliar with what an average man was like—one who actually got to know me *before* seeing me topless.

I would catch myself watching him cook. I marveled at the way he tossed food around in a pan and none would fall out. One afternoon, I watched him cruise into the kitchen with his long hair slicked back, dressed in a worn-out Zebra tank top. He was balancing his stereo, a CD Walkman, and a large bong. I shook my head and thought, *No, no, no!*

I stared hard at a filet of seared tuna and focused on the task at hand. To further complicate matters, on this particular day everyone was wishing him a happy birthday. Calculating quickly in my head, I realized he was a Pisces like me. That couldn't be good, I thought. I liked my men hard like tigers, not soft like fish. I also knew through a vast amount of personal experience that all my other encounters with Pisces men had ended badly. According to the stars, I was best suited for a Capricorn or Scorpio, the ram and scorpion both intimidating creatures of the wild. Unless Rob was a stingray in disguise, the universe was clearly trying to warn me.

Despite my inner turmoil, I snuck up on him and said, "Hey, I got you a birthday card. It's in my locker."

He moved around arrogantly, reorganizing a shelf of pots and pans with no particular urgency. I watched him stack them on top of the dishwasher according to size. "That's all you got me?"

I gritted my teeth, hating myself. "Yeah, the card wasn't actually meant for *you*, but I happened to have an extra one in my bag. For situations such as these."

He smiled as if he'd been expecting a card and said, "Give it to me later."

"Err, OK." *Does that mean I'll be seeing him later? What is happening?*

Before I left work, I went and fetched the card—feeling a little guilty about the friend I'd actually purchased it for—and scribbled, "Nice working with you since I no longer consider you a jerk." (I didn't want to be too obvious about any ulterior motives I was still trying to squash.)

"Here you go." I handed him the yellow envelope.

"Yellow?" he scoffed, wiping his hands on a rag before accepting it. "What a sissy color. There weren't any blue envelopes? Even green or purple would have been better. Shit, I gotta carry this around with me?" he joked.

"You're welcome." Why did I *like* this guy?

"Thanks." He winked. "I'll read it later."

"Later when?"

"When I leave and go home."

My heart began to pound. The thought of not seeing him until the next day left me bereft. I couldn't believe this! "So you're going straight home? Oh, that's right. I don't suppose you could go out in public holding a yellow envelope *and* a boom box."

"I could hide it in my locker."

"Well, in that case…"

"Where are *you* going?" he asked.

Franklin and T-Bone were already at the Corner Bistro and waiting for me. "Corner Bistro," I mumbled.

"Yeah."

"Yep."

"Maybe I'll join you when I get done."

"When will that be?" I swallowed hard.

"Soon."

***

An hour later, I was crammed into a small booth between Franklin and Rob. T-Bone had disappeared to order us some burgers, and I was sneaking sidelong glances at Rob while acting nonchalant. After a couple of drinks, I was so attracted to him that I couldn't look him in the eye. "Did you find a *private* place to read my yellow card?" I asked, looking down at the table.

"Yes, I did."

"I am funny, right?"

"Hysterical." He caught my eye and gave me a lopsided smile.

I wrestled with myself. *This is a bad idea. I want him. This is a bad idea. I want him.* "So, do you play any sports?" I asked. "Or did you? Ever?" It was obvious to the both of us that I had no idea how to begin a conversation with someone wearing stone-wash in the dead of winter.

"When? In high school?"

"Or college? If you went. Or just in general?"

He laughed his high-pitched bird noise and clapped his hands in response to what I translated to be funny memories. "Well, I wasn't an athlete. I guess my classification would have been more along the lines of burnout. Spent more time in the parking lot than on the playing field, if you get my drift. I made fun of the jocks, if you will."

"I made fun of the cheerleaders!" At last I had one thing in common with this guy. "Where did you grow up?"

"Long Island. Nassau County. You?"

"Jersey. Then Manhattan until now. Still growing, ya know?"

"And you, did you play any sports?" he stuttered, sounding just as stupid as I had minutes before.

"I just hung out at the mall. Before I was forced to get a job, that is."

"I see."

Having returned from the burger counter, T-Bone added his two cents. "Have Rob tell you about his *Karate Kid* moves."

I turned to Rob expectantly. He looked embarrassed. "It's called martial arts, you ignorant dick bag!" he shouted at T-Bone.

"Haaaaahhhh-chaaaaaaaa," drawled T-bone, making a stiff two-handed gesture in the air. "Whhhaaaaa-chuuuuuung."

"And I can kick your ass from across this table," added Rob, not looking too happy.

I turned to him. "What color belt are you?" I knew a little bit about the practice. (I'd seen *Karate Kid* six or seven times, having been in love with Ralph Macchio for several years as a child.)

"Brown."

"That's only one step away from black!" I exclaimed. He certainly didn't look like any black belt I'd ever met. It did, however, explain the bandana.

Rob shrugged.

"He also plays a mean game of handball!" chirped Franklin, who was eavesdropping on our conversation. "He's beaten me a dozen times."

"That's 'cause you suck, dude," said Rob.

"Interesting." I'd always thought of handball as a sport one played in an Italian neighborhood or in jail. This was an entirely different take on things. Franklin and T-Bone started to argue over who was the best handball player they knew, and I made another attempt at conversation with Rob. "I know you listen to a lot of music, but do you ever read?"

"Read what? Books? Magazines? Billboards? Signs?"

"Books. It goes without saying you have a subscription to *Rolling Stone.*"

"I do have a subscription to *Rolling Stone.* But I also read books."

"What type?"

"Mostly paperback thrillers I get from my father. Now, he's an avid reader," he said with a chuckle, clapping his hands to yet another hilarious joke I was not privy to.

"I like true crime." I wondered why I was telling him this.

"Oh yeah? Me too. Maybe I have a few you haven't read."

"I doubt it. I've read everything there is. Executing the perfect crime has been one of my lifelong goals," I confessed, thinking I should just shut up because I sounded like a moron.

"No kidding."

"Yep. In college I majored in sociology with a concentration in organized crime. I was trying to get my foot in the door, so to speak."

"You sound dedicated."

"I was."

"And then?"

"Then, I dunno. The dream fell apart."

The bar kicked us out at four, and we all staggered outside into the cold.

"Oh my God. Where's your stereo?" I asked Rob. "Did you leave it inside?" I must have appeared genuinely worried because he smiled.

"Nah, I left it at work. They won't care for one night."

"Where can we go now?" I asked. The night couldn't just end because it was late. "I might be able to get us into Halo. It's just around the corner, closer to Grove Street."

"Let's go," said Rob.

"Yo dudes, I'm going back to Brooklyn," announced Franklin. "I'm tired."

Franklin left, and I walked to Halo with T-Bone and Rob. The oak doorway leading to the basement lounge was gated and shut. "Oh, I forgot it's Sunday. Fuck. Nothing will be open." I sighed.

"I'm just gonna split," said T-Bone. "Pam, I'll take you home." T-Bone lived in the Bronx and sometimes gave me a ride home to the Upper East Side to save me from taking a cab.

I glanced at Rob, but he didn't say anything helpful. He didn't say anything at all. I knew if I refused the ride, it would be obvious to the both of them I wanted to hook up. I stood there, paralyzed. I shouldn't be hooking up with Rob anyway, I reminded myself. What was I doing?

"My car is parked on West Fourth," said T-Bone. "Are you coming?"

"Yeah, yeah," I said, but as I hurried to catch up with him, I glanced back at Rob at the same moment he looked back at me.

And our eyes met squarely for the first time all evening. And I just knew.

***

Waiting tables at Moon was a total joke. Monday nights I averaged six tables during the eight-hour shift. And truth be told, I liked it that way. I *liked* hanging around doing nothing. And I excelled at it. I'd worked hard my whole life: all through high school, all through college, and ever since. I was eleven days away from turning twenty-six, and I was primed for retirement.

This explained why I had so much time to dillydally near the locker room during Rob's expected time of arrival. When I wasn't creeping around my one table, praying nobody would ask me for anything, I was staring at the Moon bulletin board adjacent to the locker room, replaying the events of the night before. Had I imagined the mutual response in Rob's eyes? Had that look actually transpired? I was so distracted that I didn't see Rob duck by me. I only heard a small hi mumbled under his breath, which reached my ears after he'd already passed. I left my staunch post at the bulletin board and approached the locker room like a burglar. I was alert, cautious, and obsessed.

"Hey," I said to the crouched figure with a head of soaking wet hair. As I stood there, I couldn't *believe* I was making a play for this guy. Torn between longing and revulsion, I noticed he was stuffing used books into his locker.

"Uh, hi," he murmured without looking up.

"Are those books for *me?*"

He was sweating now, looking for a way out of the locker room. "Yeah, I'll give them to you later. I'm running late."

"It's so cool you remembered." Not that I'd told him to bring the books. I'd specifically told him *not to*. That I'd read everything already, and his extensive library of paperbacks could not possibly impress me.

I stared at his profile. His nose was not his best feature. I'd done a research paper on state birds during my senior year in high school, and I was again reminded of our national symbol, the bald eagle. But whatever, none of the attraction made sense anyway. He'd brought me used books! Normally, I would have been appalled, but I was thrilled. *He obviously wants me if he's loaning me a copy of* Jack the Ripper! And as soon as I had this ridiculous revelation, he ran past me, sprinting down the stairs. I stared at his locker, knowing its contents, and felt special. I felt like I hadn't felt in a long time. I wandered slowly out of the locker room and back into the dining room. How I even remembered that I was overseeing a table of six was simply fortunate for them.

During the next three hours, I had no new tables and no excuse to enter the kitchen. When the opportunity finally did arise, I descended the stairs two at a time. "Are we on the late-night menu yet?" I asked, directing my question to Rob despite the fact that Assistant Big Dick was in charge. I hadn't acknowledged ABD since New Year's Eve when he'd yelled at me for popping a balloon in his face.

"Yeeeeeessssss, we aaaarrrreee!" yelled ABD. "We've been on it for thirty minutes alreadddddddddy! How long have you worked here?"

"Just making sure. That means I'm outta here," I announced, hoping Rob would get the hint and find an excuse to come upstairs. After all, he had to give me the used books.

"Pam, can you get me a drink before you go?" asked Rob. He was holding his favorite big plastic Tupperware container.

"Coke?" This meant Jack and Coke.

"Yeah, thanks."

When I returned with the massive "soda," he asked if I was going out. "I could. Victoria wants to go to Stick Fiddle."

Rob made a face. Like the rest of the kitchen, he wasn't the hugest fan of Victoria. "Fiddlesticks," he corrected me.

"Whatever."

"Will you still be there at three a.m. when I get done?"

"I don't know. It depends," I said.

"On what?"

"If you're going to come by," I gambled. Out of the corner of my eye, I could see ABD watching our interaction.

"Yeah, I'll definitely meet up with you, but if you want, stop by before that."

This confused me. "Where? Here?"

"Yeah."

"Why would I want to do that?" I glanced up at ABD and met his glare for the first time in a month.

"I'll be the *only* one here," Rob whispered. "We could go upstairs and raid the bar."

"There's an idea. Maybe," I contended, remembering my dream about the walk-in cooler. "But if I don't, just go to Stick Fiddle when you're done.

"OK." He laughed, shaking his head.

***

Fiddlesticks kicked Victoria and me out at 2 a.m., claiming they were closing. "You're not closing! You just don't like me 'cause I'm black!" Victoria yelled at the bartender. I put my head in my hands. This wasn't the first time I'd heard her say this, nor was it still a fresh, new thing to say.

"As you can see, everyone is leaving. Even the white people." The bartender indicated with his hand the various ethnicities walking out. "See, Chinese, Caucasian, rednecks, everyone is *leaving* this bar. It's only Monday, for Christ's sake."

"It's fine." I elbowed Victoria.

"Fifty-five Bar on Christopher Street is open until four," he broadcast curtly before skipping away.

"Isn't that a gay bar?" Victoria asked me, as if I had any clue.

"Who cares? Let's just go. But we have to stop by Moon on the way and let Rob know we're changing locations. I told him we'd be here."

"Rob? From the kitchen?"

"Yeah."

"Isn't he the scruffy little one?"

I smiled. "Um, I guess."

"Oh, he's the *worst* one down there! The rudest! The meanest! Why do you want *him* to meet us?"

"He's not so bad," I said in his defense, having thought exactly the same thing two months ago. "Anyway, I invited him, and Moon is on the way back to Christopher Street."

Victoria scratched her head. "All right. But I'm not going inside. I'll wait for you outside."

"Good."

When we got to Moon, I staggered into the kitchen holding a half-empty pint of beer and an unlit cigarette. Rob was sitting on one of the counters flipping through a heavy metal magazine and sipping from the same container of Jack and Coke. Probably a refill, I assumed. His stereo was blaring something painful.

"Hey," he said, looking up.

"Hey, I brought you this." I handed him the half-empty glass of Killian's. "It was full when I left."

"Thanks. Wouldn't a bottle have been easier to carry?"

"Probably. Anyway, the joint closed so Vic and I are on route to Fifty-Five Bar on Christopher Street—"

"Yo, Rob Dog, can you make me a burger? I'm fucking starving!" hollered Victoria, blazing through the kitchen. She made a beeline for a plate of cold French fries, apparently having changed her mind about following me inside.

"I don't think we have time," I said, pointing at my watch. Rob just stared at her like he was witnessing an explosion. Loosing interest with the cold fries, she zoomed past us into the cooler to raid the raw bar. I coughed and smiled at Rob, pretending I had no clue as to who had followed me inside. "Um, you know where Fifty-Five Bar is, right?"

"Yeah. I should be there in about half an hour."

"Great. Here is my cell number just in case." I tore a piece of paper from the printer and wrote it down before fetching

Victoria from the cooler. "Wipe the cocktail sauce off your face," I ordered.

At 55 Bar, I realized I needed to come clean about my intentions with Rob, otherwise Victoria was not going to leave us alone for any small amount of time. I cleared my throat. "The reason Rob is joining us is because I like him."

"God knows why," she muttered, not getting my point.

"No. I *like* him, like him."

"Scruffy!" she screeched.

"Yes."

"What?" she exclaimed. "*Why?* He's awful!!!"

I shrugged. "I can't explain it either."

"But you guys would make a terrible couple! You're so sweet and cute, and he's such an asshole! And that fucking mouth of his, always swearing and yelling."

"The reason I'm telling you this is because if I leave *with* him, you know it's something I *want* to be doing."

"Oh my God, you might go home with him? I can't picture this at all!"

"OK, so don't try. I just wanted to warn you before he got here."

"You guys are *not* suited for each other," she reemphasized.

I sighed. "Please don't say anything. I'm not one hundred percent positive he's into me."

"Why wouldn't he be? On a scale of one to ten, he's a one and you're *at least* a seven."

"Gee, thanks. At any rate, I'd also like a little *alone* time with him, if you get my drift."

"Don't worry, I'll leave the second he gets here."

"Wait at least five minutes; otherwise it will look too obvious."

"OK. Just give me the nod."

"Fine."

Once Rob got there, boom box in tow, Victoria waited an hour and I almost killed her. I spent forty-five minutes nodding like I was having a seizure while she talked about how much she hated the kitchen staff. "You're not *so* bad," she told Rob after concluding her diatribe. "But I only just changed my mind. I disliked you *the most* before tonight."

Rob looked at me and grinned.

When he finally got up to use the bathroom, I turned to Victoria. "What the hell are you still doing here?"

"I'm trying to gauge if you two will be compatible."

"Will you leave that up to me and hit the road?"

"You're dying for some, aren't you?"

"It's almost four o'clock. I only have ten minutes to work my magic. Please, I'm begging you."

"OK, but be safe," she said, putting on her coat. "God knows where he's been."

"Good night!"

Rob was standing behind me when I swiveled back around on my chair. "Victoria had to go. What a shame," I said, sighing.

"I didn't know you two were friends."

"Friends is a loose term, but I've known her a *long* time. Too long, in fact."

"I see."

"She's actually calmed down. I used to hang out with her when she was completely crazy."

Rob sat down again and picked up his beer.

"Move your chair closer," I urged bravely. He stared at me with those huge brown eyes. "If you want?"

He complied, and our knees touched. "This took a lot of planning to finally get together," he said thoughtfully.

"Yeah, I wanted to hang out for a while now, but I had to be sure. After last night, I was more than sure," I said, staring at my hands.

"Me too, but then you left with T-Bone. You shot me a look, though. Jeez, you're already confusing."

"Well, you didn't say anything when he offered me the ride, so I didn't know what to do. Plus, I didn't know if it was all in my head."

"What? We've been flirting for two months!"

"Two months ago you wouldn't even give me a bite of your sandwich!" He had taken my hand in his and was rubbing his thumb back and forth over my fingers. I was suddenly terrified.

"This place is closing. What do you want to do?" asked Rob.

I shrugged and looked at him expectantly.

"Well, we can get a six-pack and go back to my place. I only live a block away."

"That's an option." This was the *only* thing I wanted to do.

He held my hand as we crossed Sixth Avenue and walked north toward Ninth Street.

"Wow, you live so close to work," I remarked. "How did you manage that?"

"Coincidence, honestly. The apartment used to be my cousin's. When he moved back to Long Island, he signed the lease over to me."

"Cool," I muttered.

"That's my building," he said, pointing to a brick brownstone before leading me down the stairs into a bright deli. It sold an enormous selection of beer and seemed clean. A slaphappy Asian man nodded as we weaved alongside the back coolers.

"What do you like?" asked Rob.

"Corona. Regulation. No light versions."

Rob grabbed a six-pack and glanced back at me to make sure I was following him to the register. At this point, I would have followed him to Iceland. He handed over some cash, and I stood there watching him. His ponytail was unraveling, and I thought that might be a good opening for, "Why don't you cut that shit off?" but I held back. He grabbed my hand again and pulled me out of the deli and up his front steps. I only had two

seconds to admire the decorative columns that supported his
West Village gem.

A night doorman was fast asleep in a dirty chair "protecting" the building. We sped past him, and Rob unlocked the
door to a first-floor apartment. Turning on the light, he guided
me two feet forward to what sufficed as a couch. The beer was
set down on the floor beside my foot, just like the stereo I'd
forgotten he was carrying. He opened two bottles with the back
of a hammer—and perhaps he handed me a Corona. I may have
even taken a sip or drank the whole bottle. The only thing I
remember is how Rob took my face in his hands and kissed me.
He cupped my chin and pulled me to him. There was no awk-
wardness or overzealous tongue action. We simply dissolved
into each other.

***

At 2 p.m. the next day, Rob had to detach himself from me to
go to work. We hadn't slept or spoken in ten hours. And as I
watched him skip down the street, I didn't point out that he'd
forgotten his stereo. *No tunes for the kitchen today*, I thought happily, heading uptown in a cab. I wasn't concerned that I'd slept
with him on the first "date" or that he might act differently
when I got to work later. I suddenly believed in fate.

Later that evening, he handed me a key to his apartment.
"You're coming over when you get done, right?"

I stared at the shiny piece of metal like it had magical powers. "Yes, yes. Of course."

Two weeks later, I was staring at the computer screen at
Moon during a very busy rush when it hit me like a thunder-
bolt. *He was the one.* I'd never put much stake in the expression
before, but I was suddenly breathless. A month later, I sublet
my apartment and moved into his. I began the new millennium
with a brand new life.

Part 2

PAM AND JAKE

Manhattan, NY

NOVEMBER 2002

Two hours after Jake bought Mimi and I shoes at Saks, the three of us gathered around a shiny black booth at Commune, a once-popular restaurant in the Flatiron District. Its dim atmosphere and ominous red lighting provided the perfect backdrop for our offbeat antics.

Mimi was stretching out raft-style while Jake competed for elbowroom with the wall. I sat opposite them, admiring my three new pairs of designer shoes: a short pair of burgundy boots with a skinny heel from Dolce Gabbana's latest collection, Chanel boots that came up past my knee, and a pair of chocolate brown Coach mules. I held tight to my shopping bag, inhaling the scent of new, fresh leather.

Mimi had less to be happy about, but that was entirely her fault. She had been a terrible shopper and Jake had to convince her that two pairs of Gucci heels would bring out her feminine side. Both she and I knew this was extremely unlikely, and she'd never wear them outside her apartment. I, on the other hand, was planning to buy all-new outfits to match my new shoes.

"You two did a great job of running up my credit card today," said Jake, sipping his gin and tonic. "I think, all in all, it came to twenty-three hundred dollars for Pamela and twelve hundred for Mimi. You guys took me for thirty-five hundred today. How does that feel?"

"Marvelous," I said, unable to peel the goofy smile off my face. I was high on life. Evidently there is a first time for everything.

"You, Mimi?" asked Jake.

"I would have preferred the cash."

"Well, I love my gifts!" I announced.

"Not to mention I could have bought twenty pairs of shoes in H&M for what you paid for two," added Mimi.

"Mimi, you don't get it," I said, shaking my head.

Jake looked at me as if noticing me for the very first time. "You know, Mimi told me you were crazy about shopping. After today, I can see she wasn't kidding. What is the date of your wedding?" he asked.

"The twenty-eighth of February," I said stiffly. It unnerved me how rapidly it was approaching. I felt like I was discussing someone else's life.

"Where's it being held?"

"A Long Island catering hall. Like most weddings around here."

"Well," said Jake. "I think I should buy your wedding shoes and have you walk on me with them. That would be pretty pathetic. And if you'd allow me to be a total doormat, I'd like to buy all the bridesmaids' shoes as well—and of course, the hosiery. That goes without saying."

"It does?"

"Yeah, I know a woman at Wolford on Madison who loves to treat me like the little sissy wimp I am. She'd be thrilled to pick out the finest stockings for you. At least two pairs each, in case anyone gets a run."

"Seriously?" I said.

"How many girls do you have in your wedding party?"

"Including me, only four."

"Who are they?"

"Well, Tina is my maid of honor. She's my best friend, but she lives in Montana."

"Montana? Who the hell lives out there?"

"Um, generally humanitarians and those who refuse to pay taxes. Tina falls into the first category. She's a doctor." Jake looked impressed while Mimi smirked into her cheese plate, unable to conceive of such a noble profession. "And then there's Donna," I continued. "She works with us at Lime. And Lexi is my number three. She used to work with me at Dream Girls," I added.

"It would be the ultimate turn on! I've never done anything like that before. It would mean me having to buy your wedding shoes and the shoes for your bridesmaids, just so you could go and marry someone else. And the only thing I'd get out of it would be the privilege of licking the bottoms of the shoes after the reception."

"That sounds fair," I said, laughing. "You can come to the wedding. See the shoes in action." I glanced over at Mimi, who didn't seem to be paying attention. I knew better.

"What color are your bridesmaid dresses?" asked Jake.

"Dark purplish. Eggplant. There is a fancier name for it, but I can't pronounce it."

"OK, so you'd probably want to go with black heels. Closed toe or open?"

"It will be cold so closed toe, I guess." My mind was whirling. To get my friends free designer shoes would be fantastic! But how would I explain it?

"Who's in your wedding party again?" asked Mimi. She was swilling her wine while simultaneously chain-smoking and pouring a powdery white substance into her left hand. I was surprised she still had the ability to ask questions.

I gave Jake a sidelong glance. "We just went over this. Tina is my maid of honor," I repeated. "Lexi and Donna are bridesmaids."

"Who is Lexi again?" asked Mimi.

"After Tina, she's my oldest friend. I met her in '95 when we worked together at Dream Girls." I felt like I was explaining this to a small child.

"I wish I'd known you then," said Jake, laughter in his voice.

Mimi turned away from the table to snort the drugs in her hand. "But you never even see her now," she mumbled into her hand. "I see you almost *every* day."

"I still see her; you just don't hear about it. I don't know anyone you hang out with outside of work." *Thank God for small favors.* "Anyway, what is your point?"

"How come Lexi gets to be a bridesmaid and I don't?"

I stared at her—then at Jake—then back at Mimi. The red candle on the table illuminated her gothic features, a flashing danger sign.

"I've been friends with her for *nine* years, and I've only known you a few months," I said.

"But I want to be a bridesmaid. Why didn't you ask me?"

Was I actually at liberty to give an answer here? Out of the corner of my eye, I could see Jake looking incredulously at the both of us.

"I've never been a bridesmaid before," moaned Mimi. "I've never even been to a wedding. Mine were both held at city hall!"

"Aren't you, like, twenty-six?" said Jake. "You've never been to a wedding before?"

"Mimi," I started, "I'm flattered but I'm just not sure—"

"What? You think Rob would care?"

"Well, I just don't know," I said, gulping vodka. "We're trying to keep the wedding parties small."

"So you don't want to include me," she accused. Her eyes shined like tinfoil.

"The idea just never occurred to me," I said.

"Mimi, it's not a play. It's a wedding," said Jake, coming to my rescue.

I suppose there is no reason to exclude her, apart from her being irresponsible and a drug addict. Certainly, no one else was asking to be included. Moreover, there was a space for her, since my sister had declined the invitation. "Not my cup of tea," Christine had told me.

"You'd have to get a dress," I said finally. "I don't know if it's still available."

"Donna said you got them at Bloomingdales. Jake can order me one online." *Fucking Donna.*

"Jake, are you taking notes?" I asked, raising my eyebrows.

"Well, ah, do you know the name of the designer?" he said, squinting.

"Laundry by Shelly Segal."

"How long ago did the other girls purchase theirs?"

"Back in August," I said.

"OK, so it may have been a summer item," said Jake. "I suppose Mimi could backorder it on the web, presuming you know the product number." I smiled, thinking it was clever how Jake had turned it back around to be Mimi's responsibility.

"Jake, how do you know this shit?" asked Mimi.

Jake sneaked a glance at me before answering. "Because I sometimes order clothes online. I shop with an idea of what I want. I don't just go *wild* in H&M."

"Fuck you. Can you get me the dress or not?" said Mimi, charm leaking from her every pore.

"I don't think it would be too difficult."

Mimi positively lit up. It was like Darth Vader removing his mask.

God knows what I looked like. Probably like a stunned Luke Skywalker.

I tried to pull myself together. *After all, what were the actual chances of her following through with this?*

***

I walked into the apartment, attempting to be nonchalant about the huge bag from Saks I was holding. It wasn't as if I was hiding anything necessarily.

"Hi," I said, hearing the buzz of the TV.

"Hi," said Rob looking up, one hand on the clicker, the other hand wedged in a bag of Lay's potato chips. His big brown eyes stared up at me, and I dropped the shopping bag down with a thump, signifying I was holding nothing of importance. A bag of rocks amassed in brown paper. I sat next to him on the couch and casually reached for a chip.

"Kisses," I said. Rob kissed my cheek and returned his attention to the Discovery channel. "A real kiss. Don't be stingy with the kisses."

Rob rolled his eyes and kissed me quickly on the lips. "You're home early. I thought you were 'going out on the town.'" He shook his chest, doing his impression of me dancing topless. Despite him never witnessing such a thing, it was still one of his favorite and practiced imitations. Obviously, I never should have told him about any former jobs or evenings out at Red Rock West. Or anything fun at all, really.

"We just went shopping and then out to dinner. Mimi and I. And Jake," I added.

"Oh, yeah. Where did you guys eat?"

"Commune."

"How is that place?"

"It's OK. Nothing great."

A minute went by before Rob asked, "Who's Jake?"

As if I could sum him up in a few quick words. "Mimi's new catch." I ran my tongue along the sides of my teeth.

"Lucky guy," said Rob sarcastically.

"He might be good for her. She could benefit from some stability," I said, coughing.

"She could benefit from some sleep," said Rob, and he'd only met her once when he'd given her a ride home from work. "What's in the bag?" he asked.

"Which bag?"

Rob pointed to the Saks shopping bag.

"I told you. We went shopping."

"With Mimi and her boyfriend? That's weird."

"Well, it was actually the point. This dude, Jake, his company handles one of Saks Fifth Avenue's accounts—some money management, profit-sharing type business thing. I don't know much about it. The important thing is he gets a discount so Mimi dragged him along for our sake. Cool, huh?"

"How much of a discount?"

One hundred percent. "Like, um, thirty. Isn't that great?"

"I suppose, but thirty percent off in Saks is like normal prices everywhere else. I thought you were saving all your money for this wedding. The same wedding you talked me into."

"Please Rob, it would have been ludicrous to ignore this fantastic opportunity."

Rob glanced at me warily. "OK, as long as you're coming up with your share."

"Of course, I am. I work five nights a week."

"I'm not saying you don't work. I'm just saying you spend a lot. Two different subjects."

"You think I spend a lot?"

"Pam, cut the shit."

Instead of vehemently defending myself like I normally did, I thought it wise to say nothing.

***

I pursed my lips in determination, trying to block out JT's fiery insults from across the room.

"Donna! Pam! Get over here!"

It was almost five, and we were about to open the upstairs lounge for business. I was shoving napkins under the table legs to lessen the wobbling while Donna was wiping the surfaces down. Essentially, we were just talking.

"Jesus, what now?" I mumbled, standing up.

JT charged across the floor in our direction. Before I could blink, he was standing next to me, neck vein pulsating, eyes twitching. Normally it took him a few hours to get him to this point, so I knew whatever he had to say was not going to be good.

"Your fucking piece-of-shit friend Mimi just quit! Did you know anything about this? Wolves travel in packs!" Donna and I stared at each other. For once, we didn't know anything. And if it came down to it, I knew more than Donna. "That *whore* leaves me a message five minutes before she's supposed to be here, and you two know nothing? I find that hard to believe!"

JT's nostrils were actually flaring, which frightened me into responding. "She met a guy," I squeaked.

"Well, she had better start screwing somebody for money because she'll never work here again!" JT raged. "And that bitch owes me fifty dollars!" He charged off in the pursuit of happiness.

"Did you know Mimi was going to quit?" asked Donna.

"She'd didn't say anything to me. She probably just decided this very second. I'll call her and see what's up." I marched into the bathroom, dialing Mimi's number. She answered right away, probably anticipating our call.

"Pam?" she asked.

"Is this your idea of a joke?"

"No, I quit. Fuck JT and that shithole. I don't need the hassle."

"But do you need the money? Jobs pay bills."

"Pam, spare me. I've made five thousand dollars in the past six weeks, and Jake told me if I ever wanted to quit, he'd pay my rent."

"And you know this for a fact?" Feeling a pang of jealousy, I reminded myself that if it sounds too good to be true, it normally is.

"Yes, that's what he implied."

"Implied?"

"Yeah, he said that he'd help me if I wanted to try something else."

"Oh boy."

"Pam, trust me. It's cool."

"OK, because JT is pissed. He says you also owe him money."

"Oh Jesus. I do not! I gave him fifty dollars' worth of sleeping pills last time I was there. He was just too fucked up to remember."

"OK, more importantly, when am *I* going to see you again?" I didn't want her disappearing on me just as life was becoming more interesting. Declaring her a bridesmaid didn't guarantee anything. "Are we going to do another dog food night soon or what?"

"Next Tuesday. Think of another good place to meet up. The two of us are hopeless when it comes to choosing a restaurant."

JT was near the bathroom door. I could feel his negative energy. I snapped the phone shut before he appeared. "What did that lousy tramp have to say for herself?"

"She says she doesn't need this job, she's snagged a sugar daddy, and she doesn't owe you any money."

"Give me that phone!" He grabbed it and pressed redial. I cringed and stepped back. Mimi must have picked up again because JT went off on her. "If you ever step foot in this restaurant again, I will escort you out by the neck and pummel your face into the ground!" I looked down at my nails, willing myself to disappear. "If I ever see you on the street, you had better walk the other way, honey! Because I'm the meanest gay man you'll ever meet!" he finished with a flourish. Luckily Mimi wasn't an overly sensitive person.

"Get to work!" he yelled at me. I made a mental note to give two weeks' notice before quitting.

***

Given what happened, it was no surprise JT forced me to work Mimi's Monday night shift. Under normal conditions, I would have been furious about having to work this colossal waste of time, but I agreed, hoping Jake would still come in and I could make some serious money. In retrospect, Mimi was stupider than I initially realized for relinquishing her Monday night shift. *There is always an understudy waiting in the wings!* And I was mentally prepared. Dipping my hand into the drink bucket was another story, but I was sure I'd be able to manage it with the proper incentive.

It was almost ten o'clock on Monday night when I began to think there was no way Jake was going to show up. I figured he had probably talked to Mimi over the weekend and learned of her job reversal, so I was surprised when he wandered through the door at ten thirty. Then again, Mimi could have been on a bender Saturday and slept through the last two days without alerting a soul, I considered, jumping up from the couch to reassure him we were still open.

When I sunk into the seat across from him, his surprise was apparent; he was clearly not expecting to see me. "Hey. What did you do? Kidnap our Mimi?"

"No. Mimi quit, and I'm stuck with her stupid shift. Didn't she tell you?"

"No, I haven't talked to her in a couple days. She quit?"

"Yeah. I figured you knew."

"Well, she told me she didn't like working here. Something about her boss being a jerk, but I didn't expect her to run so quickly. I mean, everyone hates their boss, so it's a difficult statement to take seriously."

"She must have had her reasons." I looked the reason in the eye.

"It's lucky that you're working, then."

"Luck had little to do with it. Donna uses the excuse she has school on Mondays, so there was no one else to ask." I wanted it to seem like an accident as opposed to a well-devised plan. "Can I get you a drink? Something disgusting, perhaps?"

"Yeah, how about a Beefeater and tonic, and a glass from the drink bucket?"

I silently cheered. "Coming right up. Do you want a menu, or did you bring your own food?"

"I brought some staples, but what's the soup today?"

"I have no idea. It's usually Manhattan clam chowder. But I'll make sure."

"OK, if it is, that's fine."

I walked through the door into the dirty dish area to check out the drink bucket situation. I'd only had six customers all night so there was very little in the bucket, but at least it looked pretty gross. I grabbed a clean glass from the rack and then thought better of it, figuring he'd prefer a dirty glass. Lifting up the bucket, I poured the filthy liquid into it, recalling the drinks I'd served that night. The dark mixture was nothing more than vodka, coffee, sour mix, and tequila. And basic bucket filth, as it was rarely washed.

Naturally, JT approached the stairwell. "What are you doing? Do you know you have a customer sitting at table sixteen?" He was smoking a cigarette and drinking Jack Daniels straight from the bottle.

"Yes. I just ordered his drink."

"Save it, Pam. Do you know who this guy is?"

"Why?"

"That means you do. He tips a lot of money, but he likes some weird shit, so you better cut me in," he said, not one to waste time.

"Fine, OK." It was impossible to hide anything from him.

"Is that what I think it is?" he asked, pointing to the glass of drink bucket.

"Yes."

JT leaned over and flicked his ash in the drink.

No wonder he'd been pissed when Mimi quit. He probably thought Jake wouldn't return, and he wouldn't be able to extort money from her on a weekly basis.

"How do you know him?" asked JT. He inhaled sharply on his cigarette and then exhaled furiously through his nose, a true evil dragon.

"Mimi told me about him."

"So you've talked to that worthless skanky bitch."

"No. Not since we both did Friday night. I knew about him before."

"Holy shit!" he exclaimed, making the connection. "That's her *sugar daddy*! Hysterical!"

I shrugged, realizing it didn't matter what he thought.

"OK, I'll make the gin and tonic while you go entertain. Shoo, shoo," said JT, waving me away. "Try not to fuck this up. Mimi was actually pretty good at this stuff."

"Whatever," I muttered. "Do you know what the soup is today?" I spoke to his back, which was like speaking to a long, thin reed.

"No. Go ask the kitchen." I scampered down the stairs and verified it was the dreaded chowder before returning to Jake's table with the "refreshments."

"What shoes are you wearing?" asked Jake, glancing down at my feet.

"Why don't you take a closer look?" I sat across from him and placed my dirty sneaker in his lap. They were streaked orange from the flood.

"Oh, these are great," he said. "You'll have to sell them to me."

"You have no idea how disgusting they truly are," I replied. "And they need a fresh spray paint."

"You spray paint your sneakers?"

"Yeah. They're actually orange, but we need black shoes for work."

"That's funny. I've never heard of anyone doing that before. Oh, here," he said dismissively, dipping his hand in his pocket. "It's three hundred. For now."

"You just saved my night. Now I'll make three hundred and five dollars as opposed to only five." I mentally calculated JT's cut. Two fifty was still better than five.

"There's more where that came from," he said, laughing.

"Where *does* it come from?"

"Working. Unfortunately."

"Ah. Yes. Very inconvenient," I agreed.

"It's too bad you don't have any other tables. Mimi always transferred her cash tabs to my check so she could keep the cash."

"She did?" That explained JT's involvement. No one had the transfer key but JT and—wait a minute—Donna! I remembered with glee, the wheels turning. "You know, you should come in on a Saturday night sometime. After eleven p.m. we have no one here but pretty little college brats, and all of them pay in cash. I can spread the word on what a loser you are. That would be pretty humiliating, no?" I sat back, pleased with myself for articulating my suggestion in such a way that might entice him.

"Young women come here on Saturday nights?" he asked, glancing around the deserted room. At that moment, it was hard to believe anyone came there.

"Women, no. Girls, yes. This place is flooded with blond highlights all clutching their Louis Vuitton wallets and smoking Gallois. It's totally ludicrous that they can afford to go anywhere and they *choose* to come here. I guess word has gotten around that we serve anyone over twelve."

"I'll keep that in mind." He handed me his gin and tonic.

I gathered up all the saliva I had in my mouth and spit just as JT walked past our table. He narrowed his eyes and kept walking. If it had been any other customer, he would have pulled me up by the ears and hurled me over the balcony.

"Who is that guy?" asked Jake. "I see him walk by a lot."

"He's the manager Mimi was so infatuated with. They broke the mold with him, all right."

"What a twig. I pictured him looking totally different."

"His appearance is deceiving. He can be quite menacing."

"He doesn't seem to mind you sitting with me."

"That's because there's no one else here," I lied, feeling the need to protect Jake from the sordid truth of the matter.

"When you bring the soup, will you also bring some bread? I was hoping you could stick it in your socks and walk around for a while. Incorporate the real flavor of the foot, so to speak."

I remained expressionless, but my eyes flickered in amusement. "It would be my pleasure. Actually, let me check on the soup. Sometimes the kitchen staff smokes too much weed, and then they have trouble reading the tickets."

Jake laughed, assuming I was kidding.

I laughed too. I was totally serious.

December 2002

The closer my wedding loomed, the more I thought about the past. With stability so close at hand, my mind yearned for excitement and missed the general ridiculousness of what used to be an average day. My world, however improved on the surface, had become boring and stale, and this nagging feeling began to seep out of my skin and into the air around me, forcing me to breathe it back in. Although I ignored this building condition and its relentless consistency, it would be a lie to say I was unaware of the gradual effect it was having on me.

I didn't know what it all meant back then, but this state of mind was preparing me for something far greater. After years of doing my best to be a good girl, I was ready to risk more and take greater chances just for the sake of making my day more interesting. I had an inkling that Mimi's downward spiral had begun, and I was eager to eclipse her position.

***

The following Tuesday arrived, and I'd spoken with Mimi the day before to confirm our 7 p.m. meeting at Gonzo Restaurant. I didn't yet have Jake's phone number, so I was relying on Mimi to keep up the communication between us three, however idiotic that may have seemed.

I was already at the bar when Jake waltzed in. "Is this a gay restaurant?" he asked, coming up behind me. "We're in the heart of the West Village, and I don't see any women." He placed his small Barney's shopping bag down on the bar, and I felt privileged to know its secret contents.

"Yes, I'm doing fine. How are you?"

"Hi," he said, smiling.

"The bartender is a woman," I said. "That usually indicates a heterosexual environment. Although who knows, nowadays?"

"Where's our fellow crackhead?" he asked, grinning from ear to ear, expecting to see her sardonic face glaring at him.

"She's not here yet."

"Did you speak to her today?" he asked, signaling the bartender.

"Last night, before she went out. I hope she's *still* out; this way she'll show up. Otherwise, she's dead asleep right now."

"The afternoon is over. Why would she still be asleep?" asked Jake, staring open-mouthed at the hard body heading toward us.

"She does that." The bartender was distracting me too. She was gorgeous and blond—two points *not* in my favor. I tried to finish what I was saying. "Basically, now that Mimi has no job, she goes out all night drinking and doing drugs until someone finally has the good sense to give her a few sleeping pills. Then she crashes into an Ambien-induced coma for the rest of the day and into the next one. When *and if* she wakes, the cycle continues."

Jake shook his head in amazement and requested a Beefeater and tonic.

"Haven't you seen her?" I asked. If I was paying someone's bills, I would like to see them occasionally.

"Not lately," he said. We both watched the hard body pour Miller's gin from the bottle. Jake didn't correct her and I doubted its authenticity in the first place.

"But I thought you guys had sort of a thing going?"

"Thing?" He shrugged. "I don't know. I like her. I saw her once last week, but I haven't heard from her since." He accepted the drink with a huge smile, setting the lime on the cocktail napkin.

"I see."

"What do you want to drink?" asked Jake, shifting his eyes from her to me, and then back to the hard body. I was outclassed yet undeterred.

"Goose martini. Dirty. Up." If not for Jake, I would have had to use a gigantic sign to get this woman's attention. Minutes later, I pried the martini from between her pale pink fingernails. *Where the fuck is Mimi?*

"You know, she's so funny," he said, in answer to my unspoken question of her whereabouts. "I can't believe her apartment. It's like a luxury rat's nest. She lives in this tiny shithole with that stupid yapping dog, and she tells me she pays thirteen fifty a month."

"I know it's crazy." *Ha! That was his goddamn problem now.*

"She did something utterly hysterical the last time I was over."

"And what was that?" I wasn't sure I wanted to know, considering her bed took up three-quarters of the apartment.

"Well, she was wasted on just about everything, and it was five in the morning and she put on the stupid uniform from Lime and tried to serve me a plate of dog food. She was balancing it on one of those cocktail trays—which she must have swiped—but her apartment was such a mess, she slipped and fell onto her dog's piss pad. Now most people fall, they get up, right?" he said, taking a large gulp of his drink. "Not Mimi. She looks up at me, closes her eyes, and passes out."

"She's a graceful creature," I murmured.

"I couldn't believe it. I thought she was kidding at first, but seconds later she was fast asleep."

"Why doesn't this surprise me?"

"She also has no sense of smell left."

Nor any sense of time, I thought, glancing at my watch, which read 7:27.

"What makes you say that?" I took a huge swig from the worst-made martini in history and quickly bit into the olive to ease the pain. I had to stop ordering these. I no longer enjoyed the first sip.

"Because each time I go over, her building smells worse. As soon as I walk out of the elevator, I'm struck with this pungent scent of decay, and she's completely unaware of it."

"Shocking." I wished for a cigarette. That was the problem with acting as if you'd quit.

"Seriously. Her hallway smells extremely bad. Like someone died and is yet to be discovered."

"Hopefully she won't be the next victim." I had my doubts. I was also sorry I had appointed her a bridesmaid in my upcoming wedding. I needed to somehow correct that incompetent mistake.

By 8:20, when she still hadn't arrived, Jake finally said, "I wonder where she is."

"She's conked out. Since she quit Lime, she has no structure."

"But I thought she was doing her photography."

"Excuse me?"

"I bought her an amazing camera for this photography class she's taking."

"Class?" Mimi and school were like total antonyms.

"Yeah, at NYU."

"Right, of course," I said, coughing.

Jake looked at the door. "Well, we've waited long enough. She knows our phone numbers if she wakes up. Do you want to go somewhere darker to eat? This place is kind of bright."

***

Two lounges and many conversations later, I realized I was having a *very* good time. At the third lounge, we tucked ourselves into a small banquet at Clarinet. Having worked there for a short time, I knew it would be another perfect location for our shenanigans: hidden corners, dark lighting, and finger foods perfect for mashing with my foot. Without Mimi's lead, I was a little shy at first, but the champagne made me brave, and before I knew it, I'd mastered the art of spitting and pissing in a glass. I also knew that the next time I had to give a urine sample at the doctor's office, I wasn't going to feel half as self-conscious.

I found I could talk to Jake freely about my past and my future and any odd thoughts that occurred to me without the usual filter I applied to most conversations. I felt comfortable with him, and his idiosyncrasies no longer struck me as irregular. He didn't pull any punches; there was no façade or walls up to hurdle over—unlike my fiancé, who had mastered the art of passive-aggression long before I ever came along.

Jake's best quality was I could ask him questions that were none of my business and he didn't take it personally.

"Are you sleeping with Mimi?" I probed.

He smiled. "Should I be?"

"From a safety standpoint, probably not, but it's none of my business."

"Well, the answer is no. I haven't yet, anyway. Why?"

"I was just wondering. I have this feeling she'd be better in bed than anywhere else."

"You're probably right," he said, looking me in the eye.

I stared back, forgetting what we were talking about. "How can you afford to spend so much money every time you hang out with us?" I asked.

"I can't."

"But you do. You have. And that doesn't include the shoes."

"Yes, but I won't be able to much longer. I do well, but not *that well*."

"So why have you been so generous?"

"Mimi wouldn't agree to it for less."

"Wow, she's hard. She's lucky you didn't tell her to go to fuck herself."

"Well, she's the first waitress I've ever propositioned, so I wasn't sure what to offer or expect."

"She was the first?"

"Yeah, I never thought about trying the role play with a waitress, but Mimi was so naturally suited for it. I had to ask."

"But you could get a high-class escort over to your house for three or four hundred bucks. Why don't you just do that?" I said.

"If I want sex from a stranger, I will. But that's not what I want."

"You want to be humiliated."

"Correct."

"I like how you admit that instead of pretending to conform to society's rigid expectations."

Jake smiled, his eyes lighting up.

"Well, I'm having fun doing this crazy stuff with you so if your money is running out, I'd rather hang out more often for less. I can't speak for Mimi, but I'd be fine with a few hundred. You've made *my* life more entertaining; I'd hate to see you disappear," I confessed.

"Yeah?" he said, staring me in the eye again.

"Yeah. As long as you give me what I would have made at work, I'll take a weeknight off anytime."

"Cool," said Jake. "That actually makes me feel better."

"Hey, I worked in a strip club for five years. I know that *no one* can keep that kind of money up for very long unless they are a shipping magnate or a sheik. Or in Miami, a major drug dealer. And I know you've got Mimi's rent to think of as well."

"Mimi's rent?"

"Never mind," I said, kicking myself.

"No, what did you just say? Her rent?" He appeared more horrified than confused.

"Mimi told me that you intended to pay her rent. She said that was how she was able to quit her job."

"Her rent?" he repeated. "What, like every month? I never said that."

"I'm sorry. That's just what she told me."

"I told her I'd help by hanging out with her on a regular basis, but I certainly never said I'd pay her rent."

"Oh."

"I did encourage her to do other things—which is why the whole photography subject came up—but I never expected her to up and quit her job. That was stupid."

"OK, sorry I mentioned it. Listen, I had better go. It's getting late, and I'm sure Rob is already home."

"Yeah, OK. We're on for this Sunday though, right?"

I remembered his promise to take me shopping for the bridesmaid shoes. "Absolutely."

***

Mimi called me back eventually. She sounded like she'd been stuck in a cement mixer for two days. Her voice kept fluctuating from high to low, alternating between yelling and whispering. Finally she mumbled something barely audible about going out with a bunch of people. I heard the words *crystal meth, cheeseburger,* and *tranquilizer,* and I had to fill in the gaps. I decided it wasn't worth my time, reminded her about shopping on Sunday, and hung up the phone.

I can't say it was a shock when she never showed.

***

The dynamic between Mimi, Jake, and myself was based on need. We all wanted something from each other: I wanted an element of excitement within the confines of my controlled lifestyle; Mimi wanted to remain the center of attention and have enough money to pay her drug dealer; and Jake wanted to be used by beautiful women and did everything in his power to make that happen. We all supplied a necessary connection, and we chased our addictions within the links of our small chain.

At this point in our complex relationship, I was still very much in control, but Mimi was slipping. To be fair, I suppose I had a few more years of life experience on her and a fiancé to be concerned about, but nothing and no one guided Mimi.

The three of us were enduring a somewhat uncomfortable dinner in the dining room of Almonds at the newly constructed Z hotel in Gramercy Park. The dynamic was off because the last two encounters Jake and I had been alone, and suddenly it was very apparent how changed Mimi seemed. She was further agitated because I'd chosen a restaurant where there was no smoking allowed—even at the bar. She spent a good amount of time bad-mouthing everything from the chef's crab cakes to the design on his custom silverware. Her tone implied that she knew him personally and perhaps had even slept with him on more than one occasion. Each time Mimi went outside to smoke, Jake commented that she was acting strangely.

"You're forgetting her temperament," I said.

"I think she's lost weight, too. She looks ghostly," said Jake, eating normally for once, a bowl of dirt-less rigatoni Bolognese in front of him. "Do you think she's mad that you got all those shoes on Sunday and she didn't?"

"No," I said, wondering if she was, indeed, furious. "If she'd been there, she would have gotten shoes too. She's an idiot."

"That doesn't mean she's not jealous." Apparently, he was well acquainted with the conflicting feelings women sometimes experience. He shrugged and poked at a little ball of hamburger meat suspiciously, suddenly concerned about what he placed in his mouth.

Mimi sauntered back to the table, both hands shoved deep in the pockets of her dark blue jeans. She slid into the booth next to Jake. "You guys were talking about me. I can tell." She glanced from me to him.

"Mimi, how did you know? You *are* a genius," said Jake, laughing.

"What did we say about you?" I asked with a straight face.

"I don't know. You tell me." Mimi folded her arms over her chest. I wiped my nose with my hand, indicating Mimi might want to do the same.

"OK," said Jake. "We were wondering if you were mad that you didn't go shopping with us on Sunday."

I giggled. He was too much.

Mimi shook her hair—which didn't move—appearing uncertain. "That's what you were talking about? I don't believe you." She reached for the only drink left on the table, my glass of pinot grigio.

"That's because you're paranoid," I pointed out.

"I am not," snapped Mimi, tipping the wine glass back like a shot.

"Hey Mimi," said Jake chidingly, "there's your food—remember that stuff you used to eat?" He motioned to her untouched plate of salmon while laughing hysterically. My smile widened. He had such a good time with himself.

"I'm not *fucking* hungry," she declared. "What did you two morons buy anyway?" I shifted my eyes toward Jake. Perhaps he had a point.

"Pam picked the shoe you'll be wearing as a bridesmaid if you ever get around to ordering the dress."

"Oh, yeah. What's it like?" Her eyes darted around the room.

"It's really not your style," I admitted.

"What—does—it—look—like?" she asked slowly and deliberately, staring at me.

"Closed toe, black satin, narrow, three-inch heel." I wished for the waitress to appear. If Mimi was going to keep drinking my wine, I wanted two glasses.

"I can't wear heels that high," she said. "I'll break my neck."

"A three-inch heel is *not* that high," scolded Jake. "Pam is wearing a five-inch heel right now. Show her, Pam." I struggled to hoist my leather boot out from under the table.

Mimi peered at it suspiciously before stating flatly, "That's a boot."

"So. A closed-toe shoe with a strap around the ankle is not going to fall off—I don't care how accident prone you are." I assumed he was recalling the incident in her apartment.

"What brand are they?" she asked.

"Vera Wang."

"How much did they cost?"

"Two eighty. Each pair," answered Jake, glimpsing at me.

Mimi shrugged as if this was a minor purchase, but I could tell she was calculating the dollars spent in her mind. "Did you get wedding shoes?" she asked me.

"Yes. They're beautiful, white satin pumps with a platform. *Valley of the Dolls* meets twenty-first century."

"Were yours more expensive?" Her chin jutted out like a boxer.

"Ah, no, about the same price."

"What about my dress, Jake? Did you order it?" asked Mimi.

Jake pushed his plate away. "No. How many times am I going to tell you? I have no problem paying for it, but *you* need to find it. I don't have the patience."

Mimi sighed, probably thinking what a massive undertaking that might be considering she was so used to doing absolutely nothing all day. "Fine," she muttered. "Can we go somewhere more fun? This place is fucking lame."

After a few minutes of deliberation, we decided to go downstairs to Almond Joy, the newly opened lounge under the hotel. It was our first time there, and we found it was perfect for all types of illicit behavior. Personal round booths with curtains for full privacy! More importantly, our waitress was pretty and scantily clad, Jake's idea of a rocking good time. Mimi's eyes flashed with anger as he handed over his first hundred dollars for the privilege of licking the bottom of her stiletto heels.

We ordered a round of drinks while Jake massaged our feet. When it was my turn, I sat back and smiled. I was having a great time, but Mimi had gone from agitated to anxious. When Jake pulled out another hundred to purchase the waitress's stockings, I thought Mimi would keel over. Her expression was such that even Jake noticed. His reaction was to pull out two folded bunches of bills from his pocket and slide one to each of us. I closed my hand around what I assumed was a bunch of twenties, instinctively knowing it was too thick to be fifties or hundreds. Mimi narrowed her eyes. "Pam, will you show me where the restroom is?"

"I have no idea where it is. The place just opened."

"Help me find it then!" I sat up, reluctantly removing my feet from Jake's lap and followed her through the mess of people. Everyone was six feet tall, bleach blond, and holding a martini. No one even noticed us two dwarfs slip through the crowd.

The bathroom was located down a long hallway, all the way off to one side. It was one of those huge rooms with low fluorescent lighting, a toilet, a sink, and a bench, in case you wanted to move your party to the restroom. We both went in, and I locked the door behind us. I assumed Mimi really had to pee, as she never had any qualms about snorting cocaine in front of us, so I was surprised when she went to the brighter area of the sink and pulled out the folded bills Jake had given her. When she finished counting the twenties, she held them out and pointed them at me. "What the hell is this?"

"I don't know. How much is there?"

"It's only three hundred. What do you have?"

I took out my money and counted it. "The same."

"The waitress is probably going to make more money than us!" screeched Mimi.

"She might. Remember how he used to hook you up," I reminded her.

"And now I don't get shit?" said Mimi, directing her anger at me.

"Ah, you're no longer his waitress."

"So! I'm *with* him. Don't forget I was the one who cut you in on this!" I gawked at her, unsure of where the conversation was heading. "If you weren't here, I'd be making all the money," she continued. "I have to cut you out!"

I continued to stare, shocked. "You're cutting me out? OK. I didn't realize this was strictly business."

"Did you tell him that he could give us less money?"

"I told him he could give *me* less. I said nothing about you."

"Why?"

"It's complicated."

Mimi continued to scream at me. "I *cut you in* and now you're acting like I'm not included, making deals and arrangements without my consent! I don't even have a job right now!"

"Whose fault is that?" I argued.

"You went behind my back and lowered my income!"

"Mimi! Did you really think he could continue to give us each seven hundred every time we went out with him?" I asked incredulously. "That's fourteen hundred a week. I was just trying to keep this a regular thing, and in order to do so, we had to take a pay cut! He's not that wealthy!"

"You were a sneaky bitch." Her eyes were bloodshot and flashing venom. She reminded me of the hungry wolf in hot pursuit of Little Red Riding Hood. Unfortunately, I was Little Red and not too jazzed about it.

"You are a not-so-sneaky idiot! If you had been with us the other night at Clarinet—instead of blowing us off—you would understand. He admitted he couldn't keep paying us as much. That's why I was playing it cool! I told him that he could give *me* a few hundred, what I would have made at work. I never said anything about *you* and your requirements. If anything, I made it seem like you still expected the same fee!"

"But you lowered your standards, and that gives Jake the edge! He can say that if you are willing to do it for half the money, why won't I? He's using you as leverage. You're nothing more than a bargaining tool!"

"Well, you weren't there, so what was I supposed to do?"

"Discuss it with me first!"

"Like I know when you'll be awake or asleep."

"If he can afford to keep giving the waitress hundred-dollar bills, he can afford to give us more money!" said Mimi.

"I don't know. That's not what he told me." She had a valid point.

"You wouldn't even be here if it weren't for me!" she rehashed, unable to see outside the box.

"Oh really? Maybe *I'm* the one keeping this whole thing together! Ever think of that? I'm the fucking producer—and director—and you're just the careless star who never shows up to rehearsal!" I praised myself on this perfect metaphor despite her continuing to catch me off guard. And she was half-right. Somewhere in the back of my mind, I was well aware that I was making myself look like the good guy. As pissed as I was at Mimi, I rather admired her for confronting me.

"I'm not being careless! I was the one who cut! You! In! If it weren't for me, you wouldn't have three new pairs of boots, and he wouldn't have bought your bridesmaids' shoes!"

"True." I attempted to lower my voice. "But I didn't ask or anticipate that. Everything so far has been his idea. If you were getting married, he'd probably pay for your entire wedding. You're the one he likes because you're so naturally rude and mean." Mimi just glared at me with her hands on her hips. "It's not as if you're going to refuse the free wedding shoes."

"But he would get them for me anyway. He doesn't have to buy everybody else's!"

And therein lay the problem.

"I don't want him to spend money on anyone else but you and me!"

"You mean *you*. I thought you were cutting me out." I was reasonably calm, considering. "Moreover, why would I want you in my wedding party?"

Mimi reached into her purse, and I half expected her to pull out a revolver and aim it at me. "Well that's fine, because I didn't know what a pain in the ass it would be. I can't even *find* the dress."

"You haven't tried to find it."

"Whatever."

"You know what?" I said, finally pushing her aside. "You involved me, and I thought you valued my expertise, so I really don't want to hear that I'm suddenly the bitch!"

"Keep in mind that the money Jake gives you is money I'm *not* getting. Especially considering that I've done all the work."

"If you think that you'd be getting more if I weren't here, you're wrong. Try studying your victim's profile longer next time." I turned on the cold water and stared at my reflection in the mirror. Under the fluorescent lighting, I looked like I could actually benefit from a couple months in Hawaii.

"I know what I'm doing, Pam." Mimi lit a cigarette.

"I know you *think* you do." I reached in my pocket and tossed my three hundred dollars at her feet, a tactical move. "If you don't want me here, then I'll go."

"Don't turn this around," spat Mimi.

"Just take it. You deserve it," I said with a crocodile smile.

Mimi finally appeared a little shocked.

"No, I don't want it," she said carefully. "Don't leave—"

Slamming the bathroom door, I walked straight back to our table. Smiling ruefully at Jake, I reached for my jacket.

"Where are you going?" he asked.

"Home. Mimi doesn't want me here." I grabbed my bag.

"What?"

"According to her, I've overstayed my welcome." I kissed him on the cheek and scribbled my phone number on a cocktail napkin. "Give me a call if you feel like it, OK?"

"OK." He was obviously confused but perceptive enough to see I was upset. I held off telling him about the money I'd thrown at Mimi's feet. I had faith that this wouldn't be the last time I saw him. If my instincts were correct, Mimi would make her own bed, admitting to Jake what happened in the bathroom, and I'd seem even cooler for not mentioning it. I turned around and walked up the stairs, wondering what the future would bring.

***

After the dramatic departure of Mimi, Jake took my advice and visited Lime on Saturday nights. I really had no choice but to take a risk on Donna. I knew she loved money more than people, so I had that on my side. I figured for all she knew, I was ensconced in prewedding bliss.

The truth was, I thought more about shopping with Jake and feeding him strange substances than I thought about my upcoming wedding. The wedding would arrive no matter what I did, but with Jake, I had something I didn't have with Rob: the power of suggestion.

I could encourage Jake to buy me something and he would. Jake believed in positive reinforcement. He rewarded me for my efforts, whereas Rob received a blowjob twice a week and I still paid half our rent, the phone bill, and Con Ed. If I had suggested to Rob that he purchase me an eight hundred-dollar Gucci satchel, he would have burst into hysterics at the preposterous notion that I might be serious.

The first Saturday Jake came into Lime was the funniest. I studied Donna beforehand, deciding how I was going to casually bring up the subject of a self-destructive hottie who was expecting complete cooperation. It was difficult to explain my involvement in the first place, but more importantly, I needed to properly convey the kind of attention Jake expected without scaring her. I had faith in Donna, but I was unsure of her limitations. I knew she was open-minded enough to accept certain behavior, but could she take an active role?

"Pam, what's up?" Donna was watching me out of the corner of her eye, her fingers punching buttons on the computer screen. "You keep fidgeting."

"Did I ever tell you about this guy, Jake."

"No. Who's Jake?"

"Just this dude I know. Anyway, he's coming in tonight and he's going to help us make some money."

"How?" she asked skeptically.

"He's going to open up a tab and we are going to ring all the cash drinks on it. He should also give us cash throughout the night."

"And *why* is he going to do this?"

I glanced at the ceiling. "He likes to be used by women."

"He likes to be used?" she repeated, deadpan.

"Yeah, he's the *opposite* of most men."

"What do we have to do?"

"OK, let me just preface this by saying that we'll each make at least three hundred extra dollars because of him."

"What. Is. The. Catch?"

"We have to humiliate him."

"Humiliate him how?"

"It's really very simple."

"Give me an example."

"Make him drink stranger's leftover drinks. From the same glass. He prefers it to be a woman's but whatever."

Donna didn't blink. Her face didn't move a muscle. "Is this another one of your jokes that you think is funny and no one else does?"

I cleared my throat. "Nope. Not joking."

"What else?"

"I don't know, ah, maybe pour him a drink from the drink bucket and laugh at him while he drinks it?"

"Has he done that before?" she asked, grabbing my arm and pulling me closer. Her brown eyes sparkled under the horrific red lighting that Lime had installed in preparation for New Year's Eve.

"Yes," I confessed.

"What else?"

"Well, if you can kick his food around on the floor, flatten it with your dirty shoes, and make him eat it, that would be good too."

"Seriously?"

"Would I lie? You can even call him a loser and dump the ashtrays into his drink. Scoop dirt onto his food and watch him eat it. Have him kiss the bottom of your shoes. Whatever you feel like, really."

"Wait, back up. Where are we supposed to find dirt?"

"He'll bring it."

"And he's going to give us money for this abuse? It seems too good to be true."

"In this case it isn't," I said. "Or hasn't been yet, I should say."

"All right, explain as we go," she agreed, distracted by the cackling voices of adolescent women approaching. An army of privileged girls, fully clothed in Prada and Gucci, were headed up the stairs, eager to make our lives a living hell. It must have been a young socialite's birthday, but I didn't care about the reason; I was grateful for the influx of nineteen-year-olds who would soon be drunk and chasing each other around the furniture. It was perfect timing, as Donna never got the chance to ask me how I came to know a man with such profound preferences.

By the time Jake arrived, the lounge was in full swing. He looked a little dazed as he approached me through the crowd of women blocking his path. He tapped me on the back. "You weren't kidding. This place is a man's paradise."

"If you like them underage and stupid," I shouted over the noise, leading him to a little table in the corner.

From that point on, Donna and I took turns sitting with Jake while we racked up his bill with numerous apple martinis and Cosmopolitans. When the many girls fumbled through their studded handbags for cash, I tapped my foot impatiently and took as many drink orders as I could memorize. For the first time ever, I didn't care if these Emilio Pucci-clad chicks tipped me or not. It was quantity—not quality—as every second counted.

Every so often, I stopped to observe Donna sitting at Jake's table. She seemed at ease, and I paid special attention to her mannerisms. Her head bounced around merrily, and it appeared that Jake's liveliness held her rapt attention. But more importantly, I could tell Jake was comfortable in her presence, leading me to believe I had made a good decision. I had counted on Donna's degree in psychology and her general curiosity concerning human nature to counter any misgivings she might have had. Of course, it didn't hurt that he was gorgeous to look at, she pointed out to me later. It was sad but true. If he hadn't been so cute, accepting him would have taken far longer.

Later on I laughed as I watched Donna dunk her hand into the drink bucket and serve him the delicacy. I had to hand it to her: she caught on fast. By the end of the night we were both sitting at Jake's table while he took turns licking the bottom of our disgusting work shoes. Everything was going splendidly until the crowd petered out and JT got wind of what we were up to.

JT rounded the corner shortly after 3 a.m. with daggers in his eyes. "Donna! Pam! What the hell do you two think you're doing!" he screamed, grabbing both of our ears from behind our ponytails and twisting them upward. Like cats handpicked from

a litter, he pulled so tightly that we automatically rose from
our seats and followed him to the DJ booth, which doubled as
a platform for copious amounts of designer drugs. Donna and
I exchanged frightened glances as JT snorted another calming
installment before letting us have it.

"Why *is it* that neither one of you lousy bitches told me
that your psycho weird friend is here?" he asked, snarling at me.
"Don't think for one fucking minute that you two can get away
with extorting the loser without cutting me in! The fact that
I had to hear it from Jeffrey and not from one of you two cunt
bags makes me think you might be stealing more than I originally figured! If I'm taking the slack from these French fuckers
over the lack of sales, then I want half!"

"It doesn't affect the sales—" I started.

"We can't give you half!" cried Donna. "We already give
Jeffrey half! If we give you half of our half, it's not even worth
us doing it!" So much for denial, I thought. If it came down to
Donna parting with *her* money, she had the tendency to become
a different animal altogether, whereas for the first time I could
see JT's point. Why should he let us get away with impropriety
if he had nothing to gain and everything to lose? It was like
giving an agent or a mob boss their rightful cut; it made perfect
sense in the scheme of things.

"If you don't, you won't be working here much longer!"
retaliated JT, lighting a cigarette with flair and shaking it in
Donna's face. "Just who the fuck do you think you are?"

I hopped from one foot to another helplessly, attempting
to intervene as Jake watched this spectacle from a distance. JT
pivoted his body in my direction. "Obviously this is *your* fault!
You may as well just leave right now, you fucking cunt!"

I ignored this statement, as it wasn't the first time he'd
called me this, and I knew he didn't *really* want me to go because
we still had to clean. I glanced over at the DJ, but the drugged
up, headphoned hipster seemed blissfully unaware that anyone
was nearby.

"What I'm telling you two slut liars—and you had better listen carefully—is that you need to take care of everyone who works here!" JT waved his hand around. "This includes *me*! This includes Jeffrey! Even that lazy fucker of a busboy, Carlos! Do you understand? And if I don't think you're being fair in your assessment of funds, I will *beat* the money out of you! Is that clear?"

"Yep. Right, Donna?" I nodded, pulling her back from JT.

"Fine," she muttered.

"Get out of here! Scram!" We scampered back to Jake's table, tails between our legs.

"What was that about?" asked Jake, glancing from Donna to me.

"Oh, nothing," I said. "JT thinks you're hot."

***

I've always hated New Years Eve. It's a bullshit holiday that extorts ridiculous amounts of money from the average person and leaves them feeling depressed and cold for the next three months.

As per usual, I chose to work as opposed to pretending to have a good time with a bunch of my drunken friends and making resolutions I would never keep. I'd worked last year's fiasco at Lime, so I knew what to expect; I had no misconceived notions as I sat around blowing up balloons with the helium tank. By 8 p.m., I had erected three and inhaled ten.

I considered calling Rob to see if he wanted to do some whippets before going to the Phish concert at Madison Square Garden. I knew he and his concert buddy, Jones, were down the block at the Old Town Inn drinking beer before the show. Glancing over at JT, however, I decided against it. It wasn't so much the calm before the storm that was brewing but the anxiety before the riot.

It would all be over in eight hours, I kept telling myself. By closing time the police would be a permanent fixture, busting gangsters for drugs and their respective girlfriends for prostitution. Perhaps an ambulance would be on call—just like the year before—equipped with exhausted paramedics trying in vain to counteract the numerous cases of alcohol poisoning. Unfortunately, the people who never went out during the entire year always chose to make a party animal debut on New Year's Eve. And Lime seemed to be the epicenter of this trend.

I watched Del-Ray trapped behind the long bar downstairs. He was taking his sweet time unloading a box of plastic champagne flutes, disgust highlighting his shiny freckles. It was his official last day, having accepted an accounting job in Atlanta. The fact that he'd lasted half a year was a miracle, and I had gained respect for him. He was the only employee who could admit that Lime was *not* a safe environment for anyone.

I would have been more disappointed at Del-Ray's inevitable departure had I not known that my sentence at Lime was drawing to a close. January was going to be my last month, and I was going to alert JT of this fact after the New Year.

After decorating Lime to the best of our ability (it looked like a brothel with balloons), JT called the staff downstairs for a meeting. This was his special time to scream and yell at us before things got too out of hand or before he swallowed too many pills. He warned us all not to drink until after midnight because we had to be "on our game."

Sure enough, by ten, we were all plastered and Lime looked like the pit of hell it was. People milled all over the place, and the upstairs was so packed I could barely move. I stayed within a one-foot radius of the service bar, serving drinks to whoever could push their way through the crowd. Thankfully, there was no food service due to a loose bottle of Jack Daniels circulating in the kitchen. Half the cooks passed out in the stockroom, and the other half were milling about with the customers, drunk and disorderly. Del-Ray had never seen anything like this in his life. At one point, he mumbled, "What did I ever do to deserve this?"

To add madness to mayhem, Lexi showed up with her new boy toy from the gym and half of Suffolk County. The phantom fiancé was *where?* I asked. She was very drunk and still drinking, which made it easy for her to act as if she didn't know whom I was asking about. I was so busy pocketing cash that I didn't notice her curled up on one of the couches practically having sex. Del-Ray had to point her out to me. "Your friend is vile," he commented, stalking away.

Del-Ray must have mentioned this to JT because he stormed upstairs with the intention to boot her out on her ass. It all happened so fast that I missed the shouting match between Del-Ray, Lexi, the unidentified boy, and JT. But as the argument ensued, I suppose JT had a chance to look over Lexi's half-naked, perfectly proportioned, tanned body and seemed to change his mind about evicting her. He probably figured she was good for business.

In addition, it wouldn't have been in the spirit of New Year's Eve if the toilets hadn't started to overflow. When a woman slipped and broke her ankle in the bathroom, two hostile paramedics had to carry her out on a stretcher.

I was cold and unfeeling toward any of this. I glanced over at Del-Ray, who looked positively green. He turned to me and said, "After tonight, I will never set foot in this place again."

January 2003

There is nothing like receiving the replies to your own wedding. Checking the mail had always been a cautious, infrequent act for me, but once the invitations went out, I soon began running full speed past the mailbox and up the stairs on a daily basis.

I suppose that once people started responding in the affirmative, our marriage suddenly felt official. Then the terror set in. My stomach lurched when I saw people were bringing guests. It was as if they had already bought tickets to a play I was starring in and I had yet to memorize any of my lines. Each day became more harrowing, and neither Rob nor I had any idea how many invitations had been mailed. I'd meant to keep track of it, but it had all become too confusing—especially when certain couples declined and we realized we could invite more people!

To further bewilder, we had the guests who responded yes but really meant, "I'm not sure, maybe," such as the ex-friend, ex-stalker-bridesmaid and a few of Rob's old buddies from back in the day of smoking around the campfire. It seemed that a particular friend of his was still toking pretty hard on the reefer because he neglected to sign his name on the reply card. All we knew was our mystery guest was bringing his girlfriend and they were looking forward to meeting me. I quietly wondered how I was supposed to create a place setting for this couple without appearing ridiculously incompetent.

It's also fun when your first reply is from someone you've never met. It's never from a good friend of the family. It's always from a random person or couple you almost didn't invite. Mr. and Mrs. Dick Walters will be attending. *How will I even know they are the real Mr. and Mrs. Dick Walters?*

And naturally, all the people I never thought would commit in a million years all planned on being there—even my older male cousin who I hadn't seen since he tried to kiss me in the backseat of his Ford when I was fifteen. Not only was he intent upon making the long trip from Arizona, but he was also bringing a guest! Funny, I thought, turning the response card over in my hands; I hadn't invited him with a guest. My mother had warned me to expect this outcome based on the fact he was now a successful bond tradesman with a very tall girlfriend who worked in aviation. I didn't see what that had to do with accepting a wedding invite, but Sarah Castle had been right once again.

I received the acceptance from my other cousin, his younger brother, on the same day. He was planning to hitchhike up from South Carolina, hence another, "I don't know, maybe," response, dependent on transportation safety. Much to my relief, he was *not* bringing a guest. Since I knew absolutely nothing about him, I figured he was either shy or perhaps he knew how to read an invitation properly.

Somewhat unanticipated, the news of my male cousins' attendance soon reached the ears of their mother, whom the family rumored was "estranged" from her two sons. The "most important day of my life" clearly piqued her curiosity because she also declared she was intending to drive up from Florida. Close by her side would be her latest in the way of husbands, whose name didn't ring a bell. I assumed this would be quite the reunion after fifteen years.

The one thing I was pleased about was that my favorite aunt would be present with her husband and their two daughters. Through sheer craftiness and solid campaigning,

I'd managed to ensure their presence, but somehow I still had the aunt I'd only met once, her mysterious significant other, and her successors joining the festivities. It was like a buy-one-get-one-free sale. You never really want or need the second pair.

***

Due to this chaos, concentration at work was at an all-time low. I was getting married in less than two months so I didn't care if some dude wanted his burger rare.

After a solid week of trying, I finally managed to corner JT near the office. "Dude, I have to talk to you," I attempted.

"Spare me, bitch," he said, blowing past me.

"I'm serious," I said.

"Do I need a drink for this?"

"I guess. Yeah, probably."

JT sighed and returned with two Amstel Lights. Both for him.

"Follow me!" I trailed him into the office. "Talk," said JT.

"Well, as you know, I'm getting married at the end of the month."

"This month?" he shouted, gulping his beer with ferocity.

"Yeah. I invited you to the wedding." (A mere formality.) "Remember?"

"I thought it was weeks away!"

"You should try reading the invitation," I suggested.

"You must be nervous, honey!" he shouted. He was half-deaf due to years of abusing loud techno music.

"No, not really. Anyway, I'll need that whole week off. The twenty-second through the twenty-ninth."

"For a wedding present, I'll order you some topnotch Valium." He scribbled a large V on the corner of his desk calendar.

"Thanks. I appreciate that. Now, after the wedding, Rob and I aren't going straight on our honeymoon."

"Get to the point, Pam."

"I'm giving my notice. The second week of February is my last week. We're moving to Hawaii."

JT actually looked surprised. "You little fucking bitch! I thought you were kidding about moving! All that stupid talk about Hawaii. Hawaii is an island! What are you thinking?!! You're a city girl!"

"Yes, I'm aware of that. It's his idea."

"Where I'm from, if you're in love, you go with your man. That goes for both of us!" JT tossed his head back and guzzled the last half of the first beer. "But you don't leave New York City!" he said, cackling and shaking his finger at me.

"Trust me, I know. We're giving up our rent-controlled apartment in the West Village. It's like knowing you have a terminal illness."

"West Village, honey. That hurts. Will your apartment be available, by any chance?"

"Once we leave, the landlord is going to triple the rent."

"Oh. Never mind."

"And leaving Lime is the icing on the cake." I attempted to keep a straight face. "I love working here."

"Shut up, Pam. You know what they say: marriage is all about compromise. Not that I believe that for a second," he muttered, hurling the empty beer bottle in the garbage. It clanged loudly before shattering in the metal can. He uncapped the second Amstel Light and took a long sip.

The phone on JT's desk rang. He rolled his eyes and picked it up, swerving his head to me. "Lime. How may I help you? Donna, what the fuck do you want?" He slammed the phone down. "Pam, your fucking table lit their booth on fire! Get out there and see what in the hell is going on. And print them a check!" Before I could blink, he'd swung open the door, charging in the direction of smoke.

Yes. *I was most definitely going to miss this.*

***

I'd come to a crossroads. Not a term I used very often. But up to this point, I'd been highly successful in keeping "the Jake counterpart" separate from "the Rob counterpart" to avoid inner turmoil. However, since I had introduced Jake to Donna, my two worlds had begun to overlap. My inner devil was crashing my angel's party. It was inevitable, of course. How long did I think I'd be able to keep Jake a secret? He was planning to attend my wedding and was currently working alongside Donna and Lexi on my bachelorette party.

When Tina came to stay with me a month before the wedding, the first thing I did was introduce her to Jake. We went back to AZ for martinis, and Tina and I took turns peeing in his beer glass. Tina, with her medical background, pointed out that drinking urine was common practice in the desert and actually considered healthy as long as the donor wasn't terribly sick or a heavy drug user. Considering Jake had withstood—and was somehow able to stomach—Mimi's heavenly varietals, it indicated to me that he had a strong immune system.

While Tina was in the bathroom, Jake leaned over and whispered, "Your friend is very cool. She hasn't blinked an eyelash."

"Why would she?" I shrugged. "She trusts me."

"I know, but rarely do I meet someone who is so naturally unaffected. Does she like the shoes I purchased for the bridesmaids?"

"Yeah, totally. Who wouldn't? Besides Mimi, that is."

"Does she know I bought them?"

"Yeah, her and Donna know, but I told Lexi that you have a work-related account with Saks Fifth Avenue and you scored us a really good discount. I told Rob the same thing, by the way."

"You know, you're always thinking. You could come up with a logical explanation for just about anything."

"I know, but Lexi doesn't believe me for a second. She's too smart."

"She sounds like it on the phone. She also sounds *hot*! And she has so many great ideas about your bachelorette party. Does she still work at Dream Girls?"

"Yep."

"You say she's a knockout, right?"

"Barbie in the flesh," I confirmed.

"Would *she* ever want to go shopping for shoes?"

"I'm sure *she* would, but frankly, I'm a little scared that she would ring up your credit card faster than the entire team of Knicks City Dancers."

"So she would take advantage of me?"

"Uh. Yeah. You have no idea. Just be careful. I love her, but she can be *very* persuasive. And she's blond," I added.

"Well, I'm going to have to take someone shopping once you move to Hawaii."

I cringed at the position of power I was stepping down from in exchange for barefoot dancing to the beat of a bongo. "Please don't remind me. I have the worst feeling about this move."

"Don't go. Say you changed your mind."

"It's too late. We gave up our lease, and Rob quit his job."

"Oh. Well I can't take Donna shopping again. She has horrible taste in shoes. Almost as bad as Mimi."

"Well you'll be fine with Lexi. She rocks out the five-inch stilettos."

"How come you've never introduced me?"

"I don't know. She has a kid, and she lives way out on Long Island. If you want to meet her, we should go to Dream Girls later tonight. I'm sure she'll be there."

"Now that is a good idea!"

"What's a good idea?" asked Tina, plunking down a glass of clear urine in front of Jake. Her pee had to be the healthiest on the planet. If we were ever stranded on a desolate island, I would beg her to trade with me.

"We might go visit Lexi later," I said.

"Have you been to Dream Girls?" Jake asked Tina.

"Oh yeah, a bunch of times, but not since Pam worked there." She took a sip from her gin and tonic. "I think everyone in our high school visited at some point to see Pam dancing on Broadway."

"That's how I used to phrase it," I said with a laugh, thinking how clever and funny I used to be.

"Are you kidding?" said Jake.

"Nope. Everyone in our graduating class considered it a very high achievement," explained Tina. "Far more prestigious than becoming a doctor or lawyer. One of our friends who works at the UN actually had his bachelor party in one of the back rooms."

"That's funny. Was that weird, Pam?"

"Nah. I'm sure it wasn't the first time they'd seen me topless." I sipped my drink, flashing back to high school strip poker games, twenty minutes in the closet, and various other sordid activities that never had a proper name.

"I can't believe you're getting married," commented Jake. "You'd never know it."

"Yeah, right," agreed Tina. "She's so calm."

"I've had a couple martinis," I pointed out.

"Rob's a lucky guy," said Jake. It was the first comment he'd ever made without laughing.

I swallowed. "Thanks." Somehow, the flattering remark meant more coming from him.

***

Later that evening we went to Dream Girls. Walking down the stairs that led to the club, I was suddenly lightheaded. Déjà vu hit me full force. I grabbed the railing and looked down. The stairs were carpeted and much cleaner, no longer slippery slabs of black concrete. Little red lights adorned the edges of the steps so people could actually see where they were going. God, was that a fresh coat of paint on the walls? In hindsight, I'd helped pay for these renovations.

After Jake paid our admission fee, we entered into the bar area of the club, and a host wearing a tuxedo checked our coats.

Coat check? How many nights had I shoved a big fat coat into a baby locker? Fuckers! While Jake and Tina handed Penguin Boy their jackets, I glanced to the right of the bar. The same patrons still occupied the same barstools. I thought of the old, proverbial theory of a tree falling in the forest; it still makes a sound even if nobody's around to hear it.

Lexi must have spotted us then because she charged over, appearing very determined. Her platinum blond hair was pulled back into a high ponytail, and she'd attached a long extension so it hung all the way down her back. A skin-tight, cornflower blue dress hugged her curvy body, and her eyes were lined with heavy black liner. Her false eyelashes were simply ridiculous.

She hugged me quickly and screamed to everyone within earshot that Casey (my old stage name) was here, as if I'd only been away on a cruise as opposed to missing in action for the last three years. She then followed it up with, "She's getting married, and I'm going to be a bridesmaid!" I got a few weird looks but thankfully, not from anyone I recognized. I glanced at Jake, who was predictably awestruck.

"Lexi, you remember Tina. And this is Jake. He's the one who finagled us the discount on the shoes." I cleared my throat at the sound of my lie while Tina glanced at me in mild confusion. I could see her recording and cataloguing the false statement for further inquiry.

Lexi led us to an empty table. "It's not so busy right now, so this is excellent timing," she gushed, pulling up an extra chair and sitting down. "I'll get my sister to take our order. I got her a job here as a waitress."

"Cute," I remarked, thinking it was more along the lines of disturbing. At one point in history, her unemployed father had considered taking a management position at Dream Girls. Known more for his philandering among Long Island nightclubs than his paternal attributes, he would have made a perfect addition to the executive team. I feared that one day I would walk into the club and her entire family would be running the place.

Lexi swept her legs up and laid her feet across Jake's lap. "You don't mind, do you?" she said, batting her eyelashes and shaking her ponytail.

"Er, no." Jake glanced at me as if to say, "What have you told her?" I shrugged and smiled. The funny part was I hadn't told her anything. She did that to everyone. Tina went off to the bathroom for the fifteenth time, and I ordered us drinks with Lexi's sister. "Can I rub your feet?" Jake asked Lexi, handing her a hundred-dollar bill.

"Please, like you have a choice," she said, plucking the money from his fingers. Jake smiled and slipped off her shiny silver platforms.

"Jake wants to take you shopping sometime for shoes," I said, stirring my vodka cranberry with the tiny straw.

"Great, when?" She looked pointedly at him. "I heard you get discounts."

"Yeah, it's a big discount," Jake said, nodding.

"He'll buy you whatever you want—as long as it's sexy," I said with a sigh.

"OK, so when?" she asked.

"Whenever you want. Maybe I'll take both of you after this wedding is over. You're not leaving for Hawaii the day after, are you, Pam?"

"No, the flights are booked for the end of March. Maybe you'd like to invest in some luggage for me?"

Part 3

PAM AND ROB

Honolulu, HA

MARCH 2003

Since we planned to honeymoon in Hawaii and then actually live there, we couldn't jet off the day after the wedding like most couples do. A month after our wedding, I was still sitting in a pathetically dirty apartment pretending to write one hundred thank-you notes.

Yeah, so I was married. I kept repeating it to myself because I didn't believe it. I didn't necessarily *disbelieve* it; I just wasn't sure it had really happened. A drunken blur from start to finish, I remembered details of the day, but how six hours of socializing could completely alter my life was a bit overwhelming. For someone who wasn't nervous before or during the wedding, I began jumping around in a state of constant agitation.

This unease surfaced three days after the big day. I was scheduled to do my taxes, and I had forgotten the time of my appointment. Since Rob was awake, I had him phone my accountant. Through my hazy slumber, I heard him say, "Yeah, my wife has an appointment today, and she can't remember what time she's scheduled."

I bolted upright in our bed. Was he referring to me? My new title fell from his mouth so naturally that it positively stunned me. And all of a sudden everything came flooding back: Father Bob had officially bound me to another human being, despite his warning looks.

I was focusing on some deep-breathing exercises when I heard Rob shout, "How many people are waiting? Thirteen! What's the point of my *wife* having an appointment if she's going to be behind thirteen people?" A valid point, yes, but I still crept into the bathroom and swallowed a Valium.

***

Besides packing up our stuff, there wasn't really a whole lot to do while I waited to honeymoon and move. Since I wasn't working, I went out every night in post-celebration of the wedding. (This form of drinking and living it up was similar to the precelebration that went on for eight months prior.) Unfortunately, Rob picked the night I was the most fucked up to confirm the honeymoon plans. I had just rolled in from a night at Crow Bar with Lexi, and he had me hunting all over the Internet for hotels and car rentals. I had no idea exactly what I'd booked until I was surveying the printed confirmations the following morning. Where the heck is Kauai? I thought, reading about my prepaid Marriot excursion to come.

Rob marched over to me, holding the calendar. "I was thinking about the honeymoon."

"What about it?" I would not have answered him at all, but it would have been rude not to, especially since he insisted on calling me his *wife*.

"We're leaving on the twenty-sixth of March for Honolulu." He pointed to the square on the calendar for emphasis. His other hand was covering a playmate's left breast. I giggled.

"What's so funny?"

"Nothing."

"I was thinking it might be better if we stayed with Brandon and Jenna for the nights of the twenty-seventh and twenty-eighth, before we fly to Kauai on the twenty-ninth."

"Those would be the first two nights of our *honeymoon*." I blinked. "Why would we want to do that?"

"Because people rent out apartments beginning the first of the month. If we don't start looking until the fifth, we might have to wait until the following month to move in anywhere."

"Is our honeymoon going to revolve around finding a place to live?" I asked in an I-might-strangle-you voice.

"No, baby, but this is something we should be thinking about."

"Let me make something perfectly clear. I am not spending the first two nights of our honeymoon with Brandon and Jenna. I don't care how nice you say they are. I'd actually pictured us in a sleek hotel, having sex all day and watching sunsets. While we are on the subject, where the heck is Kauai?"

***

Heeding my advice, Rob and I spent the first two nights of our honeymoon in a tropical, touristy environment, and we had fun. This is because we didn't know each other yet. By the third day of our honeymoon, I was getting to know Rob and experiencing a mixture of disbelief and anticipation combined with fear, which first reared its ugly head when he requested a piña colada at the pool in Kauai (apparently one of Hawaii's smallest islands known for its excessive rainfall). In the time I'd known him, he'd never ordered a frozen cocktail. Who was this man?

"Pam, do you want your usual?" Rob asked me.

I just stared at him, horrified.

"What? What did I do now?"

"I didn't know you liked frozen drinks," I accused.

"Are you suggesting I should have sat you down and told you at some point?"

"I would have appreciated the heads up." He rolled his eyes and turned back to the bartender. "I'm serious!" I exclaimed. "I should *know* if you like frozen drinks. That's an important thing to know about your husband. I'm totally freaking out!"

"Stop freaking out. I'm sure we'll face bigger problems. Are you doing your spritzer routine?"

"Yes, pinot grigio and club soda." I spritzed in the day, drank it straight in the evening. "Don't you think it's weird that this subject has never come up?"

"Are we still talking about the same thing?"

"Yes. I've only ever seen you drink beer, Jack and Coke, or gimlets, and now you pull this stunt?"

"I'm not usually lounging by a pool in Hawaii. Can we drop it?"

This conversation got me thinking in the abstract. It made me feel like I didn't know the man I married. I didn't know his earliest memory or his favorite color. In my defense, I suppose there was an awful lot Rob didn't know about me. Just how close were married couples supposed to be?

Later that evening, after an afternoon resulting in a hardly visible, slightly reddish glow, Rob and I perused the grounds of the Kauai Marriot. The landscape consisted of tall decorative columns, which provided a Spanish Victorian feel. While I was marveling at their height, Rob was sizing up their width, about to light a joint.

"Where did you get that?" I said. He couldn't have brought it from New York, much less from Honolulu to Kauai, with all those drug-sniffing dogs at the gate.

"I mailed it to myself here."

"You did what?"

"I mailed it about a week before we left New York."

"Airmail?"

"Yeah."

"You mailed it to *this* hotel?" I asked incredulously.

"It was waiting for me when we checked in."

"You're unbelievable," I said. "What if somebody had opened it?"

"Then they would have been committing a federal crime. You're not allowed to open another person's mail."

"You can if you suspect it holds drugs!"

"I wrapped it tight and flat. There's no way anyone could have suspected anything."

"What about the smell? Pot reeks!"

"Hash is practically odorless."

"Hash! You're smoking hash?"

"Pam, it's almost the same thing." I shook my head, amazed at his commitment to his addiction. And strangely enough, a little turned on by his ballsy desperation. I attempted to find out more about him. Now was a good time since he would soon be high on hash.

"Babe, what's your earliest memory?"

"Huh?"

"Your earliest memory? What is it?"

He was silent for a moment. "Climbing out of my crib."

"You can remember being in a crib?"

"I don't remember being *in* it, just climbing out. Then I crawled into the kitchen and found my parents. I can even recall their shocked expressions—my father looking up from his newspaper and laughing like a hyena."

"I think you were advanced for your age. It must have been all those episodes of *Jeopardy* blaring in the background."

"Nah, I was just a climber. I liked to climb—"

"What's your favorite color?"

"What is this? Twenty questions?"

"I want to find out more about you."

"Does this have to do with the piña colada? I'll never order another one again."

"Will you just answer me?"

"My favorite color? Probably purple."

"Why purple?"

"I don't know, Pam. It appeals to me."

"But why does it appeal to you over other colors, say blue or green?"

"Well, I like blue and green too. If you mix blue and green you get purple."

"No. Red and blue make purple."

"Are you sure?"

"I studied art." I didn't think purple would be his favorite color. Purple was a girl's favorite, and if he liked purple, *would he also like pink?* "Do you like pink too?"

"Not really. I mean, I wouldn't wear it, but if you were wearing a cute pink sweater, I might like it."

"But you wouldn't wear it?"

"No, not even to prove a point."

"I see men wearing pink a lot."

"Yeah, but they're all fags."

"I really don't think—"

"Sure they are. They're saying, 'Look at me, I can wear any color in the rainbow and I choose to wear this faggy color.'"

"For your information, some men look really great in a light pink dress shirt. Especially if they have a nice tan. My psychiatrist looks hot in pink." I felt the need to defend the straight men who dared to wear pink against Rob's biased opinions. Perhaps this was the reason not to play twenty questions with your spouse. I could see how the game could lead to arguments.

"Well, you won't catch me in it. Even with my killer tan." I stared at his bare arm sticking out of his muscle shirt. With his red and white splotches, he looked more like a candy cane.

***

Our hotel room was dark when we entered it. "The maid must have drawn the shades," I said. "I hope she pulled down the bed and left us chocolate!" I was a step ahead of Rob in pursuit of it when he grabbed me by the back of the neck. I stopped in my tracks and waited to feel his mouth on my skin. When he wanted me, he always indicated it with an unusual gesture. It was never a kiss on the lips that would start the lovemaking process but a tug at my hair or a rough kiss on my back.

He nibbled my bare shoulder and licked the side of my ear before quickly lifting my shirt up and over my head. My bikini top sprung forward, and he tugged on my breasts. I leaned back and rested my neck in the nook of his shoulder. It excited me when he was urgent. I felt that he needed me, couldn't live without me. When I sensed his desire, it turned me on.

I pressed my back into him. His cock was hard through the slippery material of his still-damp bathing suit.

I turned to face him and smiled. Between the hallway and the bathroom, I'd noticed a counter with a sink. "I want you to fuck me on this," I said, walking to it, my bikini bottom pushed to one side. I slid it off so all I was wearing were light pink stiletto heels that were hell to walk in but obviously served a greater purpose. Rob lifted me up, and I arched my back against the mirror. We fucked, the cold porcelain soon slick with sweat before he eventually collapsed, burying his face in my chest.

We never once kissed.

***

After five days away together, I was getting sick of Rob. It was the most time we'd ever spent with each other, and I was discovering he was far more anal than I'd initially realized. "How will they know our luggage is going to Maui if we have to change planes in Honolulu first?" Rob asked for the second time.

"It's an *adjoining* flight." I was hot, hungry, annoyed, and at an airport for the fourth time in one week. I had since learned island hopping wasn't the most relaxing way to spend a vacation, and I was not in the mood to deal with his paranoia.

"But how do the people in charge of luggage know we're en route to Maui?"

"Because it's printed on our tickets," I said with a sigh.

"I have a feeling our baggage is circling the carousel downstairs."

"Trust me, it's not. An airport employee is about to start loading it up through that little chute. I assure you." I pointed to the diminutive plane that was supposed to safely transport us to Maui.

"I think you're wrong. It didn't used to be this way, I'm telling you."

"That was nine years ago. They probably caught up with the times." Rob's face was ashen. "Haven't you ever taken an adjoining flight before? The luggage goes to the final destination," I said, exasperated.

"I'd better make sure."

"That's totally unnecessary," I tried, but the next second he was gone. *Making sure* for the both of us.

While Rob was off inspecting strangers' belongings, I watched our luggage board the plane. A few minutes later, I heard my name echoing from the ceiling. *Why was I being paged?* I left our bags in care of an angry man with a red face who probably assumed I was a threat to national security and went to speak to the person behind the nearest desk. She informed me that my husband couldn't get back to the gate without his ticket and ID, which were in my possession. I told her that he was just my boyfriend up until a month ago and I was having the marriage annulled the first chance I got. She believed me.

I lugged all the bags back to the checkpoint. Arriving at security, irritated, sweating, and still starving, I spotted him in line waving at me like a maniac. As if I could miss the Candy Cane jumping up and down.

***

Arriving in Maui, we picked up our canary yellow convertible. Apparently I had reserved it that drunken night on the computer, although I was fairly sure I had not requested yellow. We drove to an area called Makena in South Maui, having chosen the southern tip of the island based on the fact that it was the driest and sunniest section, receiving only fifteen annual inches of rainfall!

Upon arrival at our hotel, room service had the foresight to bring us champagne and chocolate-covered strawberries, which reminded Rob we were still on our honeymoon. I stepped out onto the balcony and looked down over acres of golf course. I wondered how the grass could be so green given the lack of precipitation. Joining me on the balcony, Rob held out a glass of champagne and put his arm around me. "Too bad we don't play golf," he said.

Setting his champagne down, he slid his hand under the front of my shirt. He kissed the back of my neck and slid his other hand under my skirt and up my thigh. I shivered. Down below, a male golfer sporting an orange cap putted a ball three feet past the flag.

Rob's fingers slid down the front of my thong. Now he had my full attention. I turned around and kissed him, unbuckled his belt and undid his pants. "Fuck me, baby," I said. He pushed up my skirt. I let my underwear drop to the floor and he entered me, pressing me up against the railing. I gave a small prayer that the guardrail was sturdy, quickly realizing this would be a very embarrassing way to die. My bare ass pressed up against the bars, he thrust in and out of me, coming in seconds.

"Jesus. Could you come any faster?" I said.

"I was really turned on."

"I'll say. You should enter a contest."

Next thing we heard was clapping and whistling from two floors above. A man and woman, both scruffy looking and holding cans of Coors Light, were leaning over and cheering. I laughed and reached for my skirt while Rob turned bright red and reached for the sliding door.

"Stay tuned for further adventures!" I yelled up.

"Pam, get in here!" He yanked me back inside. "Any minute those two will be knocking on our door."

"For what?"

"They could be swingers for all we know!"

"Drinking Coors Light? I doubt it."

"Get in here!"

***

The next morning, things went downhill. While I was hoarding pastries from the breakfast buffet, Rob went to secure us chairs by the pool. However, when I went to meet him, he was already asleep and lying diagonally across his chair with his mouth and legs wide open. Both deck chairs next to him were empty, but only one had a towel on it, so I assumed that was mine. I made myself comfortable, applied three layers of sunscreen, and read the back cover of my book for the zillionth time.

Half an hour went by. A woman about my age emerged from the pool and walked over to me. I ignored her, but water dripped off of her and onto the pages of my paperback.

"Can I help you?" I said.

"Yes, you're lying on my towel. I'd like it back, if you don't mind. And my chair as well."

Rob picked this moment to wake up and say, "Pam, what are you doing? Why are you lying on her chair?"

I stared at both of them like they were completely mad before glancing to the other side of Rob. A skinny African American dude with sagging skin was now occupying the other chair. In my opinion, he didn't even need to tan. "But—" I tried to say, watching in amazement as Rob jumped up and gave the wet girl his towel. Suddenly equipped with manners, one might have assumed his last few years were spent cooking at a finishing school in Switzerland as opposed to letting me open my own doors and encouraging me to pay for all our meals.

"Get up, Pam! Jesus! That's her chair," said Rob.

I gave him a hard look and reluctantly got to my feet, mumbling a half-hearted apology to the drowned rat still dripping beside me. "Just where am I going to lie now?" I asked, grabbing my bag. "And why on earth didn't you get *me* a towel? Naturally I thought the chair with the towel was mine."

"You should have asked me."

"You were asleep!"

"Well, while you were finishing your elaborate breakfast, she was lying there," he said, nodding to the girl. She smiled at him and reached for her suntan oil. Her tan, wet skin glistened in the sun. To my disbelief, Rob returned her smile.

"Did I miss something? I'm ten minutes late to the pool, and you're acting as if you two are a couple! You'll gladly give up your towel for her, but you didn't get me one in the first place?" I hollered.

"Lower your voice. You're totally embarrassing me," said Rob.

"I'm embarrassing *you*?" I shouted.

"Yeah. You are."

"Let's just figure this out. Where am I going to lie? It's almost noon. Every chair is taken."

"Why don't you look around? A chair is not going to come to you."

"Oh. My. God. Perhaps you could apply the same courtesy to your *wife* as you do for an absolute stranger and help me? The newlywed phase was O-V-E-R. Rob heaved a great big sigh and got to his feet like he weighed four hundred pounds. "I asked you to fetch me a chair. Not the crown jewels," I barked.

"Just take mine. I'll go sleep on the grass!"

"Fine!" At this point, every swimmer in the pool was watching us, even the toddlers. *Great, now I have to lie between a girl I hate and a snoring old man.* The three of us together made a fine picture: I was the white in the middle of tan and black. The marshmallow portion of a s'more. I turned to the graham cracker that had since pulled Gucci sunglasses and a magazine out of her ass. "We're on our honeymoon," I announced.

She raised her eyebrows. It must have been obvious.

***

Later that evening, Rob awarded me the title of Surf and Turf. I crackled like shrimp tempura and ended up begging him to slather me with aloe. Thankfully, this green-gel-inspired intimacy ended our impasse so we were able to enjoy the rest of our evening and plan the following day's Clark Griswold adventure. Relying heavily on our *Hawaii for Dummies* book, we decided to take the Road to Hana, a rather touristy drive through the Hawaiian mountains/volcanoes.

"It says here, 'The Road to Hana is the most famous off-the-beaten-path adventure in Hawaii.' I love adventures!" I said. We were lying on the bed next to each other. I was resting on my stomach, trying not to move a muscle, and he was pretending to enjoy his sunburn, still insisting on calling it a tan.

"Yes, I know the Road to Hana," said Rob. "It's an adventure, all right, but it doesn't involve sex, drinking, or strip clubs. I don't want you to be disappointed."

"I know that. It's exploring. I get it. This book says, 'A constant stream of rental cars embark on this fifty-two-mile odyssey, negotiating fifty-six single-lane bridges and more than six hundred curves.' In the convertible, it will be like nonstop action."

"OK, but it's a long ride—"

"Road trip. Road trip. Road trip." Instead of chanting these foolish words of a moron, I should have been reading the remainder of the page, where they suggested breaking up the trip by spending the night at one of their bed and breakfasts. In bold print it read, "It'll take the pressure off the drive home."

***

Driving, we had two choices: the shorter, steeper route with difficult dirt paths and hills or the longer, winding, paved thoroughfare. We opted for the first route, thinking we'd come all this way to Maui—why not get the full experience? And we most certainly did. When the car wasn't stalling and sputtering, we sailed past black sand beaches, twisted mountains, purple skies, and rocky cliffs. I took photos of Rob among the scenery while we were still on speaking terms. "OK, let's have a shot of you by the cave. Now I want you *in* the cave. Get in the cave and peek your head out."

"Pam!"

Our scenic drive was actually going pretty well until our car veered off into a ditch, directly underneath a small waterfall. Rob had been staring at the waterfall as opposed to the road ahead. This descent into a deep hole would not have been so bad if we hadn't been in a convertible, of course. Soaking wet upholstery always makes for pleasant travel. I immediately hopped out and captured a couple winning photos of Rob immersed in the vertical stream of water as he attempted to push the car out. "Stop taking pictures and come help me!" he yelled, spitting water.

"But my shoes," I said, looking down at my new Stuart Weisman flats.

"Fuck your shoes! Jesus!"

Thankfully, various tourists suddenly appeared, willing to assist Rob. I stood back and captured more winning photos.

Back on the actual road again and driving along, one thing became glaringly clear: I couldn't navigate any better than Rob could spot trenches. Soon we were lost, and it began to rain. I renamed it the Road to Hell.

"It's not raining. It doesn't rain in these parts," said Rob, still in denial.

I held out my hand and watched the drops fall one at a time. "Right. It must be a big animal above us, sneezing and traveling at the same speed as this car."

It began to rain harder. Rob looked up at the sky and then straight ahead. He squeezed the wheel and gritted his teeth. "These roads are going to be mud if this keeps up," he said, downshifting. The rain poured down, and to say we were miserable was a vast understatement. Finally Rob located the button to close the roof, and after stopping to ask directions another six times, we began to head in the proper direction, which we decided should be back to the hotel.

Four hours later, we were back. Wet, cold, starving, and ultimately pissed off with each other, we both jumped out of the car. One look at my face and the valet just shook his head. "Road to Hana?"

"You could have warned us," I snapped, stalking off in the direction of the bar.

Later that evening, I read, "The Road to Hana is like life: it's not the destination that counts but what you do along the way." *What did that say about us?*

***

After the honeymoon, Rob and I camped out at Brandon's house for three weeks. Friends with Rob for many years, Brandon had been nice enough to let us stay with him and his girlfriend in their house rental in Kamuki, a town that lies just above the touristy district of Waikiki.

In the three weeks of serious apartment searching on an island that seemed to discourage newcomers from settling in beyond their vacations, Rob and I perused *Honolulu Weekly* with vengeance and begged for the opportunity to live in a run-down apartment within our price range. Never having been to Hawaii before and lulled to death by Rob's reassurances that everyone was *super* friendly, I was unprepared for the harsh reality: Honolulu was a divided culture consisting of white upper class and minorities of lower income brackets. And *no one* was friendly.

As we drove to the apartments listed for rent, I began to realize two things: 1) white people didn't rent places we could afford and 2) despite his black belt in karate and superior attitude, Rob wasn't very street smart. He acted as if the world was a fair playing ground and everyone followed the same rules. In fact, all the landlords frowned and asked us why we were relocating from the East Coast. It was as if they suspected us of working under a Christopher Columbus regime with secretive plans to wipe out their entire native race. And Rob, who was downright naive, insisted I was crazy and simply imagining the dirty looks and side-on jeers from the old, rickety Hawaiian homeowners set in their ways.

In Rob's defense, however, the community seemed to distrust me more than they did him. Perhaps they considered me shallow because of my Dior sunglasses and skeptical attitude, whereas Rob at least looked like he could be of use supplying drugs to the neighborhood. The bottom line was we had nowhere to live.

So when Brandon's girlfriend—a Hawaiian-born native named Jenna who was eager to get us out of her hair at that point—mentioned her aunt had a cottage sublet for rent, Rob jumped on the connection. I was wary of course, not really liking Jenna and trying with difficulty not to let it show. She was the type who pretended to be friendly and fun but was really just competitive and jealous. According to her, she was a natural at everything: designing jewelry, writing for a magazine, singing in a band, volunteering at the soup kitchen, surfing, heading the rowing team to victory for five consecutive years, etc. *I mean, really, what the fuck is rowing?* I nicknamed her Lulu J. Lo, and referred to her as such. She even resembled J. Lo, which made it that much more annoying: long dark hair, doe-ish brown eyes, deeply tanned skin, an ass that stuck out perfectly, and a body fit from rowing, perhaps?

Naturally, there were a few details Lulu J. Lo left out about her aunt's apartment, such as location and price and many other nightmarish aspects. I knew Rob and I were in trouble the moment we began to ascend a steep and winding road, more accurately described as a mountain. Having left our canary yellow dynamo back in Maui, we were traveling in a small red economy car we'd rented from Hertz. Rob's "plan" was that after we'd found a place to live, we would be able to take the bus everywhere. In the twelve years I'd lived away from home without a car, I'd never once utilized a bus system, so I didn't realize just how terrible his idea was. Rob raved about it. "It's one of the best public transportation systems in the country!" And for some crazy reason, I believed him. Live and learn.

For better or worse, we braced ourselves in our shit car that was tackling the incline in second gear. Cars came zooming toward us, leaving behind smoke on the single-lane road. This mountain—ingeniously named Round Top—made San Francisco seem like flat terrain. Rob's hopes were high, but I could see them sinking when he glanced at the odometer.

"Brandon said it was five miles up this hill. We've only gone two," he declared, downshifting into first for a tight turn.

"You do realize this won't be very convenient," I commented, picturing Lulu J. Lo being cooked over a fire, pig-roast style. Rob didn't respond, too preoccupied with the sharp twists of the road. I sat back and surveyed the thick mass of green woods that ran along the inside of the mountain. The air was damp and dense, not unlike the mugginess before a rainstorm. As if reading my thoughts, Rob confessed it rained at least twice a day up at this elevation.

"I thought we were moving to a sunny island. Not the fucking Congo. It's also super humid," I added. "Can't you put on the A.C.?"

"No. I can't. Every time I do, the car stalls. It doesn't have enough power."

"Do you think this area would actually be on a bus route?" I asked, suspicious.

"Yes. The bus goes everywhere. I'm telling you." We passed a park with a sign that advertised "Deerfield Mountain Trails."

"Did you see that?" I shouted. "This is a mountain. I knew it! Goddamn that Lulu J. Lo!"

"Great, we're at the halfway point. And stop making fun of Jenna. Without her, we wouldn't know about this place."

"Exactly. Did you even ask her what the rental was like?"

"It's a one-bedroom cabin, and it won't be ready until the first of May."

"It's only the middle of April," I said.

"I'm aware of the date. But if we like it, we can get a cheap hotel for ten days."

"There are no cheap hotels in Honolulu." At the time, I had no idea I was about to become an expert on budget accommodations.

"The Best Western in Waikiki is only ninety-five a night."

"Awesome. Do you have a thousand dollars or will I be paying for our Best Western extravaganza?"

"Pam, you know I'm completely wiped out."

"OK, let's not get ahead of ourselves," I said, fanning myself with my fashion magazine—the last shred of evidence that indicated I had any connection to my old life. The altitude was causing my ears to pop.

The longer we drove, the steeper the single-lane road became until we finally pulled into a driveway at the cusp of Round Top Mountain. The odometer read six miles exactly, and that didn't include the driveway, which was an additional half mile. *Fucking J. Lo.* "About how far would you say this is from town?" I asked.

"Maybe eight miles?" he guessed, pulling into a space behind a sleek silver Lexus. Due to the huge Banyan trees, the house was sheltered from the road.

Rob opened his car door and jumped out. His exuberance was disturbing and out of character. Traipsing through the misty air, I felt trapped in a Hitchcock film with a psycho. We walked up a stone walkway, which was more like a rocky slope of beach. Looking down at my heels, I realized I was forever wearing the wrong shoes. Rob was bounding up the walkway, five steps ahead. "Would you take my hand please, before I trip and kill myself?" I warned. "It's not like there's a handrail!"

"How old are you? Eighty-five?"

I was about to lash out when an older woman appeared at the door. She looked like all the other homeowners I'd encountered so far: hostile and judgmental. She introduced herself as Rose, which I thought was a fucked-up name for a Korean woman living on top of a mountain.

We slipped out of our shoes—a Hawaiian custom, no doubt originated from wealthy Americans with expensive carpets—and entered her huge house.

"Oh, you're friends with Jenna! How nice!" squealed Rose.

I plastered a smile on my face. "Yeah, she's really great! Where's the cottage?"

"Oh, let me show you." Rose glanced down at my shoes with disapproval. "You can't walk there wearing those. Let me get you a pair of old sneakers from the shed. Every time it rains, the trail gets a little muddy."

"Of course it does," I mumbled.

Rose was back in an instant with a pair of old Keds that were too big for me. I slipped them on, and we followed her out through a back door and onto an earthy path. By earthy, I mean unkempt. Five hundred feet behind her house, through thick brush and brambles, sat the campground of my youth. Resting on the lot was a cottage slightly bigger than the Unabomber's shack. The outside wood was deep brown and brought back fond recollections of walking from my childhood tent to the community bathroom.

The cabin was in serious need of a paint job, and the trail leading to it wasn't ideal, but it had a cute little porch with a bench and a fairy-tale quality that was enticing: Hansel and Gretel before being shoved in the oven, Snow White before she bit into the apple, the Three Little Pigs, etc. I imagined Rob and I reigning over the forest Peter Pan style, protecting our home and threatening trespassers with a bow and arrow.

Half-listening to Rose's explanation for the cabin's original use, which involved some type of indentured servitude, I pictured myself on the bench with my laptop with only the sound of the woods to distract me from my goal. It was, in fact, the perfect place to rewrite Grimm's fairytales, living in a similar setting. Moreover, after I'd completed my first literary work of genius, I could move on to write a sick cabin thriller that Spielberg would no doubt make into a movie starring Jack Nicholson. Jennifer Love Hewitt would obviously play the heroine trying to ignore the alarming changes in her husband as he slowly transformed from friendly neighborhood chef into mountainside killer.

I finally stopped daydreaming when Rose said she was unable to show us the inside of the cottage. This, she explained, was because her current renter was obsessed with protecting her privacy and would strongly object. I assumed her tenant was cooking crystal meth inside and wondered if she was moving out to serve jail time. Unfortunately, Rob was as intrigued with this impractical situation as I was, and we agreed to her outrageous fixed price of thirteen hundred a month.

"You're paying extra for the privilege of being part of the Round Top community," explained Rose. "A portion of your rent will go toward maintenance of the grounds and the general tending of the mountain."

How irritating.

On our ride down, I prayed that the brakes were in good condition. The view into nothing but sky reminded me of movies where the antagonist plunges to his death over a five-mile cliff. "There is no way a bus travels up this high," I declared. "And if there is one, I can't say I'd like to be on it. How would a vehicle larger than ours make these tight turns?"

Rob glanced off to the side. "That's a good point. Maybe you should get a mountain bike."

"Are you serious?"

"Very."

"What is wrong with you? You know I am used to riding everywhere in a taxi. I haven't ridden a bike since I was ten, and even then I recall it was a disaster."

"Well, if there's no bus, you're going to have to figure out some way to get around," he said matter-of-factly. Suddenly I was not as enthusiastic to cohabitate in the island's coolest fort.

"Maybe we should think this over before agreeing to rent here."

"We just told Rose we'd take it!"

"I think *Rose* would understand if we wanted to think about it."

"Pam, we have to take this. No one else has been willing to rent to us."

"Ha! So you admit it then!" I said triumphantly.

Rob sighed. "I don't think it's because of the color of our skin. Or because we're Yankees. It's just a competitive market."

I rolled my eyes. "You're so clueless."

***

We spent the next nine nights in the Best Western, courtesy of my Visa card. By the seventh night, I was sincerely bored. Standing on the balcony, I dried my freshly washed hair with an eleventh-floor tailwind and stared out at the world. Strands of wet hair whipped across my face, casting opaque shadows over Waikiki and its overlapping neighborhoods. Peering down at the roofs of varied low-income housing and intersecting highways, I felt infinite. Limitless, like there was so much left to be discovered, so many places I hadn't been. I turned around and studied Rob's profile through the screen door, thinking he probably didn't share my enthusiasm. He was resting on one of the double beds watching TV and drinking Bud.

Stepping back into the room, I leapt onto the bed, jogging its frame and knocking a bag of pretzels to the floor.

"Baby," he scolded.

"Yes," I said, imitating his sternness.

"What's up? You're so restless. Can't you just relax for once?"

"I'm bored. Let's go explore!" I exclaimed.

He slowly pulled his eyes away from the TV and turned to stare at me. "Just where do you want to explore? Waikiki is not that big. I think we've covered it from top to bottom already."

"Yeah, the obvious areas, but there's plenty of places we haven't been. Let's go to a really seedy bar or an underground dance club. Somewhere strange!"

"Oh God. Let's not."

"Come on," I urged. "We should be discovering Hawaii's subculture, its underlying vibe."

"I'm very content not to explore Waikiki's underlying vibe. Plus, it's hard to do that without money."

"We can't let money stand in our way," I said. "That's the dumbest thing I've ever heard."

"I realize *you* think that way, Pam. Luckily, you have me to balance you out."

"I'll withdraw cash on my charge card. Please? Come take a walk with me. We'll just go into any bar or club at random. It's only nine o'clock."

"Jesus God." He looked up at the stucco ceiling. "Can't we just sit here and relax?"

"We've been relaxing. Shit, I've never been so rested in my entire life. Let's go explore!" I repeated.

"I have an idea," said Rob. "Why don't you go out and explore for the both of us? You're obviously not going to be happy just sitting here. When you return, you can tell me all about the wild times you had dancing on the ceiling, or the bar, or whatever it is you find fun. Just remember you're married now." He pointed to the platinum band on his finger.

"How could I forget?"

"Anything is possible with you."

"The adventure won't be as fun by myself. Just come with me," I pleaded.

"Will you please let me watch my fucking show?" His eyes widened in annoyance. This, coincidently, would not have been possible had he not run out of weed. "Come back by midnight.

If you insist on going out, I'm going to have to instill a curfew. You're not in New York City anymore, Dorothy. There are a lot of bad, leaky characters lurking around these parts. Bring your phone with you and keep it on. And answer it if it rings. It'll be me calling."

"Fine."

Seconds later, I was out the door. I walked past the cheesy, economy-size indoor pool and out of the hotel. Turning right onto Kuhio Avenue, I headed away from the beach and the commercialism of Kalakaua Avenue. I wanted to check out how people lived and why they lived here, what they knew that I didn't.

I hit the first cash machine and withdrew two hundred on my credit card. Then I walked in the direction of Déjà Vu, a strip club chain with which I was familiar. I hadn't been to a strip club since my bachelorette party (only about seven short weeks), and I suddenly missed the ebb and flow of negativity. I was also contemplating picking up some part-time work, and the strip clubs seemed the best place to start looking.

Déjà Vu was a corporation, with most of its locations on the West Coast and South Florida. Having visited a few already, I'd found them to be the sleazier, more bang for your buck, quantity not quality, all-nude venues and was expecting something along those lines.

I stepped into the line of guys waiting outside and shut off my phone. The last thing I needed was Rob calling me the moment I made it to the ropes. I tried to be cool and ignore the various stares I was receiving from all types of men who had ditched their wives and kids in lieu of tits and ass, but as I neared the entrance, the big, fat bouncer stopped me. "Who are you with?" He cracked his knuckles and looked straight past me. He was chewing on what looked like a straw. Handy, I suppose, if someone were to come along with an open bag of powder.

"No one. I just want to go inside. I'll pay the cover."

"Women aren't allowed in without a male escort. House policy."

"Does that mean I have to make up some elaborate excuse as to why I'm here?"

He finally turned to me, raking his eyes up and down my frame, making sure that I was aware he was giving me the once-over. His eyes settled on my chest. "An excuse might help," he said, grunting.

"Well, I can tell you that I'm considering working here, or I could tell you that I know Bobby or Tony. Which do you prefer?"

The bouncer continued to stare at my chest and coughed, rolling his eyes. "Fuck, I don't have time for this. Pay the lady inside to the left." He unlatched the rope. "And if anyone asks, you're here to audition."

I nodded and smiled curtly before stepping around a heavy velvet curtain. For a second, I thought about Rob, who probably hadn't moved an inch off the bed. Married or not, I was still an independent woman who was entitled to enter the establishment of her choice! I was not going to be one of those pathetic women unable to function without her other half. *Not this girl.*

I handed over ten dollars to a disgruntled teenager, thinking what a bargain I was getting. She stamped my hand with red ink and glared at me. I glared back and thanked her. The club was crowded and dark. Blue strobe lights assaulted my vision, reminding me of the few experiences I'd had with the police. Walking purposely over to the stage to blend, I let my hair down from its usual knot and positioned my nose in the air as if I were awaiting the arrival of twenty male office pals.

There were five dancers on the stage, each glued to a pole. All five were in good shape, tan, and saturated with sparkly lotion enhanced by the low lighting. Other dancers were walking around in tight Lycra dresses, clutching a glass in one hand, a small purse in the other. I had expected most of the girls to be of Asian descent, but only one woman appeared to be.

I studied the talent and picked who I thought was the hottest. She had long, light brown hair and big, round brown eyes, and her body was unusually curvy. I suspected she was Brazilian or Venezuelan. My gaze settled on her tits, which were full, perfectly proportioned, and refreshingly real. When she swayed and smiled at me, I grinned back, motioning for her to detach herself from the pole and move closer to the end of the stage.

I pulled out a massive amount of singles. After moving to Hawaii, my bankroll resembled Rob's—not a terribly good thing overall—but handy in certain situations. As she crouched down in front of me, the disco ball reflected in her eyes. Spotting the stack of singles, she pressed her chest in close to me and whispered, "What's a gorgeous girl like you doing alone in a place like this?"

"Good question," I answered, handing her the stack of ones.

"All for me?" she asked, genuinely surprised.

I cleared my throat yet again, trying to recall the reason I'd walked into Déjà Vu in the first place. "When you're done will you come answer some questions for me? I'll pay you."

"Are you a cop?"

"No. Just bored."

"Okay. This is my last song and I'll be right over."

Brianna stayed true to her word and slid into the seat next to me by the stage. "How can I help you?" She smiled wide and her gorgeous, white teeth glowed under the spotlights.

I didn't waste any time. "If I wanted to work somewhere in Honolulu dancing topless or all nude, but without the contact—is there such a thing?"

"You've danced before?"

"Yeah, but in New York, and not for a few years. I just want to make some quick cash, but I wouldn't be able to do any of the back room stuff."

"Do you mean just a bar with dancers on stage? That type of dancing?"

"Yeah, I guess."

"Well, sure. Honolulu has all types of bars and nude clubs but I'm not sure how much you'll make. Maybe two hundred? Possibly three? Here at this club, I make between six and eight bills a night."

I bit my bottom lip and thought of Jake. "Hmm. So where are places like that? I have until midnight to check it out."

"What happens at midnight? Your husband comes looking for you?"

"No. More like he falls asleep wondering where I am."

Brianna laughed. "OK, the best place I know is on Kapulani Boulevard. If you keep walking straight on Kuhio Avenue away from Waikiki, you run into Kapulani. Take a left and walk straight for about ten minutes. Or hail a cab. The place is called Femme Nu. I have a girlfriend who works there, and she does OK."

***

Ten minutes later, I was skipping along Kapulani Boulevard. The road was wide and long and lonely. Huge Banyan trees lined the sidewalk, protecting me from the deep black night. Halfway there, I considered turning around, but my feet rushed on, curiosity getting the better of me. Two hundred a night in cash wouldn't be too bad. And it would be honest money.

By the time I reached my destination, my skip had slowed to a hesitant stagger. The establishment was set far back from the road and didn't seem like a club at all. It was more like a square house in the middle of nowhere. Painted black and run-down, the cheesy pink lighting outlined the corners and gave it an I'm-a-block-away-from-the-airport feel. The words "FEMME NU" sparkled from a distance, but the "NU" part was blinking, hinting at its energy level. I walked toward the fluorescent sign before realizing the entrance was on the side.

Peering around the corner, I spotted an older man in a leather jacket sitting on a stool, reading a book. "Sorry to disturb you," I said. "But is this the entrance?"

He looked up from the yellowing pages of a slim paperback, which I could see now was the classic *Looking for Mr. Goodbar*. *Great.* I'd never read it, but I'd seen the movie and remembered Diane Keaton being raped and killed.

"Yep. You have ID?" he asked.

"Yes." I pulled it from my pocket.

"Cover is ten dollars, but you get a ticket that's good for two free drinks."

"That's cool," I said, thinking this was the land of deals. I handed him a ten in exchange for two pink tickets that reminded me of a long day playing ski-ball at the arcade. Luckily, I'd arrived in the right frame of mind. He noticed the red mark on my left hand and nodded gruffly, probably thinking I was on a ridiculous bender.

The inside was dark. I snaked my way to the bar, where a bunch of old men were talking about how old they were, and ordered a vodka cranberry from a female bartender, a drink I assumed would be difficult to screw up. Not the case; it tasted like water.

Two girls were dancing together high above me on a small platform. One was tall and blond and wearing a tight white half-shirt that read HUSTLER in bold, black letters. Her black leather shorts were cut high up her ass. Sucking her fingers seductively, she stared into the eyes of a diminutive Asian girl. The Asian girl appeared Filipino and was semibalanced on silver stilettos, modeling a pink leopard print bra and garter, which, coincidentally, was posted inside every bus stop along the "finer" streets of Waikiki. Her bra straps were seductively falling off her shoulders but somehow still managed to cover her tits. I marveled at this rebuff to gravity. Glancing down, I noticed she was bare under the garter. She didn't look much older than twelve. This bothered me.

Pulling my eyes away from their riveting performance, I grabbed my drink and walked to the edge of the bar so I could survey the odd layout of the club. A large square stage was centered in the room with chairs around it, some occupied by young men. Nine dancers moved on a lackluster rotation wearing bikini-style ensembles. On the outskirts of the stage, booths were set up like a sports bar. Large black benches with wooden tables held pitchers of beer and larger parties of what appeared to be regulation people enjoying a bar atmosphere.

Two things occurred to me instantly: there were plenty of women customers among the men, and there seemed to be a fair share of couples as well. Overall, the clientele appeared to be a melting pot of locals, Japanese, and people from Connecticut.

I looked back at the stage. All the dancers were natural, not one breast enhancement in the joint. *Could I pull something like this off?* I thought about Rob and chuckled.

I returned to the bar and changed two twenties in for more singles. I drank another vodka cranberry and watched men go from their tables to the stage and sit down in front of a particular girl of their choosing. These men set down a stack of singles (I assumed twenty dollars' worth) and continued to feed the same girl a few at a time, which seemed to perpetuate the removal of clothing until they were stark naked. I waited and watched, amazed at the unusualness of it all. It seemed apparent to me that many customers were simply there to drink beer and see their friends, and others were there for the ladies.

My curfew long past, I stood among the other patrons, eyes peeled. I concentrated on a woman with long, dark hair and a porcelain doll-like face, astounded that there could be so many attractive women working in such a dive. Were they all married? I walked swiftly over to the stage and sat down in front of her. She acted a little surprised, and I smiled sheepishly, quickly sticking a five-dollar bill in her G-string. This broke the ice.

She smiled at me, opened a square mat, knelt down on it, and began to seduce me from a foot away. I fed her singles, and she stripped off her clothes. She was already seminaked, but *everything* she'd been wearing came off. When my singles were gone, she spread her long, pale legs open, giving me a direct eyeline into her insides, apparently the pinnacle of her routine. I squinted, knowing she was thinking about anything other than me. I left after that, thinking, *I can do this!* All I needed was a cute little gym mat!

Down to my last twenty dollars, I walked quickly along Kapulani Boulevard in search of a cab. None came along. I reached the 7-Eleven on the corner and asked a befuddled employee eating a package of devil dogs how I might call one. He said his late-night replacement was on his way and he could give me a ride to the Best Western if I was willing to wait around while he balanced the cash drawer.

I peered at this freckle-faced kid. "Nah," I said, "but thanks anyway." I headed out of the store and turned my phone back on, thinking I might have a few angry messages from Rob and now was a good as any time to delete them. Strangely enough, I had no messages. Then something odd happened: a small black car crammed with a bunch of kids peeled past me, screaming something that resembled, "Halley—you no good white bitch!" and random objects hit me hard from a few different angles. It took me a few moments to realize these objects were raw eggs. I thought they could have been stones because that's what they felt like. One smacked my forehead, another my stomach. Two hit my left leg, and another landed on my shoulder. Thankfully, two flew over my head. My left temple stung with pain, and I stood there stunned, dripping raw egg. *Who the fuck is Halley?* I was sincerely annoyed that I resembled her in the pitch black of night.

Twenty minutes later, I walked into the hotel room wondering how I would explain this bizarre egging, but I didn't have to account for a thing. Rob was fast asleep on the same bed in the same position I had left him. The TV was on the same channel, and empty bottles of Bud lined the bedside table. I smirked my disgust. *It's a good thing he was so worried about me. One of those eggs could have given me brain damage if anyone in that car had been a decent shot.* I ran myself a bath, surreptitiously trying to rouse Rob from his slumber, to no avail.

Instead I soaked in the hot bath and thought about Brianna. *"What's a gorgeous girl like you doing alone in a place like this?"* She'd seen right through me when most people were fooled. We'd barely talked, and she knew me better than the man I'd married.

The next morning, I awoke facing Rob. He was still purring like a cat that had never spent a night in the cold. I stared at him until he slowly opened one eye.

"Hi," I said.

His other eye snapped open. "What the fuck happened to you?"

"What do you mean?"

"Your head! You're a big egghead!"

I reached up and felt my forehead. "Oh yeah." I had a huge bump.

"Oh yeah, what?"

"I am an egghead. Literally."

"What happened?" He was more alive than I'd ever seen him.

"Flying eggs. No shit."

"What?"

"I'm serious. A carload of assholes threw eggs at me." Slices of golden light radiating from the shit shades of the Best Western caused me to wince.

"Explain. Your forehead is lopsided." Rob was sitting up on one arm, entirely focused.

"I was walking home and these kids, or guys, or men, or *some gang* mistook me for someone else and socked me with raw eggs. Like a dozen—no pun intended. I got hit other places too."

"They mistook you for someone else? How do you know?"

"Because they screamed a girl's name, and then they called me a white bitch like they knew who I was."

"Whose name did they call you?"

"What does it matter?"

"It matters."

"Halley, or Hailey—like the comet—or something like that."

"Oh." A few seconds went by.

"That's all you have to say? 'Oh.' Do you know this girl?"

"Not exactly."

"What is that supposed to mean?"

"I know that 'Halley,' spelled H-A-O-L-E but pronounced the way you said it, is Hawaiian slang for rich white bitch, or cunt, rather. If they yelled that and pounded you with eggs, well, the attack was aimed at *you*."

This changed everything. I gave up on the notion of more sleep and sat up in the bed.

"Do you mean to tell me that you've moved me to an island where I'm a target for drive-by-eggings due to the color of my skin?"

Rob looked a little sheepish for the first time since we'd moved. "I'm a little surprised. I thought the natives would be a bit more evolved by now. Where exactly were you walking?"

"Kapulani Boulevard."

"What were you doing all the way over there? What did you do last night?"

"Research," I said tiredly. My egghead was throbbing.

"Research for what?"

"A part-time job."

"Oh no. Tell me about your night," said Rob flatly.

"Hmm, well first I went to Déjà Vu and talked to this hot Brazilian stripper—"

"Quit fucking around. Your jokes aren't funny."

I sighed. "I also went to Femme Nu, and I have to tell you, I think it would be a great idea—"

"Are you serious? This is just great. My wife of less than two months is hanging out in strip joints while her husband waits for her alone in a hotel room."

"Motel," I corrected.

"Pam!"

"Oh, come on. You told me to go explore on my own."

"And you missed your curfew too, by the way."

"Yes, well, what did I miss exactly? Watching you stare at the television and sip warm beer. Shit, talk about regret."

"That's not the point."

"It *is* the point. If you really cared what I was doing, you would have come with me. Anyhow, the good news is that I might have found an answer to some of the financial problems I'm anticipating."

"Oh really?"

"Yes. Maybe I could dance at one of these bars like Femme Nu. No one knows me here. It's a totally different environment and involves no contact whatsoever with the men—"

"No, Pam."

"No, wait. Listen to me. I checked it out. It's totally different than New York."

"I thought you were over this little phase."

"Phase? It was my profession. It's part of who I am."

"Who you were," he corrected. "And it was five years ago."

"Three and a half. I danced for *five.* Would you please let me finish?" He folded his arms over his candy-cane chest and turned on his back. "I spent an hour or so hanging out in Femme Nu, and the customers seemed normal. They treat it like a bar—not a whorehouse. And the dancers never left the stage. It looked totally easy. Boring but easy."

"You noticed these girls were completely naked, right?"

"Men pay to see pussy. Some things don't change."

"That's really something to commend them for."

"I'm not commending anyone. I'm simply stating a fact. Oh, come on. I've modeled worse, and those pictures are out there forever."

"Pam, I've already said no. This isn't Manhattan. You're not going to get the same caliber of people visiting the establishment. It's not going to be rich businessmen and stock-holders staring at your tits. It's going to be the guy who takes out the garbage or the man who picks pineapples all day on the Dole Plantation. You wouldn't like it anyway."

"But I'd be protected because I'd always be on stage. The dancers are all cute and clean, and they carry these adorable little yoga mats around with them."

"Wow, that makes all the difference," said Rob dryly. "It sounds like a sanitary dream."

"I'm just telling you how it works."

"I know how it works. I've been there, OK. Years ago. The girls spread their legs wider than the wingspan of an albatross. Anyone within a five-mile radius gets a good look inside. My wife is not doing that."

"Why are you referring to me in the third person?"

"You get my point."

"No, I don't. I'm willing to do this for us, and I can't make money here doing anything else. What's minimum wage here? Four dollars an hour?"

"I thought you set money aside so you could focus on your outlandish book of fairytales."

"I did put money aside, but things have cost more than we thought, and soon we'll be paying a huge rent. Are you going to be able to come up with thirteen hundred by yourself?"

"No, but I should be able to come up with a third of it."

"A third? So you're relying on *me* to pay two-thirds of the rent, and you won't let me do a job I'd prefer, in which I'd be able to work less hours and write more? Why? *You* turned down good jobs in hotels just so you can go work with Brandon in the strip mall."

"It's not a strip mall. It's a marketplace."

"It's an Italian restaurant with pink linen tablecloths positioned over a Genovese Drugs."

"It happens to have a good reputation."

"The point I'm trying to make is that *you* get to choose, so why can't I? If you could afford to pay everything then I could see your point. But you're not picking the job that's best for us—you're picking the job that's best for *you*. Considering that I still have to pay my own health insurance, two-thirds of the rent, and God knows how much else in the way of bills, you'd think you'd be a bit more open-minded."

"One thing has nothing to do with the other."

"But it does. Cooking and taking off your clothes for entertainment purposes are both just *jobs*. That's all they are. We get paid, and we go home."

"I'm getting in the shower. This conversation is over."

"I know how much you hate it when I make valid points you can't refute!"

He jumped off the bed. "I suggest you find some ice for your head. It's growing by the second."

"If you really cared, you would have already gotten it for me," I growled, following him into the bathroom. "Not for nothing, Brandon still hasn't told you when you'll be starting your job or the salary you'll be making. It's all very suspicious to me. We stayed with him and fucking J. Lo for three weeks, and he still didn't know?"

"He's finding out my schedule this week."

"Who cares about your schedule? What about your *salary?*"

"He's on it, Pam. I'll speak with him later."

***

After discovering there was no bus service on Round Top mountain—big surprise—super-savvy Rob went and bought a used Ford with a thousand dollars. Apparently he had not been "completely wiped out," as he had stated previously. He purchased this eclectic vehicle off a used car lot from a salesman named Butch. It just filled me with hope. As for me, I purchased a pair of Duck boots—circa 1989—for traipsing through the mud.

As soon as we moved into the cabin, we became aware of a few problems; primarily, it wasn't furnished. The only piece of furniture was a thin foam mat covered with one of those stupid egg crate thingumajigs that every asshole raves about. *It's so good for my back!* I denounced that theory in one night. And there was a broom, although that hardly qualified as a furnishing. I wasn't expecting satellite radio, but this place didn't even have a refrigerator. You'd think Rose could have mentioned that small detail, along with the fact that there was no phone hookup. We would have to rely on our cell phones, which only worked if we hiked to the end of our half-mile driveway.

Looking on the bright side, we were living on a warm island, so the lack of heating wasn't the end of the world. And as far as air-conditioning was concerned, Rose assured us the breeze would be more than adequate due to the high elevation. *Why didn't I totally freak out?* I think I was so out of my comfort zone that I'd simply lost touch with reality. In New York, I never would have stood for such inconveniences; I was a fish out of water and hadn't yet realized my inability to breathe.

The larger problems began after Rob and I had spent a few nights living in the wild. The thin log walls of the cabin blocked none of the outside animal chatter. In addition to the few hundred neighborhood dogs in hot debate—highest and loudest bark winning the argument—we were also bestowed with what Rose called "her neighborhood gecko," which made a unique squawking sound, louder and shriller than your average gecko. As if I had any comparative basis, knowing nothing about lizards in general. Throw in the wild pigs, wild cats, and wild boar also competing in the bark-off every morning, and it was like sleeping in the Kalahari Desert. Then the birds began chirping at dawn, raising the degree to which I hated Lulu J. Lo.

The not-so-funny part was that we were also kept awake by the *inside* animal noise. Considering we had no pets, this was puzzling. It sounded like the buzzing of a fly, but the only insects we saw were the quiet ones, spiders and red ants marching along the rotting wood floorboards. Baffled, I finally asked Rose about it. She casually informed me that the wood beams trap bees. As if there was nothing unusual about bees living inside the structure of a house.

"The bees are trapped? How can they live without food? Why don't they eventually die and shut up?" I said.

Rose shrugged. "I have them in my house too, and they've been there for years."

"Awesome," I said. "That's just awesome."

But the best was yet to come. After a week or so, I noticed I was scratching my legs constantly, and every morning I had fresh bug bites around my ankles. At first, I ignored this and tried sleeping with long socks and more clothes. When that didn't help, I applied bug spray before I went to bed, which Rob found wildly sexy, but still—still something was biting me. After two weeks, I had Frisbees for ankles, and my waist was a string of bumpy red hills and valleys. I voiced my complaints to my husband, but instead of expressing concern, he just pointed out that *he* wasn't being bitten so it must not have anything to do with the cabin. As if the two things were completely unrelated.

Each night got worse, and I scratched until I bled, cursing Lulu J. Lo and Rose and then eventually Brandon for liking that bitch in the first place. I cornered Rose and expressed my frustration by threatening to take my husband by the neck and leave unless she fixed the problem. This sent her into a tizzy of Agatha Christie sleuthing through our cabin. She had the magnifying glass up to the floor and seemed determined to figure out how the windows were sealed. Her inspection was so thorough that I knew it had to be an act.

One morning, she had me seal my socks in a plastic bag and send them to a lab for testing. I began to document everything, taking digital photos of my legs and the inside of the cabin. I went to the emergency room and created a record on file. I went after Rose like Rob Shapiro went after Mark Furman. I did all this without any help from Rob, who only claimed I was being a big baby.

***

After the doctor in the emergency room claimed I was being attacked by fleas, termites, and possibly other unidentified insects, I walked a mile and a half to an area called Ward Warehouse, home to a restaurant called Kincaid's. I sat down at the bar, ordered a dirty martini, and consequently burst into tears. I drank it in its entirety, accepting that things must be really bad if I could finish it and request another.

Then I called my mother, whom I'd barely spoken to for longer than five minutes while standing at the end of Rose's long driveway. Sarah had already expressed her blatant disapproval of my living in total isolation, calling me impractical and Rob a son-of-a-bitch. So naturally, when I told her the latest news, she went ballistic. "What the hell is wrong with you? Get the hell out of there!"

"It's really not that easy," I whimpered into the phone.

"Sure it is. Get your shit and get the fuck out!" My mother rarely cursed.

"What if Rob won't come with me?"

"Then he can stay, but *you* need to go! The fact that he hasn't taken you away already is despicable."

"Rose was the only person who would rent to us. I'm not even sure I'd be able to find another place."

"OK, listen. You've always taken care of yourself. Maybe you *imagined* Rob would take care of you once you married him, but that isn't happening. I suggest you stop acting like Robinson Crusoe and get down off that volcano. You're not fooling anyone."

"I know." I sighed and took a large swallow of vodka.

"Come home."

"I'm tempted." I hung up, even more depressed. By my fourth martini, however, I was feeling much better. I'd forgotten about the itching and had bonded with the adorable Asian bartender by sharing my tale of woe and showing him my collection of bug bites. He called a staff meeting so the employees of Kincaid's could offer suggestions to my plight. They were all shocked and appalled, and with each person who expressed their revulsion over my living conditions, I felt myself regaining power. I wasn't going to let Rob or Rose boss me around as if I was some stupid, weak idiot who didn't know my rights.

This amazing group told me about a few alternate accommodations. Ultimately, I decided on a fifty-dollar-a-night crack motel, which suited my needs perfectly. I settled in, and tried to ignore the drug deals going on outside my window. Then I placed a call to Rob telling him to come by after work to discuss our "situation."

"Where are you?" he asked with a twinge of annoyance.

"The Blue Diamond Motel off Kapahulu, next to the Pancake House."

"What are you doing there?"

"We're going to stay here until we find a new place. Rose can shove her flea-infested cabin up her ass."

"You gotta be fucking kidding me. You want us to move out over a few bug bites? What the fuck is your problem? Are you that much of a prima donna?"

"Yes!"

"Go back to the cabin. This is ridiculous."

"No way!"

"Pam, you're so selfish. I just bought a car!"

"So? It's a piece of shit. You'll be lucky if it drives another week. If this was happening to you and not to me, *I'd* be the one trampling through Rose's little herb garden and demanding she bug proof the place or give us our money back. Not only am I the victim here, but I seem to be the man too! Just continue to do absolutely nothing and I'll take care of Rose. *I'll* be the one to get our money back. And *I'll* be the one who finds our next apartment. All you have to do is get your ass here after work and spend the night with me in an actual bed! Room ten!" I screamed into the phone, fueled with anger only a mixture of vodka and frustration can induce.

***

Rob never showed up. After I realized he'd gone straight to work the next morning without calling me, I located a bus schedule and took the bus out to Kahala Mall. I longed for New Jersey and New York, and the food court at the mall was the closest thing I was going to find. I purchased a Cinnabon and reminisced about my former life.

I had spent an awful night awake, scared, and alone. The assorted drug deals going on outside my window continued throughout the night, replacing nature's hellish choir. But at least I had no additional bug bites.

I needed a friend. It was easiest to keep in touch with Tina since we were used to the distance apart, so I called and left a message. Donna and Lexi seemed so far away, and I couldn't picture them understanding. I hadn't spoken with Jake except for the two occasions he visited Donna and they decided to call me.

I dialed Jake's home number and left a message, feeling a little ridiculous. I mean, there I was, stranded on an island, and the only person I felt comfortable calling was a man to whom I'd fed dog food three months earlier. Unsatisfied with leaving a message on the machine, I dialed his cell, suddenly determined to get in touch with him.

"Hey!" he said, recognizing my voice right away. "How's it going?" he yelled over what I figured was bar chatter. I quickly realized my 2 p.m. was 8 p.m. there. "Let me just step outside. Hold on a minute."

"Sure."

"OK, I'm cool now. Can you hear me?"

"Yeah, yeah."

"So are you loving it?"

"Not exactly," I said.

"What do you mean? Isn't it like *so beautiful* like everyone says?"

"Yeah, it's pretty and it's always sunny, but I can't say I'm having the best time."

"Why?"

"Well, it's just different. I don't have any friends and I live on Bug Mountain and—"

"Wait, back up, where do you live?"

"I live in this cabin in the woods, and every night when I go to bed, fleas and termites feast on my flesh, and then I wake up and itch all day and it's hot and I can't go anywhere unless Rob drives me in this ugly, beat-up car he bought off this junkie in a parking lot—"

"Stop, stop," he choked out, dying with laughter. "Bug Mountain?"

After I'd explained the chain of events that had led me up to the point, I had sobered him up enough for him to be genuinely worried about me.

"So let me get this straight. You left the mountain, and he didn't follow?"

"Well, it's only been one night, but no, he didn't."

"And things were OK before you decided to leave?"

"Well, they weren't fantastic. I was afraid to sleep on the egg crate without five layers of clothing and—"

"Egg crate?"

"Yeah, you know, people who live in vans swear by them. We don't actually have a bed or even a mattress—"

"Why don't you two buy a bed?"

"It's complicated. Basically, Rob won't let me use the wedding money in the joint account because he says we might only be here for six months to a year, and it would be a waste of money. So if I want a bed, I have to be the one to buy it, and I guess I'm annoyed about that."

"Are you kidding me?"

"I'm not. We didn't discuss practical issues before moving. I should have asked him a few hypothetical questions concerning what he deems important in living arrangements. I just never thought."

"Well, be sure to let me know if you need anything," he said quietly.

"Don't worry. I'll be fine once I get this mess sorted out."

"So what are you going to do now?" Jake asked.

"I'm going to call him and tell him he needs to bring me my stuff even if he chooses not to join me at the crack hotel."

"Well, good luck. Keep me posted."

"I will."

"And if it's any consolation, it's not fun here anymore," said Jake. "It's not the same without you."

"*Really*? Thanks." It was the nicest thing anyone had said to me lately.

***

Rob grudgingly appeared late the next evening with all our belongings after I'd left him a scathing message on his cell phone demanding his presence at the Blue Diamond Motel. He then proceeded to lie on the bed grumpily, not speaking to me, while I thundered away on my laptop, proving I didn't need a picturesque mountaintop to create timeless prose. Apparently all I needed was rage.

The events of the last few days inspired me to rewrite the tale of Rapunzel, making her a character delighted to be kidnapped from her home in the woods. I reversed the whole story, having her chop her long hair short so a rescue by her annoying husband would prove impossible. In addition, I reinvented her captor as a handsome man with good fashion sense who dressed her in Versace and wined and dined her nightly. I was so engrossed in my clever tale that I was able to block Rob out completely and was genuinely surprised to hear his voice over the white noise of the TV. "So what is your grand plan, exactly?" he asked, lighting up a roach.

I tried not to breathe in the stench of the strong Hawaiian pot he'd wasted no time acquiring outside our window and finished typing my sentence before answering. "My grand plan consists of taking matters into my own hands."

"For instance?"

"Before you drive off to work tomorrow in your sporty little race car, you are bringing me back up that mountain. I'm going to have a little chat with our dear Rosebud. Then after I get our security deposit back, I'm planning on finding us an apartment."

"And you think it's going to be easier than it was before?"

"As long as you stay out of it! I know how to deal with people on their level," I added, thinking how low I was prepared to sink. "I'll have a place for us within the next few days, you'll see."

"Oh, right."

"I will," I repeated. "Give me forty-eight hours. And the place *I* find won't cost us an extra two hundred in mountain maintenance."

"Whatever," he said angrily. "If it were out there, we'd have it already."

***

"Rose, we want our security deposit back," I declared the next morning over the sound of her annoying New Age chimes. I stood on her porch talking to her through the screen door because I refused to take off my shoes to enter her cavernous house.

"I just told you, I'm not in a position to return your money. The security deposit is, in fact, a cushion to protect me from those who change their minds. Such as yourselves."

"I know what a security deposit is, Rose. I've lived in apartments all my life."

"Then surely you understand what you're asking is unreasonable." She folded her arms across her bony chest and her almond-shaped eyes had a hard glint to them, but then again, I'm sure mine did too.

"In most cases it would be," I agreed, "but in *this case* the living conditions of the cabin are unacceptable."

"There's nothing wrong with the apartment I've provided for you and your husband."

I smiled tightly. "So you say." I pointed to the bandages wrapped around my calves and reached into my bag for the letter. The bandages prevented me from itching, but they were also a nice touch. Like wearing a neck brace in court. However, dressed in short shorts and a button-down shirt, I resembled Bob Barker on the golf course. "I have a letter explaining the reasons we vacated the premises. My lawyer has a copy." I opened the screen door and handed it to her.

Rose's eyes narrowed further as she scanned down my list of documentation. I'd signed my name with finesse, forged Rob's squirrel-like signature, and printed an attorney's name I'd gotten from the phone book, just to be on the safe side.

Rose glanced up at me.

"I'll be expecting a check for thirteen hundred mailed within the week to this address." I handed her Rob's Italian restaurant "business card."

"I can see now that Round Top just wasn't for you," she said in a tone I suspected was meant to be insulting.

"Evidently," I said, marching down the rocky slope. Maybe I could still return the duck boots, I thought.

"Did she give us our money back?" asked Rob, reversing out of the long driveway.

"She will."

"How do you know?"

"Because no one wants to be sued."

"You threatened to sue her? Pam! That's Jenna's aunt!"

I scowled. Like I cared.

Rob shook his head and didn't say anything until we were safely down the mountain. "Where am I dropping you?" he asked.

"Drop me at the pharmacy next to the motel." I needed some supplies.

What Rob failed to understand was that women had a secret weapon most men didn't possess: the promise of sex. All I needed was a male victim, preferably of the clueless Asian descent. I figured it couldn't be *only* women renting apartments. I just had to narrow my search and prepare myself. In the pharmacy, I purchased a curling iron, hairspray, false eyelashes, a cheap body spray, and a pack of Marlboro Lights. Under the circumstances, I'd decided to officially take up smoking again.

My *grand plan* entailed searching the newspaper for management companies that were renting apartments in the Honolulu area. I then planned to narrow the list by calling first to see if it was a man or woman showing the apartment in question and what his last name was. I only had two afternoons, and I wasn't about to waste any time. With Rob, I'd been limited to looking for a specific type of apartment in an area convenient to his job. Now that we were desperate and living in a crack motel, his bullshit restrictions no longer applied.

I showered and changed into a tight blue tube top and a short pleated skirt. Scooping my hair into a high ponytail, I curled the ends and loaded on the makeup. If my hair had been lighter, I could have passed as Carmen Electra. Glancing at my left hand, I decided the rings had to go, a strategic move. I could still be married without the rings but not *un*married with them glistening in the sunlight.

Opening the paper to where I had circled a few possibilities the evening before, I began making phone calls, lining up appointments for that afternoon.

Some people say "three strikes and you're out." I always say "third time is a charm." And that's what I mumbled to myself before the third appointment when I spotted a clean little Oriental man sitting on a bench in front of a building. He was perfect for molding and manipulating, unlike the female counterpart of his race. Holding a clipboard and talking into his cell phone, he didn't notice me when I had the cab pull over.

I stuck out my chest, pulled down my skirt, and slammed on another shot of body spray before approaching the little man. It was all about confidence, I told myself; men love confident women.

Mr. Tomichi finally looked up, knocking his clipboard to the ground.

"I'll get that," I said, relishing the opportunity to bend down in front of him.

"Thanks," he said. "You're Ms. Castle?"

"Yes." I made eye contact and sized him up quickly: Asian but American, successful, probably loaded, very short—and therefore possibly insecure, a perfect handicap—and honest, as honest as one could be who managed a building.

"Great, you're on time. Please call me Ming," he said. "How did you get here? I didn't see you drive up."

"Oh, I walked over. I was actually having lunch around the corner," I lied.

"Where?"

I blinked. "The pizza place," I said automatically, hoping the little red shack I'd passed in the cab sold pizza.

"Harpo's Pizza?"

"Yes," I said, smiling.

"It's good pizza, right?" I could see he was enchanted.

"The best," I purred.

"Well," he said, turning his red face toward the building, "I think you'll like this apartment. You said on the phone you're from New York?"

"Yes."

"The actual city? Manhattan?"

"Yep."

"Were you there during 9/11?"

Ah, the dreaded question. "Yes. I had a view of the towers from my street corner."

"Oh my God."

Ming Tomichi then proceeded to quiz me on the details of the destruction while sneaking panicked looks at my legs and chest. If the living space was decent, I knew I had this deal in the bag. Satisfied by my up-to-the-minute account of living in the West Village during the tragedy, he finally told me about the apartment.

"Which floor is it on?"

"Six. The building has seven floors total." He unlocked the first gate.

"And what was the rent again?"

"Eight-sixty."

"Perfect!" I stepped through the second gate and into the elevator, giving him a sidelong glance.

"Is it just you?" he asked.

I glanced at his left hand before answering. Spying the thick silver band on his ring finger, I smiled. "My husband and me."

"Oh, OK."

"But he does a lot of traveling for his job," I lied. Eye contact.

"What does he do?"

"He's a chef, but he does restaurant consulting as well. You'd never know it by looking at him, though." I added this for my protection against the eventual disbelief Ming Tomichi would experience upon meeting him. Rob didn't look like an expert at anything, except maybe music trivia.

"And you? What is it you do?" he asked, stopping in front of a doorway.

"I came here to finish writing a book."

"Oh, that's exciting." He turned to me before placing a key in the lock. I inched a little closer to him. "Where did you say you lived before this?"

"We rented a cabin high up on Round Top Mountain. The bugs ate me alive," I said, rolling down one of my knee socks. "Look."

"Jesus, you poor thing."

"We had to get out," I said. "Right now, we are staying at this dirty hotel in Waikiki. So we really need something that could be available immediately."

"This place could be available by the end of the week."

"Great!" I squealed. It was the most utilitarian place I'd ever encountered, but I had a newfound respect for anything that wasn't made of wood. "Are these walls made of concrete?"

"Yes. It was first constructed as a state penitentiary in the early part of the century." *Mountain cabin to ex-prison?*

"Well, that's intriguing, Ming." I wandered into the bedroom and up to a huge window. Down below lay the road. A large graveyard rose above it and up a hill. "That's some graveyard."

"Beautiful, isn't it?"

I raised my eyebrows. "I suppose."

"Handy too. A nursing home is situated right next door." It seemed Ming had a sense of humor after all. "Let me show you the best part of the apartment!" he exclaimed, referring to a massive balcony. Ming Tomichi unlocked a sliding glass door, and we stepped out into the sunlight. The balcony at 426 Pensacola Avenue was the first and only thing I liked about living in Hawaii. Not only did it have a fantastic view of the mountains, but if I looked to my left, I could also see the tops of the gravestones, shrouded by clouds and sky.

"Is there a refrigerator in here?" I asked.

"Of course."

"Just making sure. Our last place didn't have one."

"You're kidding." At that moment Ming Tomichi's cell phone rang, alerting him that my competition had arrived to view the apartment.

I touched his arm lightly, "I think my husband and I would *really* like this place. It's simple and the price is right. Can we have it?" I pleaded.

"Um, let me just buzz them in. I promised they could take a look."

"OK, but can you promise it to me?" Big eyes, loose lips, little pout.

He paused, a little perplexed. "I'm sure we can work something out. Are you willing to sign a lease?"

I nodded. "Yes, and I can get my husband over here pronto."

While Ming went down to let the other potential tenants in, I dialed Rob's cell. He picked up on the third ring, and I listened to a kitchen employee yelling he was out of fresh rosemary. "Use the Italian blend!" screamed Rob in my ear. "What is it, Pam?" he asked impatiently.

"I found us a place."

"I'm not in the mood for jokes right now. This restaurant is a fucking disaster today."

"I'm not joking. I need you over here ASAP."

"Are you serious? Where are you?"

"I'm here. At the apartment."

"Where is that?"

"Four sixty-two Pensacola between Beretania and Islethorpe. Wherever that is."

"I'll have to wait until we break. How did you find a place so quickly?" he asked suspiciously.

"Don't worry about it."

"What did you have to do? Nothing illegal, I hope."

"Nope." *Not yet, anyway.*

"I'll never figure you out, Pam."

"How soon can you be here?"

"We break in half an hour."

"OK, just remember that you also do kitchen consulting for big restaurant firms and corporations. You're not *just* a cook."

"Why did you say that? Why can't you simply tell the truth?"

"Because you make nine dollars an hour. That's why."

"Lying never works. Who's supposed to vouch for me?"

"Your friends back home. The entourage, for Christ sake."

"Now you want my friends to lie too?"

"Yes. That's what friends are for."

Rob sighed.

"This is precisely why I didn't want you with me. It's this or the next flight back to New York. You pick."

Rob cleared his throat. "OK, where are you again?"

I handed the phone to Ming, who had come back to chat with me. "Could you give my husband directions from Manoa Marketplace?"

***

Ming Tomichi lived in an upscale area called Hawaii-Kai, half an hour outside of Waikiki. Rob and I were on our way back from signing the lease at Ming's house when the gold Ford conked out. As I'd predicted, three weeks driving up and down that mountain had stolen its last dying breath.

After we played hangman with chalk on the side of Highway 1 for two hours, the tow truck finally arrived, and we towed the car to Butch's used car lot in town. "I have a bone to pick with this guy," announced Rob.

I glanced around Butch's headquarters, realizing he sold more than just cars. From the looks of his desk, he peddled everything from jewelry to gasoline to gold fillings. The guy in front of us was negotiating the sale of a used coffee maker. "Six dollars and give me those filters," Butch proposed to a kid no older than twelve.

Rob hopelessly tried to get Butch's attention, and when he noticed my husband hopping up and down, Butch yelled, "I'm running a business here! Take your problem and get in line like everyone else!" *Yep, Rob is a highly valued customer.* So we got behind the last guy, who was pawning a set of golf clubs, and waited our turn.

"This is a perfect opportunity to buy a used coffee maker," I whispered to Rob. He scowled at me and crossed his hands over his chest protectively.

Eventually we got our turn with Butch, whose name described him perfectly. He had a square build and a big thick head with thinning hair, and he looked like he'd spent the better half of his life in prison. We explained to him that his prized Ford had come to an abrupt stop on the highway and smoke had billowed from the engine. Afraid of an impending explosion, we opted for a tow that we *hoped* he would reimburse, although this was obviously out of the question.

"Actually, Butch, I'd just like to sell the car back to you. We moved again, and now we don't need it. I'd be willing to take eight hundred for it at this point," tried Rob.

Butch laughed in his face while I cringed and looked away.

"Seven hundred," said Rob, the hotshot negotiator. Why he was even bothering, I had no idea. It was mortifying.

"I'll tell you what," said Butch after examining the car himself. "I'll keep it on the lot for you, and *I'll* try to sell it. Whatever *I* get, I'll give you half."

I smiled at Butch. He knew I knew we were both wasting time.

"Well, I suppose if I walked in there and paid a thousand dollars for the car, there's a chance that someone else might too. That would yield me five hundred," reasoned Rob.

I didn't comment. I didn't want to ruin his fantasy.

Halfway home Rob announced he was going to buy a bike. "A Harley?" I asked, unable to picture it.

"No. A ten-speed. That's all I rode the last time I lived on this island. The place you found for us is only four miles from my job."

"But what will *I* do?" I asked. "How will *I* get around?"

"Well at least you'll be on a bus route now."

"Oh yeah," I said. "The bus."

Three weeks later, the bus drivers went on strike, the infamous 2003 Honolulu bus strike, which outlasted the time we lived there.

***

Settling in, Rob and I headed off to Ala Moana Mall on the quest for furniture. The entrance to the mall was lined with flags, a patriotic ass kissing, which juxtaposed the overall lukewarm feelings in the air. As Rob guided me into Sears, I gathered it was only going to be the finest of furniture. He led me straight to the camping section. "What are we doing?" I asked.

"We need a bed."

"No kidding. The beds are over there." I pointed away from the tents.

"Nah—not a real bed—we might not even be here a year."

"I really hate you at this moment." And I did.

"It's a waste of money."

"A year is three hundred and sixty something nights," I stated, wondering exactly how many days were in a year.

"Jerry said I could buy an awesome air mattress here for under a hundred dollars."

"Jerry? Who the fuck is Jerry?"

"I work with him. He's a food runner. I *told you* about him. He's the one out on parole for growing weed on his property. Nice guy."

"I bet." Before I truly understood what was happening, Rob was choosing the air mattress of our lifetime. Given the timing, it seemed like a step up from the foam mat. I picked out a few charming camping chairs on the off chance we might entertain.

"How are we going to pay for this?" I asked, assuming I would be paying, but to my shock, Rob whipped out a silver card.

"What is that?" Rob holding a credit card was equivalent to him holding several solid gold bars.

"A Sears credit card. Yeah, baby!"

"Judging from the color, does this mean you're in the upper echelon of card holders?"

"Platinum, baby. Oh yeah!"

"Congratulations."

***

We also inherited a great deal of used furniture, compliments of Ming Tomichi. After we moved in, he seemed determined to make sure we—as in I—felt comfortable with the new living arrangement. Part of his wooing included him hiring two high school derelicts to move every piece of old, decaying furniture occupying his garage into our new concrete apartment, including a huge TV that he just happened to have sitting around. I appreciated the TV, but could have done without the dilapidated furnishings. Especially after I saw a large lizard jump free from a wooden cabinet and run into our bedroom, happy to relocate to a real apartment. I almost fainted when I noticed an enormous green worm inch through a hole in the bottom shelf of a "solid oak" bureau.

I didn't know it at the time, but I later found out this disgusting maggot was a centipede. And for those who don't know, a centipede is roughly half a foot long and one of the most aggressive predators on earth. A bite from a centipede can be every bit as painful as a blast from a shotgun. Yes! Even not getting the memo on this very important fact, I screamed to hell and back at the very sight of it, causing Ming to chase it out onto the balcony with the broom I'd taken from Rose's precious cabin in the woods. Then I made Ming dispose of the broom in case the worm was somehow still hiding in it. Fucking Hawaii.

In addition to the furniture, Ming seemed determined to help me find some part-time work while I was living on the island. He arranged for me to come up to the school on a day he was teaching under the pretense of picking up the mail key. I should have been more hip to his sneaky plans, but I emerged from my building and walked up Pensacola Avenue toward his high school alma matter unknowingly, carrying my little bag filled with sun block, cigarettes, and bottled water.

The hill was steep, but for the first time since our honeymoon, I enjoyed the afternoon Hawaiian breeze. The palm trees towered above me, tall and lean, and I marveled at how they swayed back and forth without really bending. The sky was a deep blue with spotted clouds, and the flowers were all in bloom, although I couldn't have told you *which* flowers.

I reached out to pick a large pink blossom. Then two things happened. First, a bee stung my ring finger, and as I was hopping around shouting and searching for the stinger, a carload of sketchy-looking teenagers came dangerously close to running me over. Although I was grateful to have narrowly escaped with my life still intact, I was not pleased when they threw a bag of McDonald's trash out their back window at me and screamed, "Haole!" Only this time I knew how it was spelled and what it meant.

There is nothing like taking a lovely walk to boost your spirits. I wondered whether I should come to expect this welcoming novelty every time I stepped out of a building and onto a street. The sun beat down on me, and vanilla milkshake dripped from my arm. I shook it off, not wanting to attract any more bees, cursed the island for the zillionth time, and vowed to avoid nature and being outside in general.

When I approached the school, I spotted Ming hanging halfway out a window. He was waving at me like a kid on television. "I'm on the third floor!" he yelled.

I stared back at him. *What a nut.*

"Take the staircase to your left when you come in. I'm in classroom three-L," he continued to shout.

"OK!" I yelled back feeling royally stupid, although somewhat relieved that he didn't have a class in session. I figured no one would act so ridiculous in front of a roomful of teenagers.

No one except Ming Tomichi, that is. His world history class was in full swing, and two dozen bored, hot, ethnically challenged students all swiveled their heads when I entered the room. My finger stung like mad, and my face turned scarlet to match. These kids did not look any nicer than the ones who had just thrown their McDonald's scraps at me. It could have been them for all I knew.

"Class, there's someone here I want you to meet," announced Ming. "This is my dear friend Pamela Castle, who has just moved here from New York." *Dear friend?* Did I miss something? "Pamela was living in downtown New York City during 9/11," he broadcast as if I were a major celebrity as opposed to being in the wrong place at the wrong time. Then to my absolute horror, he said, "The bell is set to go off in fifteen minutes, so you have fifteen minutes while Pamela tells you what it was like on that day. Any questions you have, I'm sure she'd be happy to answer." And then he left me in front of twenty-five angry sixteen-year-olds who understood I was the only thing standing between them leaving for the afternoon. Words cannot describe the fear I felt. Seconds later Ming was gone, and I cleared my throat, vowing silently to kill him after the mail key was safely in my possession.

After the longest fifteen minutes of my entire life, the bell rang, and the kids *ran* out. Ming reappeared, carefully balancing two huge trays of food from the cafeteria. He had mumbled something over the phone to me about lunch, but it was only then I made the very awful connection. He placed both trays down on his desk and pulled over a kid desk for me to sit at. Scrutinizing the side dishes of creamed corn and broccoli, I was truly at a loss for words.

"How did it go? I'm sure the kids loved you," he said with a genuine smile.

"Oh yeah. What a bunch of angels. I cannot believe you did that to me," I said, taking a seat.

"We have Swedish meatballs today. It's cafeteria food, but it's really not bad," said Ming.

"It looks delicious," I said flatly.

"So I was thinking, while you're living here in Oahu, you could be a substitute teacher at this school."

I had just picked up my container of apple juice when he said this, and I dropped it with a thud into my corn. I could not think of a worse fate. "And why would I want to do that?"

"Well, you live so close, and you're obviously very bright. I'm sure the kids would really take to you."

"I've never had any desire to be a teacher. Ever," I stressed.

"Yeah, but you'll probably want to earn a little money while you're writing your book, and the hours for substitute teachers are rather flexible."

"It's nice of you to think of me, but I'm *really* not interested." Between the smell of the food and his suggestion, I felt physically ill.

"Are you going to be OK financially?"

"Of course. Why do you ask?"

Ming looked embarrassed for a moment. "I had a long talk with Robert's boss, Eugene, and I think your husband hasn't been entirely truthful with you."

"In what regard?" I silently cursed this scumbag, Eugene.

"I'm referring to your husband's salary."

"What about it?"

"According to Rob's employer, it's actually far less than you quoted me. In fact, he's not on salary. Eugene is paying him hourly, and according to his fixed hours, he's only making fourteen thousand a year. I just worry that you might have difficulty paying the rent."

I fixed my eyes on Ming's. "There must be some mistake. Eugene must have said forty, not fourteen." I lied effortlessly.

"He specifically said Robert Trombetti was earning nine dollars an hour before tax."

I stared Ming down, disbelieving the vivid and accurate details he'd obtained from Rob's dick of a boss. I had to be careful here. "Rob has assured me he's making a top salary. And even if he wasn't, I have enough money put aside to cover us both for the next ten months." I coughed, wondering how many lies I could fit into a single minute.

"Well, I'm glad to hear that. However, I think if you love someone, you might lie to them so they won't worry. Perhaps that might be the case here?"

Huh? "Are you suggesting that Rob might be lying to me?"

"I'm just looking out for you. You seem like a lovely person, and I don't want to see you get hurt." He said this so nicely that I believed him. I even felt guilty for being the biggest liar of all.

"Well, thank you. I appreciate you telling me this. I will have a talk with my husband and make sure we're on the same page. In the meantime, I assure you the rent will be paid on time."

"I want this to work out. I'm looking forward to showing you some of the better parts of the island. You said you were interested in seeing Pearl Harbor sometime?"

Did I? Fuck. "Oh yes, I'm a big history buff. Gee, this lunch looks positively fab, but I must scoot. Did you happen to remember the mail key?" I asked.

Ming scratched his head, and I instinctively knew this afternoon had been an excruciating waste of time. "You know, I forgot it. Shoot. When's a good time for me to drop it by?"

JUNE 2003

Since I was an official tenant of 426 Pensacola Avenue, Ming Tomichi knew where he could reach me and bombarded me with invitations. Every time I checked the answering machine, I'd hear Ming's voice…

"I know of a private beach I'd love to show you!"

Sorry, I prefer pools.

"How would you like to climb Diamondhead later this week?"

Do I look like a hiker to you?

"Do you need any pots and pans?"

If you throw in a personal chef.

"I know a great place to buy cheap wine glasses."

I'm using the same mug for everything.

"There's a new sushi restaurant that just opened up!"

And I don't know about it?

"You know, we barely use our microwave. Do you want it?"

Absolutely!

So basically, if the invitation or gift was inviting enough, I accepted. I saw Ming periodically, as long as I had something to gain. I flirted with him just the right amount to keep him useful but controlled. After all, I was bored, and boredom is a precursor to trouble. The combination of living in Hawaii with no job and no friends and a husband who worked nights was a very boring existence. I had nowhere to be. And I wasn't a drug user like Mimi so I really had *nothing* to do. Sure, I had the fairytales to rewrite and expand upon, but I was learning that self-discipline wasn't my strong suit. I was my own boss and not a very good one.

The days were easier than the nights. I went to my office (Starbucks), and on the weekend days, I went to the pool at the Hilton, intent on sipping numerous mai tais, care of some unknowing guest. But come nighttime, Rob was at work and I was alone. In Manhattan, if I wasn't working, I was out with friends drinking and socializing and having a killer time. But in Hawaii, it was harder to do that, friends and money being the absent components. I considered getting a job, but it seemed like such a waste of time. I'd have to lease a car, and I'd be lucky to break even at the end of the day. I'd also have to learn how to drive, which was a terrifying prospect.

And sticking with my guns, I refused to wait tables or work in a café, so there wasn't much else I was qualified to do unless I wanted to sort books at Barnes & Noble or scoop ice cream at Stone Cold Creamery. And I wasn't really qualified to do either of those things either!

I started to slip. I took on an attitude that I could still live the same carefree lifestyle by my broke self and make it fun. I started hanging out at the mall every night as if I were still in high school and twelve long years hadn't passed. The only improvement was the mall itself, which was outdoors with three huge floors of shops. The fourth floor consisted of various restaurants and three tropical bars. I spent most evenings walking two miles to the mall and then furtively shoplifting from store to store, which eventually resulted in extreme paranoia.

When I would wake up at noon, I made small efforts to clean up my act. Obviously, there was no need to walk to the mall when I could hitchhike. That was a given. Second, I vowed to only steal stuff I could use to better myself, like instructional

writing manuals or art supplies. I got serious. And my serious-
ness paid off.

***

Despite what everyone preaches about bad things happening to
bad people and all that karmic nonsense, shoplifting at Borders
was how I met my only friend in Hawaii. Naturally, she was
from New York. I noticed her tucked away in a corner of the
store standing at a perpendicular angle to a particular book-
shelf, a position that blocked the video camera. Although her
back was to me, I knew she was preoccupied with trying to peel
the sensor off a huge hardcover book. This girl was small and
cute, with light blond hair, but the reason I cared about her was
because she was standing in my precise stealing space. Between
reference and psychology, eye to the window.

"Whatcha doing?" I asked, startling her. She dropped the
heavy book on her foot and laughed nervously once she realized
I wasn't a Borders employee. I winked at her, and she smiled
before kneeling down to pick it up. She seemed about my age,
if not a little younger. I glanced at what she'd been planning to
remove from the premises. It was a huge monster of a textbook
entitled *Parental Psychology*. She later explained to me that it
was ninety bucks and she needed it for school. Psychology was
her major at the University of Hawaii.

"I endorse stealing as long as it's for instructional or edu-
cational purposes," I said with a nod, quite stoic. "Since you're
taking something in the name of self-improvement, it's not considered shoplifting."

"How do you figure?"

"It eradicates any guilt. You *need* the book." I was happy to
share my theory of ethics with this complete stranger.

"I never normally do this," she claimed once we sat down
together at a small wooden table piled high with French cook-
books. She leaned in toward me. "I'm really an amateur at this
sort of thing."

"Well, that's obvious. How else could you have found the best spot in the entire bookstore to avoid the video camera?"

Her guilty smile spread. "And what is it *you* were so eager to take?" She glanced at the book I'd set on the table. It was a thin yellow paperback priced at $19.95 called *Understanding Efficient Uses of Grammar*. I held it up for her to see, grateful I'd put back *The Idiot's Guide to Sentence Structure*. "Are you a writer?" she asked.

"I'm trying."

"What type of stuff do you write?"

"Oh, all different things," I said. I wasn't ready to tell her about my sick, twisted fairytales quite yet. I also didn't need anyone stealing my idea at this crucial stage in the game.

"I'm Cara," she said, extending her hand. Her nails were trimmed short and painted a shiny red. I shook her hand firmly. It was a true meeting of the minds.

"Pamela, but everyone calls me Pam."

Cara stared at my wedding ring. I glanced at hers. "How long have you been married?" she asked.

"Um, going on four months. You?"

"Two years."

"Impressive." And I meant it. I considered each night on the air mattress with Rob a massive achievement.

"What does your husband do?" she asked. "He must not make much money if you have to steal a twenty-dollar book."

I chuckled even though it wasn't particularly funny. "He's a chef."

"Oh, that's cool. You must eat well."

"That's a common misconception."

"What is?"

"That chefs love to cook for their wives. Chefs love to eat out and see what other chefs are cooking. Anyway, what does *your* husband do?"

"He's a sergeant in the military base over here in Awai."

"Oh." As if I knew where Awai was.

"It's out near the airport," she explained. "Near Pearl City. We live out there."

"Close to Pearl Harbor?"

"Yeah. It's all the same area."

"I see. I live close to this bookstore. Well, sort of. Pensacola Avenue, do you know it?"

"No."

"It's in the ghetto," I said. "But my proximity to Borders is good. I usually bring my laptop and write all day," I lied, feeling pathetic. "You?"

"I only come here when I need books for school. My husband and I are a little tight on cash at the moment."

"I hear ya. Do you know the bathroom trick?"

"What?"

"The bathroom trick. It's a way of testing you have all the sensors off the book before leaving the actual bookstore. Whether it's this particular store or another."

"I don't understand," said Cara, amused. "How does the bathroom figure in?"

"In order to take the books out of the store without triggering the alarm, we need to remove the sensors, right?"

"Yeah," she said, nodding.

"Well, the reason this corporation doesn't want people taking books into the restroom is because they assume—and rightly so—that we'll shove the books in our bag and not pay for them, so they place the same alarm system before the restrooms as they do at the front door."

"OK, I'm following you."

"The bathroom can be accidental whereas the front door? Eh."

Cara smiled and nodded. She was very receptive to my wisdom.

"It's also good just for acting like the book was yours all along. You came to the bookstore with *your* book to study! You walk in the bathroom holding it and you walk out holding it.

The book *belongs* to you. Write your fake name and address in it and have a few things underlined just in case a security guard ever stops you."

"You've really thought this through." Cara nodded, and her blue eyes sparkled. Glimmered, even, and I thought of Jake. And I knew that Jake would buy this woman anything she ever wanted if I explained the situation as it had just occurred.

"Hand me that mother of a textbook," I ordered. "Did you take the sensor off before I startled you?"

"Yeah, yeah. I think so."

I leafed through it nonchalantly, making sure. "Do you have to go to the bathroom?"

"No."

I stared at her.

"Oh yeah. Yes, I do."

"OK, let's go. Grab your book."

We passed the bathroom test without a problem and sat back down at our table. Collectively, we ripped a couple corners out of *Parental Psychology*, made a few highlighted remarks, and shoved the huge book inside her backpack.

"See how easy that was?" I said. "When we walk out, you can actually feel as confident as you look, instead of vice versa."

"I am super glad we met," said Cara, her eyes still twinkling. "It's been fun."

"So am I. First impressions are everything!"

***

Cara and I started meeting most afternoons at Borders. I actually started bringing my laptop with me as I'd initially boasted. (I tried to appear nonchalant the first time I looked around for an electrical socket.) It helped to have a friend around as my wit surfaced in the spirit of the random derelict fairytale.

Outside on the balcony of Borders, she would study. And I would create literary masterpieces with her helpful suggestions.

Anyway, when we weren't being so darn serious, we would occasionally read, take turns smoking cigarettes, and utilize the bathroom. And sometimes we'd talk about our lives. She had good energy, and I was grateful. I felt Cara and I were supposed to meet for a good reason. Because I needed her—I needed a friend.

***

When Rob chose not to show up at the Blue Diamond Motel that first night—never even supplying a reason—something changed in me. I can't say what exactly; I can only describe the emotion: it was similar to feeling homesick—which I was—but I also experienced sadness mixed with fear.

I had always taken care of myself. And possibly, just maybe, wanting to get married had to do with wanting someone to take care of me for a change. I wanted *Rob* to take care of me. And for all my bitching, I didn't mean from a financial standpoint, although that would have been nice. Essentially, I wanted Rob to take control of situations, as perhaps a good father would take care of his child. Protect and cherish and stick up for me. When I envisioned the word *husband*, I pictured a solid, reassuring man who was willing to stand by his wife, even if he didn't necessarily agree with her.

I still wanted Rob but the old Rob—not the new and unimproved. As the days passed in Oahu, indifference dominated his personality. He was guarded, too defensive for me to penetrate. And I would catch myself still wondering why he never came to the Blue Diamond motel that first night. And after he grudgingly showed up, where was he in spirit? From that day forward, his kindness never resurfaced. I seemed to be just an extra person in the room, a roommate of sorts. I was alone.

When we lived in Honolulu, I suppose Rob settled into a routine and I didn't. He wanted to go to work and then come home and read his book and relax. On his days off, he just wanted to lie on the sand and continue to read his book. He didn't possess a great sense of adventure, and since we didn't have the money to go out, we didn't do an awful lot together.

I, on the other hand, never had any idea what the day would bring. I would hang by myself or with Cara. Sometimes we'd skip Borders and go for walks on the beach. We'd smoke cigarettes and talk about which antidepressants we preferred, stopping for the occasional mixed drink once the clock struck six. Each day was an adventure, and I tried to include Rob but he wanted no part of it.

Being with him at home was equally as frustrating. He didn't take any interest in me.

"Please can we play," I begged one night. It was late, and I had removed every item of clothing except for my pink ankle socks and a sheer pink thong. My tan was a deep glow provided by Sun Worship Spa in Waikiki. I looked good.

Rob, on the other hand, looked like he'd acquired ten thousand more freckles. He was preoccupied with Dan Brown's latest thriller. My fingers reached under the thin blue sheet in search of a way to arouse Rob, but he caught on and stopped me. "Come on. Cut it out. I told you I'm tired." He placed my hand back on my stomach.

"But aren't I tan? I thought maybe you'd want me more if I looked like I was fitting in."

"You actually look orange, but yes, it's very cute."

"Are you *really* tired?"

"Yes, baby."

"But you're not too tired to read," I said.

"I'm shutting off the light after this chapter."

"Your hot wife wants to bang the shit out of you. Am I being clear?"

Rob shifted his eyes to me and made a face. "You're so vulgar."

"I'm serious. I want to fuck you *so* bad."

"Stop it," he said, glancing back down at his page.

"Please, I'm literally begging. I'm dying for you. Dying."
I emphasized this by placing my hands underneath my throat
and circling my head around.

He pretended not to notice. "Pam, I said no, and I don't like
when you tell me we *have* to. We don't *have* to do anything."

"I know, but it would be nice once in a while."

"Oh please, you act like you're sex-starved. I hate it when
you say things like this."

"Why, because I'm direct enough to ask for it? It's a shame
that I *have* to ask."

"When you ask me—or tell me, rather—it turns me off,
OK? It should just happen naturally."

"Yes, but it doesn't! The only way it ever happens is if I
initiate it! If I don't catch you off guard and start sucking your
cock, we never have sex!"

Rob turned a page in his book and continued to read. I
stared at him, livid. *How can he still be reading?*

"Rob, please fuck the shit out of me."

"You know your language is crass. You make everything
sound dirty."

"That's probably because I'm not getting laid," I said.

"Just shut up because you're really starting to annoy me."

"My sincerest apologies. Either the Hawaiian weed is taking away your sex drive or you've *got to be fucking somebody else.*"

"You have no idea what you're talking about," he said
calmly.

"The truth is that you haven't wanted to fuck me since we
moved out of the Best Western and into the cabin from hell. It
was like the cabin was haunted and you're possessed by evil. It's
like *Amityville Horror!*"

"*Amityville Horror*," he said, snickering. "You live in a dream
world."

"I can't even stand to look at you right now," I said, staring
at him.

"And what makes you think I feel any differently?"

"Wow. Nothing, in fact." I grabbed the copy of *Angels &
Demons* out of his hands and held it over my head.

The way he stared at me then stopped me dead in my tracks.
I tossed the book back at him, thoroughly disgusted. Then Rob
picked the book up off the floor and hit me in the stomach with
it. Hard.

"I can't believe you just did that," I said.

"You hit me so I hit you back," he said viciously.

I swallowed. "First of all, I didn't hit you. I tossed the book
back at you. But even if I had, you're not supposed to hit me
back. It's taboo, for God's sake."

"If you hit me, be prepared to be hit back."

I glanced down at the white mark the book had left on my
naked stomach and felt sick. Turning away, I hauled myself off
the air mattress—not the easiest or most graceful maneuver—
but appearances no longer mattered.

Not feeling much of anything, I pulled on the most accessi-
ble clothes and shoes and wandered out of the apartment. I didn't
have a bike like Rob, so I went for a walk in the projects instead.
At that time of the night, it was practically a suicide march.

I walked and walked. Walked and smoked. I drifted up
Pensacola Avenue into the hills past the assorted seedy housing
developments toward Round Top Mountain. I moved on auto-
pilot, feeling a foot above the ground.

Sure enough, I tripped over a broken, rusted washing
machine and almost fell. Cursing, I buried my cigarette butt
into its once-white exterior. Then I kicked the dying appli-
ance—kicked it until my foot hurt—until I could *feel* something, the pain seeming radically better than the emptiness.

I then slowed my walk, lit another cigarette, and limped
past a soaked mattress. A half-bent lamp was balanced on top of
it, so I kicked that too. It rolled onto the ground, barely making

a sound, and I began to feel invisible. I was coasting, detachment my only friend. I glided past a homeless man who was half-dressed and clutching himself under a tree.

Scooting under a little bridge, I wondered about the likelihood of a car running me over, but there were no cars and I knew none would appear. I smoked and walked until I felt I could no longer breathe.

***

Whether it was boredom, the fresh air, or that fact that I had to coax Rob to have sex with me, the days passed and I brewed with resentment.

It was an afternoon like most. I went to the gym. I met Cara at Borders. Keeping to our ritual, we were hanging in the outdoor area, surrounded by unpurchased books. I had my computer on and Cara had her huge textbook open, yet neither one of us were doing any work. Just chatting.

"Matt's away," she said casually, referring to her husband.

"Oh yeah? Where did he go?" I asked. Maybe it was the bright sunlight, but Cara looked younger that day. She was wearing a yellow T-shirt dress and gold eye shadow. It clashed, but I liked it.

"He's training some cadets down on the big island. He won't be back until Monday."

"I wish Rob would go away," I said. "Not that I don't feel alone when he's home."

"Do you two ever do anything fun?" asked Cara carefully.

"Nope. We are broke, but I did point out the other night that having sex with me is actually free. Unfortunately, that doesn't interest him either."

"Maybe he doesn't want to risk deflating the air mattress," quipped Cara, who had been a guest one evening in our camping apartment.

"The air mattress is not helping matters, but couples who want to have sex find a way to have sex," I said. "Rob would rather read his book."

"Huh?"

"He'd rather be *reading* than fucking me. I swear he's caught some rare tropical reading disease. He's averaging a book a day."

"I've never heard of anything like that. Where is he getting these books?"

"He's stealing them from Cheapo Books. That used book-store near the college. Only he calls it 'borrowing' as he plans to return them all. Isn't that totally pathetic? At least you and I take *new* books in search of higher education."

I shut my laptop. My screensaver was a photo of my mother and me standing in front of Short Hills Mall in New Jersey, loaded down with shopping bags from upscale stores. I decided the image was subliminally putting me deeper in debt.

"I know what you should do," said Cara excitedly. "Take a break from him. Come over to my house, and we can get some wine and cook dinner. Matt won't be there, so it will be just us."

"Um, do you know how to cook? Because I can't say I'll be much help. I do excel at drinking wine, though."

"Yes, I know how to cook."

"OK, but you live so far away. How will I get home later?"

"I'll drop you back later or you can just sleep over. Whatever. It might make Rob miss you a little. It'll be fun!"

I peered at her longer than usual when she said this last part, and something in my spine tingled as I accepted her invitation.

***

The thing about Cara was she thought she'd been seducing me when, in fact, it was the other way around. Women were sexy and beautiful creatures, but only men could seduce me. But I was thankful for Cara, thankful for the diversion. She was a welcome distraction from a mediocre existence in a strange land.

Before long, two empty bottles of Chianti were lying in the recycling bin, and the pasta, which never quite made it to fruition, lay uneaten and sticky in the sink. As I followed Cara into her dark bedroom, the smell of jarred spaghetti sauce and the melody of *David Gray* became distant in the background. My heart thumped, and waves of heat passed through different sections of my body. We'd gone from friends to flirting to about to get it on within the last few hours. But we knew what we were doing.

Cara sat me down on the edge of her bed, kneeling on the floor in front of me. Her hands resting on my knees felt unusually cold. She peeled off my dress. I let her. Then she pulled down my bra straps and glanced up at me before taking my breasts in her hands and bringing each to her mouth. She flicked her tongue back and forth over my nipples while I wriggled around. Her physical touch was changing the composition of my insides; it felt like it was raining inside my body. Her arms encircled me, and I grabbed her face. Lips smashed together, we kissed like savages. My tongue reached under her front teeth and to the back of her throat, and we breathed into each other's mouths as we twisted and spun around on the bed.

I yanked the yellow dress down off her shoulders and immersed myself in her. I cupped her tits and pulled on her nipples until she began to moan. Her breathless sounds turned me on so badly that I reached up under her dress, pulled her soaked underwear to the side, and plunged two fingers deep inside her. I felt like a cheetah, devouring my prey.

Cara reached for me, and then we were both lying on the bed, making each other come. My long hair trickled in waves down her bare stomach, and I held onto her like a raft in the vastness of the Pacific Ocean. Which is what she was, figuratively speaking.

I could hear my short screams as thoughts flashed in front of my eyes. I saw Rob looking furious, Cara in the bookstore, Brianna on stage, Jake buying my wedding shoes, the cemetery across the street, my swollen ankles, the homeless man—and by then the luxurious feeling had subsided. I blinked twice, feeling the blood in my face, and noticed Cara studying me. "Pam."

"What?"

"You are so . . ." Cara struggled for the right word. "Undervalued," she said finally. I felt the left side of my flushed face but said nothing. How does one measure their value?

***

I was twenty-two before going to bed with another girl ever even crossed my mind. I suppose most women have the chance to experiment in college, or the idea comes in the form of a suggestion from a boyfriend, but neither of those opportunities ever jumped out at me. If I hadn't gone to work at Dream Girls in '95, I may have never been exposed to the idea. I'd only ever been physically attracted to men my whole life, but after a year of working alongside hundreds of beautiful half-naked women, it began to dawn on me that I had options.

From 1995 to 2000, the women of Dream Girls were sexy and desirable but consumed by their insecurities; it was clear that most of the girls felt guilt, shame, hate, self-loathing, and envy on an average day. And I was no exception. It was comforting to have coworkers who understood the mental difficulties of the job, and bonds were formed. Although it was hard to trust and make solid friends in a setting that will forever breed jealousy and competition, a mutual respect for one another did exist. Perhaps that was partly because we shared the same common enemy: the clients we were torn between needing and hating. The reasons we needed them were grounds for hating them; we desired the surplus of cash but despised the men because they could buy us. And deep down we despised ourselves, because we approved our own sale. Money cast a powerful spell over me, and I would often find myself trapped in a power struggle I had single-handedly created.

Combine this element of understanding and mutual common ground with a considerable amount of sexuality and flattery—and for most, drugs—and fantasies often became a reality. It is yet another aspect of my life where I can say I was a product of my environment.

One night, a beautiful coworker named Jessica, who in retrospect was basically an emotional disaster—albeit one gorgeous example—pulled me alongside the front bar and told me she would consider hooking up with me if I lost five pounds. I can't imagine the look on my face when she said this, but what surprised me was my sudden willingness to lose five pounds. It wasn't as if I was overweight. I may not have been the skinniest twig on the planet, but I'd never had any complaints directed my way. However, it was the late nineties, and models like Kate Moss and actresses like Calista Flockhart were changing the country's perception of thinness. Super skinny was in, and Jessica was just that. Her long, narrow legs snaked up past her hips and curved inward, revealing a hint of a waist, and her long, curly black hair hung down her back in perfect ringlets.

"A lot of girls here think you're sexy," she told me, "but you'd look better if you dropped some weight."

"Really?" I tried to digest this bit of friendly advice, as she didn't mean to be insulting.

"What are you doing later?" she asked me.

"I don't know," I said.

"If you want, we can hang out."

"I'm not sure I'll be able to lose five pounds that soon," I'd answered, biting my lip nervously. She laughed at what she assumed was humor and pulled me over to dance with her for one of her clients.

Jessica took full advantage of the situation she had just created. She caressed my body, and I followed her lead as we danced song after song for this bald old man who resembled Sean Wallace from *Mork & Mindy*. At first I was slightly embarrassed and grateful for the dim lighting as I was suddenly conscious of

those "extra five pounds" circulating my hips, but when Jessica
kissed me full on the lips, I knew she'd be coming home with
me despite my weight.

At 5 a.m. that morning, we had sex on my small, grimy
futon in the East Village, squashed between my door and
the wall. The next afternoon I awoke and she was gone. She
didn't leave a note. I lay there wondering if I'd been used
but decided it wasn't important. If I had been, at least I'd
enjoyed myself.

After the first time, it was easy. I didn't make a habit of
it, but there were other girls, all gorgeous, sexy, and lonely.
The only consistency was it never developed into anything more
than a one-night stand. It was simply about finding comfort in
another, even for just a few hours.

***

Cara and I lay in her air-conditioned car, two blocks away from
my apartment, parked behind the graveyard. Through the window, I could see the laundromat that doubled as a pawnshop.
Handy, considering I was now hocking all my jewelry. I stared
past it at the rows of used furniture that were most useful in
blocking our partially naked bodies from the street. "Your
neighborhood is really not so bad," said Cara, twirling a piece
of my hair with her slender fingers. (This wasn't our first time
loitering behind Honolulu Suds.)

"Luckily, I have a stun gun in my bag if anyone smashes
your window." I'd purchased it online and had felt much safer
when hitchhiking to the mall.

A lone streetlight lit Cara's face. I could barely see what
I was touching, but by then I knew. On her backseat, we
stretched out like two cats in the wild, minus the screeching. I
shifted the majority of my weight onto her. My bra was unfas-
tened and carelessly wrapped around my shoulders, revealing my pale breasts to the world. Cara's shirt was shoved up
over her tits so she resembled a Penthouse model. I grazed her

jean-clad crotch with my knee and pressed into her, running my left hand along her flat stomach. "If only Matt could see me now," she said, stretching her neck up to kiss me. "I've been telling him for years that I like girls, and he never once acted on it. Dumb ass."

I smiled. "At least he acts on you."

"Look what I've been missing," she whispered. Her mouth was wet, and her tongue was convincing. But her lips were soft. She breathed life into me.

"You are so hot," I said.

"What makes you say that?" She reached a finger under my shorts and along the edge of my thong. Her touch was light, like a butterfly resting.

"You just are. You have that innocence that fools the people at the bank, but if you look closer, you have all this sexual energy."

"You're pretty hot yourself." With her thumb grazing my clit, she slowly pushed a finger into me, and I gasped. Before Cara, it had been years since anyone had fingered me. Rob refused to do it. *It's squishy, and I don't like it,* he'd said once. "I want to go down on you," said Cara. Yet another thing Rob never did. I merely blinked, as we hadn't gone that far yet. At least not sober, and certainly not in her black Le Sabre with the tinted glass.

"OK," I murmured. I was almost embarrassed by how much I wanted it. Needed it, like I'd been sexually deprived for years. A weighty possibility, looking back.

"That was amazing," I said, minutes later. I said this because it felt amazing, but whether it was amazing because it was *with her* was still up in the air. I was indifferent, separated from myself. Adapting. She smiled coyly, and I robotically lowered my body down on hers. I didn't necessarily feel like returning the favor, but she had earned it.

***

Being with Cara was fine. It was intimacy, and I craved it.
But I didn't relish in any afterglow and rarely thought about
our moments together when we were apart. However, it did
make me feel desirable again. I took this newfound confidence
and tried to apply it constructively to my marriage. Sounds
bizarre, but I was running out of ideas. And I figured if I was
having regular sex with a girl instead of a guy, it wasn't really
cheating.

My overall plan was to act as unresponsive and lackluster
toward my husband as he did to me and see what happened. I
had sex with Cara twice a week and then went home before Rob
finished work. The other nights I went out drinking and would
arrive home after he was already asleep. My overly optimistic
hypothesis was that if I didn't *initiate* sex with him, eventually
he would. So I waited.

Weeks went by. And with every day that passed, my resentment grew. How could he expect me to last a year on a tropical
island without any affection or sexual satisfaction? Was he completely out of his mind? Why was he changing so much? And
why wouldn't he talk to me about it?

One night I tried a different approach—a romantic dinner
for Rob and myself, minus the food. When he got home, I was
wearing only black lace underwear and a black lace bra with
black thigh highs, and I had lit jasmine-scented candles among
the camping equipment. I had also dressed up the air mattress
with satin sheets, which at the time I didn't realize was not the
best idea in the world. (Unbeknownst to me, the bed was about
to become a slippery pond.) I also picked up a bottle of Laurent
Perrier and two perfect champagne glasses.

When Rob walked in the door, pushing his goddamn ten-
speed bike, I was ready. I sat perched seductively on the largest
camping chair with my legs crossed, smoking a cigarette.

"Are you conducting a séance?" he asked, wheeling his bike
past me and leaning it against the wall.

"No."

"Those candles smell funny."

"They're scented." I was waiting for him to look at me. Back in New York, black lace and stockings would have sent him over the edge. But New York was just a memory at this point.

"Maybe it's the cigarette smoke mixed in," he said, turning up his nose. "Can't you smoke on the balcony?"

"You never do," I pointed out.

"Yes, but pot doesn't leave a stale smell."

"That's true. Pot only stinks like a skunk and can't be smoked around small children for fear of potential brain damage." I reminded myself I was supposed to be wooing, not antagonizing. "Come sit with me. I missed you."

"I've got to take a shower, baby. It's like a hundred degrees out, and that hill on Manoa Drive keeps getting steeper. And I'm hungry. Did you buy any food?"

"I bought champagne and satin sheets."

Rob turned on the kitchen light and opened the refrigerator door, ruining the romantic lighting for which I'd strived. "I'm so sick of peanut butter," he muttered, removing the jar and what was left of the bread.

"If you want you can take a shower and I'll order something for you. The Chinese place delivers," I said, kissing his ass. I actually wanted to punch him, but that was not the right way to go about things.

"Nah, that's OK," he said, spreading peanut butter over two slices of bread without looking up. I walked over.

"Champagne?" I asked, holding two glasses.

"Where did you get those glasses?" he asked immediately.

"The Glass Shop on Kalakaua. They're nice, right?"

"Yeah, but we can't take those back with us."

"So we should live without glassware?" I sighed. "Can I pour you some?"

"Sure, OK. I'm going to take a shower," he announced for the second time.

"I'm going to wait for you in bed. OK? I bought fresh new sheets."

"I don't see where you get the money to buy all this stuff."

He hadn't said anything about my outfit so I followed him into the bathroom. "Do you like what I'm wearing?"

"It's very cute," he said, stepping into the shower.

Cute wasn't the word I wanted to hear. Puppies were cute. Baby chicks in a basket were fucking cute. I grabbed the two glasses of champagne from the kitchen counter and slugged one back, pouring myself more before bringing them both into the bedroom. I glanced around, wondering where to place them. That was the problem with sleeping four inches off the ground: it was difficult to have a night table.

I had already made the bed with the silver satin sheets, but this was my first time actually testing them out. They felt nice and smooth on my skin, but I found it hard to get comfortable. As soon as I found a good position, my weight would slide into the center of the mattress. It was fine for one person, but I knew Rob was not going to want to share the middle of the bed with me. *Oh well.*

I stared at the ceiling and reminded myself this all came down to strategy. I couldn't be too aggressive. If I pounced on him, it was never going to work. I was just going to lie there pretending to read and see what happened.

I opened up my recent acquisition from Borders, *Fairytales for Those Who Can't Remember Their Youth*, and took out my high-lighter. I would not be pushy. Be coy and sexy but also aloof. I kept repeating this mantra until Rob slid into the middle of the bed with his book.

"Shit. These sheets are slippery," he said.

I highlighted a passage from *The Princess and the Pea*. I highlighted the whole page before I realized I was seething mad. It just wasn't fair. I was a sexy, attractive woman, still under thirty—just barely—wearing black lace, and I was lying on an air mattress with a man who seemed intent not to make the first move. I would wait it out, I vowed silently, turning the fluorescent yellow page.

"How's that book you're reading?" I asked. He seemed so engrossed that a low-flying missile could have zoomed in our window without gaining his attention.

"I don't know. I just started it. I'm only on page eighty." Great. He was reading *The Hunt for Red October.* Twelve hundred more pages to go. A hundred pages a day equaled twelve more nights *just like this.* This realization weakened me, and I slid closer to him. I told myself I was just being sexy and coy; I wasn't making the first move. Kissing his neck would be a blatant first move. I wasn't going to do that. Not this time. No way.

Ten minutes later, I was seriously considering it. Fifteen minutes later, I was doing it. I kissed it soft at first. The kisses he used to love. And then I started kissing his neck harder. Rob held tight to his book. "Come on, baby. I'm in the middle of a chapter here."

"Fuck the chapter."

"Stop it. I don't like this game you're playing, OK?" he said, pulling away. "Dressing up. Buying champagne. You just won't stop."

"I'm trying to be endearing! And sexy! And coy! So you notice me! I've been playing hard to get for weeks to see if your famous let-things-happen-naturally theory might have some credence. And you know what? It doesn't. It's bullshit!"

"So you just want to get fucked! Is that it?" He hurled his book against the wall and grabbed my hair roughly.

"Yes. Yes, I do," I said meekly. In truth, he was frightening me. Before I knew it, he was crushing his lips down on mine so hard it hurt. Between mean, hard kisses, he said, "This is what you want? Fine, I'll give it to you."

I was so stunned I could barely react. He yanked my hair back, and my lips stung with his loveless behavior. His motions left no room for reciprocation of any kind. I simply lay there while he ripped off my bra and underwear in one swoop, tearing the sheer pretty lace I'd chosen with care. He squeezed my left breast and twisted it so hard that I thought it might just tear off in his hand, and then he was inside me, fucking me hard. "You keep pushing me, this is what happens. How do you like this?" he screamed, holding my head back. "You make me do something that I don't feel like doing so there!"

I was speechless. Every part of me was dry except for my face, which was wet with tears. And then he came inside me, and I truly hated him.

"Feel better now? You got what you wanted?" he said angrily, rolling off me.

I shook my head. "That wasn't what I wanted," I gasped.

Rob turned off the light, and I lay there with my eyes squeezed shut, afraid to move. Afraid to talk. Afraid to think. Afraid to be. Seconds went by and eventually minutes. I heard him sleeping soundly. I took deep breaths. Regrouped. Calmed myself down. At least he hadn't been indifferent. He had finally showed some raw emotion, I thought, trying to look on the positive side, had there been one. The cocoon that encased him had cracked, and out had emerged what? A demon butterfly? A killer moth?

It's just this island. This is not the man I married. It can't be. I need to get him back to New York, and quickly. Just like Shelly Duvall had to get Jack Nicholson out of that damn hotel. The sick cabin thriller that I hadn't yet written was becoming my life. It had been almost six months, and every day Rob was getting more withdrawn, angrier, and meaner. I stared hard up at the ceiling. Resolute.

***

"We're leaving," I announced the next morning. I wasn't actually talking to Rob, but we were still speaking.

"Leaving where?"

"Here. Hawaii. I'm done," I stated. He laughed like I'd just made a joke. "Hawaii turned you into a fucking asshole so we're moving back home."

"Well, in case you've forgotten, we signed a lease for another seven months. So we're here until May. Whether you like it or not."

"I don't think so."

"What?"

"The lease is just a document. Just like our marriage certificate. People break their leases all the time as they do *other* documents. I'm a pro at breaking leases."

"Oh, are you?"

"You lose your safety deposit. That's all."

"We're not going to lose our safety deposit. That's for damn sure."

"It's one month's rent. If you choose to stay here, you'll lose *me*." I smiled grimly, watching him search for the peanut butter. I'd thrown every one of his possessions away the moment I'd woken up, the only exception being his clothes, simply because he couldn't move back to New York in his birthday suit.

He looked up sharply. "Pam, did you throw the peanut butter away—"

"Rob, just in case you're not putting six and four together, I officially *hate* you now," I clarified for him. I was not allowing myself to recall the night before because I would have had a nervous breakdown. And a breakdown was not going to get me out of this mess. In a matter of ten hours, I'd gone from detached to hard. Apparently, one must hit rock bottom before realizing one has the ability to fight back.

He paused and scratched the back of his head. He looked slightly guilty, but we were past the point of apologies, so I carried on. "Personal feelings aside, I've depleted my savings and am now drowning in debt. So you have two options. You can leave when I do, which will be as soon as possible, and still have a chance to repair this marriage, or you can stay without

me, paying all the rent and bills yourself. That means you'll
have to stop smoking so much pot and get a higher-paying job.
The choice is up to you. Otherwise, I'll get us out of the lease
without losing our deposit. Which is *my* money anyway, which
is the only reason I care."

"What are you planning to do? Fuck our building manager?"

If that's what it takes. I peered at him, my eyes cold, green
slivers of glass. Like broken shards of a Heineken bottle. "That's
a low blow."

"I was only kidding."

"I'll take care of it. Just like I've taken care of everything
so far."

Rob sighed, finally afraid. I walked out on the balcony and
looked out past the graveyard, having won the battle. It was a
shame I'd already lost the war.

***

The only problem was I had to break the lease without losing
our security deposit. The money wasn't so much the point as the
act of proving I was capable.

In any case, I had two points in my favor. One was the fact
that Ming Tomichi wanted to have sex with me. The second
point was that I was willing to do anything to leave Hawaii. So
pleading my case on a deserted beach prepared to sunbathe topless was my starting plan.

After Rob disappeared out the door with his stupid bike, I
dug Ming Tomichi's cell number out of my purse. I regretted
blowing him off for the past three months but decided to forge
on, as he was my only ray of hope. He answered on the second
ring. "Tomichi here."

"Hi. It's Pamela Castle. Remember me?"

"Pamela . . . oh, of course. How are you? How's everything
going?"

"Well, it's going all right." Still on the balcony, I stared at
the graves, remembering how nice he'd been to me.

"Everything's OK in the apartment, I hope."

"Oh yeah. The apartment is great. Really solid. We love it."

"So what's up?"

"I just wanted to call and apologize for being so busy these past few months and not making time for you."

"Oh, I understand." He coughed. "You're busy. Totally understandable."

"Yes, well, things have calmed down here, and I was wondering if the invitation to the deserted beach on the North Shore still stood. Ever since you left that message, I've been dying to check it out," I gambled, hoping he wouldn't remember how long ago that had been.

A few lengthy seconds passed. "Um, sure. I mean, yes. That would be great. When would you like to go?"

"I'm free tomorrow." I watched Rob bike up the hill in the direction of his restaurant. He was pedaling standing up, and if I hadn't known better, I would have assumed it was one of the high-school kids, not my thirty-four-year-old husband.

"Tomorrow? Ah, OK. Tomorrow is good," Ming stammered.

"You could pick me up at, say, noon? I'll bring lunch."

"Perfect. I'll bring the beach blanket."

"Great. This will give us a chance to catch up," I said. *And a chance for me to get the hell off this island.*

***

The next morning I walked to the supermarket to purchase supplies. Each planned encounter with Ming Tomichi had me putting on an act of profound proportions. The first meeting with him was to secure the prison apartment, and now it was to leave it without penalty.

At the supermarket, I purchased a huge bag of ice, a loaf of French bread, a wedge of Brie, some plastic plates and utensils, a pint of blueberries, grapes, and two decent bottles of champagne. The one redeeming quality of Hawaiian supermarkets was they stocked a huge variety of liquor, catering to the obvious demand.

Once I got home, I threw the ice into my largest backpack, packed up the food and drink, and then heaved the backpack into our empty freezer. Then I got ready for my date with Ming!

By the time his car pulled into the lot, I was dressed in a black bikini, Brazilian style, and a sexy baseball cap that said *Support Your Local Strip Club*. My bikini top created a cleavage that I didn't possess naturally, and the bottom was simply a triangle of black with a thong in the back. A silk black wrap around my waist hid this feature for the time being, but when I swirled around, the soft, floaty material flared, revealing the excuse of a bathing suit. I made sure I did a little swirl before jumping into the front seat of Ming's black BMW.

"Hi! You didn't even give me a chance to come around and open the door for you," he scolded, kissing me hello on the cheek. "You look great!"

"Oh, men still do that?"

Ming laughed as he pulled back onto the road. Driving down Pensacola toward the freeway, he glanced at me. "You look ready for the beach." His eyes lingered on my cap and then eventually settled on my cleavage. Since he knew that I *knew* he was staring at my tits, he quickly jerked his head up again, blushing as only an Asian man can blush. I noticed a slight rise in his beach shorts, and my smile widened. *So far so good.*

"I was actually a little surprised to hear from you," he confessed.

"Oh, Ming. I'm sorry. Living here has been *such* an adjustment. I had to discipline myself to get any writing done at all." *Keep the lies consistent.*

"I hope it's been a worthwhile experience."

I stared straight ahead, not wanting to allude to any details during the car ride. "Do you mind if I smoke?"

"Smoke? Mind? No. No, I don't mind," he said, rolling down my window. "Do you need the car lighter?"

"No, I have one." I lit a Marlboro Light and then appraised Ming from the corner of my eye. Overall, he wasn't a bad-looking guy. He had nice skin and straight teeth. And a deep tan, which offset his bright eyes. I wasn't the least bit attracted to him, but I figured any physical contact would be relatively painless.

"What's in the backpack? It appears to be dripping."

"It's just the ice melting. Makeshift cooler." I stared out the window, gazing at the various mountains in the distance while I polluted the crisp, clean air with nicotine.

"I really hope you like this beach," he said. "It's one of the most uninhabited shores on the island, and it's managed to stay that way. Very few people know about it."

"That's wonderful. You must keep it a secret so the tourists don't find out."

"You got that right."

I kept the conversation light while we drove north on H-1 for the next forty-five minutes. Finally Ming made a sharp turn down a narrow dirt road lined with thick forest on either side. "I'm going to try and remember where this is. But I won't tell anyone," I added. "I'm good at keeping secrets."

"I trust you," he said, grinning. The dirt road twisted steadily downward until it came to an abrupt stop. "This is where we get out," he said, shutting off the engine.

"Where's the beach?" I asked, undoing my seat belt.

"Just through those trees," he said, pointing.

I waited in the car until Ming opened my door for me. Then I climbed out and watched him reach gingerly for my backpack. He held the bag outstretched in front of him, and I followed him down a rocky little trail. I was happy he was leading the way so he didn't see me sliding in my sandals and holding onto nearby branches for balance.

The ground finally stabilized, and calm, indigo blue water suddenly surrounded us. "Oh, wow. I see what you mean. This is really beautiful," I said. We stood on fresh green grass, five yards of sand separating us from the still sea.

"We are standing in an inlet. It stretches half a mile."

"How did you ever find this place?"

"My wife knew about it. She showed it to me when we were growing up. About thirty years ago."

"That is awesome. Where should we set down the blanket? I'm partial to shade, as you can see," I added, pointing to my bone-white stomach. The self-tanning had been a one-shot deal, given the outcome.

"This spot is fine," said Ming. "Considering it's a weekday, we might get lucky and be the only ones here."

"That would be super," I said, thinking that would be *fantastic*. Hopefully Lulu J. Lo. wouldn't row past us with her crew.

Ming spread a cherry-red quilted blanket down over the soft green grass, and I waited until he sat down to remove my wrap. When I gracefully undid the knot and pulled the silky material away from my body, Ming's mouth acted like a drawbridge, slowly opening to full capacity and then closing again. He pulled himself together and babbled some nonsense about the North Shore verses the South Shore while I reached for my forty-five sunblock.

"Would you mind?" I asked, using the oldest cliché in the book.

"I'd be delighted." He clumsily poured the lotion in a liquid stream down my back. "Wow. This comes out fast," he remarked, working quickly to rub in five times the amount of lotion that was actually needed. His hands felt small as he rubbed the excess cream in circles.

I poured the champagne into two large plastic cups, and we cheered.

"I love champagne," said Ming. "I really shouldn't drink it. We Asians don't have much of a tolerance," he said, laughing. "But I love it!" He took a nice long swig, and I smiled. I liked his enthusiasm.

After setting out the food and chatting for a bit, I finally got down to business. "As much as I wanted to check out this secret beach, I had an additional motive in meeting with you today," I mentioned casually.

"Oh?" he mumbled, staring at my tits. I decided to raise the bet.

"This beach is so *private*. Any objections to me sunbathing topless?" Ming swallowed and proceeded to drain his entire cup of champagne, finally choking on eight ounces of carbonation. I didn't wait for an answer and simply untied my bikini top, letting it fall. "Ah, much better. Tan lines are so eighties." I reached over and refilled Ming's cup, allowing him to stare.

"Ah, what did you say about a motive?" he stammered.

"I wanted to tell you that you were right about Rob. That day in the classroom when you told me what his boss said, you were right. I didn't want to believe it at the time, but he *had* been lying to me." I took a long sip of champagne and considered my next statement carefully. Ming squinted and nodded, and I could tell he was trying hard to concentrate on what I was saying. "Hawaii isn't working out for me," I said, staring at the water. "From a financial standpoint *and* a relationship standpoint. As a couple, we're not doing well."

"I'm sorry to hear that," said Ming, not sounding too sorry at all.

"We need to get back to New York to straighten things out. And the sooner the better." It wasn't as if I was lying. But I was so mixed up, the truth often sounded like lies. I paused while Ming considered this. He pursed his lips and attempted to look at my face. "I realize you were worried about this from the beginning, and since I reassured you in every way that we had things covered, I feel very much to blame," I continued, using my initial disadvantage to my advantage.

"When do you have to leave?" asked Ming, guzzling more champagne.

"What's left of my savings will last us until the end of this month." A more positive way of saying *the amount I could borrow might last until the end of the week*. He peered into the bottom of his plastic cup, and I refilled his champagne despite his flushed face.

"Thanks," he muttered.

"If you could look for someone to rent the apartment, that would be a tremendous help." I leaned into him and touched him on the arm. It felt smooth and young, almost like a little boy's arm. Ming glanced up at me then, and his eyes widened. I stared back. "I'm so lonely here in Hawaii, and with Rob acting so differently, I just want to go back home."

"Why doesn't your husband get a better job? Isn't he qualified?" demanded Ming suddenly.

"He absolutely is, but he refuses."

"But I don't understand *why?* On this island there are so many good hotels in need of a qualified chef from New York, and they pay like sixty grand a year to start. You mean to tell me he *prefers* to work part-time making nine dollars an hour?"

"I know. It's ludicrous. There may be other things going on that I am not privy to. I just don't know."

"If I had a girl like you, I'd want to do everything to keep her happy."

"Oh, Ming. You are too cute. That means a lot to me." I felt like a snake for being so manipulative. He was a nice person. I paused, debating whether to elaborate. "There is only one reason why my husband doesn't seek better employment, but if I tell you, it has to stay between us."

"Of course," he said, taking another large gulp of warm champagne. He threw in a few ice cubes from my backpack, a brave move, and stirred it with his finger.

"He says that all the high-paying hotel jobs test for drugs, and he refuses to be a lab rat to society. His words, not mine. Basically, he doesn't want to give up his mainstay of marijuana every couple of hours." Ming just gaped at me, probably afraid of what I might do or say next. "And it's not like he does hard drugs," I reassured him. "He just smokes pot, but he smokes at least ten times a day."

"That's a lot," slurred Ming, appearing significantly redder.

I continued my monologue despite Ming's body language and questionable comprehension. "In New York, he wasn't like this. He made love to me. He desired me. Now he couldn't care less about me, and it's extremely hurtful," I said, biting my lip. My acting ascended to the next level of sophistication when I began to cry, although I had no idea if I was still acting.

Ming Tomichi struggled to put his arm around me and squeezed my shoulder reassuringly. "None of this is your fault," he comforted.

"I'm so glad you understand," I said through tears, burying my face in his small shoulder. "I *hate* Rob for doing this to me."

"No you don't."

"Yes, I certainly do!"

"Well, hey. We'll work something out. Don't worry."

"Can we?" I choked, perking up considerably.

"Yes," he said, and then he touched my face. "I can't believe that someone as beautiful as you is so lonely. I have always wanted to be with a girl as striking as you." And as he was speaking these accolades, his eyes began to cross, and his upper half became limp and collapsed backward onto the beach towel.

I smiled and let him sleep. I put my bikini top back on. Finishing the rest of the champagne, I ate some cheese and fruit and waited.

Eventually he awoke. "What happened?" he asked, rubbing his eyes.

"You just took a cat nap. Before that you were telling me how you were going to help re-rent our apartment. You really are the best," I crooned. "Thank you so much!"

Ming nodded, somewhat bewildered.

Rob and I left at the end of September holding a check for our security deposit.

Part 4

PAM AND JAKE

Queens, NY

OCTOBER 2003

Achilles was barking. Again. That damn dog. *How can this be?* I wrestled around in the tiny bed I was sharing with Rob in his parents' spare room. I knew I was going to get up and take the little Snoopy outside, but my mind was simply denying that I had already made such a choice. I opened one eye and glanced at Rob, who was sleeping like he was connected to a morphine drip. "Tell me you don't hear that dog," I said, poking him in the ribs. He grunted and threw a lazy arm over me.

I pounded my pillow and turned over, still aware of the quiet whimpering in the background. *This is exactly why I don't have pets—or children, for that matter.* Although no one could describe Achilles as a simple pet; he was more like a full-time job. Rob's mother had once mentioned that she and Paul could have purchased and trained a thoroughbred racehorse for all the time and money Achilles had cost them. After staying at their house for seven weeks, I finally understood the gravity of the situation.

I removed Rob's arm and wearily got to my feet. It was an early morning in October and still pitch black outside. Treading carefully down the hallway and into the living room, I felt my way around in the semidarkness until I reached his cage. I unlatched the door and scooped him up with both hands.

Every time I had to deal with the little guy, I wondered who was responsible for naming him Achilles. Blind in one eye and paralyzed from the hip down, he hardly fulfilled the image of a great warrior. Achilles' heel, maybe.

I carried him outside into the unusually warm morning. One floppy ear to the grass, Achilles began a succession of rolls, and I shut my eyes in an effort to block out the events of the previous day. While Rob had settled back into his old job at the Copper House without a hitch, I was the one hopping the Long Island Railroad every day and hunting for an apartment. Again! Not that I wanted to live with his parents forever, but compared to living in Oahu, it wasn't so bad.

With my eyes still closed, I began to count in my head the things I didn't have: a place to live, a job, any friends who could get me a job (discounting waiter or stripper positions), a car—which I really didn't want but was probably necessary—and oh, *money*! Trying to be positive, I forced myself to recall the things I did have. Unfortunately, only troubling things came to mind: huge debt (thanks Rob), some half-assed modern versions of fairytales, a warrant from the IRS due to back taxes, and sun-and-chlorine-damaged hair that was fine for the beach but *not fine* for making lasting impressions in the Big Apple. I also had reddish farmer tan lines from walking everywhere the past six months, along with the premonition that my tropical tan would one day lead to irreversible skin cancer.

I snapped my eyes open, remembering Vicki, the real estate agent I'd discovered the day before in Astoria, Queens. Vicki Vancowski lived in Kew Gardens with her two kids and was the toughest businesswoman I'd ever had the misfortune of randomly contacting. She was Polish, sharp as a whip, and reminded me of one of those Pekinese dogs that can never sit still. She had a small, heart-shaped face, pale white skin with scattered freckles, and long, fluffy red hair, and she jogged along instead of walking. She also drove her enormous gray Buick like a maniac. (In the two hours I'd been a passenger, she rear-ended two cars and side-swiped another.) When I wasn't holding my breath in her backseat, I was either racing to keep up with her or standing there awkwardly while she talked a mile a minute into her cell phone. It had been a long, tiring day and hadn't amounted to anything. And I was supposed to spend another entire afternoon with her.

***

I took the train into the city, but I never made it to Astoria. I directed the cab straight to the Four Seasons and called Vicki to reschedule everything for Monday, Rob's day off.

"Do you want me to show you apartments in Astoria only? I have a few two-bedrooms that opened up in Woodside if you're interested," she said.

"Where's Woodside?" I stirred my Bloody Mary with an oversized celery stick.

"West of Astoria. Off the LIE as opposed to the Grand Central."

"That means nothing to me. How far is it by subway from the city?"

"It's the seven train, about thirty minutes from the East Side."

"Too long. Forget it. I have a better idea," I said, deciding to appeal to her sneaky immigrant, money-hungry side. "You said you had a nice one-bedroom in the trendier part of Astoria, correct?"

"Yes, off the Broadway stop."

"OK, on Monday I'm going to bring Rob. All you have to do is take him to a few of the apartments you showed me yesterday off Ditmars and *then* bring us over to the nice building near Broadway. Don't say anything to him about it being a one bedroom. He's hung up on this two-bedroom idea. But I think once he sees how it's comparable in square feet—but with a renovated kitchen and bathroom—you'll have the rental and we'll all be happy."

There was a pause on her end of the line while she tried to gauge my sincerity. "Do you have first month's rent and the security deposit ready to go?"

I calculated quickly in my head. "Yes."

"And the broker's fee in cash?"

"That can be arranged."

"OK. Monday at noon. My office," she said, about to hang up.

"Oh, and one more thing," I said quickly. "Do you know the band, the Grateful Dead?"

"I'm Polish, not stupid."

"OK, this is a lot to ask, but if you go by the apartment for rent on Broadway in the next few days, could you put a Grateful Dead sticker on its door? Those stickers are easy to find, and Rob would see it as a sign. Trust me on this one."

"You're right. That *is* a lot to ask," she snapped, hanging up. Oh well, it was worth a shot. *She'll do it.* I smiled and sipped my drink. If I always had to figure everything out, we were going to start doing things my way.

The bartender handed me a lunch menu, and I opened it just to be polite and feel important. I knew darn well that I shouldn't even be having a drink there, much less eating. I glanced down at the first appetizer on the list.

Tuna Sashimi Ravioli, Goat Cheese Center, Soy Honey Reduction. $24.95

As I read this this, it felt so good to be back in New York. Wasting no time, I dialed Jake's work number.

I entered his extension at the beep and waited for his voice. "Jake Hennessey."

"Jake, it's Pam. Hey."

"Hey you. Tell me you're back."

"I'm back and I'm never living anywhere else ever again."

"But you loved it there," he joked.

"I loved it like a farmer loves a drought. Like a communist loves freedom. Like a—"

"OK, got it. Are you in the city?"

"I'm sitting at the square bar at the Four Seasons, drinking a bloody Mary, about to order some very expensive food."

"It's good to see Hawaii hasn't changed you."

"Oh, *it has,*" I assured him.

"I work a block away from there."

"I know. My plan was to come here and call you." I motioned to the bartender that I would like another twenty-dollar drink.

"You're lying. You never have a plan."

"That's true." I grinned at the accuracy of his statement.

"I have a client meeting in five minutes, but I can come by after. Order something to eat in the meantime."

"How long will you be?"

"Thirty minutes. Can you wait that long?"

"Of course." I'd waited seven long months already. What was an extra half hour?

***

By the time Jake located me at the bar, I was enjoying my third bloody Mary while slicing duck confit off a large bone. I was the happiest I'd been in months. "What are you eating there, Fred Flintstone?" asked Jake, startling me from behind.

I dropped my knife and gave him a kiss on the cheek. "Duck. You want some?"

"No thanks." He looked the same. With the chiseled face and full lips, he was still James Spader. Only he was wearing a double-breasted navy blue suit with a crème-colored tie. Good-looking men in suits are like apples dipped in caramel: an ingenious way of improving an existing product.

"Sit down," I urged. "It's so good to see you."

"You too. You look tan."

"Just my arms and legs."

"But what's up with your hair?"

"I know it's awful. The sun fried it."

"You left a brunette and now you're practically blond."

"It's closer to orange, but it's fixable," I reassured him. "I wouldn't trust my hair to anyone on that island."

"You didn't get your hair done for six months?" I glanced around self-consciously as anyone near me probably had a personal stylist who made biweekly visits to their Fifth Avenue penthouse.

"There was really no point. Believe me, my hair was the least of my problems."

"I don't know how you survived." He pulled out a polished barstool and sat down.

"So what's new? I'm so relieved to be back. I actually feel like myself again."

"Oh, nothing's new. Each day is just another smoldering example of the mundane. And now, to further restrict social opportunities, it's getting cold outside. I can't believe you went to Hawaii from March to September."

"Yes, my life has never made any sense. Have you spoken with Donna?"

"Yeah, I visited her last week at her new job."

"How is she? She was terrible at keeping in touch. Not that I was much better."

"She seems good. She went back to school, and I think she's working a lot."

"Where?"

"She's waiting tables at this Irish bar downtown. Its biggest attraction is the dead moose hanging from the wall."

"Nowhere could be worse than Lime," I reminded him.

"At least Lime attracted female customers. Her new place is just a bunch of stockbrokers drinking pints and patting each other on the back. Its location is also totally inconvenient—*the financial district*."

"We have to go once I get settled. Order a drink."

"OK. I don't drink gin and tonic anymore. I switched to vodka soda."

"Atkins? That's so feral," I exclaimed, a little surprised.

"How did you know?"

"Oh please. That's the first thing everybody does on that stupid diet. They say good-bye to wine and beer and *hello* to vodka. You're a textbook case." I requested a Kettle and soda from the bartender. "Is it working?"

"Is what working?"

"The diet."

"Oh, I don't know. It's only been a few days, and I haven't been following it to the letter. I just need to trim a few pounds off my midsection. I don't want to wind up like my father, not being able to tell which socks are on my feet."

"What about dirt and dog food. Is it low on carbs?" I teased.

"Good question." He seemed to be mulling it over as he accepted the glass from the bartender. "We'll have to see."

"Have you been doing anything humiliating lately? With anyone new?" I tried to appear nonchalant. I was hoping he was still unusual but *not taken*.

"Here and there. Donna works with a girl named Nadine. She's pretty cool." Just her name sounded tall and thin and tan and sexy and Brazilian, and I hated her instantly.

"Nadine, you say? Where is she from?"

"South America. Brazil, I think."

"And Sarah Castle names me Pamela. Where is the love?" I took a long pull on my drink, and my eyes started to water.

"Pam's not such a bad name. Look at Pamela Anderson," Jake pointed out.

"True. However, I once bought an orange bathing suit and was seriously disturbed by how different my body looked in it. Anyway, Miss Brazil? Does she encourage your atypical behavior?"

"Yeah, she's hung out with us a few times. Donna and I have taken her to the Tribeca Grand and the Penthouse Club, and she's a lot of fun."

I wrinkled my nose.

"She's young though. Just barely twenty." *That makes me feel so much better.*

"Any word from Mimi?" I asked, changing the subject.

"Yeah, she was calling me for a while after you left town."

"That figures. Where is she now?"

"Your guess is as good as mine."

"Did you see her at all?"

"Oh yeah." He laughed and sipped his vodka.

I smiled, realizing how much I'd missed his laugh. "Tell me." I pulled on his Armani sleeve.

"Well, you know how she was plowing through her savings, right?"

"Yep."

"I'd given her about fourteen grand when all was said and done, and she spent it all on blow and didn't do anything but party and sleep for six months. I mean, who doesn't work for *six* months?"

I shrugged my agreement despite the fact I hadn't worked in *eight* months. But that was totally different. I was a serious writer enduring the elements of a cracked-out island. Not snorting coke and watching TV all day long.

"When her money ran out, her calls became more regular. I kept telling her that when she got a job, I'd consider hanging out with her again."

"So, did she?"

"No, not at first. Another two months went by before she even started to look. At this point, she'd slipped into serious debt. Her mom had cut her off, and her drug dealer—who was an heir to some soap company—actually moved into her studio apartment, but she explained to me that he was only *giving* her drugs and she still had to pay her rent. Like he was the problem, not her. I reiterated that if she got a job, I'd consider helping her."

"That was nice of you."

"So finally, she starts hosting at a Lebanese restaurant in the Garment District. Now, Mediterranean is one thing, but who the fuck eats Lebanese food? So I forced myself to visit her at this disgusting joint that advertised belly dancers and smelled like a sidewalk vendor, and Mimi had on this ridiculous outfit. She was wrapped in dark silk from head to toe. She looked like she'd been mummified in navy. And she proceeds to tell me it's her last day because she can't work anymore; she's *come down* with hypoglycemia." Jake rubbed his eyes with his fists as if to wipe away the memory. "Everyone knows you don't catch hypoglycemia like you catch the flu. Six days on the job and she's already thinking up pathetic excuses so I'll give her money."

"I give her credit for trying," I said under my breath.

"I told her, you don't have *hypoglycemia*, you just take too many drugs and you don't eat and your sugar drops and that's the big disease you think you have. She argues with me. I leave. She quits right there and follows me back to my apartment— still wearing that ridiculous outfit—and I don't realize until I get home and she jumps out of a cab behind me, yelling my name."

"Oh my God."

"Yes. So I tell her to get lost and she keeps saying she's really sick. Like *dying* sick, because of this high-sugar bullshit. 'I have all the symptoms,' she kept repeating. It was obvious that she'd self-diagnosed herself by taking a few sample symptom tests over the Internet."

I nodded.

"Anyway, I got annoyed and bet her a thousand dollars that she didn't have hypoglycemia. Meaning I'd give her money if I was wrong and I'd get nothing if I was right. I was that positive."

"Did she have it?"

"Of course not. She lied and said she went to the doctor— that she had all this proof and she was faxing it to me." I studied Jake's perfect chin as he raged on, thinking how we both appeared like civil adults enjoying cocktails in the epicenter of the world. "A few days later, I received a fax with no doctor letterhead and several spelling mistakes. *At work.* So it changed hands five times before it landed on my desk."

"That was the last you heard from her?" I practically missed the bitch.

"Yeah, she's a lost cause." He shook his head and stirred his drink. "Do you and Rob know where you're going to live?"

Who's Rob again? "No."

"Are you looking in Manhattan?"

"No, I wish. We've decided on Queens. Yet another compromise since he's already working back on Long Island. Hopefully Astoria."

"Why Astoria?"

"I picked it because it has the cutest restaurants. I'm actually supposed to be there right now viewing apartments, but I just couldn't deal with it today."

"I had a feeling you were supposed to be somewhere else," he said. "Why don't you live in Brooklyn instead? It's supposed to be much cooler. Not that I've explored it."

"Well, they say that Astoria is on the up and up as well. Although I hardly believe it."

Jake laughed. "Hopefully you'll get settled in somewhere soon so we can get back into a routine." I perked up, liking what the word *routine* implied. "We definitely need to go shopping. I haven't bought you anything in so long. Did I tell you I took Lexi and Celeste shopping for shoes?"

"Her younger sister? The waitress at Dream Girls?"

"Yeah. Those two basically emptied my wallet. I bought them both the same pair of heels. It's a Gucci sling back with the emblem on the back so when you walk in front of someone, it peeks out. They're sexy. I purchased a pair for myself too."

I gulped. "What do you wear them with?" I asked.

"My maid's uniform."

I stared at him, clearly a step behind.

"You haven't seen me in that, have you?"

"I most certainly have *not*! You've been holding out on me!"

"I don't get to wear it much, which is a shame."

I sucked down the remainder of my drink and struggled for a mental picture of this gorgeous man squeezing into such an ensemble. Apparently his fetish had not lessened in my absence.

"Well, as soon as you move, we're going shopping. So find a place fast."

"That's pretty good incentive, Jake. Monday, Rob and I are meeting the realtor together, so cross your fingers."

"If the apartment is really dirty when you move in, I can come over and clean it," he offered eagerly.

"And how much would that cost you?" I laughed.

"I could pay you on an hourly basis. One hundred an hour sound OK?"

"Very reasonable," I said, nodding. *Damn, I need a place to live. And fast!*

"What are you going to do for a job? You're not going to wait tables again, are you?"

"Not if I can help it. I was thinking maybe retail, but to be honest, just the idea of it bores me. I guess I'm really hoping I can publish my fairytales. Did I tell you I rewrote Cinderella from the perspective of the prince? I gave him a foot fetish, and the story makes a lot more sense now."

***

Rob picked me up at the train station, eager to know how my day went with Vicki.

"She cancelled on me." I turned up the radio. Tiffany's "I Think We're Alone Now" was playing, and I still really enjoyed that song.

Rob rolled his eyes and lowered the volume. "What do you mean she cancelled on you? You didn't see any apartments?"

"Nope," I said, turning the music back up.

"So what did you do all day? It's eleven o'clock at night," he exclaimed, switching off the radio and turning on the CD player. Iron Maiden blared.

"I went to lunch, walked in the park, saw a movie—"

"Did you reschedule with Vicki?"

"Yes, for Monday."

"Pam, that's my only day off next week."

"I know. I figured you should come with me so you'll have a better idea of what's actually available within our price range."

"I do not want to spend my day off schlepping around Queens," he said, sounding tired and angry.

"Hey, newsflash! Nor do I!"

"Well you're the *master* at finding apartments; I don't see why you need my help."

"You're coming with me on Monday. I do need your help," I lied. It was the only way I was going to be able to manipulate the situation.

＊＊＊

Rob and I drove to Astoria together on Monday. "I just want to warn you about this woman," I said, referring to Vicki Vancowski. "She's not your run-of-the-mill real estate agent. Or maybe she is. I don't know that many, but she's definitely crazy."

"What do you mean?"

"She doesn't waste time."

"That's good, no?"

"I suppose." I'd let him be the judge.

Once we parked, Vicki buzzed us into the building. Even her quick finger on the intercom system screamed impatience. We entered and climbed the crooked, concrete stairwell to the third floor.

"Come in, come in, come in," she urged, appearing at the doorway to her office. "I'll just be a second." We took seats in front of her enormous Nixon mahogany desk and listened politely to an argument she was having with a potential client. I glanced over at Rob and smiled, but naturally he was engrossed in free reading material.

I uncrossed my legs and glanced up when I heard Vicki click shut her phone. Oddly enough, I noticed a swift change in her demeanor after I introduced her to Rob. She was practically *nice*. "Pam tells me you're a chef out in Long Island. Where is it that you work?" she inquired softly. I blinked.

"The Copper House. It's in Glen Cove."

"And what kind of food does it specialize in?" I watched as she delicately ran her hand through her long, red hair. Could she really be interested in the cuisine of a place named the Copper House? It sounded like an Irish Pub.

"It's really just upscale bar food. We have the typical lamb, steak, and duck entrees, but we don't specialize in anything, per se."

"Is it kid friendly?"

"Oh sure. It's a family restaurant. Very big around the holidays."

I attacked my cuticles for something to do.

"And how long have you worked there?"

"Well, not including the six months we were in Hawaii, a few years now. They just rehired me two weeks ago."

"So you have a history there? Good. Most of the management companies in this area like to know you've held the same job over a good span of time." *Ah, a trace of the old Vickster.* She then informed us that we had to go and rushed us out the door.

I had warned Rob we were going to be backseat passengers, so I was surprised when she offered the front seat to him. Apparently she had taken me for an ax-murderer on my many visits. I climbed into the familiar backseat and stared out the window onto Thirty-fifth Street, thinking Rob was in for a treat. While Vicki peeled out of her parking spot, he and she discussed how real estate was booming and I began to count the number of bakeries in the neighborhood. It seemed we might be moving from pineapple country into the pastry belt.

Vicki asked him specifically what he wanted in an apartment, and I was grateful he was there to explain his excessive requirements. Hoping Vicki was sticking to my plan, I was just waiting to see the place over on Broadway. I was positive it was going to be the answer.

Once Vicki began to show us the apartments I'd already seen, I think she forgot about me completely. I was grateful for this. From the way Vicki hung on Rob's every word, one would have thought he was the next Donald Trump as opposed to penniless. Finally, she turned up Broadway toward the more populated area. To her credit, she was working the situation like I had asked her to.

"The block of apartments I'm taking you to now is called Oak Towers. It's a great building, and I try to get as many clients in here as possible because they are always very satisfied!" said Vicki, giving Rob an oblique glance. Rob nodded as if to say, *I'll be the judge of that.* "The superintendent is also extremely attentive. He keeps the building in magnificent shape," she added, glancing back at me in her rearview mirror.

"Yes, I'm still here," I announced.

"What's that, Pam?" said Vicki.

"I said, 'Are we near?'"

"Yes, next block."

"And how much do these apartments run?" asked Rob.

"I'll be able to get them down to thirteen hundred," she said, turning to him—and I swear she batted her eyelashes.

"Great," said Rob. "I'm anxious to see something on the newer side." I smiled and covered my mouth, thinking what a fucking idiot he was. I could have sensed a setup like this a mile away, and he had zero clue.

However, once Vicki ran the superintendent's buzzer and the alleged Mr. Attentive opened the door, all my thoughts went away. Vanished like Houdini. Disappeared like Hoffa. There in front of me was Stanley Kowalski from *A Streetcar Named Desire*. His features were deep-set and angular. He had a shock of black hair and a thick, muscle-toned body—like someone who'd spent serious time in jail, rather than at the gym—and an accent I couldn't place. His mouth hung with confidence, deserved or not. He was like a hot piece of meat waiting to be served up at a barbeque. I stared openly while Vicki raced past him, thanking him profusely.

Holding the elevator door open for me, Rob smiled. "It's a nice building. I like the courtyard in front." *Did it have a courtyard?* I was too distracted picturing Stanley Kowalski fixing my kitchen sink: on his back, face close up to a pipe, possibly some grease on his thick arm as he twisted some stubborn screw. Fucking the shit out of me was just a mere reflex on his part, as he was obviously capable of rewiring a building and having sex with two women at the same time.

"What do you think so far, Pam?" asked Vicki.

"What's the superintendent's name again?"

"Bruno. He's here every day and is always available if you have any questions or need a repair." *If so, I'm 100 percent broken.*

"Do you like the building so far?" Vicki asked more pointedly.

"Oh yeah, it's great," I said, my mind still on Bruno.

The elevator door opened up onto the fourth floor, and we followed Vicki to a dark green door. I coughed when I saw a sticker over the door handle. There was a green bear holding hands with a purple bear holding hands with an orange bear.

"Look!" Rob pointed. "It's the dancing bears! Good omen! Right on!"

I exchanged a quick look with Vicki and did my best not to crack up. She seemed merely amused, as if tricking your husband was the most natural thing in the world.

Unlocking the door, we walked under a tall archway and followed a long hallway that led into an empty living room. I noticed the floors were not only level but also nicely polished wood. There was a big bay window in the kitchen, and I walked over to check out the view.

"Look, you can see Manhattan from here," I said, stepping out onto the fire escape.

"Oh yeah," muttered Rob, seemingly disinterested, the view somehow exempt from his massive criteria. "This is a really nice kitchen. I love the deep sink," he said, touching it lovingly before feeling the temperature of the water.

Vicki shuffled alongside me. "What do you think, Pam?" she whispered.

"I really like it," I whispered back. "Let's see if he *notices* there's only one bedroom."

"So, what's the verdict?" asked Vicki, minutes later.

"We really like it," volunteered Rob. "But is it a two bedroom?"

"No. But the square footage is comparable to the other apartments I've just shown you." She intentionally avoided my eyeline while I inspected the ceiling. "I don't need to tell you that the rentals in this building go quickly. I'm showing it three more times today, so let me know if you're serious as soon as you can. Like in the next few minutes," she finished.

"I think we should go for it!" I exclaimed. "It's *perfect* for us."

Rob was acting stoic and moving his lips around in contemplation, but I could tell he liked it too. He finally shrugged. "OK," he said.

I didn't bother to hide my huge smile.

*****

We had dinner with Rob's parents later that evening. His mother set down a huge plate of steaks and a vat of gravy. "Did you have any luck with your realtor today?" she asked hopefully. Neither one of us responded because we were not speaking to each other, which made speaking to others awkward.

"Why so quiet?" demanded Rob's father, Paul. "Lover's quarrel?"

"Rob is mad at me because I have bad credit," I said, taking a bite of mashed potatoes. "It's like being mad at me for breathing."

Rob stared at his food.

"Pam, pass me the gravy," said Paul.

"We did find an apartment we liked," said Rob finally, slicing into his steak. "We just might have difficulty qualifying for it."

"Does this have anything to do with the warrant from the IRS I had to sign for last week?" Paul asked me. "That could screw up anyone's credit."

In bed later, Rob refused to talk to me. "I can't do anything about my credit right now. I'm sorry."

"We might not be able to get the apartment because of you, Pam. We might not be able to get *any* apartment."

"Yeah, I know, and I feel bad enough as it is."

"You're just so irresponsible."

"Um, excuse me, I had enough to deal with in Hawaii without worrying about what was going on back east. I had no phone half the time. No Internet access. I was twenty-five thousand miles away with a six-hour time difference, and frankly, keeping track of everything wasn't the easiest task."

"You really have some nerve making your problems mine, you know."

"Well gee, I'm sorry. I thought that's what married people did. Take on each other's problems. But what do I know?"

"Just because I married you doesn't mean I'm obligated to support you. It's not the dark ages anymore."

"No, but it does mean you're supposed to stop living like you're single."

"You're just trying to cover up the fact that you were careless enough to let seven months go by without following up with the IRS. If anyone knows anything, it's not to fuck with the IRS. How stupid can you be?"

I could feel myself hitting an all-time low, which often inspired me to think dangerously and without mercy. It was that moment that I vowed to do things for myself. Rob did exactly what he wanted, taking his old job back for less money and no health insurance just because he wanted to work with his buddies again.

From this point forward—while I accessed if I was still going to stay married to this person—I was going to do exactly what I wanted. I was ready to give him a taste of his own poison. I wasn't going to work in some pathetic café or in the Gap just because he didn't want his wife doing anything *inappropriate*. I thought of all those wasted nights in Honolulu where I could have been stripping for money instead of paying for my own drinks, and he probably would have been none the wiser.

My anger was so brilliantly focused that I suddenly felt stunningly alive, awash with clarity, free to live my life without restrictions. And he was completely unaffected by what he didn't yet know.

***

By some grace of God, we managed to qualify for the apartment. To be fair, Rob's squeaky-clean credentials qualified us, and the management company looked the other way where I was concerned. We were able to move in the following week, which, quite naturally, Rob turned into a huge production.

Since we had stored the majority of our stuff in my mother's garage during our extended stay in Hawaii, it was up to us to retrieve it. This included all the gifts we'd received at our wedding shower and basically everything I owned. Fortunately, it was all still waiting for us when we arrived at Sarah's house in South Jersey. Well, almost everything.

Rob and I were surrounded by cardboard and freezing our butts off in Sarah's garage when this mishap started to take form. "You know, Pam, there are all these boxes, but I don't see the All-Clad set of pots and pans my parents gave us," said Rob. *Us?* A pot to me was either a weapon or used for storing candies.

"Of course the pots and pans are here. We just have to get to the bottom of all this stuff," I said, thinking it would have been smart to label.

"But I don't see any boxes big enough."

"Well, Sarah might have stored them somewhere else in the house. I don't particularly think she has a system," I muttered, surveying the chaotic balancing of various objects.

"Well, if they're not in this garage, they'd better be somewhere else," he stressed.

"Calm down. My mother did not have a yard sale with your beloved cookware. It's here somewhere."

***

A week later, I awoke in the new apartment to Rob sitting on the edge of the bed, staring off into space. He was freshly showered and dressed from the waist down. Beads of water still clung to his back and neck. He looked cute. How I could still like him *at all* was a mystery to me, but I was too scared to analyze it. "Baby, is anything wrong?" I asked. *Surely Rob's silence can't still be over the missing pots and pans?*

He shook his head from side to side.

"Is it the pots and pans?" I felt ridiculous asking this as if it were a serious question.

He nodded gravely.

I couldn't believe this discussion was still on the table. Especially since I had reordered the pots and pans express shipping three days ago. As I watched him feel sorry for himself over a problem I had technically fixed, I felt he'd chosen the wrong career. He should have gone into politics or the military, where he could have won awards for this type of rigid, pig-headed behavior.

"It's about responsibility," he said heavily. "They were *our* gifts."

"Oh Jesus. I've heard it already. It's a broken record. A Starbucks CD! If I ever remarry—which it's looking like I might—I'll be sure to hire security at the wedding shower. A designated present watcher! An ex-cowboy would be ideal! He'd have to be fast on his feet, quick with a gun, and an expert with the lasso—"

"Don't be a wise ass."

"I'm serious. I'm not going through this again."

Without another word, still sans shirt and slightly dripping, he scampered off to the bathroom and locked the door. *Fantastic*, I thought. *I've made a drastic mistake in marrying this man.*

***

The morning I was set to go shopping with Jake, I woke up with an unusually stiff neck. *Annoying.* I dialed his number. "What time are we meeting, sissy?"

"Who is this?" he said jokingly.

"I need to know when to catch the train. I live in an *outer borough* now. I can't just skip over to Bloomingdale's."

"One o'clock. Fourth floor. Designer shoe salon."

"OK, just so you know, my neck is a little screwed up—"

"So you're going to treat me like your personal wimp today and humiliate me in front of the salesgirls?"

I smiled. Jake always brought the focus back to himself and how pathetic he couldn't wait to feel. "You bet. And we'll purchase some girly lingerie to go under your maid uniform. Hopefully they'll have your size, you undersexed giant!"

"I love when you call me that."

"See you at one."

***

"I can't help but admire these Kate Spade boots. Did you know she makes shoes?" I said. "She's turning into quite the entrepreneur. I'm so sick of these multi-talented people who continue to make the rest of us feel like we do nothing."

"Incidentally, Kate Spade also designed the original flight attendant uniform for Song Airlines. I've heard the outfits are very cool. You know how god-awful those things can be." Jake picked up the boot and studied the heel. "Did you see anything with a pointier heel? It's got to be sharp; otherwise it won't leave a mark when you walk all over me."

"Oh, so we're taking that figure of speech and making it literal?"

"You should have been walking all over me from the very beginning, leaving heel prints on my forehead."

"Wasted opportunities," I said, sighing. "Oh, I also spotted a sweet pair of snakeskin Ferrangamos, but they only come in brown."

"Get a salesgirl over here. Find the prettiest one. What are you going to tell her?"

"You know. The usual," I said, twisting my whole body around in hopes that a hot salesgirl would saunter by.

"What's wrong with you? Why are you acting so rigid?"

"I have a stiff neck."

"What?"

"I slept funny, and my neck is all fucked up."

"You're walking like Frankenstein."

"Stop being so damn observant. You're my pathetic doormat, loser wimp who is going to lick my floor clean with his tongue this Friday."

He looked rather surprised. "You just tactfully put things back in perspective."

"No kidding. I'll tell her something humiliating, bordering on mean. I might even mention that you'll be cleaning my apartment this Friday in your so-called 'maid's uniform.'"

"Good, good. I'll be over here," he said, motioning to a glass case of Chanel bags.

Spying a short blonde in hot dispute with an old lady over in the Prada section, I reminded myself there wasn't much I wouldn't say for a pair of nine hundred–dollar boots. I approached her, waiting patiently while she finished up with this Judge Judy lookalike. Might have been her, actually.

"Melissa?" I said, reading her nametag.

"Yes." She was cute—not a stunner—but she had a certain Kylie Minogue allure. I raked my eyes quickly over her tailored navy blue suit, trying to assess whether she was really that conservative.

"Do you want to make a fat commission?" Her eyes lit up despite a suspicious twist of the mouth. "See that guy over there?" I continued, pointing to Jake, who had drifted from bags to clutches.

"The good-looking one wearing Hugo Boss?"

"Yes. He's my little bitch, and he'll buy me whatever I want." *Am I changing or is this abhorrent behavior getting easier?* "If you work with me, we'll both be happy. Get my drift?"

Melissa seemed a little stunned but took it in stride. "Ah, what do I have to do?"

"Not much, really. Just act as if he's beneath you. Also feel free to recommend certain styles you think are hot. Don't worry about cost. He loves to be used."

"You're serious."

"Very. Stiletto heel only, please. Size seven."

"Coming right up," chirped Melissa. I hoped for her sake this wasn't her first day; otherwise she might assume her job was always going to be this good. My cell phone rang then, and I hastily picked it up without thinking.

"Pam, I'm having a crisis!"

"What is it, Lexi?"

"It's my fiancé. I think he's seeing someone else."

"You met him at Dream Girls. He probably is."

"Pam, you met your ex-boyfriend at Dream Girls!"

"No I met him at a sister club."

"That's even worse!"

This was true. "What is the reason for your call again?"

"I just found seventeen calls to Aruba on his cell phone bill totaling over three hundred dollars."

"Lex, I'm standing in Bloomingdale's and I can't move my neck. I'm going to have to get back to you."

"You're with Jake?" she asked, her whole mood brightening.

"Yes. We just got here."

"Does he remember I'm a size six?"

"Probably. I'm surprised you didn't tattoo it on his arm when I was incognito for seven months. Can I please call you later?"

"Yeah, totally. Shoes come before anything. I understand that."

"Good, I'll talk to you—"

"Pam!" she screeched.

"Jesus. What?"

"Just remind him that I'm a size six."

"Good-bye!" I shoved the phone back in my purse.

I walked over to where Jake was suddenly sitting. He was doing his typical squirm combined with his suspicious glance around. His good looks and fine dress never seemed to hide his obvious insecurity. I walked over to him and sat down, placing a calming hand on his head. "Good boy," I said, patting him.

"Who was on the phone?" he asked.

"Lexi. She could smell the fact we were shopping. She wanted me to remind you of her shoe size."

"I don't need reminding. No one heard you other than the salesgirl, right?"

"Of course not. I was discreet and to the point."

"Is she cool?"

"Yeah, she's fine. I have yet to encounter any salesperson who doesn't understand the universal language of *money*. This is never going to be a losing proposition for us."

With Andrea in the lingerie department, I used a different tactic. Tall and statuesque, her big brown eyes and long, expressive face revealed a serious case of boredom. The fact that she was standing there eating raspberries out of a cardboard container also indicated to me that her job was *not* her biggest priority. Uninterested and irresponsible! The ideal salesperson for our needs!

"Here's the deal," I told her while Jake stood there, listening for a change. "I've looked around. I realize this is not Barneys, but this loser next to me will spend money. He is a pitiful, pathetic runt of a man who gets his kicks being taken advantage of, so just bring out the best stuff you have. This shop closes in thirty-five minutes. Don't waste your time or ours. Shop for me first. Then him."

Andrea swallowed and capped the container of fruit. "What are you? Like a size four? Meet me in the dressing room," she said, rushing away. I smiled sweetly at Jake and maneuvered my way to the back of the store, where I took a seat on the waiting room bench. *I really love these precious moments.*

Andrea was back in two minutes flat with a five hundred–dollar Ms. Antoinette corset. It was black satin with hand-embroidered red roses running up and down the seams. "I hope I can do this justice," I fretted, taking it from Andrea's willing hands.

"Honestly, our stuff is crap," she said. "This is the only nice thing we stock. I also have it in pin stripe. We only get very few, and they're usually gone within a few days. We used to carry La Perla and Eres, but the market just isn't here for it anymore." Andrea helped me lace up the corset.

"Great, maybe this will get my husband's attention."

"Do you want to show him?" said Andrea, mistaking Jake for Rob.

"Oh no, I'm married to someone else. Jake is just my little toy. I treat him like shit, and he buys me stuff. We're more like business partners."

"Does he have a brother by any chance?"

"Nope. OK, so I'll definitely take this. Friday Jake will be cleaning my apartment in his maid's uniform. He needs—"

"*That guy* is going to clean your apartment? In a maid's uniform!" she hooted.

"Yep. He needs a bustier-type thing to go under it. Would you have anything that might fit him?"

Andrea rubbed her chin thoughtfully. "I think so. He's probably smaller than a lot of women who shop in this department. Let me go take a look."

"Cool. While you do that, I'll show him what he's buying me."

I stepped out wearing the corset. Jake was lurking around the corner and stopped dead when he saw me. "That looks amazing on you."

"Thanks. It's sucking the life out of me, but I suppose that's its purpose."

"Your waist is the size of my calf." *Ah, lovelier words were never spoken.* I swooned.

"Andrea went to find you undergarments to go under your maid's uniform. Oh, and I hope you don't have plans for this Friday because I'm serious about you cleaning my apartment."

"Great," he said, gulping.

When Andrea returned, she was carrying three types of tight black slips, complete with matching underwear. "Do you want to try these on?" she asked Jake.

"Can I return them if they don't fit?"

"As long as it's within fourteen days."

"OK, I'll just take them all. And the corset," he said, pointing to me.

Andrea smiled. "Doesn't it look great on her?"

"It certainly does," said Jake. I basked in the compliment, feeling sexy and admired. Something told me Jake was hard as a rock, and I used all my self-control not to glance below his belt. I didn't stop to consider why I cared. Or what made me think of it in the first place.

***

When Bloomingdale's closed, Jake and I went to dinner at Serafina. We were hunched over a large pizza, drinking champagne, and I must have been positively glowing. There is nothing like spending somebody else's money all afternoon to give you the feeling of being reborn. I had just taken a bite of pizza when Jake said, "I like the idea of cleaning your apartment, but Friday seems a long way off. It's only Saturday."

"I chose Friday because Rob works late, so it's the best night to do it."

"OK, but let's do something earlier in the week."

"Like what?" I asked.

"Well, since you're not working yet, let's take it up a notch."

"What did you have in mind?"

"I'm really anxious to wear the maid's uniform, and since you had the great idea of purchasing those undergarments, I think we should test them out."

"What you want to do? Give me a fashion show?" I laughed.

"Nah. A spanking might be fun, though."

"Jake, that's a sweet offer, but I don't want a spanking."

"Not you, silly. Me. You'd spank *me*."

I set down my slice of pizza. "I can't say I have much experience in that area."

"There's only one way to spank someone."

"I feel there might be many ways."

"It's just an idea. I mean, that would be pretty humiliating. Picture it: me in my maid's uniform, you spanking my ass. You could even give me a wedgie between hits." I squinted, trying to produce a mental image. "Haven't you ever just wanted to spank the shit out of someone?"

I thought about this. "I can't say I have."

"It would be totally pathetic if I was giving you twenty bucks each time you took a crack at me." I blinked and quickly did the math. If I spanked him twenty-five times, I'd leave with five hundred. *Why the fuck not?*

"This will be at your own risk, you realize. I can't be held responsible if anything goes wrong," I said.

"What could go wrong? As long as you don't swing at my head, we should be OK."

***

On Tuesday afternoon, I walked along Steinway Avenue in Queens, still checking out the new hood, disappointed that my main drag consisted of mostly assaulting cell phone storefronts and beauty supply stores. A few people had verified to me that Astoria was one of those "up-and-coming" neighborhoods, but in my opinion, it had a ways to go.

Spotting a large Delbartin's on the corner, I turned in, thinking it might just do the trick. Jake and I hadn't actually discussed *what* I would spank him with, so I was simply brainstorming. Obviously, I was an amateur; I was thinking more along the lines of a tennis racket or a bat. Black leather and S&M paraphernalia hadn't even crossed my mind.

Not a fan of Delbartin's, I perused the filthy store feeling out of place since I wasn't a rapper or a member of any particularly threatening gang. Navigating my way through yards of stretch pants, I unearthed the tennis section. Only this particular Delbartin's was short on space. Among tennis balls and assorted sweatbands peeked golf clubs and fishing poles. I considered a golf club for a brief moment before thinking better of it. If I swung too high, I might kill him. Stuff like that was always on the news, and I didn't want to be remembered in the same light as that Kennedy cousin.

Throw in the maid's uniform, and I would have a real fiasco on my hands.

I was searching for the likes of a whiffle-ball bat when I bumped into the sharp corner of a Ping-Pong table. Picking up the sample racket, I stepped back and sliced the air, chuckling as I envisioned my target. It felt natural, nothing like playing *Ping-Pong*, but I was suddenly confident in my ability to smack some ass.

***

When Jake opened the door to his apartment, I hesitated before stepping in. In the time I'd known him, I hadn't yet been to his home, and I was both curious and nervous.

"Can I offer you a drink? I have wine, vodka, rum, gin, scotch, etc. But no mixers." He grinned. I smiled and glanced from his face down to his white collar, to his waist, wrapped tight in black polyester. I took a step back and put my hand over my mouth, a mere reaction to keep from shouting.

"What?" he said. "I told you I'd be wearing my sissy outfit."

"Yeah, I know what you told me! Telling me didn't necessarily prepare me!"

"What did you expect?"

"I don't know. You look bizarre—but not bad or anything," I added. "I mean, you wear it well." I shut my mouth. To be fair, he still looked like Jake. I must have appeared perplexed because he repeated his invitation for a cocktail.

"A glass of white wine, please." I regrouped and inspected his apartment. The interior consisted of brick and wood paneling. A perfect rendition of a Vermont ski lodge. My eyes eventually settled on the wood fireplace. I stared at it, the foreign object that it was. "Is that a working fireplace?"

"Yes, but I rarely use it." I nodded, speechless. "Why are you not talking? You're never quiet." Jake uncorked a bottle of sauvignon blanc with a high-tech stainless-steel opener. He set down two elegant glasses on the hardwood table and poured.

"I'm catching my breath from the fifth-floor walk-up," I said, not wanting to seem too nervous, too inexperienced, or too impressed. All of which I was.

"I thought you went to the gym every day."

"What's the connection?" I ran my fingers along the soft dark brown leather of his couch.

"Well, one would assume you were in shape enough to handle a fifth-floor walk-up."

"Oh no. Being in shape and going to the gym have nothing to do with each other," I clarified, accepting the glass of wine.

"Is that so?"

"Two totally different concepts."

***

Fifteen minutes later, I was positioned in front of a huge wall mirror peering intently at myself as I flexed my newfound spanking powers. Jake had produced two neckties and insisted I tie his hands to the leg of the couch to limit his movements. He was full of ideas.

I acted like I knew what I was doing. I guessed that yelling was the key to this. "Jake, look in the mirror when I spank you! Don't look at your feet—you little pussy! Just because you're not licking the bottom of my shoes doesn't mean you can slack off!" I smacked his bare ass with the Ping-Pong racket. His butt was stark white with the exception of a woman's black lace thong, which hugged his package tightly. His Wolford stockings were down around his ankles. It was a true Kodak moment.

"What the hell are you spanking me with? It feels like sandpaper," yelled Jake, his back to me.

"A Ping-Pong racket."

"A what?" he said, twisting his head around as far as he could, being tied up and all.

I displayed the racket proudly. It did have a sandpaper-like quality to it. The back of it was fake wood paneling.

"Well, that's original," he said.

"Is it?"

"Yes!"

"With what do you normally get spanked?"

"I was expecting an instrument more along the lines of a paddle."

"Oh." *A paddle?* I associated paddles with something Lulu J. Lo might have framed on her wall. I shrugged and whacked him again.

"For God's sake, Pam, use the other side."

"Hey, who's in charge here? If it ain't you, it must be me." *How irritating, him telling me what to do.* He was such a contradiction.

"Yes, mistress. Tell me what a loser I am."

"You don't get to make the rules. Shut the fuck up!" *Whack.*

"But only a loser would let you spank him like this," he pleaded.

"No kidding. Your ass will be good and red by the time I'm done." I giggled. I had the upper body strength of a squirrel. My hits probably didn't even hurt.

"So I'm your personal doormat and you're just going to use me for the rest of my good-for-nothing life?"

"Something like that."

"This is so great. To be spanked by a beautiful mistress."

I was wearing a low-cut white blouse, skin-tight black pants, and a pair of high black boots. Holding the Ping-Pong racket firmly—tossing my mane of long black hair—it was a kicking image. Very X-Men. I yanked Jake's girly underwear higher up his ass. I felt ridiculous doing this, but I did it anyway.

"You look so hot," said Jake, our eyes clashing. With him stooped over, wrists tied to the couch, stockings down around his ankles, his good looks were seriously compromised. It was a true testament of my character that I didn't crack up laughing. "How would you feel about letting me be your personal slave from now on?"

"Downright ecstatic."

"No seriously. Does it make you feel empowered?"

More like ridiculous. "Totally empowered."

"Maybe I should make your phone calls and book your appointments."

Oh sure. I have so many engagements. Other than seeing you, I do virtually nothing. "That's a great idea. Start with booking me a facial. And a haircut. And one for Donna. She needs one. I'll let you pay for hers too!"

"I can see you'll have a hard time with this."

"I was born to take advantage of you." I aimed the racket and followed through, thinking the tennis lessons in the ninth grade finally paid off. "How does it feel to know your true calling?"

"Fantastic. I live to be your slave." I took a step backward, switched the racket to my left hand, and worked on my back-hand for a while. The exercise in concentration was invigorating. It was the equivalent to meditation! I realized excitedly, feeling very Zen. Apparently I was experiencing such enlightenment that I didn't hear Jake when he said, "OK, that's good. Yep, you can stop!"

He hopped back and forth to escape my range of motion. Still tied to the legs of the couch, he resembled a fly deciding on which piece of fruit to land. "I think your left arm is more powerful than your right," he said. "My ass kills!"

"Oh." I knelt down to untie him, and he pulled up his stockings in a quick fit of modesty.

"How about you scratch my face before we go out? This way I can feel like a sissy loser in public. Then we'll go see Donna and tell her what we've been up to."

I made a face and considered his next idea, feeling apprehensive. Playful spanking was one thing, but scratching seemed cruel. Moreover, with what would I scratch? Thanks to the stress of living in Oahu, my fingernails were tiny specks embedded in flesh.

"You could use the heel of your shoe," he said.

"With it on my foot? Balance is not my strong point, Jake."

"I could lay down, and you could stand above me and drag the edge of it along my face. Like you're stepping on me."

"This is not your first rodeo, is it?" Before I had time to think, Jake was down on the ground staring up at me expectantly. "All right," I said, relenting. "But it would not be wise for me to balance on one foot for this exercise." I sunk into his soft leather couch, slid off one of my boots, and dangled it over his face.

"You're not going to keep it on your foot?"

"I'll have better control if I hold it," I said, surprised at how knowledgeable I sounded. "Just where exactly do you want this sissy mark? Cheek? Forehead? Chin? Where?"

Jake studied the boot looming over him. I could see from his facial expression that he was deliberating over this very difficult decision. "My right cheek," he finally said. "Press the heel in and twist, as if you're putting out a cigarette."

"Yes sir." I saluted and turned the skinny, stiletto edge of the heel into his face, which felt rugged and worn beneath his chosen apparatus of destruction.

"You have to twist harder than that. I want it to leave a mark."

"Jesus, you're a pain," I said, twisting it harder. "This is going to cost you."

***

An hour later, we were downtown at Donna's awful new job. A loud Irish pub filled to capacity with Wall Street's choochy attitudes is always something of a roll-your-eyes experience.

It was weird seeing Donna again. We'd been so close before I left the city, but we'd hardly spoken in eight months. And upon arrival, she hugged Jake before she hugged me. She sat us in a dirty booth, safely away from the wannabees crowding the horseshoe bar. "Did you happen to notice Jake's face?" I asked her.

"Yeah, what the hell happened?"

I shrugged and Jake smiled smugly. "Can I have a Beck's?" he asked.

Donna glared at me. "Is this a secret?"

"That mark is a heel imprint. And no, it's no secret," I said.

Donna took her hand and tilted Jake's chin toward the light. "That's hard," she said.

"Excuse me?" said Jake.

"It would take a *hard* person to do that," she clarified, raising her eyebrows at me. I ignored her, considering she would have done the same thing for a roll of quarters. Donna studied us with mild confusion. I usually didn't play the role to this extent, but Jake had urged me to be more outspoken.

"You should see what I made him wear underneath his clothes." I reached up and undid the first two buttons of Jake's shirt to reveal the top of a black lace bustier. "It's nice and tight. Perfect for keeping his body streamlined during a spanking."

Donna gave me a poisonous look before turning on her heel to fetch his beer. When Jake got up to use the bathroom, she scurried back over to me. "It's becoming more sexual," she said.

"When wasn't it sexual?"

"Before your wedding, it wasn't like this."

"That was nine months ago. These shenanigans have to either escalate or vary. Otherwise he'll get bored. Common sense," I explained. "Eleven months ago you peed in a glass for him and watched him drink it on several occasions. What is the difference?"

Donna mulled this over. "It's still kind of weird."

"Don't be judgmental. It was *always* weird. We need to raise the stakes. Otherwise he'll move on." I hadn't thought about this too much, but as I spoke the words, they rang true.

Jake took his seat again. Out of the corner of my eye, I could see him scanning the table for his still-missing drink. Donna handed it to him.

"Pam, does your mother still live in Jersey?" he asked me.

"Yes, *why?*"

"I just had an idea."

"An idea that involves Sarah? In the bathroom, you had this idea?"

"What is it?" asked Donna.

"I could take Sarah shopping. She's a good-looking lady, and it would be ultra humiliating. I mean—not only do I have to keep Pam and her friends in new shoes—but also her mother!"

"Why did this occur to you in the bathroom?" I asked again.

"I don't know. I get crazy ideas all the time. Do you think she'd let me buy her a few pairs of shoes?"

"*Sarah Castle?*" I coughed. "I don't think she'd have a problem with it."

I changed the subject. "Donna, Jake is going to pay for us to get our hair cut. Won't that be fun?"

"I totally need a haircut!" She beamed. It was like pulling a light switch in Giant Stadium. "Can we do it tomorrow?"

"When you make the appointments, make sure you tell him your fashion slave will be footing the bill," said Jake, his eyes sparkling.

"I thought you were going to make all my appointments from now on, sissy?" I said.

"Oh yeah, just tell me who to call and when you'd like to go."

"Tomorrow." I turned to Donna. "May I get a drink too?"

***

Seeing Jake's number on my caller ID, I glanced around for Rob before picking up. "Hello?" The sun streaming through the window signified it was morning and I was still in bed.

"Did you know that scratch on my face got even more prominent?" exclaimed Jake. I lowered the volume on my phone.

"Scratch?" I asked, still half asleep.

"The *scratch* mark you made with your heel last night before we went to that disgusting, hellhole."

"Oh yeah." I yawned. "How humiliating for you."

"It's super humiliating!" he said excitedly. "Everyone at work is avoiding looking at my face!"

"Congrats, Jake." It was too early for me to be thrilled about his peculiarities.

"I'm going to tell everyone I bought a cat."

"There's an idea." I stared at the clock. "It's ten fourteen! Fuck, it's fucking early! Why are you calling me so early? Have you talked to Donna?"

"Yeah, she did a complete one eighty from her judgmental stance last night."

"Figures. What did she say?"

"She left a message for me saying she wanted to know how embarrassing it was for me to go into work with scratch marks all over my face."

"Interesting."

"Yeah, and she also suggested that she and you have a contest to see who can mark up my face worse."

"Oh, did she?" It was a no-brainer that she could smell money.

"She just needs to get used to an idea, and then it doesn't bother her as much. I think her initial reaction is always more of shock and judgment, and then she gradually becomes less narrow-minded."

"She likes money. Like I do."

"Hey, when you get a chance—maybe today after your haircut—I scheduled you both for two o' clock, by the way—could you shop around for a riding crop?"

I opened one eye. From Ping-Pong racket to whip in only a day! Yikes! A vision of me in front of Jake's enormous mirror wearing black leather and holding a whip was unsettling, albeit amusing. "Let me guess—so I can whip your sorry ass?"

"Lash marks last a couple days, so it would be a constant reminder of what a little sissy you're turning me into."

I sighed and considered this, one eye still shut. Spanking could be considered sporty. And whipping—in its purest form—was practically a sport, kind of a cross between fly-fishing and horseback riding. "Let me see what I can find."

"You could stop over after and we could test it out."

"Maybe." I could tell he liked to coerce me into doing things. "I'll think about it."

"I'd love to see you standing over me with a riding crop, whipping and insulting me."

"Fine, but it will cost you," I whispered.

"Honestly, when you were spanking me, I felt I could hand over everything to you. All my cash."

I opened both eyes, somewhat programmed to respond to certain words, *cash* being one of them. "Hey, Jake, one day let's hit each boutique along Madison Avenue." It has been said that people think clearer in the mornings, but I never believed it until that moment, hearing myself speak.

"Nice idea. When do you think you'll be over?"

"If the appointments are at two, between five and six."

"Do you like me paying for your general maintenance?"

"Jake, let me explain something to you. You should pay for *all* my beauty expenses. Think *Pretty Woman* with no perks." I heard the shower come to a dripping halt. "Bye."

Minutes later, Rob stormed into the bedroom and whipped his head around to look at the clock. He did this every morning and responded the same way *every* morning. "Ten-thirty already! Fuck, man. Where does the time go?" A towel wrapped around his waist, he was dripping from the neck down.

"Good morning."

"Have you seen my John Lennon shirt?" His eyes frantically searched the room. Piles of clothes hid most of my new shoes from view.

"The one with the holes in the armpits?"

"I only have *one* Lennon shirt, Pam, and I'm lucky to have it. It's hard to squeeze out more concerts after you're dead."

"Haven't seen it." *Did I use it to clean my boots?* "Where are you going in such a rush?"

"Work. Where do you think?"

"Oh."

"I know you're unfamiliar with the concept."

"You must wonder what I do all day, since you never ask," I said. "You must also wonder how I have no trouble paying my share of the bills."

"Yes, it's all very mysterious. This never-shrinking safe-deposit box from back in the day of shaking it." He stuck out his chest and shook it quickly.

*He is so stupid. I make money without really working—**and** I have a personal fashion slave. How many people can say that?*

***

I met Donna on the corner of Eighth Street and Sixth Avenue, and we walked over to my hairdresser's salon together. I noticed Donna was wearing a long skirt and ugly brown shoes, so I complimented her skirt.

"Thanks," she chirped. "I got it at Barneys when I returned a pairs of boots."

I raised my eyebrows. "Care of Jake? Which pair?"

"Just this impractical boot. Too high. You were in Hawaii."

"Why did you choose them in the first place?"

"It was the most expensive. A Chanel snakeskin pump. I knew that if I were to return them I could buy clothes for Ken and myself."

"Ken? Are you nuts? Why should he benefit? Why would you waste Jake's money on your boyfriend? I would never return a pair of designer shoes to buy Rob clothes."

"Yes, but Ken cares about fashion. He doesn't just wear old concert T-shirts." Walking along Christopher Street, we passed a storefront with male mannequins wearing leather thongs and

police caps. Then we passed another store with male mannequins wearing leather thongs and police caps.

"Are you sure Ken's not gay?" I asked. "Ken is kind of a gay
name, and he's really vain."

"Yes, I'm sure. You've asked me that before, you know."

"That's because I've wondered it before."

"He needs to dress well. He's trying to start up his own
company," she further explained.

"You don't have to justify your actions to me. But what if
Jake wants you to wear those shoes out one night?"

"They'll be getting professionally cleaned."

I laughed. "Are you going to give him the same excuse each
time he asks?"

"I don't know, Pam," she said wearily. "He'll probably never
ask."

"How much were they?"

"Thirteen hundred."

"He's gonna ask. Just wait."

"The only person he asks about is *you*. When you were
away, you were all he talked about." This statement came out of
nowhere, and I didn't believe her.

"Yeah right. He seemed plenty entertained by you and Lexi.
Between the shopping and the strip clubs, it sounded like you
two morons had all the fun while I hung out by myself—or on
better nights, with complete strangers."

"No, I'm telling you. He has a picture of you in his wallet.
He really adores you."

"Get out!" I stepped over what looked like a used condom
and somehow restrained myself from kicking it.

"I'm serious. I saw it."

"Where would he have gotten a picture of me?"

"I don't know. Aren't you plastered all over the Internet?"

"Very funny."

"I assumed you gave it to him."

"I don't go handing out pictures of myself."

"Well, he got it from somewhere."

"Interesting." A picture of me in his wallet? That was a sign of utter adoration. Girlfriend-boyfriend type shit. Initials in the sand. *How flattering!*

***

After my haircut, my hairdresser told me where I could purchase a whip. The woman working at Fantasy Extreme sold me a few other items, including a thin whip that folded up—I guessed for the submissive on the run? It was portable and small, and I liked it because it was cute.

I hailed a taxi and headed over to Jake's apartment. Five flights up, he stood before me clad in his maid's uniform and Gucci stilettos. This time I didn't bat an eyelash. Instead, I threw a pair of crystal handcuffs at him. "Put these on, you sucker." I kicked the door shut. Gone were the formalities.

"These are cool," he marveled. "But how do they attach?"

"With this chain." I removed a thick, shiny, silver chain from the shopping bag. It was so wide and thick that Rob could have used it to lock up his ten-speed bike. I attached it to the leg of the couch and admired the strength of the Velcro. This was quality stuff.

Since I was now a pro and short on time, I guided him in front of the mirror and mercifully yanked his stockings down before removing the hand-stitched leather whip from the bag. The handle felt different from the Ping-Pong racket, softer and more briny. "Look in the mirror when I do this. I want you to witness your punishment." I was feeling rather confident for a person who'd never used a whip before. *Any type of whip!*

"That thing is cool looking. And you all in black, you really look the part," said Jake.

"Wait until I put on my mask." Slipping it over my head, I surveyed my image in the mirror. I looked better than Zeta-Jones. Only something about my appearance was agitating me. I felt detached and a little out of control.

"You did good," said Jake.

"Shut up. Bend over." I applied the first few lashings to Jake's bare ass, trying not to giggle. "Does that hurt enough, or should I do it harder?"

"You can do it harder. And stand further back. It will give you more leverage."

"Silence. Your place in life is handcuffed to the bottom of your sofa."

"So I'm your personal loser to be solely exploited by you?"

"And my friends and family." I let the whip fly.

"Ow! Yeah, I can feel it now." He coughed. "Are you sure you've never done this before?"

"Yes. I would remember."

"Ow!"

This idiotic exercise carried on for the next half hour, but time flies when you're whipping someone. "I can't believe it's seven o'clock already!" I shouted, dropping the whip. "I have to go. Write me a check!"

"Are you going to uncuff me?" Jake asked nervously.

Minutes later, I was hailing a cab back to Astoria, a check for five hundred in my pocket and a nervous tick in my left eye. *I must not forget to pick up Rob's dry cleaning!*

***

I was excited about collecting my hourly fee to watch Jake clean. Hence, I took great pleasure in preparing for our night by first purchasing dog food for Jake, since he intended to eat it out of his own personal dog bowl (a gift from a prior mistress).

When I asked him which kind of dog food he preferred, he requested a can of Reward. Having compared it to other brands in the past, he insisted it was the nastiest-tasting on the market. I took his word for it. Combined with some dirt he had dug from a local dog park on the Lower East Side, he felt this would be an appropriate dinner to reflect his current pitiful status.

Who was I to argue? As long as I didn't have to eat his divine concoction, everything was technically going very well.

I waltzed into the Thriftway on Thirtieth Avenue in Astoria with strong-willed purpose and cornered a tiny Latino dude who was stocking cleaning supplies on a ladder. "Dog food? Which aisle?" I asked this question in a serious tone, one of a devoted pet lover.

Still holding his price gun, he turned to me. "Is your dog big or small?"

"He's quite big. Why?"

"Aisle three stocks cans more appropriate for small dogs and aisle ten stocks big bags of economy dry food for larger dogs."

I stared back at him with admiration. Not only was his English perfect, I'd obtained a detailed explanation from a kid on a ladder concerning a dog I didn't own. Normally kids just point weakly in a direction and you're on your own. I headed to aisle three, figuring it was a little too soon to start buying economy.

Staring at the yards of cans, suddenly the flavors became critical. Would Jake enjoy Alpo's beef tenderloin in gravy or prefer Pedigree's chunky beef, bacon, and cheese? I weighed my options, distracted by a picture of Mimi's stupid dog gazing up at me from a can of Classic Chef. This five-pound reflection of obnoxious white fur advertised filet mignon with bourbon sauce. Since that sounded a little bit too good to pass up, I grabbed it. Unable to locate Jake's favorite brand, I settled for a backup: Mighty Dog's classic chicken delight.

Heading to the register, I noticed a box of Milk-Bone dog biscuits in a variety of colors. Perfect for incentive and luring! And then I wondered if it all looked a little odd. If I actually had a dog, would I be buying only two small cans of food? They were only sixty-nine cents each. Just as I was thinking this, the older, wise-ass Greek woman behind the cash register lowered her bifocals and inquired, "Is that all you're having for dinner this evening?"

I smiled at her, blinking rapidly. "I'm on a diet."

"That's what they all say." It was like I was invisible. I felt she knew much more about life than I ever would.

**

Jake knocked on my door around 8 p.m. holding the fundamental ingredients for a swinging good time: maid's uniform, newly purchased bodysuit, a black thong—the essential undergarment—a size-Q pair of women's stockings, and his special dirt.

I welcomed him inside and poured the mixture for two Cosmopolitans into a large shaker while he changed. I was thrilled to be using Rob's and my new wedding martini glasses, even if I would be spitting, and eventually, pissing in the glass.

Jake returned to the kitchen, having rid himself of masculinity. (I was now rather accustomed to seeing him in the maid's uniform.) "Put on the Gucci heels," I urged. He dug into his Neiman Marcus shopping bag and slipped on the four-inch stilettos. "Oh, by the way, the checkout lady at the supermarket told me to enjoy my dinner."

"Did you purchase only one can of each kind?"

"Yeah."

"That sometimes makes them suspicious."

"Them as a species? Cashiers at the supermarket?"

"Yeah," Jake said, shrugging. "You have to buy a whole bunch of cans at once. It's not like they're expensive. And you don't look poor."

I spit in one of the Cosmopolitans and handed it to him. "Here."

"That was weak," he said.

"Like you're in any position to judge, standing there dressed like a maid. You douche."

"Touché," he said. "Why don't you pour this Cosmo on the kitchen floor and I will lick it all up with my tongue."

Removing the martini from Jake's grasp, I lowered myself to the ground and gently poured it out. The pink liquid swirled on the uneven surface and then gradually sunk into the cracks in the circular white tiles. It was actually quite pretty, like a bunch of strawberry cream Life Savers. "On your knees, motherfucker. This is your place in life."

"Where's your camera?" he asked.

"Right here." I stood up and grabbed it from its place above the stove.

"Is that where you normally keep it?"

"Yeah, every time I attempt to cook, I document it to prove to Rob. Hey! Did you *not* hear me? Get on all fours and lick that floor clean," I said with a raspy edge. I was striving for Kim Basinger, but supervising such shenanigans didn't necessarily mesh with sexy, suggestive tones.

"Yes, mistress," said Jake, dropping to the ground.

I attempted to get comfortable on any available dry tile while Jake lapped up dirty pink vodka. I sipped my Cosmo from the glass, wondering just how much money he was going to give me.

"I think the ground should be my glass for every drink. What do you think?"

"I make the rules around here. Not you."

"That's correct, mistress. I can only make suggestions. This is very cool. You make everything cool," he added.

"No shit."

"Why don't you step on me with those pointy Kate Spade heels we bought the other day?" suggested Jake.

"I would love that!" I rolled my eyes. "Kate Spade, right?" I tripped into the bedroom and grabbed the boots. Zipping them up, I laughed as I surveyed my bedroom. New shoes spilled from every corner.

I returned to the kitchen to find Jake stretched out horizontally over the sticky tiles. "It's important you walk on me between the countertop and the stove. This way you'll have something to hold onto," he instructed.

"Right." I reached for the box of Milk-Bones on the counter and tossed an orange treat at him. "Fetch, loser." He smiled and crawled over to the dog bone. I watched him and grimaced. "I hope I don't hurt you—or myself—doing this extraneous exercise."

"No, just go slow," he advised, back in place and crunching on the bone. "Step lightly at first. You can't stand on me for real in those shoes."

"Shall I keep one foot on the floor and just position my heel?"

"Slide the heel over my face. Just like the other night. This way it will leave another mark."

"Fine." I was a little annoyed he was telling me what to do again. It seemed I was following *his* directions and not the other way around.

"Yeah, it's Friday. I have the whole weekend for it to heal."

"You rock star." I angled my boot down alongside Jake's face and scratched. It was daunting to feel his tender skin underneath the thin spike, knowing I was disrupting the cells beneath the surface. It was like driving a car. In a split second, I could decide to drive off the road.

"That's great. Perfect. It feels amazing."

I kept this routine up for a few minutes until I started to see long white welts forming on the side of Jake's face. "Um, maybe you should look in the mirror and tell me if you want me to continue."

"Don't worry. My skin might look raised and bright for a while, but it will go down. The cool thing is it will leave a statement."

"I would hope." When Jake's face began to throb, we stopped. Sitting at my kitchen table, him feeling his face, I handed him a sheet of paper with a printed menu on it. "Ready to eat, bitch?"

Prix-Fix: Special High Rate for Sissy Losers.

Designated Cocktail: Girly drink with extra spit.

First Course: Classic Chef filet mignon with bourbon sauce served in a personalized dog bowl.

Second course: VIP Thoroughbred Mighty Dog chicken delight. Dished up in the same bowl. No cleaning in between courses.

Dessert: Dirt brownies, stepped on, feet essence.

"Hope you're hungry!" I quipped, rubbing my forehead.

Jake squinted and read it over. "This menu is great. Can I keep this?"

"You can frame it for all I care."

"Good idea."

I ripped off the top of Classic Chef's filet mignon with bourbon sauce and dumped it in the silver, ceramic bowl on which Jake's name was engraved, trying hard not to think about what I was doing. I was entitled to every last penny he was giving me. His filet mignon with bourbon sauce looked disgusting. Even Jake was horrified as he turned on his side to eat it like a dog would. "This is dog food? It's so gelatinous."

I was once again trying to get comfortable on the floor, now gripping a glass of wine—when I wasn't taking massive gulps from it.

Jake went for it despite its appearance. He made a face as he chewed, and we both almost threw up. "You know you really don't have to eat this," I pleaded. "Seriously, it's the intention that's admirable." I winced, unable to look anywhere other than the ceiling.

"That was the worst thing I've ever tasted. Where is the Mighty Dog? We know that's good."

"*You* know it's good. Not *we*," I said.

While Jake used the restroom, I jumped to my feet and washed my hands twice before eating a Kraft single. I stared at the picture of Rob stuck to the refrigerator. He was six years old, balancing on a skateboard, and he had hair past his shoulders. I unwrapped another piece of cheese, thinking it was time to put up a recent photo. Jake's return reminded me that he was still a priority in a financial sense and I better not screw it up. In truth, he was all I had, and I was positively lucky to have him.

"Chicken Delight in brown gravy," I announced, replacing the rejected dog food with a worthier supplement. "This should definitely be better. Do you need salt?"

"Yeah, I might."

"OK, let me get it."

Jake dug in while I counted dollars in my head, still gulping wine. "Is it OK?" I asked after some serious time had elapsed.

"Miraculous compared to that other shit."

"Good. I'm glad you're enjoying it."

"Thank you. I feel honored to eat like a dog in your presence. I'm truly your slave.

***

An hour later, Jake and I sat quietly at my kitchen table appearing once again like two responsible adults enjoying a cocktail together. Jake had changed out of his maid's uniform and was looking refined in black jeans and an expensive shirt. We were discussing politics when Rob burst in the door.

"Hey, what's going on, guys? I soooooooo have to piss," he yelled, flying by us. This behavior was typical, as Rob always had to piss on arrival. Drinking as many beers as he did during the car ride home guaranteed his sprint to the bathroom. I winked at Jake, and we continued to discuss George Bush in detail.

Rob returned to the kitchen and tripped over the salt. "Pam, why the fuck is the salt on the floor?"

Fuck. "I hate to tell you this, Rob, but I think we may have ghosts. This is an old building."

Rob sighed but thankfully dropped the subject when he noticed his three hundred–dollar prize steak knife in the sink. "Pam, what the fuck? I told you this knife is killer sharp. It should only be used for meat and poultry."

"But why?"

"That's what it should be used for."

"So I have to use a dull knife to cut a lemon?"

"Yes. It's also safer for you. Hey! There is lemon everywhere! Sticky lemons attract bugs," warned Rob. I had just fed a man dog food and he was worried about the odd ant making its way up to the fourth floor. "Where is the tinfoil? And what have I told you about this towel? Keep it on the stove rack. It doesn't belong on the floor."

The towel actually fell to the floor when I was scratching Jake's face, but whatever. The All-Clad towels—which came *free* when I repurchased the seven hundred–dollar missing pots— were his little *darlings*. It was weird. Some guys had a dog or a plant; Rob cherished two little hand towels.

"Seriously, Pam, what did you do with the tinfoil?"

"I told you my theory about the ghosts."

***

The following Saturday, we greeted Sarah Castle in the shoe department of Bergdorf Goodman. My mother appeared as sharp as ever in a black turtleneck, a long black skirt, and square black boots, which I was dying to replace.

"Oh, Pam, this is positively the most gorgeous store I have ever stepped foot in!" She picked up a Chanel sling-back and twirled it in her hand. "Gorgeous," she said airily, glancing at the price tag on the bottom. "Oh my God." She set it back down again.

"Mom, please. Money is only paper," I whispered in her ear, kissing her on the cheek as I scanned the room.

"Sarah, nice to see you again." Jake casually extended his hand. His natural mannerisms always floored me, as the contrast between his counterparts was beyond extreme.

"Oh Jake, you mustn't buy any shoes for me. I'm happy just to have your advice," cooed my mother. I knew she didn't mean it, but I still gave her a look. "Pam tells me you're a fashion expert."

He ignored the compliment. "I think we should buy you at least two pairs of shoes: a pair of boots for the winter season and a pair of heels for dressier occasions. Judging from the size of your feet, I think Manolo Blaniks would look nice on you." He stared down at my mother's dainty feet disguised in an unfortunate—yet accurate—representation of South Jersey.

"OK," said my mother excitedly, trashing the false diplomacy.

"What size are you? Six and a half?" guessed Jake.

"Yes! How did you know?" gushed my mother. I couldn't tell if she was genuinely impressed or had done this before.

Jake leaned into me. "I only met your mother once, but I forgot how adorable she is. Let's replace those boots first thing."

"Let's," I agreed, watching Sarah wander off into what I like to call "shoppers' trance." Similar to sleepwalking, unknown forces guide the body in random directions. The only difference is the cognitive state: wide-awake and in great financial danger as opposed to deep asleep in your own kitchen microwaving leftover food.

"When you get a salesgirl's attention, make sure she knows to drop off the shoes and get away. I'll help Sarah with the fitting," said Jake.

Jake picked out some styles, and the Hungarian salesgirl began piling up boxes beside them. Jake stared longingly at my mother's stocking-clad feet until I finally said, "Jake, get down on your knees!"

Upstairs in designer women's clothes was where my mother really mastered the craft. "Jake, get me this in another size!" she ordered repeatedly, tossing various garments over the dressing room door.

"Which size, Sarah?"

"Four." "Six." "Two." "I don't know my exact size!" Every item flung at him was preceded by an exact direction, and Jake took off in search of it. I stayed put in the dressing room. "Look, I'm just ordering him around. Where are my manners?" said my mother.

"Don't worry, he likes that. You're making his day," I said, yawning.

"He's such a sweet man."

"No shit."

"How's Robert, by the way?" I helped her zip up a Valentino silk skirt.

"No clue."

"That's what I figured. How does this look?"

The highlight of the evening for Jake was giving my mother a foot massage in our regular booth at Houston's. "I don't know how you can stand my feet in your face, but it feels wonderful," said my mother, having no idea how her words placated him.

***

Two days later, my female cousins, seventeen and fourteen, sent pairs of their oldest and most disgusting sneakers to Jake's home in exchange for Louis Vuitton purses. I happened to be there when he received the unique package.

"Awesome!" roared Jake, ripping through the brown paper and tape in seconds. "I can't believe that I'm going to let these kids take advantage of me like this. I think they're the youngest girls I've ever let use me! And these shoes are filthy! Look at them!"

I cringed and forced a smile. "Yes, they are," I concurred.

"I mean, seriously, these are almost as bad as some of *your* sneakers."

"It must run in the family." Jake laughed at my wry atti-tude, but I could tell he was impressed.

"It's pretty humiliating that it's branched from your friends to your mother to your cousins. Wouldn't you say?"

"It's too bad I don't have a bigger dynasty. What should we do tonight?"

"Do you want to go look at cages at Petco?"

"Did that just occur to you?"

"No. I was in Petco checking out the dog collars, and I noticed these large cages."

"Like how big? You're larger than an average dog, you know." *He wants to be locked in a cage.* I was to the point where nothing surprised me and no idea was too farfetched.

"It would be the ultimate in humiliating. You and your friends off at a nice place, enjoying yourselves on my tab, while I sit trapped in a cage!"

"How could you think of that as fun? There's nothing *to do* in a cage."

"No, it would be cool. And there is plenty to do."

"OK, I won't ask, but what if you needed to get out and you couldn't? What if your building caught on fire?"

"I've lived here seventeen years. It's not going to catch fire the one day I decide to spend in a cage."

"You don't know that for sure."

"Come on, it's not as if I'm *actually* a dog or a cat. If there was ever an emergency, I could just reach around and unlock it."

"Fine. But only if we can go to my favorite Italian restau-rant afterward."

"Yes."

"Deal."

***

I didn't know a pet store could be so much fun. When you have a man for a pet, the experience must be heightened.

Jake led me to the back of Petco and pointed to the cages. I had to admit, they had a nice selection. Since I was in charge of the negotiations with a female member of the staff, I scanned the massive store, finally luring my victim away from the cash register. She was small with short, punk, purple hair and an impish face. I smiled at her and hoped she was as crazy as she appeared. "What's your name?" I asked.

"Cathy."

I peered at her. "You don't look like a Cathy."

"Call me something else then." She registered no emotion.

"Would Raven be OK? It needs to be edgier."

"Raven is fine," she said. Jake hung ten feet away to effectively eavesdrop.

"At any rate, we need some serious advice regarding these cages," I continued, nodding in Jake's direction to indicate we were together in this obscure adventure. "Which is the best? Do they fold up?"

"Well, the chrome cages look cooler than the black, but they both fold up equally well. And as you can see, the sizes range," said Raven. "How big is your dog?"

I pointed to Jake. "If a dog could stand up, roughly his size."

"I see. Then you might want to go with the six-foot by four-foot cage. It's really our largest and most popular."

"Raven, can I level with you?"

"I'm listening." She pointed to her Petco nametag.

"The cage is for him. It's unusual, but I appreciate your help."

Raven shrugged. "I gathered that."

"I didn't know this was a common occurrence." *When did everyone get so wise?* Knowing that Jake was listening with rapt attention, I spoke up. "I'd rather he not have too much legroom. Just enough space for his dog bowl and water." I was starving, and my mind kept jumping to the best pasta in the city. I decided that I would eat at Isle of Capri whenever Jake wanted to spend quality time in his cage.

"I think we should still consider the larger size," said Raven.

"I want him to be uncomfortable for hours." I snapped my fingers. "Jake, get over here." He slid over in three large side-steps, and a smile slipped through Raven's thin purple mouth. "This is the size I'm putting you in," I told Jake, pointing to the smaller cage.

"Do they fold up?" Jake asked. (This feature was our top priority.)

"Yes, any cage here could slide under a bed or be shoved to the back of a closet."

"OK, we'll take the black one," said Jake.

I cleared my throat. "Ahem, *I* decide which cage you get." I nodded at Raven. "We'll take the black one."

We walked outside, holding the huge cardboard box between us. Barely. We were both bent over like elderly people and shuffling along at the rate of turtles. The stupid cage was heavy, and Jake's fifth-floor walk-up was not cool. As we burst in the door, we both dropped it on the floor as if we'd been carrying a vat of snakes across the Sahara. I went straight to the refrigerator and grabbed the bottle of Kettle One from the freezer, pouring two gigantic shots into coffee cups.

"To another fine purchase," I said, handing Jake a mug. Clinking porcelain, we slugged it down. "One more."

"Grab two beers as well. It could use a chaser."

The both of us not being particularly handy, it took us over an hour to assemble the cage. I made him jump in and out for a while, timing how fast he could unlock it from the inside.

After dinner we went to the Coral Room on the West Side. The club advertised mermaids who swam around in a big tank behind the bar. We watched a fair-skinned woman in a sleek blue bikini swim gracefully among exotic fish and coral. Her long brown hair swirled around her as she performed her mermaid

sequence. The tank hardly allowed for state-of-the-art synchro-
nized swimming, but she appeared elegant and managed not to
bang into any of the decorative reefs. *I wonder how much they get
paid to float around?* Practical job ideas never occurred to me.

"I could totally do this," I said.

"Can you swim?"

"Of course. But swimming is barely required for this job.
It's like asking me if I can bathe."

"With your hair and body, I think you'd look great."

Great, he likes the idea. But why do I care?

"God, can you imagine me in a cage while you're in a tank?"

"Yes," I said, glancing slyly around the room, aware that I
was with the best-looking man there and women were noticing.
I wondered if people assumed we were together. If not for Rob,
would I have gone for someone like Jake?

December 2003

Jake and I sat together at a divine mahogany table in the candlelit environment of the Tapa's Room. I was still happily unemployed, so Jake and I spent most evenings together. It wasn't purposeful; we just fell into a pattern. He was giving me money, and I was accepting it with glee. My respect for Jake was mounting, and so was my fascination with a man who seemed unafraid of the most disgusting tasks. In short, as his requests became more humiliating and pathetic, my admiration grew.

Despite my debt—which I was making good headway on reducing—I was still technically financially afloat, so life was good. I was back on familiar turf and surrounded by those who made me laugh as opposed to cry. In addition, Rob was immersed in his six-day work schedule, which meant he no longer had time to read a book a day, much less keep track of me.

Jake and I were eating coconut shrimp and downing tropical martinis when he said, "Pam, I've known you for over a year now, right? Almost a year and a half?"

"Yep," I answered, crunching on a shrimp tail.

"And I've purchased a few things for you during that time, no?"

Yeah, duh, our relationship is based on it. "Yes. You've been very generous."

"Well, I was just contemplating the idea of you destroying something I've given you. You'd make me watch."

"Like destroy? As in wreck? Ruin?" I narrowed my eyes.

"Yes. You could choose an outfit or a pair of shoes, damage it beyond repair, and then tell me I have to replace it with something more current and fashionable."

I pursed my lips. "I'm missing the overall point."

"It would be utmost embarrassing. As if the money I spent on you really meant nothing."

I considered this. Everything Jake had ever bought me I cherished. Everything else I owned was theoretically garbage. "Did you have anything in mind?"

"It should be up to you. You could come over wearing something that's no longer in style and slash it to pieces. I'd feel like such an idiot!"

"But you're already an idiot for buying everything for me in the first place," I said, still a little confused. I wasn't keen on ruining something I loved just to make Jake feel stupider.

"I know, but this would reinforce the concept. You could light fire to it and tell me what a total doormat I am."

"Light fire to it? Are you serious?" I gulped, recalling Sharon Stone's rampage in *Casino*. Her self-constructed bonfire had been an impressive display, but they were all Robert De Niro's belongings—not hers.

"I'm speaking figuratively. God knows I don't trust *you* with a blowtorch. But yes, you'd demolish it in front of me. And of course, I would purchase you something more current and hip in exchange."

I smiled tightly. Smugly. This was an opportunity of a lifetime. Yet another one, falling in my lap. "I suppose I could give this some thought." An image slammed to the forefront of my mind. *Dior.* Christian Dior, who had previously catered to the rich, geriatric population after Liz Claiborne had run out of ideas, had transformed into the hottest, cutting-edge designer

with a hard-core theme of powerfully punk and expensive acces-
sories. But what to give up?

"Is there something you wouldn't mind parting with just to
further humiliate me?"

"There's got to be something I don't wear as much." I visu-
alized my rows of hangers. "Yes, the rehearsal dinner dress!"

"That dress was twenty-four hundred dollars," said Jake.

"I know, but it was itchy."

"OK. We should take advantage of the fact that I spent so
much money on it. To see you destroy it would totally put me
in my place."

I nodded and watched Jake toy with his blue martini, focusing on his strong hands. *I must have the red Dior handbag and
matching wallet!* I relayed his new orders, and he readily agreed.
"Can we do this tomorrow? First thing?" I asked. "Christian
Dior opens at eleven."

"First you have to destroy the dress in an elaborate cere-
mony to emphasize my pathetic life."

"Oh yeah." My mind was already jumping ahead.

"Tomorrow night, you can do it. I'll go to Dior over the
weekend and buy you the purse."

"And matching wallet!" I chirped. I stuffed a miniature
meatball into my mouth, disbelieving how life often fell right
into place.

***

The next evening, I showed up at Jake's building before him. I
tried my best to appear poised and classy, wearing the rehearsal
dinner outfit I so hated. In addition to its itchiness, it was
tighter on me than it had been a year ago. Was I getting fat?
I did eat out every night—not to mention—swill liquor in
alarming quantities.

I pulled a Nat Sherman mint cigarette from my silver case.
I'd even upgraded my cigarettes, replacing Marlboro Lights

with sophisticated natural tobacco. I lit the narrow cigarette and continued to glance around.

When Jake reached his doorstep and discovered me there, he took a step back, almost colliding with the fire hydrant. "OK, this is not allowed," he said seriously.

"What? Smoking in front of your building?"

"No, for a woman to look so crazy beautiful on my doorstep. It's got to stop."

I extinguished the cigarette with my boot. "And what are the repercussions, exactly?"

He pointed to his front door. "Get upstairs." Still dressed in his business attire, he looked suave. A change of pace, considering I was now used to him dressed up like a maid. I had almost forgotten how good he looked in regular clothes. He resembled a responsible man who took care of his family and wore sexy aftershave on the off chance his secretary might decide to jump his bones in the middle of the afternoon. I was aware of this, but it wasn't a priority. Christian Dior was my main concern.

Inside the apartment, Jake poured us wine, and I sat contemplating how I'd look without the dress on. I knew I looked decent in clothes, but clothes hid the body and I wasn't twenty-one and in stripper shape anymore. Nor was I tanned, tucked, or toned.

"What's up?" asked Jake.

"Nothing." I rarely felt shy about my body, but the damn dress was tight!

"You sure?"

"I'm about to rip a couple grand to shreds. Not for nothing, it takes a little mental preparation. Do you mind?"

"Did you bring an extra set of clothes in case we want to go out afterward?" he asked.

I blinked. "That would have been smart."

"I'll take that as a no."

"It's a big no."

"That's OK. We'll order in."

"So how are we going to do this?" I asked.

"I don't know. I figured you'd just start insulting me, strip off the dress, and every time you cut a piece, abuse me some more. I'll put on some music," he said excitedly, jumping up. "What do you like to listen to?"

"Anything except jazz. Mostly female vocalists. Bands like the Indigo Girls and the Sundays." I sounded very bohemian, the liberal opposite of my personality. "I don't know—anything really. I like rock and metal too."

"Tom Petty OK?"

"Sure. Where do you keep your scissors?"

"Kitchen drawer. Left of the sink."

I glanced around his tidy kitchen. It was compact but very clean. "How often do *you* hire a maid?" I asked.

"Once a week."

"Is that standard for all bachelors?"

"I don't know. But speaking of which, should I change into the maid's uniform?"

I let out a long, slow breath. I really liked how he looked in the business suit, but I was supposed to be humiliating him, so technically I should make him change. *But I really don't want him to.*

"I like this newfound quietness," said Jake.

"Are you making fun of me? I'm *thinking*. Jesus."

"Not at all. It's cool. You're at a loss for words."

"Just because I'm wielding a gigantic pair of scissors, about to destroy the most expensive dress I've ever owned, does not mean that I'm at a loss for words." Tom Petty's "American Girl" blared from Jake's sound system.

"If you say so."

"You look really good in business attire," I said with hostility.

"OK, so I won't change."

"Fine. Sit the fuck down," I said.

Instead he dimmed the lights.

"Why did you just dim the lights?" I asked.

"Because it's too bright in here."

I looked at him suspiciously and uttered a small guffaw. Everyone knew that lowering the lights was a romantic notion. If he thought this was going to be a tender interlude, he was crazier than I originally figured.

He finally took a seat on the brown leather couch, so I walked over and stood in front of him. Sucking in my stomach, I touched my throat, reaching for the button-up collar. The lapel itself consisted of thick gray wool that fell in attractive folds around my neck. I had purposely chosen a dress that disguised my neck, knowing this would be the first section the plastic surgeon would eventually target. I stared Jake straight in the eye as I did this, fumbling with the seven, small mother-of-pearl snaps running from the top down. "I figure this collar alone cost you three hundred dollars—maybe five," I said throatily.

"God, this is truly humiliating," muttered Jake, still completely poised.

I licked my lips and lowered the floppy material down over my collarbone. I grabbed it and pulled hard, attempting to rip it off in one shot. Nothing happened. I would have had better luck tearing my grandmother's drapes leftover from the war.

"Nice try," said Jake.

"Don't speak." Grabbing the scissors off the coffee table, I snipped down the length of the collar. I cut slowly and methodically, more because I was holding the scissors so close to my neck than for seductive reasons. As the collar broke away, I held the coarse cloth in my hands and waved it in front of Jake's somewhat panicked face. "Look how much I care about what you buy me, you little sissy. I'm turning your hundred-dollar bills into rags right before your very own eyes."

"Tell me how pathetic I am," begged Jake. His breathing ran shallow, and I could literally see him drowning in the role he had designed for himself.

"Your money is as useless as you are. How did you expect me to wear last year's Alexander McQueen? What were you thinking?"

"I wasn't. I have no original thoughts anymore. I'm just a slave to you." His eyes pleaded with mine.

"That's right, but just in case you harbor any doubts, I'm going to prove it." Proceeding to cut the wool into thin strips, I let each narrow piece flutter to the floor. As I cut, I watched his expression change. He was drifting to a deeper place. I reached for the zipper that ran down the left side of me and pulled it down halfway, revealing my black lace bra.

Jake swallowed.

"A pathetic wimp like you must have one helluva hard-on, watching the money you work so hard for be destroyed." My words surprised both of us; they seemed to topple from my mouth with no safety net to catch them. His mouth dropped open. I kicked the right side of his chin. I needed to break the accidental spell I'd put him under.

"What did you say?" asked Jake, still dazed.

"Are you hard, asshole?"

He smiled a lazy smile and drank the rest of his wine in one long swig. Setting down the empty glass, he said, "It should be obvious."

"Answer the fucking question!"

"Yes, I'm hard as a rock."

I could feel his eyes on my chest, and I shifted my stance. I was reluctant to admit I liked his intensity or lack thereof. Something out of place fluttered in my stomach. Something large, perhaps a liver or kidney.

I decided to put the scissors to use. The material remained coarse as I cut into the sleeve from the base of my left shoulder. "Here goes the first four hundred–dollar sleeve. Touch yourself, loser." *I am out of control.* Jake simply chuckled. "I'm serious! But keep your pants on! Keep those fucking pants on, cocksucker! I don't want to see your small, pathetic dick right now—or ever. You ridiculous waste of life!"

"Ha! You're getting really good at this."

"Thank you."

"Are you having fun?"

"I'm not here to have fun. I'm here to take your money and abuse you," I said, avoiding the question. I didn't know if I was having fun or not.

What followed was an awkward silence, which neither one of us made any effort to cover up. I was still standing there, dress halfway down, expensive, lacy bra now in full view. One sleeve and neck disposed of. Mr. Petty's lyrics wailed from Jake's surround sound.

It's all right if you love him.
It's all right if you don't.

I grabbed the remaining sleeve and began hacking away at it. "You're reckless," Jake said.

"You're a fool, and I'm cutting up your money. Do you feel like a useless commodity yet?"

"I am useless. A victim to the female race."

"No, a victim to *me*! And you haven't seen anything yet." Getting carried away, I unzipped the remainder of the dress and stepped out of it, revealing my black lace underwear. "I was destined to destroy this dress all along. How could you think I would wear it a year later? You sad fool." I began butchering what remained. Jake watched in amusement as threads and seams flew in all directions. His ski loft apartment resembled the mice's sewing room in Cinderella.

"I'm sorry that I had such ludicrous expectations." He smiled, his eyes suddenly fixated on my crotch. I felt heat in my face, but it wasn't entirely unpleasant.

"You should be," I muttered.

As the music pierced the air, I stood straight and still before him, rocking slightly on my black Gucci pumps. "What are you thinking right now?" I asked.

His eyes drifted upward from my black lace underwear before landing squarely on my face. "I'm thinking of a pair of shoes I want to buy you. They would look great with what you have on right now."

"Do you ever think of anything besides feet?"

"Rarely."

"Describe the shoes."

"*Goddess*. That's how they're labeled. Hundreds of black strings hold the heel to the foot. It's an architectural drawbridge in the form of a shoe."

I blinked. "They sound like a bitch to get on and off."

"I'll show you on the website. I can't believe I want to buy you more stuff after you've just destroyed the most exquisite dress ever made."

"What else is going through that crazy mind of yours?" *And what is it, exactly, that I want to hear?*

"How long your legs look."

"I'm five foot two, Jake."

"No, your body is perfect."

I just smirked, feeling prickly inside. Then I dropped to the floor and began inspecting pieces of scattered material. "Look! Your hard-earned money is unrecognizable!" I said, throwing a bunch of gray ribbons into the air. The threads of material fluttered, suspended on invisible tension.

"This is incredible."

And then, like the clap of a hand from a hypnotist, Jake became alert again. "Let me show you a picture of the shoes," he said, jumping up.

"Huh?"

"The shoes that will turn you into a true goddess."

***

Sometimes you wake up in the morning and think, *This is just going to be another day.* A repeat of yesterday and the day before that. And usually the day unfolds just as you originally expected, until you're trapped in a moment unlike anything you've ever experienced. There's a revived freshness in the air, your lungs swell, and your senses are positively heightened. You are filled with expectation, and its resonance is overpowering.

When I started to spend every available minute with Jake, I was drifting into a fresh new territory of expectation. I might have told myself the allure had to do with the money or the attention, but that is a prime example of the excuses we tell ourselves rather than dealing with the reality.

I had always been a creature governed by dreams, a mere puppet to my greater subconscious. So when I awoke from the dream that morning, I embraced it. In my glorious sleep, I lay on a tan suede couch, care of a penthouse suite in Trump Tower. The surroundings were linear: crisp, clean lines, vivid colors exploding on carefully placed white canvases. Oriental rugs lined the walls. Mirrors ruled the ceiling, and a thick white shag carpet silently begged for a bottle of Château Lafite-Rothschild to taint its holy perfection.

To my right, a slender, rectangular glass table teetered unsteadily. Rolled dollar bills and lines of cocaine lay evenly spaced out, a discreet addict looming close by. An empty bottle of Cristal lay on its side, gently rolling back and forth to the sound vibrations of Portishead. The music sunk in and out from the dark abyss of the stereo.

To my left, buckets filled with bottles of chilled Goose vodka and fresh lime melted in the sexual heat of the apartment. It was obviously a gathering of magnificent wealth and privilege; one of those swinger parties where high-end escorts received huge amounts of money to accompany rich—and no doubt twisted—businessman. Invariably, the evening would result in an assortment of sordid and illegal activities.

In my dream all the women were tall, slim, refined, and mostly of European decent, although I did notice an unusual-looking Oriental woman lying naked and alone on the flawless white rug. Her large round breasts startled me, obviously fake and atypical for an Asian woman. In another corner of the room, a young redhead with porcelain skin was giving head to a dude who was the spitting image of Rick Springfield in his heyday. The man held a condom over his huge cock as she slid her mouth up and down expertly. I watched them in awe for a bit but was distracted by cryptic moaning coming from the other side of the room. There, another good-looking couple was fucking in slow motion, producing sounds that rivaled any porn video.

I suppose all the nudity and sex inspired me to look down and see how I was dressed for this stellar occasion. I was semi-covered with a murky charcoal silk bra and thong. Black lace stockings hugged my inner thighs, and my legs appeared shockingly thinner, pleasing me immensely. Following my eyeline past my legs sat Jake. His position on the couch was such that he seemed to be sitting underneath me as he caressed my stocking feet. I watched him gaze lovingly at my ankles as he massaged deeply. My breath caught in my throat, as if anticipating a shift in the spectrum. Jake's hand traveled from the arch of my foot and up my leg, slowly tracing the seam of my thigh-high until it rested on the bare patch of skin just below my triangle of silk. His touch on my skin sent tingles through my body. He rested his hand there and looked up at me, expectant. I nodded slowly. In that flash of a second, I wanted his hand resting there forever. My heart began to race, and all thoughts tumbled into one lascivious stare.

The pulsing in my groin woke me up, a dream-induced pleasant sensation of near orgasm. I reached down and touched myself, feeling the need to confirm my wetness. I was soaked. I opened one eye wide and got my bearings. Cleared my throat. Noticed Rob sleeping beside me in a Grateful Dead T-shirt with his mouth wide open. Remembered who I was and how I got there. And later that morning when I awoke again to start my day, I felt that it might be different from the day before; that it held the promise of something unusual, something exciting

and powerful and compelling. Something I instinctively knew
I'd been waiting for.

***

I was walking to the gym when Jake called me on my cell.

"What's up?" he said. "Are we still on for tonight?" We had
tentative plans that revolved around another trip to Petco and
the dog cage.

"Yeah, totally." A charge ran through my body. I cringed,
recalling my dream. *Come on, Pam, the guy licked your kitchen floor
clean. Don't get any crazy ideas,* I told myself, walking faster.

"I had a brainstorm," he said.

"Another one?" I quipped.

"Tell me if it sounds crazy, but it just came to me. I thought
I'd run it by you."

"Go for it."

"You know how you used to dance?"

"Yes."

"And sometimes you tell me how you miss it."

"Yes."

"I was thinking that maybe you could dance for me, but
make it more of an exercise in humiliation. That's all that stripping business is anyway, women in control making men hand
over their money. I have this old business suit and I thought
perhaps you could rip it to shreds and smack me around a bit.
As you danced, I could keep feeding you twenty-dollar bills."

"I love that idea." I really did. It was brilliant.

"Do you really? Would you feel comfortable? I mean, you
wouldn't have to strip or anything, you could just dance."

"I think that would be wicked fun," I said, giving the dark-
ness around me a confused glance. Why did this feel like an
admission?

"OK, so eight o'clock? My place."

"Sure." Glancing at my watch, I saw I had time to pull an outfit together. The done-to-death schoolgirl image popped to mind. Maybe I could just put a spin on it?

"Oh, and bring a pair of scissors. I think we broke the last pair destroying the dress. Won't this be totally demeaning?" His voice vibrated with pent-up excitement.

"Yes," I croaked. *Probably for the both of us!*

***

Later in Jake's bathroom, I changed into a short black skirt and a white button-down shirt and braided my hair into two ponytails. My white knee socks looked terribly cute, but I replaced them with black thigh highs, the subconscious dream seeping into the realm of my conscious. I stared at myself in Jake's spotlessly clean mirror and watched the blacks of my pupils engulf the green of my irises. I felt like I was on speed, racing to an inevitable conclusion. I slipped on Gucci stilettos, tucked in my shirt, and returned to the living room before I could chicken out.

True to his word, he was holding a bunch of bills, dressed in what I assumed was the old business suit—although it appeared brand new. He laughed haughtily at the sight of my innocent getup. "Goldilocks meet Janet Jameson," he said, whistling. Trying not to break down in hysterics myself, I ignored him and waltzed my scantily clad ass over to the stereo, my heart thumping to the beat of machine guns. Slipping a Dido mix into the CD player, I waited until I heard a semblance of sound and then approached him with my legs shaking.

"You look hot!" he said.

"I look like I'm ten, but whatever."

I placed my hands on his shoulders so I wouldn't have time to think. It had been a while since I'd done this, but then again, I sensed I would never forget how. Keeping my eyes peeled on his watery brown ones, I lifted my right leg and slid it down his crotch. He was already hard. From that minute on, it was as if I never quit dancing—and apparently, I hadn't. My body took on a natural languid movement, and I moved my lips close to his ear. "Do you think you deserve a table dance, you pathetic loser? Because I have other plans for you."

He just watched me, expressionless. I climbed on top of him and dug my heels into his thighs. "Ah, shit!" he yelped. "That hurt."

"I know. It's supposed to. Little wimps like you enjoy pain," I reminded him, sliding my body down his and pressing the buttons of my shirt into his face. Then I knelt down on the floor and rammed my head into his balls.

"Ah, Jesus!"

I glided my fingers up the side of his tailored plaid shirt and ripped the pocket off in a single swift tug. "Eat this!" I stuffed the piece of flimsy fabric into his mouth and reached for the space of flesh the pocket left exposed. Jakes eyes widened as I tore the shirt all the way down to his waist. "You're pathetic."

I stood up and turned my back to him. Sitting in his lap, I leaned my head into the nape of his neck, sliding my ass up and down over his cock with gentle precision. My technique was still top ranking. My lips a mere centimeter from his neck, I brought my heels up to the sofa, balancing myself in a perfect arch. Jake reached for my feet, and I exhaled in his ear, feeling perfect. Untouchable. On top of my game.

I pulled away and slithered back down to the ground. Jake remained mesmerized as I ripped a pocket off his pants, revealing a gaping black hole. "Sissy!" I cried. "What kind of wimpy businessman wears stockings under his suit?" Dido's voice was suddenly louder, her lyrics almost too prophetic.

Then I deserve nothing more than I get
'cause nothing I have is truly mine.

"Gosh, this is like my theme song. 'Nothing I have is truly mine,'" said Jake.

"Got that right." I unknotted his tie. Then I seized it and whipped it across his face while he sat there, stunned. To counteract my actions, I caressed the small red mark the tie had left in its wake. Push/pull. Love/hate. I reached for the scissors and sliced the tie in half. Paisley silk rolled down his body.

"I guess I won't be wearing that again," said Jake.

The corners of my mouth flickered in the form of a smile, but I tried to remain serious, straddling him instead. "You don't deserve such a good lap dance. That's why losers like you have to pay."

"I deserve nothing other than to have my suit destroyed and my body tortured."

"You're such a pussy," I hissed. Slinging one leg around his neck, I thrust my pelvis region into his face. His eyes stayed glued to my feet. The arch of my ankle. The Gucci emblem that had cost him six fifty.

Trying another approach to get Jake to notice something other than my feet, I again climbed onto his lap and wrapped both my legs around his neck so he had no choice but to stare into my panties, which I'd kept simple for the occasion: Hanes briefs, a vibrating, pounding, universal play on young and innocent. As if I were either. Jake lifted his eyes and looked quizzically at me. Like he was considering something. Something he hadn't considered before. I wondered then if he felt that today was a different day, too—a day that carried distinctive promises and would affect each day forward. Expectation. My eyes burned his and silently asked these questions, unaware of the obvious reciprocation. Dido's "Here with Me" blared from his stereo.

I am what I am. I'll do what I want, but I can't hide ...

If only every interaction could be so beautifully simple, I thought, expressed solely by music and actions alone, without words to confuse and disarm. I pressed the soles of my shoes into Jake's face, slowly retracting toward the floor. My body language symbolized my initial denial, thoughts I didn't yet want to entertain.

I was hot. Temperature wise. I could feel beads of sweat under my eyes and moisture on my back. I wasn't used to dancing, much less in clothes. I stood up again and faced him before reaching for the top button of my blouse. Jake sucked in his breath and slowly exhaled as I undid each button, revealing the matching white cotton bra.

Once I began to undress, I couldn't stop. I unbuckled my skirt, letting it fall. There was nothing dramatic about my movements. If anything, I must have seemed ridiculously sure of myself. Still watching Jake, I kicked off my shoes and peeled off the stockings. For whatever reason, I had removed all traces of black, an attempt at purifying a polluted situation.

I leaned into Jake and unhooked my bra so my breasts fell close to his lips. It stunned me that I could be forever unabashed in an act that embarrassed most. He studied me as I danced around topless, occasionally crushing my tits into his face. Finally, he reached his left hand up and touched me carefully, like a young girl reaches for a glass doll. He ran his hand lightly along the side of my breast, down my waist and over my hips, resting on my thigh, and I forgot to keep calling him names. I forgot to keep ripping at his clothes. I forgot everything and let him touch me. I must have wanted him to. I must have willed him to.

At some point, he mechanically handed me a stack of twenties. It broke the spell. I grabbed it out of his hands and counted it in front of him. "I suppose that's enough. I love charging to abuse you." I smacked him across the face to further exercise my point. I carried on in this manner for quite some time, remembering to destroy the remainder of his clothes and inflict more pain. This shouldn't be about me, I thought, despite the fact I was losing myself in the obvious chaos. His suit was in shreds. Torn material scattered like feathers after a pillow fight. In two sessions, I had mastered the art of destroying clothes.

Finally exhausted, I plunked my butt on the sofa and slipped my shoes back on, pretending this was all normal behavior and I wasn't another man's wife who was topless in a different man's apartment preparing to walk on him in stilettos. Out of the corner of my eye, I could see Jake gazing at my feet. While he got into his favorite position (on the floor), I stared at the rug until my eyes glazed over and the colors ran together. Rust and yellow blurred into an orange mustard glow, and I allowed myself a few seconds of tuning out from the new world I was co-creating.

"Grab a chair. You can lean on it while you step on me," said Jake. He was facedown on the rug with his arms down along his sides.

"I'm not moving from this couch, so just scoot closer to me." I then began lazily dragging my heel over his face. It seemed cruel, like scratching a red crayon across a Monet. "Turn over."

"Yes mistress."

I ran the heel of my shoe over his inner thigh. I was still topless, but his attention was fixated on my feet.

"That tickles."

I continued to do it until he grabbed my foot and stuck my shoe in his mouth. "Do you think about this stuff when you go to bed at night?" I don't know what made me ask this, but then again, I didn't know why I was there to begin with.

"I think about it all the time." He kissed the Gucci stiletto lovingly.

"So that means you must think about me all the time," I concluded.

"Yes, I do."

I blinked, feeling the impact of his words in the pit of my stomach and lower. "Do you know that Rob thinks I'm at the bookstore doing research?" I said.

"You're not lying. Living life *is* research."

"That's a positive way to look at it."

***

"It's getting late. Are we still going to do the dry run with the cage?" Jake asked from his position on the floor. I was stretched out on his sofa, and he was massaging my feet.

"Yep." We'd been talking for at least an hour, and I might have been stalling. It was hard to say. The plan was he was going to get inside the cage and I was going to pee in his mouth from above the cage. In theory, it seemed rather straightforward, yet I had my doubts. I wasn't the best with coordination and precision.

"OK, I'll change into the maid's uniform."

"Great." I closed my eyes. I thought of my dream and Jake and me on the tan suede couch. I wanted him to stroke my thigh right then, and dancing for him had only stimulated these ridiculous thoughts. *He is changing into a maid's uniform, for God's sake.* I shook my head in despair and flicked open my eyes, suddenly aware of nothing pressing on my bladder. How in the hell was I going to piss in his mouth from on top of a cage if I didn't have to pee? Normally I had to pee every two minutes.

I needed to pound a couple sodas. Pronto. Otherwise it was not going to be as fun as Jake probably imagined. I opened the refrigerator, uncapped a beer for Jake, and poured myself a Coke. I couldn't believe I was going to attempt this sober, but I figured it could only build character. I hated telling myself that I wouldn't have done something so bizarre had I not been drunk. That was a pitiful excuse, and frankly, I'd spent ten years overusing it.

"Do you have to pee yet?" asked Jake, returning in his standard getup. I peered at the cuffs, the pearly white buttons hiding his manly wrists. *Am I crazy or is the maid's uniform looking a little worn and shabby?*

"Soon. I feel it coming on," I lied. My bladder had a serious case of stage fright.

"How are we going to do this? Do you think the cage will support you?"

"No. Well, possibly. Let's assemble it and see."

Jake fetched the cage from under his bed, and we assembled it in two seconds. Take away the vodka and we were construction experts. I placed my hands on top of the cage and leaned my weight into it. "There's no way I could balance on this wire anyway."

"What if I pulled the coffee table over to the cage? You could stand on that."

"It would be easier if I had something to lean on. Like a railing, perhaps."

"I could move both the table and the cage closer to the wall. This way you could keep most of your weight on the table and have one leg up on the cage. You could use the wall as your railing."

I considered this. "That might work."

We rearranged the furniture together as if we were just doing a little redecorating.

"Hey Jake, I've never peed in anyone's mouth before. What if I miss my target?"

"Maybe we should put some plastic down. This is a four thousand–dollar rug."

"Plastic. Good idea! I'd prefer not to wind up owing you money." I was now guzzling soda at a disturbing rate. Then Jake opened the closet door and pulled out a plastic roll of paper. "What the hell is that?" I asked.

"It's a drop cloth."

"You have an extra one on hand?"

"I own the building. Trust me, these things come in handy. And I suppose we can't be too careful. I've never done this before either."

His confession made me feel better. "OK, so let's put it down. Then afterward, we can paint the apartment.

Jake smiled as he watched me drink another soda.

"Get in the cage," I finally said. "Let's get this over with." I pulled my underwear down over my heels and flung it onto the couch.

Jake got on all fours and climbed in the cage backward while I tried not to laugh, balancing myself on the coffee table.

"Do it slow. I want to drink as much as possible."

"I'll try. I've never had to frigging time it before." The leg I had extended over the cage was already shaking.

"OK, so just tell me when you're ready to start."

"Are you ready?"

"Yeah, I'm ready."

"You're not looking up."

"I know. I'm waiting until it hits me. Then I'll know exactly where it's falling."

"Oh my God. All right, let me concentrate. I feel like I just had an operation and the anesthesia hasn't worn off and some nurse is waiting for me to pee before I can be discharged from the hospital."

"So what you're saying is that you're enjoying it so far."

"Be quiet. Let me focus."

Jake did as instructed, but I had to guess that his heart was thumping. Mine was similar to a shamanic drum roll when they were inducting a new ruler into the kingdom. I told myself to relax and pretend as if I were simply squatting in the hills of New Jersey like the old days.

"I felt a couple drops," said Jake.

"That was the teaser. The sprinkle before the storm. My bladder doesn't like being put on the spot."

After about five embarrassing minutes, I finally got myself to the absolute point and said, "Here goes," and watched as a stream of clear liquid fell on Jake's head. Then I stared in complete horror as Jake arched his neck back and drank it as if he were starring in a Gatorade commercial. It almost would have been sexy had it not struck me as so disgusting! Apparently, this realization caused me to move slightly, because my stream of pee began to ricochet off the wires of the cage in all directions.

"Oh great." I attempted to stop midstream.

"Ah! Fuck! I got some in my eye," shrieked Jake. "It stings!"

"Are you OK? Should I stop or keep going?" I hoped he was going to tell me to keep going because I wasn't sure if I could hold it long enough to get off the cage, back onto the table, and into the bathroom.

"You can keep going. Just stay still, for crying out loud, and pee slower."

"Right." This was the true meaning of taking direction. I was now eligible for any movie role where peeing in public was pivotal to the story line. Finally, I was finished. With two feet firmly back on the table, I looked around for a tissue or paper towel, kicking myself for not thinking about it beforehand. "You don't have any paper towels?" I shouted, whirling around.

"Ah, probably not."

"You have an *extra* drop cloth, but no fucking paper towels?"

"Well, I can't go buy any right now. I'm in a cage. Just use toilet paper." But I was already in the bathroom. And just for the record, it's weird to enter a bathroom after you've just peed, as opposed to before.

After I regrouped, I went back into the living room and sat on the sofa. Most people would have put their underwear back on, but I didn't see the point. I crossed my legs and surveyed Jake's appearance from behind bars. He was drenched and rubbing his left eye. "Jake, your hair is soaked."

"I know," he said, touching it. "It's stiffening a little."

"It's a good thing we bought that puppy shampoo the other day."

"Good thing."

"How's your eye?"

"Still stinging."

"You should have kept them closed." I uncrossed my legs and leaned back.

"Well I didn't know it would sting. It's not every day I get pee in my eye."

We both cracked up. "It's interesting to talk to you through the cage. It adds a whole other dimension of superiority," said Jake. "Did you like doing that?"

"I haven't decided yet."

"When are you going to decide?"

"I don't know, Jake. I suppose it was OK. It might have been more empowering had I not been so profoundly embarrassed."

"What do you like best out of all the shit we've done?"

"Dancing for you. Definitely. It turned me on." I felt that pang in my gut again. I knew I shouldn't be giving myself away. It weakened my sense of mystery.

"That was very cool. You know what I'm thinking we should have done?"

"When? When I danced for you?"

"Yeah. After you tore up my shirt, I should have had you write 'loser' all over me in red pen. We just weren't thinking."

"It's hard to cover all the bases."

"I'm really enjoying talking to you from inside this cage."

"What about hour after hour when you're in there by yourself? Aren't you going to be bored?"

"No."

"But what will you do?"

"The only thing there is to do in a cage."

***

By the time I got in a cab, it was almost midnight. I called Rob to let him know I was on my way home. He sounded pissed. "What's up?" I asked.

"I am pissed."

My stomach clenched. *Has someone seen me at Petco lately?* "What's up?" I repeated.

"Remember that milkshake you made me last night?"

"Yes. What about it?"

"Where did you throw it away?"

"In our garbage. Where else?"

"It leaked everywhere. I went to take it out, and I got it all over me. I just spent an hour cleaning it up. I don't see how you could have left it like that."

I paused, struggling to ascertain why this was such a big deal. Obviously nothing really bad had ever happened to this man in his entire life. "Um, sorry."

As stupid as Rob was acting, relief washed through me. He was worrying about a little spilled milk—quite literally—while his wife was balancing on top of a dog cage, practicing the art of peeing into someone's mouth.

***

In the days after I danced for Jake, my thoughts were in a tizzy. *It's no big deal. It doesn't mean anything,* I kept repeating to myself like a mantra. This subtle form of self-denial worked until two o'clock on Sunday when Jake phoned and told me he was on his way to Gucci to pick up the Goddess shoes. "The other night was really fun," he stated. "Did you have a good time?"

"Yeah, it was cool. The dancing, not the cage," I clarified.

"What do you want to do later?" he asked, assuming I had nothing planned. Annoying but accurate.

"I don't know. Hard to top our last adventure."

We were both silent, trying to read into each other's cryptic nonchalance.

"I can't wait to see the Goddess shoes on your feet," said Jake. "They're going to look sexy as hell."

"Should I dance in them?" I said, holding my breath.

"Sounds good to me. When do you want to come over?"

Now. I glanced at my watch. "Seven?"

"Well, it's Sunday. How about five?"

"How about four?"

"Three is fine with me."

"See you in an hour." So much for playing it cool.

***

"How are you doing?" asked Jake, greeting me at the door.

"Ah, well, thanks," I said, feeling like an idiot. What kind of question was that? *Entirely too personal after the cage excursion!*

"Do you want to try on the shoes?"

"Oh. Yes. Definitely." Spotting the Gucci box on the table, I walked toward it, riveted. Jake had left the box open, and the shoes were lying on top of the thirty-five-dollar tissue paper. "Pictures do *not* always say a thousand words," I marveled, lifting a shoe from the box. I held it gingerly. The shoes were made of tight black strings. I turned to Jake. "Put them on me, slave."

Jake automatically dropped to the ground. I stuck my left leg out, and it started shaking all funny. Cool as a cucumber, as usual.

"Why are you shaking?" he asked.

"It's just the angle." I shrugged, giving up and sitting down on the leather couch.

After he'd placed both masterpieces on my feet, I marched around, admiring myself in his gigantic wall mirror. Five added inches can boost one's morale. For a split second, I felt positively lithe.

"Let me suck your toes," said Jake.

"Stop beating around the bush." I pranced back to the sofa.

"Lie on my bed. It's easier."

The nerve! "OK." Jake led me into his Icelandic room. Designed to look like an igloo, I admired the white brick walls before collapsing onto the stark white comforter.

I lay on my back and stared intently at the white stucco ceiling.

"Lie on your stomach."

"Yes sir." I saluted.

Jake peeled off the Goddess shoes. He took my pinky toe and slid it into his mouth. An electric jolt passed through me, and I melted. When I'd hung out with him initially—pre-horrific Hawaiian experience—he'd done this many times and I'd felt nothing. Proving once again sex is as mental as physical.

Jake massaged, kissed, and sucked my toes until I thought I was going to fuck him right there on the pristine white comforter. I forced myself up and announced I was going to change into my dancing gear, a clingy, black button-down sweater that fell past my thighs and stockings that screamed North Philly back streets. Black fishnet with red trim, the ultimate in slut-wear. With the new shoes, I would have blended in nicely among those hooking along pre-Giuliani Forty-second Street.

I pranced into the living room, anxious to remove it all.

Jake muttered something about me looking like a hooker—but a *fantastic* hooker—as I sashayed to the CD player and popped in an October Project disk. He was dressed in a casual light blue shirt and jeans, looking very South Beach for December in New York. He had already assumed his place on the couch, so I stood like a pencil in front of him waiting for the music to start. There is nothing like the first few seconds without sound to make one feel completely ridiculous. Especially dressed how I was.

Jake watched me with pinpointed fascination. At the sound of the first few melodic notes, I gripped him firmly by the shoulders and draped my long perfumed hair forward.

"Your hair is so soft." And for a second, I thought he reached his hand up to touch it. But then I realized they were both touching the outside of my legs, an assumption he hadn't made the last time. Our relationship had shifted. The geographic plates rotating the earth were traveling at an astronomic rate per second. "God you're sexy. When Mimi first told me you were a dancer, I couldn't see it. You just had none of the mannerisms, and your personality didn't give you away in the slightest."

"And I'm sure the militant dress code at Lime didn't suggest anything other than 'be all that you can be.'"

"Yeah, that uniform was ridiculous. And you always wore your hair up. When I first saw it down, I couldn't believe how much better you looked." *Gee, thanks!*

I stepped back and slowly unbuttoned my sweater, glaring at my willing subject. Fully unbuttoned, I leaned into him and engulfed him in the soft wool, forming a small, dark cave around us. I could smell my own perfume in the trapped air.

Jake's hands drifted up from the outside of my thighs, up my side, and onto the ridges at the edges of my bra. "Thank god you came back from Hawaii," he said.

"I didn't think anyone missed me."

"I did."

I began to unbutton his shirt with rapid precision. As if I'd done it a hundred times. "I had a dream the other night."

"Was I in it?"

"No, I thought I'd tell you about a dream I had with another guy."

"So what was it, smart ass?"

I paused, deciding against it. "You were buying me haute couture in Bergdorf Goodman," I lied.

"Ah." He slid his hand across my ribs, and the sweater fell to the floor. "How did you look all dressed up?"

"Oh. Fucking hot. Amazing. Very classy. Totally Jackie O with the hat and everything," I rambled. "Am I ever in your dreams?" *Say, lying on a tan suede couch at a sex party?*

"I never remember them." I undid my bra and brought my chest up to his face. "I should try to recall them. Maybe I've been dreaming about you all along and haven't known."

"Maybe." We were both quiet for a moment while I focused on not falling over in the Goddess shoes. It was like dancing on stilts.

I unsnapped my bra, and he slid his hands up my body. I stiffened, willing him to touch me. My jaw went slack, and my lips parted. I felt high and giddy with arousal. I wanted him to caress my breasts and suck on them. He seemed to sense this and stroked my back and side until finally pushing his hands up over my tits with gentle urgency. His desire excited me, and I swayed over him as he explored every inch of my chest. When he held each breast in his hands, I felt like he was balancing both parts of me. The yin and yang. The good and bad. The sane and insane. And when he finally traced his fingers gently over my left nipple, I almost came. I bit his ear and breathed out hot, bottled-up air.

I managed to pull away long enough to straddle his waist with my legs. I could feel his erection through his jeans and through my lace thong, which I was grinding into him. The pressure on my clit was mounting so quickly that I had to jump off him again. It had been so long since I'd felt any sexual excitement that I was almost unable to recognize these bizarre sensations. I stripped him down to his boxers and resumed my position, keeping the thong on, afraid of what would happen if I took it off.

It was difficult to insult him during this intense scenario, so I settled for scratching up his stomach and legs with my scrawny nails. Every so often, I pressed my hand into his cock and waited for him to push back against me.

"What are you getting my mother for Christmas?" I asked, distraction my only weapon against my own destruction.

He laughed. "I don't know. You'll have to make a Christmas list for all the people you want me to buy gifts for."

"It might be a long list this year, Santa. What do *you* want for Christmas?"

"Your Christmas stockings."

"Will you eat them with turkey and all the trimmings?"

"Just with cranberry sauce. Are you going to tell your friends what a loser I am after I buy them all presents?"

"Of course. Just think: you want me, but you can't have me. If you buy all of my friends gifts—and they know this—you'll appear even more pathetic."

"I could get very used to this dancing."

"Won't you get bored of me?"

"No. Never. This could go on for years." I gave him a funny look. Since my return from Hawaii, it was as if every day was a new adventure. I couldn't think past the next twenty-four hours, much less years down the road. I wondered why that

was, why my life had shifted its emphasis to the present with
suddenly no respect for the past and no regard for the future.
In fact, I couldn't envision a future at all. I seemed only capable
of living each day as it sprung itself upon me. As if on a train,
I planned to ride it until something or someone forced me off.
"On the days when Rob has off, you should call me up at work
and tell me to work later. Make more money for you, while
you're busy fucking your husband."

"We haven't been having much sex lately," I muttered, a
little taken aback. Somehow, I didn't feel discussing Rob was
appropriate right then.

"Actually, what you should do is call me after you fuck him
to tell me what a failure I am," he said, fixated on his new perverse suggestion.

"Would that turn you on?" I looked at him carefully, trying
to decipher if this was how he really felt. I also wondered if he
was just saying this to let me off the hook. Or perhaps to warn
me not to think beyond what was real and what existed only in
self-created fantasy-based situations.

"Absolutely," he said.

"So you *really* want to know about the mornings I wake him
up and start sucking his cock?"

"I like to know I have to give you everything and I get nothing back in return."

"Except a hard-on and an overdrawn credit card," I finished
for him. At that point, I could only discern that I was dealing
with the best-looking, nicest, and most generous *maniac* in the
tri-state area. And despite all the sick, fucked-up behavior I had
encouraged for money, I desired him.

"Exactly." He began to caress the inside of my breasts as if
he was petting a cat.

"I should really handcuff you," I suggested, wishing my
body didn't automatically tingle in specific areas when he
touched me.

"How would I have any fun then?"

"Maybe a blindfold would be better. I'll bring one next time."

Jake played with my nipple as if he were trying to pick a slippery pea off a plate. I was dying. I could feel my wetness seeping through the burgundy lace. I slung my right leg over his left leg and pressed my crotch down on him to stop the pulsating. The squares of the fishnet stretched into rectangles, and my white flesh struggled to make a breakout appearance.

"Imagine if you had a few more slaves like me," he said. "You would make so much money."

"But I have you. What do I need others for?" On my more business-minded days, I had already considered trying to find a few more willing participants but had negated the idea due to safety reasons and my overall obsession with Jake—who was, indeed, a full-time acquisition.

"I think *you* have the best life," he said. "You have a husband who loves you and a slave you can take advantage of. You're doing pretty well."

"Do you want my life?" I was only aware of his hand suddenly on my thigh.

"No, I like my current position as your slave."

"Then you have a good life too," I said.

"You're right. How does it feel to have your own slave?"

"Like I finally caught a break."

"Be serious."

"I am being serious."

"Am I different than other relationships you've had?"

I coughed. There were so many selfish, narcissistic idiots in my background, not including my current indifferent, unmotivated, unappreciative husband, that I didn't even see the point in embellishing. "You could say that."

"How am I different?" he asked, fishing for compliments— or insults—same difference where he was concerned.

"You treat me like I'm the most important thing in the world."

"It must be satisfying to know you have someone to buy you the stuff you deserve. Someone to worship you. Someone to tell you you're beautiful."

I whipped my head around. "You never told me I was beautiful!"

"I'm telling you now. I can be the person who lives solely for you. You give me purpose."

"Oh yeah? You haven't known me that long. Who were you living for prior?"

"You. I just didn't know it yet."

"Oh."

"What do you like doing the least when we are together?" He squinted at me.

I perched in his lap, thinking. "Probably feeding you dog food. It's just gross."

"Do you like when I drink your piss?"

"That doesn't bother me. But only from the glass. The cage was too tedious."

Jake laughed.

"Actually, it's rather flattering. No one I've been with would have ever *considered* doing that. Slave or otherwise."

The October Project disk switched over to the Dido CD that was still in the player from the days before, and her voice was again reverberating through the apartment. *"Nothing I have is truly mine."*

"This really is my theme song," said Jake. "It's right on the money."

I shook my head and snuggled into him, taking comfort in the way he stroked my back. The way he pulled me closer.

***

We walked over to an Italian restaurant in his neighborhood. Not exactly Isle of Capri, but we didn't feel like trekking to the East Side. The host seated us in a corner booth, and a waiter marched directly over to light our tiny wax candle. I nervously peered at the other patrons, reassuring myself that all of Rob's friends were Long Island bound, in bed with their wives or girl-friends or both. They were anywhere but in Midtown West at six o'clock on a Sunday.

I'd never cared if anyone had seen me out with Jake before I had the dream. I really felt I had nothing to hide, except a bizarre arrangement better kept out of the *Daily News*. But since my feelings were changing, I was no longer exonerated from the hypercritical public eye; I was technically guilty of cheating. Because as fantastically skilled as I was at self-denial, I understood that the path I was currently galloping along would lead me directly back to Jake's snow-white bed. And now it wasn't for the money—or the shoes. It was to be with him. Jake appreciated me and made me feel important. I was, once again, this sexy, desirable creature, confident and self-assured. I looked forward to the next day—and let's face it—I looked forward to seeing Jake.

Once I had scanned the restaurant, I felt safe to inch closer to him. Need and desire were trapping me in a narrow vor-tex. Each time I nudged closer, he would rub my back, and my stomach would skip. I rested my left hand on his knee.

Jake turned to me. "That was the best dance I ever had."

"I'm glad you thought so."

"Seriously, you looked incredible."

"Must have been my hair covering my face."

"That wasn't why." He placed his hand on my cheek and turned it toward him. His eyes were so close to mine that I blinked, collapsing from tension.

"No?"

"No. That comment came out wrong. Your face is beautiful. Your hair just accentuates it." *Beautiful.* There was that word again. I cleared my throat and picked up my menu.

"Right. Well. Thanks. I'm glad you enjoyed the dance—if one could call it dancing. And I liked how you touched me," I added, glancing down at the menu, afraid to meet his eyes.

"I couldn't help it."

"I was serious about what I said the other night. When we were at the Coral Room watching the mermaids."

"That you wanted to be a mermaid and swim in the tank?"

"No. Not that." I gave him an accusatory look.

"I'm sorry. Nothing's coming to me. Will you remind me?"

"When I said I might like you if I wasn't taken."

"You didn't say anything like that!"

"I didn't?"

"No. I would have remembered that."

"Oh. I must have just thought it."

"What *exactly* did you think?"

"I think being with you would be lots of fun. It's just that Rob and I got married. In that church with all those people around."

"Your friends and family, you mean?"

"Yeah. Them."

"Like me. I was there."

"Yes, you were one of the hundred and sixty witnesses." I stared down at the dark red tablecloth.

Jake picked up his menu. "What do you want to order?"

"This place won't be as good as Isle of Capri," I warned.

"We don't know that."

"I do. Do you miss me when you don't see me?"

"Yes. From the second you leave me. From the moment I get out of the cab. From the minute I hang up the phone."

I would have pushed my chair back in shock had I not been sitting in a booth. I gaped at Jake, disbelieving that he—maid uniform–wearing Jake—could be capable of such poetry. And toward me! I was his inspiration. "I had no idea you felt that way," I finally said.

"I almost said something to you before you got married."

"Are you serious?" The tall, looming waiter instinctively knew not to disturb us and set our drinks down without a word.

"Yes, but there was so much wedding energy circulating, I couldn't. And you seemed so excited. I would have otherwise."

I took a sip of chianti. "It wouldn't have done much good back then. I was on a mission. Obsessed with something I thought I needed to feel complete. And I didn't feel the way I feel about you now. If you had said something before the wedding, I probably would have thought you were crazy."

"Right, it's much better that I'm telling you I want you *after* you're married."

I jabbed him in the ribs. "Hey! What was that for?" He rubbed his side. For someone who liked abuse, he acted surprised when things actually hurt.

"Because half the time I don't know whether you're kidding or serious, so I'll just pretend every word out of your mouth is a joke. It will be easier that way."

Jake shrugged and signaled the waiter over to our table. Then he ordered for us while I sipped my wine and looked around furtively. The conversation alone could have incriminated me for plenty of wrongdoing.

"What was it that kept you interested in me, Jake? Especially since I wasn't even here for half a year." He had touched my face before, and I could still feel the energy of his hand.

"I don't know. I like the way you think. I like the way we always laugh at the same things. I like the way you move."

The conversation was making me breathless so I switched the subject. "Do you know what I like? I like that unshaven look you have today. You look rugged. Do you always do that on weekends?"

"No, just sometimes."

"It's sexy. You should grow a beard."

"I used to have one. I shaved it off when I saw my father in the mirror one morning."

"I'm telling you to grow it."

"I like when you tell me to do things."

"If you do, I'll dance naked for you. On your bed."

"Well there's an incentive." I watched him seriously ponder this, rubbing his chin for emphasis. "I guess I'll grow it."

***

When I got back to Astoria, Rob was trying his best to make a credit card payment on Dead Net, the local Grateful Dead website. I helped him do that in exchange for the use of my computer.

I was typing something to Jake about what a great night I'd had when Rob came out of the kitchen, complaining about two dirty forks in the sink. I was about to tell him to shove them up his ass, but his next statement caught me off guard.

"With all the mess you leave around here, it's like you're trying to enslave me!"

MARCH 2004

When Rob left for work in the mornings, I immediately jumped up and made the bed. This proficient exercise in homemaking implied I wouldn't leap back in it the moment he left the apartment. I hoped that as long as he noticed me simply *flat-out* doing productive activity, he wouldn't get on my case for not having a job.

One morning I took this diligent, self-motivated, early-to-rise image a step further by cleaning the toaster while Rob wolfed down two bowls of Fruit Loops. I then took out the trash! Grabbing a fresh trash bag from under the sink, something colorful caught my eye. *The Milk-Bone dog treats.* I stopped and stared. Could I have been so careless? Did I not throw them out—or at the very least hide them? It appeared so.

I glanced over at Rob and shut the cabinet. His head was buried in the gossip section of the *New York Post*. I knew this much: I wouldn't have stuck the leftover box under the sink without a care in the world, which indicated to me that Rob had discovered the Milk-Bones in one of my ingenious hiding spots. Then he must have moved them somewhere obvious to see what I would do. I snuck another look at him. Raised on a complete breakfast of eggs and French toast his whole life, he hardly ever ate cereal.

I glanced back at the shut cabinet, straining for a quick excuse lest he inquire this very minute. My on-the-spot excuses were usually outlandish, unbelievable scenarios, which generally encouraged his overall superiority complex. I wrestled with this inner turmoil, still rooted to the floor. A special gift for Achilles? But why would the package be open? It's not quite like taking a can of salted cashews over to your in-laws and admitting you snacked on a few in the car. Another ghost? I'd been rather adamant about their ability to move items around the apartment, but could Casper actually drift to the supermarket, peruse the pet aisle, and snag objects for which I had no obvious use? *Yep, that is my story, and I'm sticking to it.*

Trying to act natural, I took a seat next to Rob at the kitchen table. "Pam?"

"Yep."

"Which nightlife promoter is on the outs with Ford Models because he lures underage girls to certain clubs, which pay him per model?" he read directly from page 6.

"How should I know?" I asked, shrugging.

"Well, *you* are out every night. Surely you know this guy."

"I'm not out at stupid clubs. I'm not eighteen anymore."

"It says here, 'One sixteen-year-old beauty—abandoned unconscious on the sidewalk outside a well-known club—was taken away by ambulance to St. Vincent's Hospital.'"

"So."

"The girl's only sixteen, Pam."

"What does that have to do with me? I didn't encourage her to take drugs and drink herself into a coma."

Now it was Rob's turn to shrug. Apparently this was just his opening to something more relevant. "Is Lime still open?"

"As far as I know."

"Have you considered asking for your job back?"

"Fuck no. That would be like telling them what size handcuffs I wear. I shouldn't venture within five hundred feet of the place. Which totally sucks because I've had to avoid the restaurant across the street, and I really miss their steak tartare."

"The owners found out how much you were stealing?"

"I told you this. We were in Hawaii when all hell broke loose. That's why Donna left. She got *fired*. Thankfully, I funneled all my cash into our wedding so they won't be getting anything back from me—not that they have any proof, of course."

He nodded, and I detected a hint of a smile. There was something he enjoyed about me—however small. "Have you been looking for a job?" he asked, ruining the moment.

I sighed, having cleaned the toaster for nothing.

***

During this time, Lexi was toying with the idea of quitting dancing. Her fiancé wanted her to work in a field that didn't require her to be topless. I was wary, having done it myself and still weighing the advantages against the disadvantages, years later. She called the following afternoon. "Are you positive you want to do this?" I asked her.

"The New York strip club world is dead, Pam. It died with Clinton and was buried by 9/11. You don't know because you got out before it all started to go downhill. Why do you think I'm getting married, for God's sake?"

"But a downhill strip club market is still better than a *real job*," I stressed. "You just have no idea."

"Well you did it. It must be possible."

"Possible, yes. Easy, no. Fun, definitely not."

"Well, I could cocktail waitress like you did. In the big clubs, the girls make almost as much."

"No they don't. And they work a lot harder. And you're treated like shit. I'm warning you. You say good-bye to your self-respect."

"I know this new place opening up, Pam."

"You're not listening to me."

"It's a new, big lounge in the Flatiron District."

"What does this have to do with me?" I asked, sighing.

"Interviews are Wednesday between four and six. Do you want to go?"

"You mean interview?"

"Yes. You still don't have a job, right?"

"Well, no, but waiting tables is something I want to stay clear of. Remember my vow?"

"Yes, but seriously, what else did you plan on doing? You didn't marry a guy with any money." I swallowed a lump in my throat and looked down at the fairytale I was revising. It did all seem a little hopeless. "No offense, but you need to get your shit together," she added, further annoying me.

"Jesus, Lexi. I should drop you as a friend."

"Will you just come with me? The outfits are going to be adorable! Black bodysuits and platinum wigs!"

"That's your selling point?"

"The customers won't be able to tell us apart. All we have to do is drop the bottle of vodka off and disappear with our own bottle."

"You do put a good spin on it, but I don't know. What's this place going to be called?"

"I'm not sure. I only know about the outfits. Just come with me—even if you don't want to work there. At least you could tell Rob you went on an interview."

"That's true. It would look like I was trying."

"Great. I knew you'd come."

I was only thinking of Jake. "When is it again?"

***

It was snowing the day we went for this interview at the mysterious club that was keeping its name a big secret until the grand opening on St. Patrick's Day of all classic mistakes. This resulted in us trekking through sleet and snow in our high-heeled boots and push-up bras. Of course, by the time we got there and removed our many layers, we realized we were dressed identically: tight, short black skirts with tight, low-cut black tops. I was simply making an appearance, but I supposed it couldn't hurt to be hired. Considering that I hadn't officially worked since before I got married, I needed a cover for future endeavors with Jake. If by some freak mistake the company hired me, I could work two nights a week and see him the other days.

After the interview, Lexi and I slid into a booth at Houston's. All the world-famous authentic cuisine in New York and we preferred conglomerate chains with mass-produced food. Go figure. We ignored the menus lying on the table.

"Tonya unnerved me. I'm not even sure why," I said, referring to the interviewer as I glanced around for Timothy, our favorite gay waiter.

"I know. She was intimidating. Not to mention a *total* bitch."

"Isn't she your friend?"

"Like, yeah. *I know her.* She was my connection there. So much for that. I was only going to work there until Joe got me pregnant anyway," she admitted. "A month tops."

I stared at her. She was the most manipulative friend I'd ever had. "Well, thankfully Tonya hated me on sight. I have no chance of getting this job." I smiled and waved at Timothy, who was poised with one hand on his hip, yelling at the bartender in Spanish. "If this place gets their paperwork screwed up and accidentally hires me, it might be rather embarrassing. I distinctly recall telling everyone that I would rather die before waiting tables after I'm married. Do you realize what an idiot I'll look like?"

"To whom? Who else do we know?"

I scratched my head. She was right.

***

An hour later Lexi left for work, and I remained at Houston's to wait for Jake. My phone rang, and I jumped. "Hey Pam, the subway is all jammed. I'm going to walk so I'll be there in fifteen," he said. He was walking in a blizzard just to see me! *He was smitten!* Then I recalled that he designed his bedroom like the North Pole. He was smitten with Icelandic conditions, more like it.

By the time he arrived, I'd read an entire issue of *Marie Claire* and consumed two more glasses of wine. I was not a good sipper, but thankfully I had the tolerance of a rugby player. He hurried over to my table, covered with snow, and proceeded to elaborate as to why he was so late, but I didn't care. He was here and I could breathe again. I told him about the interview.

"If you get this job, I'm never going to see you again," he said, seeming disappointed.

"I'm not going to be hired. And if for some reason I am, I'll work one day, hate it, yell at everyone, and then quit—which is what normally occurs."

"You're always so positive. That's what I like about you."

"I am being positive."

"It does sound like a cool place."

"It will be cool for a few months until people catch on that it's run by all the same crackheads that ran former clubs, in which case it will either go under or maintain just enough business to attract mostly residents of outer boroughs on a Saturday night." Jake just blinked. I cleared my throat. "All I know is all the girls will be wearing blond wigs, so I'm sure you'll dig it. I seem to remember that you prefer blondes."

"Not anymore," he said, smiling.

Much to our waiter's dismay, we hung out for hours talking before we moved our small party to Almond Joy, home of the famous fight with Mimi. Our private little room felt different than it had a year ago. For starters, the noise from the bar was loud and boisterous, with a negative edge, and hip-hop was blaring from all seventeen jacked-up stereos. Although we were separated from the crowd by a flimsy curtain, the place had essentially become a club, and we discussed its cultural decline until we received our cocktails from a Spanish dude in a white shirt who spoke zero English.

Jake turned to me, his face puckered with disgust. "What the hell happened to this place?"

"The same thing that happens to every cool spot. It's like I was saying earlier. I'm just glad we got a table."

"If we hadn't gotten a table, we wouldn't have stayed." He dangled his arm around me, and we sat, knees touching in the corner of the little room. The wicker candles gave off a green glow, making us appear ghostly. I was about to make a joke about it, but my proximity to Jake caused my stomach to flip-flop with desire.

"OK." I took a deep breath. "So you know how I was dancing for you on Sunday?"

"Yeah, a ha, thanks for that, by the way."

"My pleasure."

"What about it?"

"I liked it. I would have done it for free." Dangerous words. Bordering on idiotic.

Jake glanced down at the beer in his hands and pulled at the corner of the Heineken label. "What are you telling me?"

"I think you know."

"Please explain it anyway. Guys are stupid, and I'd rather not assume."

"Let me put it another way. If I kissed you right now, would you be mad?"

"No. Fuck no." He banged his bottle of beer on the glass table. Seconds later we were kissing. We kissed until the four-foot-tall Spanish kid poked his head in.

"I've wanted to do that for a long time," said Jake, glaring at the waiter. He got the message and left us alone. "It's too bad it's so late. And it's snowing. Why did we stay at Houston's so long? How stupid of us."

"We can't help ourselves. We love it there."

"This is true." He stroked my face, and we resumed kissing until Jake broke away suddenly, claiming he'd been kicked in the leg from an unknown element beyond the curtain.

Jake grinned. "I have to admit something," he said sheepishly.

"What?"

"I was shopping in Wolford last week, and you know how they display the newest lingerie on the mannequins?"

I nodded.

"Well, I kept imagining you in each of the outfits."

"So what are you waiting for? Dress me up."

"I'd like to. This weekend, maybe?"

"I think I'm free."

***

When I arrived at Jake's apartment the next night, I wasn't sure how to act. Do I give someone who is now aware I want him a kiss hello? Or do I pretend that I never declared my love for him in the land of hip-hop?

I avoided eye contact. Choosing to stare straight at his chest instead, I saw he was wearing a plaid shirt. During the last few visits he'd abandoned the maid's uniform, and I was relieved. Obviously, I wasn't opposed to hooking up with women, but I preferred my men to look and dress like men. I finally mustered up the nerve to glimpse at his face. "Wow, your beard has grown significantly."

"It grows quickly when it's inspired."

"I guess I owe you a naked dance." He sat next to me on the couch, lifted my legs, and placed them in his lap. Gently he removed my heels and began to massage my feet. I was wearing leopard print Manolos. In the past, I'd always associated leopard print with "kicking it" grandmas hitting the town, tossing back amaretto sours with abandon—largely due to my own family legacy—but that year the major designers had revamped and revolutionized the animal to the point of probable extinction.

Minutes later I was easing myself into Jake to the sound of Counting Crows. As long as I was dancing, I told myself I was still in control. I called the plays, no one else. But then again, just how good was my coaching?

"You smell fantastic. What is it that you wear?" he asked.

"Red Jeans by Versace. Unbutton my shirt, slave." He complied, the fickle buttons parting the way for his eager hands. He brushed his fingers along my back and lifted the shirt over my shoulders. It slid off my arms like liquid.

"I love being your slave."

"I know." I turned around and rested my weight in his lap.

"Careful," he said, jostling his hip to one side.

"Huh?"

"It's just painful."

"What's painful?"

"It's my right ball," he said, shifting again. "It's killing me."

"What?"

"I think you head-butted me too hard last week. It must be bruised or something."

"Yikes, sorry." I frowned. If I was the dominant one, why was I always apologizing? At times he had a strange way of making me feel stupid. He traced my collarbone with his fingers before setting his hand on my bra. "Unsnap it," I ordered. This time I could barely feel his hands on me. It didn't provide the same thrill as it did the first time, but I still wanted it. Every time I moved in close, he brought his lips to my breasts and gently sucked on my nipples.

Jesus. *I am married to Rob. Why is that so hard to remember?* I pushed my lace thong down on one side and brought my bare hipbone up to his face. His lips formed in a kiss, and I pulled back, teasing him. Then I lowered the other side so the tiny piece of cloth rested dangerously along the tops of my thighs, revealing half of my secret. He looked at me with amazement and admiration as I bent forward at the waist, pressed my lips to his ear, and let the thong drop to the ground. The white lace fell around my ankles, draping the leopard print like a miniature tablecloth. I stood there unabashed, letting him take me in, and wondered what was going through his mind. Did he want to reach out and touch me or just plunge his tongue inside?

I waited until he stared back up at my face to move in closer. I could see his dick was hard, and I carefully straddled myself around him. I didn't want him yelping in pain over his stupid sore ball. He reached for the back of my neck and guided my lips toward his. I opened my mouth to receive his tongue and pressed myself into him, unable to get close enough. Sore ball, material, and mind-set were my biggest obstacles.

I pulled away, kneeled in front of him, and placed my mouth over the pant material covering his cock. "Tell me what a loser I am," said Jake. "How you can tease me with your body but deny me any closure."

"That's right. You can look and feel it, but you can never have it," I said, despite the fact I was about to offer it to him right on the couch. "Too bad for you because I know you want to fuck me, you miserable failure."

"I love it when you call me that."

"That's what you've amounted to," I said. All the insults seemed silly now, as I was no longer convincing.

"So the best I can hope for is slave status?"

"Yep."

"Would you like to step on me?" he asked in the same manner as, "Would you like a cup of coffee?"

No. Why must you torment me with these bizarre requests? I was fairly positive I looked as bored as I felt with this repetitive suggestion.

Before I had even agreed, Jake stretched his lean body out across the imported rug from Italy. (Thank God for that drop cloth!)

I yawned, not bothering with the scratching. I removed both shoes and glided my stocking foot down his face, down along his torso, and underneath his four hundred–dollar Valentino belt. I was juggling hand grenades but not inclined to stop anytime soon. He unzipped his pants and pulled them off, surprising me with his initiative.

I pulled his Calvin Klein underwear down his legs, unleashing his proud member, and then proceeded to run my silky foot over the size of it. Not bad, I thought. His dick felt velvety under my foot. I liked how it looked. Hard and pulsing, throbbing at the sight of me. Or rather—at the sight of my foot. Still me, I reassured myself.

"I should really make you jerk off while I shove my feet in your face."

He smiled, studying the length of my leg. "That would be amazing."

"I'm kidding. We could do more than that."

"Let's go in the bedroom. Is that all right?"

"Lead the way."

We both looked toward the bed, and Jake said, "How do you want to do this?"

I glared at him, my frustration obvious. Here I was, naked and offering myself to him, and it seemed he'd rather engage in an act I'd only joked about.

"What's the easiest way for you to have your feet in my face while I jerk off?" he asked me, only making my disappointment a spoken reality. In addition to the lack of romance, I wasn't too thrilled about it being more technical than spontaneous, but he had a point. If he really wanted my feet in his face when he came, it wasn't a position one stumbled upon naturally.

"Let's see. I knew geometry would come in handy one day. I think you at the head of the bed and me at the bottom might do the trick," I said flatly.

"Will you ridicule me and tell me how pathetic I am?" he asked, his cock twitching at the mere mention of his inadequacy.

"Sure. I won't be lying. I feel that you are beyond pathetic at this moment."

I lay down on my back with my feet covering his face and indulged him with ridiculous banter, a foot fetish mockery of a lifetime. It was beyond dull, but I was counting on him to return the favor. With all the added frustration, I thought if I didn't have an orgasm soon, I might kill him. "So, in conclusion, that is why you'll never experience anything more in your lame, sad life other than routine jacking off. The best you're going to get is a bottle of lotion and an issue of *Maxim* magazine, you pitiful wimp of a man!"

Judging from the sounds he was making, this last statement induced the finale. I didn't watch him come because I figured he'd only appear ridiculous. He got up to clean himself off, and I scooted over to the left side of the bed, waiting for him to return and lie beside me. Instead, he reemerged and sat down near my feet. *What the fuck is he doing?*

"So," I said. "My turn." He looked confused. Then frightened. "You can get me off just by fingering me. And you should do that. *Now.* Considering you didn't want to fuck me."

"Really?"

"Yes, really."

I guided him through it, thinking again how textbook this experience was turning out to be. I reminded myself that the first time with a new lover was never the most comfortable. Eventually I came, but I only achieved it by recalling the scene in the movie *Gia* where a young Angelina Jolie convinces her female makeup artist to have sex with her. That scene never failed me.

Once again, readjusting my attention to Jake, I enjoyed the tender way he stroked my body from top to bottom, feeling my dips and ridges and tracing them with his fingertips.

"I had a dream you were doing this," I mumbled. "A while back. You were stroking my thigh. We were at a party."

"I still can't remember my dreams. When I wake up I see images, but they vanish."

"I'm sure I'm in your dreams," I boasted, fluffing my hair.

"You could be. No wonder they're so fleeting."

"How do you mean?"

"Time with you. It won't last."

"Sure it will. What are you, a fatalist?"

"No, a realist. Don't you feel guilty?"

"Not exactly. Otherwise I wouldn't be here."

"I feel guilty. That's the only problem I have with this. I mean, if Rob was an asshole I wouldn't care, but he's a really nice guy."

"*Really* nice is pushing it. You didn't live with him for six months in Hawaii. I did. Honestly, he wasn't that nice."

"If we have sex, I'll never be able to stand in the same room with him."

"And you would hold up just fine now?" I said. "Just for your information, we're already cheating on him. I don't think the specific act of intercourse will be the straw that breaks the back of that damn camel."

My tone of voice must have reflected my irritation because he began twirling strands of my hair around his finger and changed the subject. "I remember when I first started thinking about you all the time."

"When was that?"

"About two months before your wedding. We were all having so much fun, and then you left for Hawaii. Everything just went flat, and I realized how much time we'd spent together. I was so depressed, and it was because you weren't here anymore."

"But you knew I'd be back."

"That's what you said, but I had no idea. I thought you would fall in love with the lifestyle and I'd never see you again. But then I called you and you told me about living on Insect Hill."

"Bug Mountain. And you didn't call me. I called you," I said.

"Whatever. You told me what it was really like and how the natives were tossing McDonald's scraps at you out of car

windows." I grimaced—still not completely over the humiliation. "I was just so glad you wanted to come back to New
York." Jake's hand rested on the edge of my stomach. "God, I
like the way you think. You're different."

***

Later that night, I concluded Rob had out-stoned himself. Or
maybe our darling realtor had left a tab of acid on the floor to
match the sticker. I wasn't sure, but he threw me on the bed
and made love to me like a wild man. I kept the light on to
make sure it was really Rob and not some nut with a key to the
apartment.

The next morning I stared at the motionless body beside
me. I recognized aspects about it: the tilt of the arm, the wide,
gaping mouth, the slow, rhythmic breathing. All of Rob's features existed independently, and those elements I could identify
with. It was the person as a whole that I no longer liked. He had
made it that way.

I stared at Rob's silhouette under the light of the full moon,
and all those years—me working my ass off—seemed wasted. It
was 4 a.m., and I was wide the fuck awake, appraising a product of my own demise. I turned over and stared out the dark
window, partially covered by a cheap crooked shade we never
bothered to correct. It struck me as symbolic of our relationship; something we never worked on to improve.

My thoughts reverted back to my wedding: my mother
meeting Jake for the first time. I watched her obvious confusion
transform into enchantment, his approving nod and twinkling
eyes the ultimate compliment. So charmed, in fact, was Sarah
Castle that she barely chastised me for sneaking a piece of lob-
ster cocktail off her plate.

I glanced at Rob again, my heart in my throat. I was married to a good man. He wasn't Vanity Fair material, and he
certainly didn't worship the ground I walked on—but I knew
he loved me in his apathetic way and I was living in the past,

reliving history when I should have been plowing headstrong into my future. Working on making things right between us. Taking him to court or putting the past behind me.

But wait—hold on—what was the definition of a good man? Just how many terrible moments was each "good man" allowed? The night he raped me in Hawaii, was he good? And did his constant rejection give me the right to engage in these other acts in the pursuit of happiness? I didn't know anymore. What was right? What was wrong? And what was truly necessary?

Instead I ignored these facts, chasing that indescribable element called "fun." It was wrong and hugely selfish, but my body and mind were galloping along in the spirit of betrayal, and I wasn't putting up much of a fight.

***

I shifted my body from one side to another, about to give Jake a private showing of Wolford's latest collection from the sanctuary of the igloo. He'd come good on his promise to dress me up and had taken me to Wolford earlier that day.

I surveyed my image in his dresser mirror. Fine clothes make average bodies look *very* good. That's why it's all so expensive, I reasoned. The dark lattice over the crème-colored silk created skin a la Nicole Kidman, and the underwear actually minimized the size of my ass for a change. The crème garter belt interwoven with black lace added a touch of racy to its classic design, and I concluded the skimpy three-piece outfit was worth twelve hundred dollars.

I turned away from the mirror, my heart thumping. No one had ever dressed me up like this. I was now officially Pretty Woman without the disproportionate smile.

"OK, you can come in now," I shouted, afraid to move in case anything unsnapped. Jake's footsteps echoed in the hallway, and he entered his bedroom. He didn't say anything at first, just dropped to his knees and ran his hands over the garter belt and over my thighs. My body instantly responded, yearning for more. I was hoping that this was going to be *it*. No more silly foot charades and bizarre discussion.

After about five minutes of this caressing, I said, "You are disappointed."

"Yeah, I'm really disappointed," he responded sarcastically, tracing his fingers down the sheer silk masquerading my crotch. I froze with desire. "This looks amazing on you. Amazing. You're stunning." He looked up at me before running his lips over my stomach.

No one had ever told me I was stunning. Not even my mother standing there with the Polaroid before my first prom. I remained motionless. With the window slightly open, it smelled like the start of spring in his room. I struggled to hold on to the fantastic feeling of sexually charged anticipation.

"Why is this the first time I've ever dressed you up?" said Jake. "I can't believe what I've been missing."

I entwined my hand in his thick dirty blond hair, pulling him up off the floor. I needed him close. Eye level close, to prove it was real. He cradled my face in his hands, and we kissed until I felt dizzy.

"Let's lie on the bed," he said, taking my hand.

He explored every part of my body. I could barely breathe as he glided his fingertips over and under the sheer material. I struggled to get a grip. I knew I was slipping into a realm I could no longer control or justify.

"Do you like me dressing you up like this?" he asked.

"I do. I love when you take care of me."

"I should have always been doing this. You're beautiful. Truly beautiful."

I melted. If he kept saying that, soon I'd be *his* slave.

Jake pulled at the edges of my bra, unleashing my breasts from the restrictive lace-up job. His shirt came off, and his hands were inside the crème underwear, touching all the spots I'd instructed him on only days before. Drawn by how wet I was, his fingers plunged deeper into me, and I pushed against him, creating sparks of pleasure.

Jake slowly lowered the crème silk down over my knees, leaving it to dangle around my ankles. There was something urgent and sexy about it never coming off completely. He placed his hand under my stomach and stroked lightly up and down. Drifting his hand down past my belly button, he paused. "Is this the spot?"

"Almost." He slid his hands over me, pausing at certain places to massage and explore.

My senses were on overload. "I can't wait to fuck you," I mumbled. He was quiet as he paused his fingers over my clit and began to rub me up and down. I closed my eyes, and minutes later my body ruled my mind completely. "Don't stop. I'll keep coming," I moaned. I lost track of how many orgasms I had. Lost track of everything.

"I found the spot. You're so sexual. It's so hot."

I was sweating and panting, much to my dismay. I wasn't one of those women who kept a cool exterior in the throes of passion. He stroked my tits, running his hands over my nipples, which were still hard like bullets. I undid his belt and whipped down his pants. He hadn't worn any underwear. Great, he was ready to go. But what he did next pissed me off. He scooted up to the top of the bed. "Put your foot in my crotch," he said.

"You're not going to fuck me?" I said, disbelieving.

"Not yet."

I blinked. "Then when? Is this a planetary thing? Are the corresponding moons not aligned?"

"It has nothing to do with astrology."

"Then I don't get it."

"One day, one day when you're not married."

I'd been sucker-punched. "You're serious?"

"Yes."

"But you had no problem doing that other thing," I said, referring to only five minutes ago when I was coming all over his bed.

"No. Of course not. I loved that. Making you excited. Pleasing you."

"So I don't get it."

"You're about to please me, too. Just do what I tell you," he urged.

I shrugged, feeling bizarrely out of sync, and inched my way down to the end of the bed. I stared at his semierection before placing my stocking foot on his thigh and holding my palm up in the air to indicate he could use my foot however he saw fit. I didn't get how this could possibly be as fun as screwing me, but then again, he enjoyed eating my dirty stockings over linguini, so what the fuck?

He took my foot and placed it into his mouth while I squinted, trying to figure him out. I watched, curious, as he sucked and kissed my foot through the glossy stockings. "Tell me what a loser I am," he said, glancing down the length of the bed at my face.

I sat up a little and penetrated him with my stare. "Do I have to? I'm really not thinking that right now." Could it be the only way to turn him on?

"Only a pathetic loser wouldn't fuck your brains out."

"I guess."

"It's true. I'm a total wimp."

I sighed. He certainly wasn't speaking those sentiments to hear himself speak. He was prompting me to begin a barrage of insults pertaining to his character, which would no doubt excite him to the point of orgasm. *Fucking tiring!* Why couldn't he just behave normally for once—just enjoy me without any peculiar agenda? I was offering him my body, and he wanted this shit instead.

Against my better judgment, I spoke, the irritation in my voice genuine. "That's right. Only a sad, pathetic fool would prefer to suck my feet instead of making love to me. You're not a real man. You probably can't even get it up if you're not being humiliated. Only the lowest specimen..." I continued on in a repetitious fury, insults flying so quickly out of my mouth that I will never recall what I said. I was only aware that both my feet were on either side of his cock, and he was using both hands to manipulate them up and down. With a final clutch of my heel, he came all over my seventy-five-dollar stockings. *Yick!* I yanked my feet away. *Give me those back!*

"Oh my god, that was great. I love it when you talk to me like that."

I stripped off my stockings and dropped them on the ground. "I want these dry-cleaned."

***

It wasn't until I got home later that I realized Jake hadn't given me any money all week. Was he supposed to? In the past, if he'd taken me shopping, he hadn't paid me—but then again, he hadn't benefited from the purchases. I thought about this carefully. At Almond Joy, the night after the stupid job interview, why had I told him I would dance for free? *So dumb.*

The repetitive degrading was a major drag—an enormous effort on my part—that wasn't worth it if he wasn't writing a check. It was a twisted subject matter requiring mental concessions. Like having to run the fifty-yard dash with a set of hurdles as opposed to a straight run. It was draining. Suddenly Rob seemed great; he just liked to fuck. If only occasionally.

If Jake had just slept with me like a regulation guy, money wouldn't have crossed my mind. Maybe he didn't even like sex. Despite the endless questions in my head, I decided not to say anything. But as it turned out, the issue of money was already on the table.

***

Jake called me from work the next afternoon, and we arranged to meet at Isle of Capri at 6 p.m. He reserved a small table in the back, and as soon as I saw him, all my insecurities and anxieties fell away. He was still in his work clothes, his Monday dark suit and tie. He looked sexy and efficient but a little nervous. Did men get nervous after having sexual encounters with married women?

"How long have you been here?" I asked, pulling out my chair and glancing at his empty bottle of Moretti beer. There was also a full glass of white wine waiting for me.

"Not long. Not long," he repeated, holding up the empty bottle, signifying to a nearby waiter that another one was needed. ASAP.

"Hey, you better watch it with that Moretti. That beer has a higher alcohol content than most. Just like Italian men are harder to control. You'll be on the floor before you know it. Mumbling incoherent statements and pulling your pockets inside out."

"Nice to see you, too. I ordered you a pinot grigio."

"Thanks." I searched his face for clues.

"You look nice."

"I know," I said. The red, clingy button-down dress was killer.

"Very sexy," he said. "But we know that already."

Our discussion soon turned to the day before on his bed. He brought it up. "So, I can't stop thinking about you. You're on my mind constantly."

"Same with me. You, that is. Not myself."

"I keep picturing you on my comforter all dressed up like that, and I just—"

"Just what?"

"I wish you weren't married. You're perfect for me. I have so much fun with you. You *understand* me."

"I often forget I'm married. When I'm with you, it rarely enters my mind. I know that's bad, but Rob doesn't act like a husband. He does his own thing. It isn't quite what I envisioned."

"Well, he obviously doesn't know what he has," said Jake.

"He's indifferent. Unless he's yelling at me for leaving his kitchen in disarray. He only gets emotional if anything is out of place, or god forbid, on the floor. Like that damn All-Clad towel! You were there when he was freaking out over that thing. And the lemon—and the fucking tin foil. Clearly, the kitchen is the *only* thing he's passionate about."

"His priorities are all out of whack."

"Do you know he didn't talk to me for an entire day after a milkshake spilled in our garbage? He's *still* upset about it. And lest we forget the debacle over the pots and pans, way back when."

"No, that will go down in history. It seems that he's intentionally harping on these minor incidents and blowing them way out of proportion. Like he's mad at something else so he loses it over the little things. Could he be mad at you for anything else? Did anything happen in Hawaii, maybe."

"No. Nothing he knows about, anyway. In fact, he was a bigger asshole in Hawaii. You don't even want to know. He's relatively nice now in comparison; he's just indifferent—like I said."

"I don't get it. He's got this pot of gold in front of him, but he barely glances at it, much less thinks to invest."

I smiled.

"Indifference is fine to a point, Pam, but after a while, indifference becomes ignoring, and ignoring becomes insulting. It's like he's resentful of you."

"I concur. He hates that I'm not working. That I can pull it off. Every time I quit a job, he gets pissed."

"Well, that explains it."

"I just hate when he acts as if I'm irresponsible when I've never once asked for his help."

"Speaking of which, there's something else I've been feeling weird about," said Jake.

"What's that, now?"

"I didn't know whether you expected money after our past few encounters?"

I looked up sharply.

"I just want you to know that I don't pay for sex. To write you a check didn't feel right. I care too much about you." I listened, clutching my fork. Convenient how suddenly everything fell under *his* version of sex. "And I hope that's OK with you. I mean, the gifts are different. I'm always going to spend money on you, but if we do something intimate, I won't be able to write you a check every day like I used to."

"I understand. I'm not in the habit of receiving money for sex either, by the way," I said.

"I know. I wasn't insinuating you were; I just didn't want any confusion."

"OK," I said, shrugging.

"OK, what?"

"That's cool. Whatever you want to do."

"You don't know how much better I feel right now."

"What did you think I'd say?"

"I don't know. I can't even speak." He took a long swig of beer.

"Do you want to be my boyfriend, Jake?"

He stared at me, his eyes bloodshot. "Ideally, yes. But you're taken."

"If I wasn't?"

"Yes, I just told you that. I love you."

I dropped my fork. It clattered on the porcelain plate louder than the ringing of the Liberty Bell.

"Did I just say that?" His face was bright red. An English parody.

"Yes."

"Maybe you are right about this Moretti. It just kind of slipped out."

"I love you too. I think about you all the time as well."

"That's cool," he said sheepishly, not meeting my eyes. "You're just so great. I like how we think the same things and laugh at the same stuff. And God, I love how you insult me. It turns me on just thinking about it. No women talk like that. You say all the right things."

No girls talk like that unless they are getting paid. "You do understand that since our relationship has escalated to a new level, I'll have to get a job."

"I figured you might say that."

There was an awkward pause, and because we were seated near the back door, we could hear the wail of sirens in the distance.

"Pam, those sirens just gave me an idea regarding all the petty bullshit Rob keeps giving you grief over. You could pull an outrageous stunt that would definitely let him know enough is enough."

"Like what?"

"Here's what I was thinking…"

***

I waited until Monday, Rob's day off, to put Jake's and my plan into action. Rob was still sleeping when I tiptoed into the kitchen and joyfully dropped the All-Clad dishtowel onto the middle of the tiled floor. Getting down on all fours, I traced the outline of the towel with thick yellow chalk and placed a piece of cheese near it. Feeling a little bit like Mark Furman, I also circled the slice of cheddar and stepped back to admire my handiwork. *This is good.*

The last move was to block off the crime scene with yellow tape, which I'd since discovered was sold in every hardware store in Astoria. (The law of supply and demand, I suppose.) I closed off the kitchen, crisscrossing the tape over the entrance so it was the first thing Rob would notice after realizing his path to the refrigerator had been impinged.

Assuming my role as acting officer, I typed up the list of possible suspects and their respective motives. Chuckling to myself, I tacked this list to the doorframe just above the yellow tape.

Then I went back to bed. Rob and I were planning to spend the day lounging around because his long-overdue and twice-postponed Christmas party was planned for this lovely evening in *March* at the infamous Bowl-A-Rama in Minneola.

At any rate, I waited until Rob woke up at the crack of 2 p.m. and followed behind him as he stumbled toward the kitchen in search of cold water. He came face-to-face with the crime scene and looked back at me, confused.

"What's going on?" I asked innocently. He peered through the tape and spotted his prize towel on the floor.

"Looks like the police were here," I said. "Look at the detailed report they left us."

Rob scowled and pulled the report from the wall. "You think you're pretty funny, don't you?"

"What's this about?" I said with a straight face.

Rob gave me a steely look before settling on the couch to read the transcript.

Crime scene: The kitchen of Apartment D-4. 3034. Thirty-ninth Street. Astoria, Queens.

Description of victim: Caucasian All-Clad dishtowel discovered on the floor beaten, bruised, and left for dead. No positive ID as of yet.

Age of victim: Appears to be roughly four months old, given the few oven stains.

Alleged time of death: Coroner assesses time of death at 1:15 a.m., March 22, 2004.

Most obvious clue: Piece of cheddar cheese located near the victim.

Who has killed the towel?

The possible suspects are being held in containment. Recorded in order of highly suspicious recent activity:

The two dirty forks. Numerous sightings of delinquent behavior, and silverware drawer cannot confirm alibi for the morning of the twenty-second. Currently out on bail.

The container of sea salt. Shows signs of excessive relocation and has a past history of elusive behavior.

The tinfoil, also in violation of switching positions frequently. Reckless behavior being tracked.

The garbage pail. Criminal record lists an incident concerning a run-in with a milkshake.

The other All-Clad towel. The oven reported it fleeing the scene just moments before the crime took place.

The All-Clad Pots and Pans. Motive extremely high. Earlier admission of anger due to lack of use. Statement claims rush delivery was unjustified.

The large knife (designated only for meat and poultry). Insignificant alibi during coroner's alleged time of death.

The one and only saucepan Pam Castle and Rob Trombetti use. Given the amount of grilled cheese it yields per week, the saucepan complains of overuse and harassment.

The coffee maker. A recent addition to the kitchen. A background check is in progress.

ROBERT TROMBETTI. Our only living suspect. Prone to swings in temper regarding his kitchen. Possibly resentful of towel mismanagement. Strong motive.

I read the report over Rob's shoulder, thinking how clever I was. Rob's mouth flickered in the way of a smile a few times, but he managed to remain stoic and act annoyed as he scanned down the list. He finally grinned and set down the report. "You know what I'm more concerned about?" he said.

"What could be of more concern than the towel's safety? Do you think we should hire security?"

"I'm more concerned by the fact you had enough time on your hands to concoct this bizarre scenario." He tossed the report at me.

"We need to keep a closer eye on our appliances from now on. This is no laughing matter."

"You've made your point, Pam."

I giggled. He sighed. I chuckled. He rolled his eyes. I grabbed his hand and tried to kiss it. He pulled it away and grabbed me around the waist. Before I knew it, I was in some martial arts trap, and I couldn't move.

"Let me go," I screamed. "I need to go to the gym. Strengthen my bowling arm."

"You're not going anywhere, Detective."

"That's lieutenant," I squeaked.

"OK, Lieutenant. I'm going to need you to suss out the suspects. Starting with Robert Trombetti. A full examination."

"You can't make me!" I screamed, laughing.

"Oh no?" he said, squeezing me harder.

"OK, OK. I'll do it." He picked me up and carried me into the bedroom.

***

Naturally, Rob and I were the first ones to arrive at Bowl-a-Rama.

"Jesus. Is the fucking heat on? It's freezing in this piece-of-shit Nissan." My legs were actually shaking.

"I'm not running the heat in the parking lot, Pam. It wears down the battery too fast."

I growled. "Rob, I have to warn you. I can't remember the last time I went bowling. I think I was in high school."

"I wasn't planning on picking you for my team."

"You're not going to pick your own wife!"

"I hadn't intended to."

"Great. So I'm going to be the last one chosen. Just like gym class. That's awesome."

"I hate to break this to you, but bowling isn't usually a team sport."

"Sure it is. All those leagues competing."

"Well, I don't think it will be tonight. I mean we have dishwashers and porters and waiters who can't walk straight all participating. A team situation would be unbalanced no matter how it was decided."

This made me feel better. I looked down at my outfit. "Am I dressed appropriately?"

Rob glanced over at my preppy Lacoste rugby shirt and Seven jeans. "Yes, somehow I knew you'd do your best to appear sporty."

I shook my head at the sight of the blinking, red neon sign: BOWL-A-RAMA. Everyone else I knew enjoyed civilized Christmas parties in the month of December, which utilized hotel lobbies and back-room restaurants, and my husband's "party" was taking place in March at a rundown bowling alley four yards off the Long Island Expressway.

Rob's eyes roamed the near-empty parking lot, looking for familiar cars. "At least I have time to roll a joint," he said.

We waited in the dark parking lot with no heat until three of Rob's excited coworkers arrived, slit-eyed and confused. Following Rob inside, I veered off when I spotted a dirty little bar in the corner. Rob caught my hand. "Wait until we get situated."

"Fine." At the shoe stand, I was more than a little nervous handing over my five hundred–dollar heels in exchange for five-dollar flats. What incentive did the little dude have to *not* steal my shoes? His job? I didn't think so.

Slowly the rest of the Copper House crew, all shapes and sizes, filed into Bowl-A-Rama, clueless and searching for the rest of us. Some were carrying their own bowling balls. I marveled at this, wondering if my participation was actually necessary. Perhaps Rob's boss would let me just sit and drink quietly while the perverse evening unfolded.

"Shit, I should have borrowed my father's ball," Rob muttered. "I wasn't thinking."

***

Once the party was over and we were back in the car, I concluded that I reeked of alcohol.

"Rob, I stink like vodka."

"I know." He made a show of rolling down his window.

"I'm serious. It's horrible."

"I'm serious too. *I know.*"

I recapped the top funniest bowling moments. "Your little victory dance was so weird! Like an ant shaking," I howled. "I can't believe *you* won!"

"Pam, I bowled a one twenty. If my father knew I took down the Copper House with that score, he'd disown me."

"Well, what's a good score? What does he bowl?"

"I think the lowest my dad has ever bowled in his life is two hundred. And he's seventy-eight years old."

"Oh."

Rob pulled into a 7-Eleven. Luckily, this didn't require any movement from me. I suddenly felt sicker than hell.

"Pam, I'm going to get a coffee for the ride home. Do you want anything?"

"Yeah." I was surprisingly hungry for feeling so sick. "Get me a bagel."

"It will be from the morning. Old and dry. You won't like it."

"Yes I will. I'm starving!"

"OK. Anything else?"

"Yes. A water. A big one." I rested my eyes while he went inside. A few minutes later, he emerged with a bagel in a brown paper bag and tossed it in my direction. "Where's the water?" I asked.

"You said a bagel or a water."

"No, I didn't. I wanted both."

"You said either—or."

"I did not! How ridiculous. A wet water or a dry bagel!" I screeched. "They're complete opposites." Rob reopened the car door and jumped back out while I convulsed into hysterics.

"Here's your big three-dollar water," he said, jamming the key into the ignition.

"A bagel *or* a water!"

Rob stared at me with a look of amusement. "I think my baby is drunk."

"I drank a dozen vodka grapefruit. Maybe a baker's dozen," I slurred.

"At least you still have your clothes on."

I stared at him. *Why would that be a good thing?*

We headed out of the parking lot, and I took a bite of my bagel. It was so dry it stuck to the roof of my mouth. "I can't eat this!" I tossed it out the window.

"I told you," said Rob.

"Wow! Look at that sign for VIP strip club. Now, that's what I call advertising. We're still an hour away from the city," I shouted.

"It's amazing the things you concern yourself with. Do you really think that billboard attracts business?"

"Hello! Yes! The power of suggestion? I mean, come on. I noticed it, and it makes me want to go there right now."

"Yeah, but you're twisted. There's another sign for you." Rob pointed to a billboard that read *Penthouse Boutique*. "That looks classy. Right next to the Cracker Barrel. Where comfort meets food."

"Next exit. Can we stop?"

"Maybe another time."

"You're no fun."

"I somehow how feel getting home safely without a DUI might be more important than sifting through nudie magazines and prize dildos. But that's just me," said Rob, turning up the music.

I turned it down again. "I had fun tonight. Unexpected, pure fun."

"Glad to hear it." He turned the volume back up.

I got serious again, realizing I hadn't thought of Jake all night. Thinking of him made my body twitch. I watched Rob drive, weaving in and out of cars expertly. "Did *you* have fun tonight?"

"Yeah. I think we made the most out of it."

"With me, I mean? Fun with me?"

"Sure. Why?"

"I don't know. We don't do much together. Do you still find me fun?"

"Of course. Even when you're a drunk, silly baby bowling strictly in the gutter."

"Hey, I didn't do so bad. Fifty-two is a high score for me. That means I hit a few pins."

APRIL 2004

I was in a mad search for a brown skirt. Wearing black with brown leopard print was like giving up, and I knew eventually Jake would point out the discrepancy. So I gritted my teeth and entered Canthropologie on Sixth Avenue. As a rule, I boycotted this particular store. In my opinion, it was unorganized and overpriced, and the employees never remembered to remove the sensors upon checkout. Nevertheless, Donna had mentioned that the cutest brown pencil skirt hung in the window, so I made an exception.

After much deliberation over its exorbitant cost, I purchased it. Since my last encounter with Jake, all I cared about was how hot I looked. I was still living like a socialite but without the steady stream of cash. Everything I tried on, I imagined Jake approving. If I didn't think he'd like it, I didn't buy it.

I stepped outside, attempting to leave the hectic, mismanaged store. *Beep! Beep! Beep!* "I'm *never* shopping here again," I stated aloud. Naturally, Jake picked that particular moment to call me back, just as the manager and the security guard began rifling through my many bags.

"What is that noise in the background?" asked Jake.

"It's the alarm system at Canthropologie. Can I call you back? I have to find my receipt."

"Sure, no problem."

With all my shopping bags, it was like looking for a movie ticket while holding a basket of popcorn, Milk Duds, Twizzlers, Klondike minis, and a large soda. *The store should change its name from Canthropologie to I-Owe-You-an-Apology.* I presented the receipt with bitter flourish.

I called Jake back when I was safely across the street. "What was that about?" he asked.

"I bought *one* item, and the teenage moron who rang me up left all three sensors on it. They must do it for their own personal entertainment. When are you leaving work?"

"Um, that's the thing. I have to work late. I probably can't hang tonight."

"Oh." I tried to hide my acute disappointment. It was a Wednesday, and I hadn't seen him since Isle of Capri. He'd been away on business, and more than two weeks had elapsed.

"Something came up with one of our biggest clients and I have to correct the problem, pronto." He sounded pissed.

"Sure, I understand."

"As of right now, my company has lost more than sixty grand, and I can only hope to regain half of it back, which means in one day I've lost thirty."

"So just call me tom—"

"I'm also in a really bad mood, and I'm no fun to be around when I'm mad like this. I'm the reason the company revenue is so high, so therefore, I'm the one who feels it the most when we lose money."

"Yeah, OK. I get it. It's OK." I was still standing on Sixth Avenue, and if I wasn't going to see him, I needed to hightail it to the train.

"It should be OK! I have responsibilities, and I can't just do nothing if an emergency arises."

"I said it's *fine.* I'm not mad."

"You shouldn't be! These are things I have to do. I run this firm!"

"I'm not mad, but you sound like you think I am." I was really confused. *What was happening?*

"I'll talk to you later." The phone went dead in my hand.

When I arrived home, I couldn't find my keys.

I managed to get into the building due to one of the dozens of accommodating neighbors who would have unknowingly laid the red carpet out for Bin Laden, but I couldn't get into my actual apartment. So I sat outside my door and went through all my purchases, hoping my keys would miraculously appear. Nope.

I sat on the concrete stairs and looked around, dumbfounded. I called Jake and left a message. Then I called everyone else I knew, with the exception of Rob. No one answered.

Tapping my foot manically, I went to see if Bruno could be of any help. He was a little slow in the social skills department, but he was still hot as hell. He suggested we go down the fire escape and see if my kitchen window was unlocked. I wasn't in the mood for any moonlit cat burglary antics, but I figured it was worth watching him. And it was.

Of course, after climbing down the roof backward in the pitch black, there was no feasible way the window could be open. That would have gone against God's unique plan for me. Bruno did, however, hold onto my shopping bags, which was helpful.

Eventually I had to do what I dreaded most: call Rob and tell him I didn't have my keys. This had spurred many arguments in the past and always—no matter what—reinforced his assumption that I was irresponsible. Dialing the Copper House, I decided the sympathy route might be my best bet.

"I was mugged!" I hollered into the phone.

"Where? Are you OK?"

"Yeah, I'm fine. The bastard didn't get my wallet, but he got my keys. And my Louis Vuitton keychain! You know how I adore that thing."

"Where did this happen, Pam?"

"When I was getting off the train. The guy must have been a pro because I didn't feel him take anything."

"You have to be more careful."

"I was holding tight to all my purchases! My keys were in my jacket pocket."

"OK, well, I'm in the middle of cooking for this party, and the main course hasn't gone out yet. You're going to have to wait for me."

"I guess I'll go back into the city." I was really thinking that now I had a legitimate excuse to see Jake. *I was mugged!*

Jake called me back when I was standing on the train platform. "What happened? Your message said you were mugged?"

"Yep."

"What happened exactly?" I explained it to him in the same heroic manner as I had to Rob. "So what are you going to do?"

"Borders Bookstore. My second home. They are open late. Where are you?" I asked casually.

"I'm leaving my office now."

"Do you want me to take the train near you and we can get a drink instead?" I said, paying no mind to our earlier conversation. After all, I'd been mugged. *This changed everything!*

"I'm hungry. I have to eat. Are you hungry?"

"Sure, I could eat."

"Do you mind eating Mexican?"

"No, why would I?"

"No one I know ever wants to." The train was pulling up, and I could barely hear him above the careening noise. "Do you know Arriba Arriba on Ninth Avenue?"

"Yep."

"I'm going to take a cab there now."

"Fine, see you there."

I was becoming obsessed and I knew it, but I was too obsessed to curtail my obsession. By the time I'd taken my seat across from Jake at a wobbly wooden table, I knew I'd made an awful decision. He had a thirty thousand–dollar problem on his mind and not much else. Usually I was the focus, and frankly, I was jealous. I complained about my day to fill in the gaps of silence, but it wasn't much of a conversation. I mean, how much could I really complain? I'd spent the entire day shopping. The "mugging" was not exactly a poignant description worthy of a write-up in the newspaper, and my exaggerated tale of dangling from the fire escape didn't even elicit a smile. If it weren't for the two baskets of chips and salsa he was shoveling into his mouth at breakneck speed, his expression would have remained a permanent frown.

Trying to break this off-putting cycle, I went to put my foot in his lap. As soon as he felt my shoe in his crotch, he grabbed it and placed it back on the Mexican tiles. "I have on really good pants," he said. It was awkward. To further increase the tension, he then looked down at his designer trousers to make sure they weren't affected. I ordered a second Cosmopolitan to mask my embarrassment. He then looked at me like I was an alcoholic breaking my ninety-day streak of sobriety.

"What?"

"Nothing."

I gritted my teeth. He certainly wasn't very considerate about the fact I had just been mugged! *Lucky to be alive, for God's sake.* The evening continued this way, and I focused on discovering bits of chicken in my vegetarian taco enchilada until I noticed Jake glance up at the bar and scowl.

"What's up at the bar? Why do you keep looking over there?" I asked. The bartender was female and decent looking but not a knockout.

"See that big guy? The dude wearing the horrible flannel shirt. Looks like he chopped down half of Pennsylvania's forest reserve."

"Yeah." I made a face. "What about him?"

"I was saving you a seat at the bar before because I wanted to watch the game, and that fucking guy took your seat. He didn't believe I had a friend coming to meet me. He kept saying, 'It's been two minutes. Where's your friend?' I finally gave him the chair and sat over here just to get away from him."

"I see."

"I mean, who the fuck wears flannel outside their apartment?" *Um. The majority of New England. Actually most of the North. Even I wear it on occasion.* I kept quiet, however, because I sensed wearing flannel in public was more insulting to Jake than the actual relinquishing of my barstool.

"So why do you keep looking back there? It's done."

"I don't know. The guy pissed me off."

I felt so ignored. I glanced at the bartender again, thinking Jake's story sounded a little made up. Had I interrupted other plans of his? Finally, I had a brainstorm: if I took my shoe off, I could place it in his lap without it endangering his good pants. He accepted it but acted like he was making a concession. That's when I decided I should really go. I hailed a cab and got the hell out of there. I was slowly learning that Jake had a one-track mind, which was fine as long as I was the only one riding the train.

***

The next day I didn't turn on my cell until 5 p.m. I had two messages from Jake. The first one was at half past three calling to see what I was up to. He managed to speak three minutes without actually saying anything. I could hear it in his voice: he was wondering if I was mad at him.

The second message: "Hey, where are you?" He sounded like he was laughing—in a sweating bullets sort of way. "It's four thirty and I haven't heard from you. I hope you're not mad at me or anything." As I was listening to it, my call waiting went off. I clicked over to him. "Where have you been?" he asked.

"Home. Why?"

"Are you mad at me? I was in a really bad mood last night."

"No big deal," I said frostily. *Asshole.*

"Work has been utterly ridiculous. Yesterday we were down sixty grand—like I told you—so today we put together a full sales team to get a better sales quota, and we actually lost more business. Another client backed out of a written agreement, so we're down another twenty."

I don't give a fuck. "What are you doing later?"

"I'm going out for a drink here in Midtown. My sales team wants to go over some bullshit strategy for the next few days with a few of our associates. Do you mind?"

"No, I have plans," I lied.

"OK, so how about we talk tomorrow?" My breath caught, and tomorrow stretched in front of me like the Chilean coastline. "Or later on. I'll give you a call later tonight," said Jake, sensing my mood.

"Sure. Whatever." That was the precise moment I knew my situation was bad. Because I really missed him.

I needed practical advice/an ass kicking, so I called my mother. When I'd completed what seemed like the most far-fetched tale—leaving out explicit details, of course—I completely cracked. "I mean, we didn't have sex, but that's only because he didn't want to! Sarah, am I a terrible person? I haven't even been married a year!" I didn't feel sad necessarily, just doomed.

"You're not bad. I think you're terrific."

"Still?"

"Yes, you are who you are."

"What is that supposed to mean?"

"It means you can't help *who* you are. You make certain choices on how to conduct your personal life, and your choices eventually make up your personality." Something resonated when she said this, and I wasn't sure she was complimenting me.

"So you think I'm making bad choices," I deduced.

"I think it's a little dangerous."

"But I don't want to stop."

"That's why it's risky. You might get caught."

"Shit, what if Rob does find out?"

"He won't. Just don't *tell* him." She phrased her next words carefully. "What is it you like about Jake, exactly? Besides his wallet."

"He's really nice to me."

"He makes you feel special?"

"Yep."

"So you like the attention?"

"It makes for a nice change. I'm just surprised I developed feelings for him. I mean seriously, he likes to be used and humiliated. I thought these attributes would act as a buffer and I wouldn't fall for him."

"Do you enjoy when he does these unusual things?"

"No. It's annoying. I want him to be normal."

"But you're still attracted to him?"

"Yes."

"So let me get this straight. You like him regardless of his odd behavior simply because he's nice to you? And obviously, buys you gifts. Which, by the way, is a fabulous trait of his. There is no question. I wear that Valentino skirt once a—"

"Sarah! Focus. This is my life. Am I every bit as strange as him?"

"He's the one with the fetish. Not you."

"Right."

"Pam, people who have fetishes are damaged people."

"Jake doesn't seem damaged."

"It doesn't mean he's not a great person. It just indicates there is something painful in his past that drives him in these peculiar directions."

"Does that mean I'm damaged too?"

"We just went over this. *You* don't have the fetish."

"But if I condone and *encourage* the behavior, aren't I just as bad?"

"Don't overdramatize this. You're getting free stuff. Great free stuff! You're not driving the getaway car to a bank robbery."

"True."

"Would you do it for no money?"

"I wouldn't want to."

"Then it's just a job for you."

"It started off as a job, but now I like him. He's not going to keep paying me."

"Why not?" demanded Sarah.

"I don't know. He explained it to me, and it made sense at the time."

"If you don't take his money, he's no longer going to interest you, so you don't have to worry. This will all go away sooner than you think."

"How do you know that?"

"Because if the money flow stops, you'll have to get a job like everyone else." It was no secret that we both detested working.

"He's really putting me in the worst position."

"I told you to go to law school and meet a nice lawyer."

"I know. And when I said I wasn't going to do that, you told me to just hang out in the law library! Ha!" I laughed, recalling her clever advice. "Those were words of wisdom."

"Pam, this has been great chatting, but I have to go to bed. Just ask yourself what your relationship with Jake is really based on."

***

My obsession with Jake grew. I felt we had a deep connection that transcended years of knowing someone. He was all I thought about, and I was needy. I'd lie awake at night, wondering whether my feelings were reciprocated or if I existed solely for his amusement. And after the last earful from my mother, I started to question myself. What was our relationship based on? Just what emptiness was Jake filling? If he had no money, would I still like him?

***

I hadn't seen Jake since the awkward night at Arriba Arriba. So when we met up two nights later, I wanted him to throw me on his bed and take me. Unfortunately, he was on a different page, claiming intense hunger again. He appeared tired and anxious to eat, so we sought out another Mexican joint in his neighborhood. I was already wary as I'd made the connection that he craved rice and beans when he was in a bad mood.

It was a cooler night for April, and we walked there quickly, heads down. At the restaurant—which was more like a take-out burrito stand with a few tables—we ate virtually in silence, watching each other the whole time. He kept his hand glued to my knee, and I rested my hand on his. It felt like we were an old married couple. Older than Rob and me, if one could imagine.

"My ankle's been hurting lately," I said, eager to make some sort of conversation, even if it wasn't the most intelligent or quick-witted. "I think it's partly to do with wearing such high heels all the time."

"Oh yeah?" He was holding a fat steak burrito up to his mouth, trying to control the unwieldy red-dyed tortilla. Rice flew out of the corners and onto the matching red plastic plate. Classy joint. I made a face. I hated messy food and didn't particularly appreciate eating off of synthetic material. I could do that at home.

"Yeah. I need to see a good doctor this time."

"How did you hurt your ankle again?"

"I twisted it three years ago attempting to roller-skate out of the Roxy Nightclub and home to Ninth Street. When I stopped for a halfway-point beverage at Pete's Tavern, I skated back out onto the street and skidded right into a stopped UPS truck."

"Oh, that's right. You thought it was moving and induced falling. I remember this story."

"Yeah, and I was obviously too fucked up to feel anything because I skated home as if nothing was amiss. At any rate, it's bothered me ever since and often contributes to my overall clumsiness."

"I know a good orthopedist."

"Is he in New York?"

"Yep."

"Write his name down for me later."

Jake nodded, wolfing down his burrito at an alarming speed. *Screw hot dogs. They should have the fastest eating burrito contest.* Black beans and shredded cheese flew in all directions, and I jumped up to retrieve more napkins.

We lapsed back into silence. I examined my cold cheese quesadilla. I needed more guacamole and sour cream but felt self-conscious asking for additional servings that would be called out through a loud speaker. Call it a sixth sense, but something told me not to ask for it.

After he paid the bill, he suggested we go to McHale's, a popular Irish bar down the street from his apartment. There was obviously a sports game of ridiculous importance being televised for him to suggest going to an Irish bar. Glancing at my watch, I saw it was already ten o'clock.

"Or we could go to your apartment." I still wanted to be close to him despite the way he handled a burrito.

"We could do that," he said, relenting.

"OK, so let's." Back at his place, desire was coursing through my body. I pulled him onto the couch and began kissing him. I wanted him bad. "Take off my shirt."

"If that shirt comes off, you're going to be here until one thirty in the morning," he said sounding scared.

"So." I rapidly unbuttoned his shirt and began kissing his chest. He shut his eyes. I took this to be a good sign and continued.

"God, I'm falling asleep here," he said.

"Are you serious?" He obviously wanted me out so he could watch the game.

"Yeah, I had a bad day yesterday. And the day before that. And the day before that. I didn't get much sleep."

"So let me put you to bed," I said, trying to hide my obvious frustration. "You need a good night's sleep."

"No, let me walk you out."

"It's OK, you don't have to." I felt angry and rejected.

I walked ahead of him and down five flights of stairs. He placed me in cab and said, "So long." He didn't give me cab money, and I didn't call him from the taxi or e-mail him when I got home. Instead, I lay down in my bed next to my husband. Rob woke up and reached for me. I must have left the kitchen clean because I didn't even have to persuade him.

***

I woke up the next afternoon realizing one thing was all too clear: Jake hadn't been appreciative of me lately. I was making myself too available. I needed to have somewhere to be so he felt privileged to hang out with me. Preferably a place that would make him jealous and remember what a fascinating, incredible woman I still was.

Donna kept telling me to look on Craigslist under the "et cetera" category. Like that was going to be my big career break. However, feeling desperate, I finally did. The job site was full of random, unrelated job "opportunities," and I perused the list, trying to keep an open mind. I read through a bunch of ads for escort services and dirty massage parlors and was about to click off the site completely when a headline caught my eye.

Pretty Girls with Pretty Feet Needed $100 per Hour (NYC)

My immediate thought was Jake had placed an ad and was paying random hot chicks to play with their feet. I double-clicked on it mainly for this reason and read on.

> *If you are an attractive girl with pretty feet, discover how you can make one hundred dollars per hour having your feet kissed and worshipped at foot fetish parties and foot fetish private sessions.*

Before you send us your photo for consideration, please note that we only work with girls that are over eighteen, very attractive, have pretty feet, and are open to new adventures! Girls with experience are also welcome.

We have work available immediately. NO NUDITY! NO SEX! We are very professional, friendly, safe, and classy. The energy is great, and your feet will make you money! The girls that do this love it! If you are interested, send a clear photo of your face and your contact number, and one of our representatives will be in touch with you very soon. See you at the party!

I was still thinking of Jake when I finished reading. There was no way he was throwing parties in that spotless apartment of his. Was there?

The job sounded too good to be true. The euphemism "new adventures" was a bit vague, but how bad could it be if there was no sex and no nudity and they didn't require a picture of your body? All considered, maybe this was a perfect place to meet other people like Jake. After knowing him, it seemed perfectly natural that there might be other generous men with foot fetishes.

I e-mailed my picture and contact info over to them right away, not expecting the organization to get back to me anytime soon. I figured they probably received two thousand pictures a day and took forever to weed through them. Therefore, I was surprised when I got a call on my cell an hour later requesting an interview. "Can you come tonight to this address?" asked a guy named Mack. He sounded easygoing and normal. Moreover, he seemed sincere.

I scribbled down the address he recited. The place was on Vesey Street in Tribeca. He told me which train to take and said he and his partner would be interviewing all night because there was a party scheduled for the following evening. "We want lots of hot girls there," he said. "And don't be worried about coming here for the first time. It's a safe commercial building with doormen and cameras."

"OK, which floor are you on?"

"Eleven. It's the penthouse."

"Suite number?"

"We rent the entire floor. Our space is huge," he said.

"Um, OK." It was all happening very fast.

"Great," said Mack. "From your picture and your voice, I can already tell you're going to love it!"

I had to admit I was intrigued. Women's feet must be a lucrative business if these two men could afford to rent an entire floor in one of the world's highest-rent districts. I told Mack I'd be there and pushed my plans up with Jake, emphasizing the fact I had a job interview.

***

I arrived just before 7 p.m. and was relieved that the building appeared commercial and architecturally sound. It was cool that Mack hadn't lied to me. The entryway sparkled with newness.

"Miss, I need to check your ID," the door attendant called after me.

"Oh, sorry," I muttered, further impressed with the security. I handed him my expired New Jersey license from ten years earlier and glanced up, hoping he wouldn't look at the date. "I like your hat." (The art of distraction.)

"Why, thank you. And what floor will you be heading to this evening?"

"Eleven."

His eyes lit up, and he passed the ID back to me with a knowing smile. "OK, when you turn the corner, you'll come to a set of elevators. Take the second one on your right," he instructed. Biting my lower lip, I wondered what I was getting myself into.

I stepped out onto the eleventh floor and found myself in a dome-shaped entranceway. The ceilings were high, and cameras were installed in all four corners. The door I was about to enter had some odd lettering in crayon, and I quickly wondered about the authenticity of all this. I did not want to be disappointed at this stage in the game.

I knocked hesitantly, to no avail. I knocked again with more force. I had a feeling I could easily be interrupting a private orgy, in which case knocking was not going to do me much good. I tapped my foot and peered into a glass panel on my left. An electronic voice boomed through the walls.

"Ring the doorbell, and be patient!" the voice thundered.

I jumped and pivoted back to the door with the crayon scribbling. I wasn't going to contest an invisible force. I waited until a very sexy man finally opened the door. He appeared to be Persian or Latin, and his perfect skin was the color of coffee, heavy on the cream. From the sound of his voice, I knew he wasn't Mack. This dude was refined, an obvious pacifist. A devout vegetarian and obviously didn't vote Republican.

"Come on in," he said. "I'm just interviewing someone right now, but I'll be with you shortly. Take a seat, and make yourself comfortable. I'm Jacquin."

"Pamela." I shook his smooth hand. He was almost pretty.

Plopping down in a plump maroon chair, I inhaled the setting. The high ceilings continued, giving the loft a cavernous feel. Large white candles cast shadows on the walls, and lavender incense burned in the background. The oak hardwood floors descended in three levels, and the bottom plane showcased a suggestive canopy. Flimsy white material floated over four large poles, creating a tent of sorts. Useless in the great outdoors but romantic inside a penthouse loft. Underneath, assorted fluffy pillows lay pristine and unruffled. I stared at the canopy, wondering if this would be where my first foot fetish experience would take place.

I thought of Jake. I hadn't told him what my interview was regarding, and I wondered what his reaction would be. He'd either be intrigued or jealous; I just didn't know which.

Eventually it was my turn to speak with the beautiful boss. "Have you done this kind of work before?" he asked.

"Yes, in Miami a couple years back," I lied. I didn't want him to think I had existing clients in New York for fear of him putting two and six together. If he thought I was going to steal his clients, he wasn't going to hire me. Of course, that was exactly what I intended to do, but that was beside the point. You know things better at twenty-nine than you do at twenty-one. I imagined they hired girls with no experience simply for that reason.

"OK, so you understand the drill. Men will massage your feet, suck on them, and you might walk on them, give a foot job," he further explained.

"Sounds pretty standard." I coughed, trying to give the impression that this didn't disgust me. As if some fucking loser was going to get a foot job from me. Not for a hundred bucks, he wasn't. I'd only just performed my first foot job on Jake by pure accident, and I was *into* him.

"Of course, whatever you decide to do is completely up to you. You're the one in control," emphasized Jacquin, reciting from his manual on how not to get arrested by a female undercover cop. "Every woman who works for me has her own set of guidelines."

I nodded and smiled. Of course she does.

After our interview, Mack showed up. He looked like the average guy I was expecting, still a boy who excelled at sports at his suburban high school. The only difference was he was hot for women's feet and extremely open about it. He took an instant liking to me, and I had my "audition" with him under the large canopy. I quickly learned that audition meant worshipping my feet free of charge, but whatever. As long as he wasn't jacking off on my perfectly shaped toes, I didn't care. I needed a job for a few weeks until Jake got the fucking point.

Mack massaged and caressed my feet (which was fab), sucked on my toes (which was interesting), and then carefully cleaned my entrepreneurial jewels with witch hazel. I concluded he was a stand-up guy. He told me he and Jacquin had scheduled a party for the following evening and asked if I could be there at eight o'clock.

"How does it work?"

"It runs just like a regular party. You mingle, and the men have the option to ask you for a foot session. A session runs about ten minutes, and during that time, they worship your feet. Similar to what I just did. The party we're throwing tomorrow is going to be a smaller one with just regular clients. We won't be doing any advertising, but it will be a good chance for you to meet some of the steadier clientele and quite possibly negotiate a few private sessions."

"I see. During a party, what do most girls normally yield?" I asked pointedly.

"Most of our girls average at least two hundred, but some make more. Once you get the hang of it, you'll start making some serious money."

"What percentage of my earnings goes to the house?"

"At the parties, you keep everything. We charge a hefty cover."

"And these private sessions? What's the deal with them?"

"An hour session booked through us costs the guy two hundred dollars for an hour. You get half that."

"So you throw the parties so the men can meet the women and eventually book private sessions?"

"Yes. The more you build up your clientele base, the more we also benefit," he said, nodding slowly. "That's our business."

"OK, I'm down."

"What's really important is that you enjoy the whole foot fetish experience. The more you seem to enjoy it, the more the guy will like you." *Why does this "company" keep reiterating this?*

"Well, there's nothing I like more than a man worshipping my feet."

***

I didn't leave the Foot Palace until after nine. I waited until the host seated Jake and me on a wooden bench at the Tapa's Room to tell him my exciting news.

"But why do you have to do that? Can't you do something else?" I could tell by his stricken expression that he was not pleased.

"Not for a hundred dollars an hour."

"You can't waitress again?" he said, sounding rather like Rob.

I bristled. "No. Duh. I hate waiting tables. I would rather let some dude play with my foot for a hundred bucks. Which part aren't you understanding?"

Jake nodded gravely. He couldn't fault me for being honest, and all things considered, he hadn't given me any money in weeks.

"If I don't have a problem with it, why should you?" I said.

"Are you telling me you have zero problems with this?"

"Jake, I have a problem with *working*—period. It's a major inconvenience. But I'll have less of a problem at this foot place than I would serving the lunch crowd at Gramercy Tavern. Getting there at ten in the morning and polishing silverware. Fuck that."

"Well, I'm going to be jealous with all these other guys touching your feet and stuff. Can't you think of anything else?" he whined.

"You'll be jealous? Are you kidding?" I acted as if this was the craziest thing I had ever heard. Meanwhile, I'd executed my plan to perfection.

"Absolutely. I don't want you to do it. Anything else would be better. Now I'm just going to be like any other guy."

"That's not true. I'm with you because I want to be. The money is the problem. Having other dudes worship my feet will just be a *job*."

"What if you get really good at it and don't have time for me anymore?" asked Jake. "I'm going to have to come up with some other type of arrangement." Ah, the magic words, spoken at last.

Jake nodded seriously and rubbed my back. I looked up seductively and picked up my wine glass. I was so busy laying on the bullshit that I hadn't taken a sip yet.

"Well, just to reiterate, I really hate the idea of you working at this place."

"I haven't even started yet. I'm just going to see how the party goes. I have nothing to lose." I shrugged, feeling very independent.

When our check arrived at the end of dinner, Jake plucked a twenty from his wallet. "Cab fare, in case I forget to give it to you. I've been out of it lately."

"Thanks." I tucked the bill in my pocket, smiling triumphantly. My clever strategy was already working brilliantly. He'd been the one who wanted to enter into the world of financial slavery. I was simply granting his wish.

***

On the night of the party, I rode up in the elevator with another woman. She stared straight ahead and didn't acknowledge me, despite the fact we were obviously heading to the same event. Her hair was long and blond and had been straightened one too many times. Her makeup matched that of a MAC advertisement: glitter and gold, green shadow fusing with yellow, black eyeliner penciled upward like a Siamese cat—not that I was staring or anything. I couldn't determine whether she looked gaudy or glamorous. Sneaking another sidelong glance, I decided the wet, heavy-glossed peach lips tipped her over the edge into slutty; she was the type of chick men who paid for sex were attracted to. Not that that was a bad thing, necessarily. However, standing next to her in my Sigrid Olson baby blue jacket, I resembled a Jewish princess in comparison. Her navy blue trench concealed her outfit, but lowering my eyes, I was able to inspect her hot pink suede boots. Interesting choice, I thought, wondering if my basic Gucci pumps would be acceptable to fellow foot worshippers across the land.

We both exited the elevator onto the eleventh floor to find the door with the crayon lettering wide open. Badly recorded soul music blared out, and I found myself face-to-face with a mousy-looking woman holding court. She sat in a fold-up chair, legs crossed, balancing a clipboard on her knees. The girl from the elevator walked past her without so much as a glance, but I stopped. Under her clipboard, she was holding tightly to a lockbox, the type shown in crime movies that inevitably leads to murder. I assumed she was collecting the cover charge from the "regular clients." I smiled at her, feeling timid suddenly. What was I doing there again? Oh yeah, making Jake jealous. And Rob furious, on the off chance he was to find out.

"Is this your first party?" she asked me, peering at me through rimless spectacles. Was she working the fetish angle too, I wondered, or did she think she was old enough to need those things?

"Yep."

"OK. Through the hallway, there are closets to your right. You can leave your stuff there, but keep your valuables on you," she said, scowling.

"Thanks."

Consumed with trepidation, I considered turning around and leaving the way I had just entered, but I reminded myself I had nothing to lose. The longer I stayed, the more believable it would be that I had showed up at all. I brightened, recalling the fact that Jake was miserable over this.

Empty-handed with the exception of a Judith Leiber clutch—perfect for clutching nervously—I hung my coat in the paneled closets and entered the large room where I'd had my interview the evening before. The lofty space was lighted much darker, and my eyes took a while to adjust. Some creative genius had transformed the corner of the room into a makeshift bar, and numerous bottles of cheap liquor lined the back of a big wooden desk. In front, plastic liters of juice and soda were uncapped and half-empty. An older woman with a well-maintained body and huge tits was tending the desk, so I figured I might as well get a drink before I explored any further. I had a feeling that a strong cocktail would expedite my transition into this dark, disturbing foot world.

"Welcome to hell. What would you like to drink?" asked the desk-tender, unable to mask her boredom. I looked behind me. This was an encouraging start.

"Um, do you have any wine back there?" I asked stupidly.

"Not for consumption. Cleaning, maybe. Stick with the hard stuff," she advised, her gray-streaked hair slipping in front of her eyes. "I got Jack, rum, and vodka."

"Right. Vodka it is. Splash of orange." There was no reason to specify which vodka. Ten bottles of Gordon's finest were staring me in the face.

"No orange juice. We have cranberry and cranberry. Or soda."

"I see. Cranberry's fine." I smiled.

She reached for a plastic cup and poured from both plastic bottles at the same time, creating a fifty-fifty ratio.

"No ice, huh?"

"Nope. Mack brings the ice, and he ain't here yet."

"No sweat." I'd worked at Lime, so I was familiar with cheap liquor, warm cocktails, and unpleasant surroundings. I was, technically, right at home.

She shrugged and jerked her head in the direction of a rust ceramic tip jar. Once upon a time, it might have housed a plant of some sort. I managed to find a couple single dollars in my purse and plucked them in.

The dark room was empty, with the exception of a few women sitting around kicking it with warm cocktails. I took a seat next to another woman on a long, thin ottoman. I needed some guidance, and she didn't look particularly busy. "I like your shirt," I said to her, starting with the most basic of nonthreatening conversations. It was white lace and cropped just above her belly button. It looked similar to mine, which was black lace and cropped just above my belly button.

"I see you're wearing a similar style." She sized me up with round, clear-blue eyes. Her medium-length brown hair was parted in the middle and hung in two ponytails around her shoulders. "Is this your first party? I don't think I've seen you before."

"Yes. Will I make any money?" I inquired.

"You should. It's usually pretty good. What's your name?"

"Pamela. Call me Pam."

"Li Li."

"Cool. What are the clients like here? I see a couple odd-balls lurking around."

"Well, it's still early. For the most part the men are OK. But they arrive later. The losers are always the first ones here."

"Is it by invite only?"

"*This* party is, but Jacquin throws all types."

"How much do these jerks pay to get in?" I asked.

"One-fifty."

"Dollars? Jesus. No wonder the die-hards are here smack at eight."

"It's good. It keeps out the riffraff."

"Right. Pure logic." I nodded my agreement.

There was a lull in our conversation as I surveyed the room. Little blue lanterns flickered on the windowsills, and I noticed a few scantily clad girls waiting their turn to receive warm cranberry vodkas. A few nondescript men were hanging back along the walls, glancing quickly from one girl's foot to another.

"Do you generally approach the men, or do they approach you?" I asked Li Li.

"Both. Some guys are shy—while they're still sober, that is—so it's better if you feel comfortable going up to them. The beginning of the night always winds up feeling like a high

school dance. See that short guy with the salt-and-pepper hair?"
Li Li pointed to a short dude with white hair.

"Mostly salt?" I said, laughing. A second ago, they were all losers, but now she was being polite?

"Yeah. He's into foot worship but more into being tortured."

"Oh, right." Torture was a broad scope.

"And see that skinny, tall dude in the corner? He's got a long beard."

"Yep."

"He's totally ridiculous but always good for a session. He likes to tickle girls. Starting with their feet."

"No kidding. You must know most of the regulars, then."

She shrugged. "These parties are only once a month. It's really all about the private sessions."

"That's what I figured. But the chances to meet these men can only happen at a party—correct?"

"Pretty much. Unless you're on the website and someone requests you."

"How do I get on the website?" I was getting ahead of myself, considering leaving the party was still a viable and appealing option.

"That's tricky. Jacquin has to approve you."

"Ah," I said, wondering what that entailed. It really was a dog-eat-dog world.

A man approached us and tapped Li Li on the shoulder. She recognized him, apparently, and I watched as he led her away through a glass-paneled door. This signified the end of our conversation and my decision to get back in line at the desk. I ordered my second cocktail, wondering where the fuck Mack was with the ice. That's when I spotted the "tickler" glancing at my shoes. Grabbing my beverage, I scooted over to him and said, "Are you staring at my feet?"

"I haven't seen you before. Are you a new foot model?"

"Yes. Do you want to tickle my feet?" *Give me twenty bucks!*

"Are you ticklish?"

"Yes," I crooned. *"Crazy* ticklish."

"Your feet?"

"Especially my feet." I couldn't remember the last time I'd been tickled.

"Have you ever been tied up and tickled? On video?"

"No. But it's always been my dream," I deadpanned.

"Because that's what I do in my studio in New Jersey. I call it tickle torture."

"What's the relation to the feet?"

"Feet are the most ticklish part of the body. I find most of my girls through these parties."

"Fascinating. Do any of them make it back from Jersey, or do you drop them off sweetly in the Hudson River after the video commences?"

"It only takes about twenty minutes to get to my place, and it's a quick, *easy* hundred bucks."

"There's nothing quick—or *easy*—about getting back and forth to New Jersey from Manhattan," I said.

"I live in Secaucus, right over the river."

"I'm sure it's picturesque."

"I'm Josh, by the way," he said, sticking out his hand.

I was planning to tell every dude a fake name, and I needed one I could remember. "Lexi," I said. *Ha!*

"Would you consider being in my video?"

"Sure." I lied smoothly. My drink was almost finished. I judged this by the ease with which I could talk to this crazy whack job.

"So, you'll consider it."

"Well, I'll tell you one thing. If I was going to hike out to New Jersey on a frigging bus to be stripped down and tied to a bed before you tickled my entire body—all captured on video—I'd require *a lot* more money, and it would have to be wired to my account beforehand. But yes, I'll consider it."

"Oh, I see. You're a businesswoman."

"There's easier ways to make a hundred thousand cents."

He grimaced, probably annoyed I was ten times smarter than he was. "Well, let's see if you're as ticklish as you say you are. Do you want to do a session?"

"I thought you'd never ask." I followed him into the same room into which Li Li had disappeared. A large four-poster bed with a maroon comforter accounted for most of the space, and red light bulbs housed in clear, ball-shaped lampshades provided eerie faint light. Couples were spilling over each other on the bed—and around it—camped out on the floor and propped up against the walls. I had to watch where I walked for fear of stepping on random strangers' limbs.

"It's too crowded in here. Let's go into Saturn," said the Tickler.

"Excuse me. Where?"

"This room is called Venus. The other room is called Saturn. Follow me."

I raised my eyebrows and followed the tickler into outer space through another glass-paneled door. I felt like Alice in Wonderland, a diminutive novice not knowing what next to expect.

Saturn was brighter, being the bigger planet and all. However, space was still limited, with couples vying for legroom. Thankfully, the terrible music helped hide the sound of foot sucking and various other begging noises. We managed to procure a corner of the bed, and I braced myself for what was to come. A few of the girls in Saturn were rolling their eyes in my direction and giving me sympathetic looks—just more encouraging signals!

Glancing furtively around, I spotted the short, salt-haired man sitting in the corner. He had an entire set of toes in his mouth. Every few seconds, the woman he was worshipping kicked him in the chest with her other foot. He looked more fun than the tickler, and I made a mental note to chat him up later.

The tickler motioned for me to sit on the side of the bed and placed my feet in his lap. He slipped off my shoes and began to tickle. He was good at it. I howled with laughter, alerting everyone in the room that I'd transformed into an extremely ticklish person. He was right about it being torture. I'll give him that. Once he started grabbing at my sides and under my arms, I was officially screaming. It almost hurt, he was jabbing me so hard. I made an estimated guess when I thought ten minutes had expired and wondered to myself if I could withstand an hour session with him. Where were all the men who just wanted to massage my feet and tell me how beautiful I was?

After ridding myself of that monster, I crept back to my cozy position near the desk and officially introduced myself to the desk-tender. I figured if she was going to pour me drinks all night—no matter how awful—I should know her name. Teresa handed me another vodka cranberry, complete with ice cubes this time, and I stood by myself contemplating my next move.

I spotted the woman who had been kicking the dude with salt hair and introduced myself. She told me she danced topless in New Jersey and was just up for the evening. Apparently it was her first time there as well. Her hair was long and tangled, and her hazel eyes had a tired shimmer. She reminded me of a single mother doing her best to stay on top of things. The effort some people went to in order to survive and provide for others always amazed me. I compared it to myself, who just did weird shit because it was easier and didn't require much responsibility.

I'm not sure whether it was fate or pure luck, but on my way to the bathroom, I managed to corner a polished Hispanic man near the kitchen. He was short and cuddly and had good skin, but more importantly, he was receptive to my cheesy advances. And his foot session was a swim in the Caribbean after what I'd just been through with Josh. I'm not sure whether he was just good at sucking my toes or if I was getting a taste for the whole thing myself, but I found myself tuning out. Singing along to Al Jones. I told Ernesto that he sucked the best feet in town, and he asked me to go to the VIP room with him.

"They have a VIP room here?" I said, incredulous. "Where?"

The VIP room reminded me of a fort I might have constructed in my early childhood. Ernesto and I had to climb a rickety wooden staircase to reach the diminutive storage space. It was called Pluto, obviously named after one of the smaller planets. Once at the top, I was delighted to see it was a dark little hole, equipped with a mirror, a bottle of lotion, paper towels, and a bottle of witch hazel. It had all the comforts of home. The space was literally four feet by seven, with a whopping four-foot ceiling, which ruled out standing. Ernesto, however, seemed overjoyed with its thrill-seeking capabilities. Holding onto a cylindrical pipe running through the length of the cave, I held up my upper body and pressed my toes over Ernesto's face. He grabbed both my feet and held them tightly to the sides of his face, causing my arms to utilize muscles I didn't know I possessed. The encounter got even more interesting when Ernesto began to voice some of his concerns about his foot fetish.

"I don't know why I like this so much. I just do. Should I be ashamed?" Ernesto cried in broken English.

"Of course not. Feet turn you on, no big deal. Better feet than small boys."

"But I have a wife and kid."

"Can't you kiss your wife's feet?"

"No. She think sick behavior and need doctor."

"OK, I wouldn't tell her about these parties then."

"She say I belong in cage like dog. She don't know I like cage," he said, his broken English collapsing into key words I could decipher.

"Some people do." I nodded, ripe with newly acquired wisdom. "It doesn't mean anything is wrong with you. You probably find it exciting!" I was on a roll of sorts, given the environment.

"Yes, yes. I find exciting."

"Well that's fine. You're totally normal."

Emerging from the glamorous VIP room, I bumped into the salt-haired man. It was no accident. "There you are," he

said, kneeling down before me. "I have already begun to worship you from afar. Thus, will you grant me time alone with
your feet?"

I stared down at him, watching his fingertips touch in
prayer.

"Sure. Where is your favorite place to worship in outer
space?"

"Follow me."

I trailed this raving nut into the Venus room, and he pointed
to a large chair in the corner. "That's my favorite place to worship, but it's taken," he said bitterly. "I guess this will do."
We plunked down on the edge of the maroon comforter, and I
speculated when it was last washed. Adjusting my short skirt,
I dangled my legs off the edge of the bed. "I'm Patrick, by the
way," he said, kneeling in front of me.

"Pa—Lexi," I replied with a smile.

"So, just to tell you a little bit about myself, I'm into punishment," he said proudly.

"OK." I was thinking about my next cocktail. Did I want
straight vodka or another vodka cranberry?

Patrick went on to elaborate, and I tuned out completely.
All the characters I met were nutty and utterly uninteresting
despite their predilections to various fixations. I went along
with it, smiling like they were the most amazing men in the
world. Three hours later I had a clientele and four hundred dollars in my pocket, and I was home by midnight. I couldn't wait
to tell Jake how great the night had been!

MAY 2004

Much to my chagrin, Jake didn't come up with a plan or present me with another alternative like he'd alluded to, so when a few of the crazies I'd met at the party requested private sessions, I found myself agreeing, hoping to prove to Jake I desperately needed money.

As far as Rob was concerned, it was simply easier to tell him what he wanted to hear as opposed to the truth, which was only good for starting arguments. "Did you get a job?" he asked stupidly when I was missing in action three evenings in a row.

"Yeah, I did."

"That's great."

"I thought you'd be happy about that."

"When did you start?"

"A while ago."

"And what is it you're doing again?"

"Modeling work. High-end shoes, stockings, socks, you know..."

"Is it for print or runway?"

I looked at him quizzically. *What the hell do you know about modeling?* "It's for retail buyers," I said.

"That's cool."

"I know." *It's better than any job.*

"If it's retail, shouldn't it be daytime hours?"

"I'll work a few afternoons."

"Oh, so why the night hours?"

"The retail buyers are clients, so most of the shoe modeling revolves around schmoozing them over dinner and New York nightlife." *There are no retail buyers. I step on most dinners, and* nightlife *can be drinking warm vodka to meet more lunatics.*

"Oh," said Rob.

***

After a couple of weeks, I realized Jake was calling my bluff. I couldn't believe it. I thought surely he'd mention some type of payment plan to me so I wouldn't have to endure other men worshipping my feet, but it seemed as the days passed and more strangers booked me for private sessions, I had no choice but to carry on. Jacquin was making use of me because I was new and didn't give a shit how ugly the guys were as long as they were respectful and clean and didn't try anything funny. Many of the girls were snobs and only wanted to session with hot Calvin Klein model types. I was all about the money and could not have cared less about the client's lack of hair or social graces. Considering the foot fetish market was ripe for whackos, it didn't shock me that the dudes were less than stellar.

Instead of Jake rushing to my aid, he began to give me grief. "What have you been doing all day?" he asked me over the phone one afternoon. Like it was any of his business—as much as I wanted him to inquire.

"Nothing. I haven't left the apartment."

"You weren't at the Foot Palace all day?"

"No. They haven't called me in today."

"I'm surprised. I thought you'd be there all day."

"What is that supposed to mean?"

"You love that place."

"I do not love it. It's a *job*. You're at work right now, and I'm not giving you a hard time about it."

"OK, I can see you're defensive. Are you coming into the city tonight?"

"I don't think so. It's supposed to snow."

"I bet if the Foot Palace called, you'd charge through a blizzard to get there."

"I highly doubt that." I scoffed.

"You'd put on your hiking boots and shovel your way through the snow."

"First of all, I don't own hiking boots, and second, I wish you'd stop making fun of me."

"I'm just kidding."

"It doesn't sound like it." My call waiting went off. "Hold on a sec." It was Jacquin calling to see if I wanted to do a session with a dude named Carl. He liked to tickle feet with a feather, and it was the easiest hundred bucks short of stealing it from French employers.

"Was that the Foot Palace?" asked Jake when I clicked back over.

"Yes, dickhead."

"Are you going in?"

"Yes."

"See, I told you. You'll come in for that place but not to see me."

"You didn't *ask* to see me."

"Yes I did."

"No, you didn't. You *asked* if I was coming into the city. You didn't say, 'Hey, Pam, would you like to go out to dinner tonight?'"

"That's what I meant."

"That's not what you said."

"OK, let me try this again. Do you want to meet up with me after your *session*?"

I thought about this. I wanted to see him, but once I was at the Foot Palace, a spontaneous foot voyeur usually booked me again. That meant I would have to say no to additional money if I agreed to meet Jake. Jake always insisted on an exact time.

"All right. Where do you want to meet?" I relented.

"What time do you think you'll be done?"

"The session starts at eight so I could meet you by nine-thirty. We could go by Lexi's latest job if you'd like."

"She's not at Dream Girls?"

"No, she's at some dive bar, waitressing. Insisting she can leave the business."

"Oh yeah, that's right," he said, and I wondered briefly how he knew that. I didn't remember telling him. "OK. I'll see you there at nine thirty. I can't believe you're making time for me. It's such an honor."

I hung up the phone. He was really missing the point.

***

Lexi's "temporary" place of employment was an Irish booze fest—somewhat similar to Donna's—only this place boasted hearty food and was filled with Europeans dressed in rugby chaps. A place in which she was spending an awful lot of time, considering how *temporary* the job was supposed to be.

"Tell Jake to come up front so we can sit in your section," I told Lexi on arrival. She was waiting on the tables in the front of the restaurant, and Jake was dicking around in the back court-yard. "You look cute," I added. Seeing her wearing an apron reminded me of her French maid act.

Lexi left and came back. "He says for you to go back there. He doesn't want to move."

That figured. It was his way now. I got it. Even through my drunken haze, I distinctly got the picture. *Shouldn't have done that last tequila shot.* I stumbled through the restaurant in search of Jake. Carl—the feather holder—had arrived with a bottle of Patron Silver to highlight—or rather obliterate—the foot fun.

I located Jake in the back courtyard, looking annoyed. I glanced at my watch. Nine thirty on the dot. I said hi and sat down—or at least there used to be a bench there. I swear there was. Jake didn't even try to help me up but merely glanced at me sprawled on the ground like I was some crazy stranger who wiped out right in front of him.

"Are you all right?" he asked in an annoyed tone after I'd pulled myself up without any help from him. "What the hell is wrong with you?"

"Nothing! It's fucking dark, and there used to be a bench here! I don't know where it is now," I mumbled, glancing around the courtyard, looking for it.

"But there *is* no bench here."

"There *used* to be," I said.

"But the fact that there *isn't* anymore should have deterred you from to trying to sit on it."

I stared at him. Technically, what he was saying made sense. "You're absolutely right. It must feel good to be right all the time."

Jake looked around again and ran a hand through his hair, giving off a signal to the rest of the patrons that he still had no idea who I was. I mean, I was still standing, and Jake clearly wasn't jumping up to find a chair for me. *Was I back at the pool with Rob in Hawaii?*

Thankfully, one of Lexi's coworkers had seen my ass kiss the ground and arrived with a wooden fold-up chair in tow. I smiled at her gratefully, wishing I could recall her name. Jake studied our table with extraordinary attention, ignoring me.

"Sorry. It'll never happen again. Jesus." I pulled the chair out carefully, sat down, and focused on finding my cigarettes.

"What are you searching for?"

"My cigarettes."

"When did you pick up smoking again? You're like a chain smoker now."

"Oh please. I've been smoking on and off since I met you. And if memory serves me correctly, you encouraged this self-serving act."

"But when did you start again? You weren't smoking before you got married."

"I picked it back up in Hawaii. You would have too."

"But you've been back in NYC for months. Why do you still have to smoke?"

"It's not that I have to. I like to. I enjoy it."

"Are you going to enjoy having lung cancer one day?"

I was drunk, but not to the point where this diatribe wasn't insulting. "What a stupid, ridiculous, insensitive, moronic thing to say."

"You should think about these things instead of just drinking and smoking yourself to death."

"Do me a favor and save me the lecture. I didn't cut my evening short at work for you to chastise me. I came to have fun with you." I reached out to touch his arm, but he pulled away faster than Kennedy pulled air support during the Cuban Missile Crisis.

"You know what? You're just like Mimi," said Jake.

"What do you mean I'm just like her?"

"You are. You don't know when to stop. You're not taking care of yourself. You look like shit, and you're an embarrassment."

"First of all, I don't look like shit. I look great. I went tanning today, my roots have just been done, and my makeup is fresh. I'm a little drunk, yes, but that's because I drank shots at work and I'm not used to drinking tequila."

"Shots of what?"

"I just said."

"I couldn't understand you. You're slurring."

"Cosmos."

"You said tequila."

"I thought you couldn't hear me? That was a test."

"I asked you which shots you were doing."

"Are you trying to trick me? Tequila," I said.

"How many did you have?"

"I don't know. A bunch."

"You're just like Mimi," he repeated.

"I am not!" I exploded. "The one day I show up a little wrecked and you reduce me to her level? How insulting. We've complained about her collectively for over a year."

"It's just your whole attitude. The way you're dealing with everything. It's unappealing."

"What's unappealing? The fact that I have a job now and *you* don't take top billing?"

"You know, you're so messed up you can't even see how bad you are."

"Keep up the compliments. Really, this is a total ego booster."

"E-go. Not eggo—that's the waffle. You can't even pronounce a simple word."

"I can't pronounce a lot of words when I'm *not* drunk. And guess what? I fall all the time too when I'm not drunk! Maybe I don't see so well."

Jake set down his empty beer bottle. This was not going well. I followed his eyeline and realized that he'd been staring at a blonde in the corner all this time. "She's pretty," I said. "Very cute. Looks like a young Loni Anderson. Whatever happened to her anyway?"

"I'm getting a check."

"We just got here."

"You're not fun anymore."

"Gee, thanks. I can't say you're much fun either." I disbelieved we were ever friends. Or more than friends. He motioned the check sign to another one of Lexi's teammates who was hustling past.

"I'm not leaving the waitress fifty dollars either—like I did last time. I don't understand why you made me do that."

"I've never been here. You must be confusing me with someone else. And since when don't you hook up the waitress? You used to be a tad more generous."

"And you used to dress up when we went out. Now you're just loose shirts and baggy jeans."

"Listen, if you're bored, you can just say so. You don't have to compare me to Mimi and make me feel like shit. You also don't have to pretend to leave just so you can come back here without me and chat up the blond chick. I'm fine leaving by myself."

"You're fucking paranoid! Just like Mimi was. I've looked over at that blonde twice, just like I've looked at every other girl in this place. I'm not staging a departure to come back. I'm ready to go home. And you're more than ready."

"I sure as hell am," I said, jumping up as the check arrived. Unfortunately, I knocked over the fold-up chair when I did this, which required me to bend down and pick it up. *Is there never any end to my embarrassment?*

***

After five years of living with Rob, I still didn't really *know* him. I knew a lot about him, and I certainly embraced enough odd quirks and tendencies to qualify me for my role as his wife, but all things considered, I didn't know a thing about him. In a roundabout way, I was lucky. He wasn't terribly complicated, and what I didn't know, I couldn't dislike. He had annoying habits, sure. He was anal-retentive and a stickler for cleanliness. He couldn't hold his liquor, he was addicted to marijuana, and his voice always got louder toward the end of the night. But those were things I could live with. His priorities were mixed up in Hawaii and he had a couple really *bad* moments, but there was still something very nonthreatening about him. He might not have been pleased about the things I hoped he'd never find out about, but he was wise enough not to ask deliberate questions that would lead to disturbing answers. I began to realize the finer attributes of my husband the more I hung out with Jake and got to know *him* better.

Wrong as usual, I assumed I knew Jake because I was an integral part of his private fantasies; I knew the gory details about his most private moments. Unfortunately, I soon realized that under no circumstances did I know him. That became very clear once our relationship hit the last fatal stage.

I hadn't anticipated that Jake would get on my nerves. Rob, yes, Jake, no. I've since learned that the longer you know someone, the greater the chance this has of occurring. The first glimpse of Jake's dark side—which I found impossible to ignore—was the day I had locked myself out of the apartment. His attitude was about more than losing money. It was about me. I was suddenly attainable, available, and willing. Once this became clear, all his fantasies flew out the window. The truth nagged at him, causing him to be moody, irritable, selfish, and unkind. His disposition would change if he didn't get his way. Despite his claims of wanting to be used and manipulated, anything that went slightly out of his control elicited a nasty response. And I began to notice mannerisms I'd previously ignored.

There were other hints I chose to ignore. I realize now that even when he took me shopping, he would only buy me shoes or clothes of which he approved. It just so happened that he had great taste, but if my preference swayed from his on a particular design or label, it would never see my foot. I suppose the thrill of receiving any designer shoes in abundance glossed over this fact, but gradually he went from fairly open-minded to "take it or leave it." Despite the crush to my personal style, I came to terms with this considering I had no one else waiting in the wings to charge hundreds of dollars onto his personal credit card. Eventually I let him pick out whatever he wanted, only for him to berate me if I didn't wear the item often enough. Don't get me wrong—I was still happy Jake shopped for me. He used his money to string an intoxicating web, and I made the most of its sticky restraints.

In short, even though Jake claimed to want to be the wimp, the pussy, the pansy, the sissy, and forever treated like a doormat, his behavior contradicted what he preached. His belittling nuances were subtle at first: a snide comment here, a correction there, and the occasional look of reproach. He had the ability to make me feel stupid at the slightest misunderstanding.

A few times out with him, he mentioned that I dressed too casual.

"What are you wearing?" he'd ask me on my way to the train, twenty minutes before I was due to arrive at his house.

"A ribbed dark brown shirt with velvet slacks and the Chanel boots you bought me."

"Oh. Why don't you ever wear a skirt?"

"Because I'm cold."

Silence.

"Would you *like* me to wear a skirt? I'll have to go back home."

"Yeah I would. I can't remember the last time I saw your legs."

"OK, no problem," I'd say, totally pissed off.

Eventually whatever I wore was never good enough. If I was dressed in a pleated skirt and a tight-cropped half-shirt, he'd say, "You haven't worn a bodysuit in a while." If I wore black pants and a skin-tight bodysuit from Wolford—both purchased by him—he'd say, "Why don't you ever show any skin?"

To make matters worse, his memory retained every detail of the evenings I was dressed "inappropriately." He took these occurrences, catalogued them, and never forgot them. Hence, on the days he approved of my wardrobe, I received no recognition. He stopped saying, "You look nice today" or "Those shoes look hot on you."

I acquiesced to the majority of Jake's requests, but even though I appreciated the new clothes and shoes, I didn't appreciate him telling me what to wear and when to wear it. It wasn't even so much his endless requirements but the superior looks of annoyance he cast in my direction. As if I were truly incompetent. And he was sneaky too, always hinting at his disapproval through the form of a question.

"How come you've been wearing your hair up lately?" This was his subtle way of expressing he liked it better down, so why didn't I always wear it down? Considering that I only wore my hair up on the days when I hadn't had time to wash it, this request was always more complicated than he realized. Or perhaps this fact was Tiffany-window clear and he liked to put me on the spot. When I refused to remove my carefully pinned French twist right away, I'd irritate him further by making up some lame excuse. Then he'd push the subject, saying he couldn't understand why women *ever* wore their hair up, as if women's hair existed solely for men's visual pleasure rather than protection of the scalp and major brain functions.

The end result: I slowly became resentful. Why wasn't I good enough the way I was? Was he just bored of me? After the night he accused me of turning into Mimi, it was as if he really believed it. I'd made one drunken mistake, but my time had ended weeks before when I began to reciprocate his feelings. That was when everything became serious, when money was no longer involved in the equation. My mother had been wise to warn me—if only I'd listened.

As far as Mimi was concerned, she hadn't been hip to Jake's game from the start, and it suddenly seemed no coincidence that she hadn't lasted long in his world. The same was true with Donna. Her style was so opposite of what Jake wanted in a woman that he dropped her the second I left for Hawaii. Instead he sought out Lexi, going for gorgeous and stylish, and more importantly, snotty and unattainable.

To further complicate the situation, a small part of me was afraid Jake was right. Perhaps I was intentionally testing the boundaries of our relationship, letting myself go a bit. Maybe deep down, I felt we had reached a stage where my image shouldn't have been as important. When in fact, my presentation was his foremost concern. Considering this, I had to admit that he viewed our liaison differently than I did. I knew of couples loving each other with different degrees of intensity, but in a different sense altogether? Had I jeopardized my marriage for someone who only wanted me in a certain way? It appeared so. Rob would never have told me to let my hair down or change my pants. He never even commented—much less noticed what I was wearing. I was always the same to him. Did a man in the middle even exist?

Suddenly Rob's lackluster attitude toward me seemed like a wonderful low-stress quality as opposed to an act of negligence. Rob never cared if I wore lingerie or made an effort to look sexy. He said I was naturally sexy and preferred that I crawl into bed naked, forgoing the time-consuming ritual of undressing me. In fact, since we'd narrowly escaped the island of Oahu, he called me his sexy baby no matter what I looked like.

***

Two weeks after my drunken incident, I was sitting opposite Jake pondering these issues. We were seated at a small black lacquer table in the Church Lounge of the Tribeca Grande, and I was dressed totally wrong of course, dirty hair up in a bun.

"Pam! What's distracting you? Dina's come back for your drink order three times!" said Jake over the distracting jazz music. I hadn't even noticed our favorite waitress lurking around the table, so deep were my disparaging thoughts.

"Right. Sorry, girl." I looked up into Dina's positively concave face. "Bellini, please. Light on the peach juice." I smiled sweetly up at her before giving Jake a dirty look. He was the most impatient man on the planet. What was the massive rush?

"Coming right up, darrrrling," she purred, returning my smile and pivoting on her heels back in the direction of the bar. She was a lithe, stunning creature with legs longer than the host stand. I enviously watched her prance away, wondering why she wasn't modeling in Milan for some renowned Italian designer.

"Maybe you should switch to vodka sodas," suggested Jake.

"Excuse me? Are you talking to me?" I glanced behind me. I detested such drinks.

"Who else would I be talking to?"

"Why would you suggest I begin ordering vodka when you saw what hard liquor did to me the other night?"

"Champagne makes people fat."

"Well tequila made you hate me, so I'm not taking any more chances."

"I'm just saying."

"What are you saying?"

"Champagne makes women fat," he repeated.

"Really?" I leaned back into the plush chair. "Is that why models drink it by the case? Because it's *soooooo* fattening."

"Models are shoving so much blow up their nose they can metabolize it. Plus, models don't eat," he said.

I bristled. "OK, so I won't eat anything tonight." In front of him, that was. "What *exactly* are you trying to say to me?"

"Nothing. You just look like you've gained a few pounds. Nothing extreme—just something you might want to keep an eye on."

I stared at him without blinking, my insides on fire. Some people see red; I saw his neck in a vice. I saw Jerry kicking me out of Dream Girls four years ago. And in that instant, everything was clear. It was over. Whatever we'd been doing—whatever had formally existed between us—had been completely wiped out. He looked away, my deliberate silence being more than he could handle.

I cleared my throat. "Everyone said I was too skinny when I came back from Hawaii. Now I'm too fat!" I hissed, just as Dina set down my drink.

"You're not fat!" said Dina, acting as if she'd just been the one insulted.

"I didn't say you were fat," said Jake. "You're still, ah, thin, you just look healthier. Like you've filled out a bit." I stared hard at the Bellini in front of me. He'd just sunk all my battleships, and I somehow had to return to base without drowning.

"I'm sorry, Dina. Could I exchange this Bellini for a Pellegrino? I'm apparently too fat to sip champagne because I eat three meals a day. Keep it on the tab so Jake still has to pay for it," I said. "Of course, if you want, you can drink it."

"Huh?" she said, finally realizing she'd interrupted a conversation of major importance. "You really want me to take this Bellini away?"

"Yep." I stared Jake squarely in the eye.

"OK," she said. "Thanks. I'll slug it down in the back."

This conversation would not have been so terribly devastating had Jake not been stating the facts. Half the reason I'd been dressing so casually was because my clothes didn't fit. But how could I admit this? I suppose now I could admit it, considering he'd noticed the extra five pounds anyway. Jesus, he had to be the most observant man on the planet. I fumed. Sensing his mistake, Jake reached for my knee under the table.

"It's no big deal. You still look great!" he gushed with fake enthusiasm.

"If it was no big deal, you wouldn't have mentioned it," I snapped. "And the fact that you did just ruined us. Actually there is no 'us.' There never was."

Dina reappeared, set down an empty wine glass, and poured from a small green bottle. "Is this OK?" she asked, giving me a sympathetic look.

"Yes, it's perfect!" I whipped the lime off the glass and onto the table. "I adore carbonated water!" Dina left us alone, leaving us to duke it out. I took a long sip, suddenly quite thirsty. "Oh, it's delicious!"

"I didn't say, 'Don't drink.' I just said, 'Drink something less caloric.'"

"I know what you said, Jake. I'll remember it for the rest of my life. I have a memory for these things. Not for nothing, you're not supposed to tell a female that. If a woman has gained weight, she is aware of it without some superior asshole pointing it out."

"Hey, don't get nasty. I just thought you should know."

Why is it that someone always feels the need to point out to me when I've put on a couple pounds? My whole life, friends, family, employers, and mere acquaintances had felt the liberty to let me know where I stood on my own personal weight demographic. It had to stop. It was stopping now. Today. This exact minute. Jake scowled and stirred his vodka soda. I almost poured it over his head. "I have an idea," I announced. "Why don't we go back to your place and I'll practice my boxing moves on you?"

Jake glanced up and laughed nervously, trying to gauge if I was serious. It had been a while since I'd humiliated him. "I like that idea. Would you insult me between punches?"

"Nothing would give me greater pleasure. And it's gonna cost you."

As I flagged down a cab and pushed him into it, none of the old moral questions I'd struggled with in the past resurfaced. I felt no guilt or hesitation. He wanted me to do it, and I was just the bullet, not the one pulling the trigger. "These are damaged people," my mother had said. She was right, and nothing was going to change this fact.

"Thank God you suggested this," Jake said, minutes later. I was alternating between punching him in the face and kicking him in the balls.

"You missed being smacked around, didn't you?"

"Totally. I thought you didn't want to do the role play stuff anymore. We haven't done anything in ages."

"Yeah, I was a little mixed up. I understand things better now." I kicked him so hard that he actually winced.

"Relationships get so stale and boring without the role play. No offense," he added.

"No offense taken." I made a fist and plowed it into his right cheek. Rob didn't think life with me was boring. In fact, he complained there was never a dull moment.

"It's just that all my other girlfriends—once they became my girlfriend, that is—they didn't want to continue the humiliation, so it never worked out."

"I guess that's the hazard of becoming too involved," I commented, thinking how stupid I'd been to become *too involved*.

"Well, I don't know what it is, but it's happened before," he added.

"I bet. Luckily you're not my boyfriend and I'm married to someone else. By the way, this session is going to cost you a thousand dollars. You heard me, sissy." I smacked his left cheek with gusto.

***

When I got home later that night, the check still in my pocket, I lay in bed and reflected back on the last few months and what it all meant. I thought I had been in love with Jake. The mind plays tricks on us when there is something missing from our lives. We mistake attention for caring, generosity for respect, and worship for love. But despite my questionable behavior in the whole relationship, I suddenly understood Jake had been necessary. Without him, I might not have realized Rob wasn't enough.

I remembered when I felt passionately about Rob. All those years ago. How excited I was before our first night together. Tears rolled down my face while I remembered some of our better times. But times had changed. He had changed. But moreover, *I* had changed. And I didn't know if I could get those feelings back.

I did know I needed more from a marriage. I was better off alone, without Jake and without Rob, so the right man could find me. And that was the real question: When the spaces were filled, could no one else enter? Just what did the universe allow?

An unhappy marriage was just a flimsy piece of paper holding two scared prisoners together. That wasn't me, or who I aspired to be. I'd come full circle, but at least my mind-set had changed. Independence was a gift. *I better not throw it away this time.*